THE KROEMAEON LEAGUE:

The Book of Idar

BY

DAVID CLAY

PublishAmerica
Baltimore

First printing

Illustrations by Eric Reitzer

ISBN: 1-60441-463-4
PUBLISHED BY PUBLISHAMERICA, LLLP
www.publishamerica.com
Baltimore

Printed in the United States of America

Acknowledgments

I wish to thank my son, Eric Reitzer, whose hard work in creating the illustrations for this book has allowed Idar's world to come alive. Roger and Diane Severson, the captain and the admiral, also deserve my thanks. Their mini lessons in sailing have permitted me, a landlubber, a glimpse into life on the water. In addition, my sister-in-law, Eva Dunn, deserves my gratitude as her editing skills not only helped me through my first two years of college, they have been of great assistance in preparing the final draft of my manuscript. A second thank you goes to Diane Severson who also aided me in editing and revising my work. Finally, I need to express my gratitude to my wife, Bobbie, who believed in me and encouraged me to continue working on this book through all the months when I felt it would never be published.

Introduction

Shellah 17

I am Koron, a medic. Miku was killed last night, and I am now the only one remaining alive who has not been incapacitated by this strange disease we have encountered on this planet. If the native aliens attack again tonight I do not think I can hold them off alone.

It seems strange for us to die this way, for with us will die our whole civilization. Yet we tried our best to preserve our culture, and now we must accept our fate. We came to this planet in peace; but, as on our home world, we have found nothing but violence and death. What is our purpose in coming here? I do not know, yet for some strange reason I believe good will come of this some day.

We had hoped we would begin anew like the ancient Miku expedition which led to the founding of the Kroemaeon League. But now this will never happen, for we await our deaths either at the hands of these intelligent (yet primitive) aliens or by a slow death from this disease.

I shall put this log with the other records we brought with us. Maybe one day the descendants of these aliens will find them; and, if possible, they will translate them. This may well be our purpose in coming to this wretched planet, to assist a new and emerging civilization, to give the ones who now kill us an opportunity to benefit from our mistakes.

This ends the history of the Kroemaeon League. No one knows what happened on that fateful night of Shellah 17, nor will anyone probably ever know. The ship used by this band of space voyagers has not been found, nor may it ever be; for we have no idea where it landed. The box containing the records Koron mentions was found on the bank of the Amazon River deep in the heart of South America in 1957 and shows signs of having been washed down river with many successive floods making it extremely difficult, if not entirely impossible, to trace the journey of the box back up river in order to find the landing site.

It took another ten years for this box to come into my possession; and I have spent the better part of the last forty years attempting to decipher the alien script and decode the totally foreign language in which the contents of the box were written. Thus, now that I have been successful in solving the mystery behind Koron's box, I have felt myself compelled to share it with the world; for it tells a story which began centuries (or even millennia) ago on a planet in an unknown solar system and ended on our own world likewise at an unknown time and place.

What follows is a translation of a story found in the records contained in the box left by these extraterrestrial visitors. It seems that at least part of Koron's "prophesy" of Shellah 17 has been fulfilled since we, the savage aliens, have advanced enough to decipher the message left by this long dead civilization. However, the rest is left to the future, for only time will tell if we will profit from the message hidden within their history.

In making my translation, I have tried to follow the original Kroemaeon text as closely as possible; and so I have used, whenever I could, the words and terms utilized by the Kroemaeon themselves. At the same time, I have also incorporated many English expressions and colloquialisms into the text of my translation as I felt that these best conveyed the patterns of speech found in the original Kroemaeon.

In a similar vein, I have also used a mixture of words, both English and Kroemaeon, for measurement of time and distance. It was my feeling that using too many Kroemaeon words for these could confuse the reader. For this reason, I chose, in many cases, to use more familiar terms yet ones having a similar meaning. It should be noted that there is no way of actually knowing the length or duration denoted by such words, and the reader should not view them as having the same length or duration as their counterparts in English.

David Clay
September 2007

Book One
Alna

Chapter I

Warm, I lay warm in my mother's womb, moist and secure as I lay in fetal darkness listening to the ever pulsing heart. I was happy then, happier than I have ever been since. And now, in this land of exile, I long for those days of my fetal infancy.

In the height of my security in that darkened world, there came a time when sharp contractions drove me from my home. They forced me through a narrow passageway into the dazzling light. There I lay, naked and helpless. My cord was cut, and I was alone.

For a time I lay in semi-warmth and nursed at my mother's breast, yet I was chilled. And there I heard the ever distant pulsing of her heart which now was forever far removed from me.

I was in hazy darkness, for my eyes did not fully perceive the light about me. But gradually light seeped in through those eager youthful eyes, and I saw.

§ § §

Red flames rose from the sea as the sun, exhausted from the day's flight through the sky, bathed its body in the cool waters just off the shore; and smoky clouds reflected back the last dying embers of the day. I sat by myself on the side of a hill overlooking the sea and watched the sun set. The orange brightness of the many mehalee, which were in bloom, surrounded me; and the whole hill seemed made of them as if reflecting the rays of the dying sun.

To the right and left of me were the dark outlines of the hills which, far off, circled outward toward each other, almost touching at one point just in front and to the left of me, thus forming the protective enclosure of the bay. The bay itself lay still, dotted with boats which grew difficult to see as the light of the day faded away into the infinite past.

Along the shore of the bay yellow sand held back the water from the green coolness of the hills. The sky, now a dark blue just turning indigo and violet, was reflected in the water as the land prepared for the deep slumber of the night.

This was Theo in the reign of Shuman, her last king, when I was in my tenth cycle of the sun. It is here that I will continue my story; for, from my birth until that time, nothing of great eventfulness occurred to me. But in the days after my tenth harvest, a farmer by the name of Aeshone moved his family the forty leagues from the village of Teuwa on the eastern border of Theo to my home village of Alna in the west.

Of course this event, as so many countless others, went unnoticed and unrecorded in the vast passing of time; and to me also, at the time, it had no meaning. Yet with Aeshone came Aarad, his son and my best friend, as well as his daughter Illiad, who was to become my wife.

And so, as I rose to return from that hill to my home in the village, as Aeshone may have returned home from the fields in Teuwa—possibly to tell his family they would move to Alna in the autumn—I knew not what fate lay before me. I was but a boy, with the mind of a boy, thinking only of play and food and sleep. There were no thoughts of marriage in my mind, nor could I in my wildest imaginings conceive the tragedies which would befall me. Thus, as I walked through the grass, naked but for a light blue tunic, I was innocent of the future yet to come.

It was Theo that those shining boyish eyes beheld from their earliest moments; it was Theo that those weeping eyes of a distraught young man beheld as he stood for one last time on the deck of a ship watching his past fade forever from view; and it is Theo, and those happy times of my youth, which these decaying eyes so long to see. Far off in both time and space is Theo now; and I, a lonely exile, lie in my grave—a canyon, rocky and barren, gaping between me and what has been.

Oh, if that innocent boy walking in the twilight could have known the horror of the future…no, it is better he did not know. For anxiety about what will come destroys the joys of our past when they are our present. It is better, yes far better, that that boy could gaze in innocence on each dying twilight—each itself the last he would ever see, yet one closer to the end of all such twilights.

Chapter II

Warmly glowed the dying embers of the fire; and I, a child, sat in the darkness pondering the fading warmth before me. It was cold away from the hearth, and I sat huddled close to it and thought. I felt great peace on those evenings by the fire as I sat with my mother and father. I knew peace, yet there was a place within me that nothing could reach, for I was alone.

I did not know the depth of my aloneness then, since in life we never see things clearly. It is only in death, in the restful contemplation brought by death, that we finally place our lives in their true perspective. In life we are so busy living we do not take the time to understand what we are doing; and it is only when the pleasures of life are no longer there for us to enjoy that we can clearly see all we once had.

It is cold in this clammy tomb, though my senses feel nothing. For cold is but the lack of warmth, and all warmth left me when these hollow shells of bone last saw the light fade from them forever into death.

I lie now in rest and contemplate those warm hearth side nights and their peace which was present from the very first of my perceptiveness, for they are forever pressed into my heart. At first I lay in a basket placed on a table near the fire, and my mother only took me out to feed me or to change my soiled cloths. Yet each night my father would sit by the fire and hold me after my bath. Though at first I knew not who he was, he was warmth to me, and my body yearned for him and all who touched me.

Happy were those infant days, yet not wholly. For in spite of all the warmth I knew and the security I had, it was not the same as in those long lost days before my birth. My heart cried out from its very depths, and all my being reached out for someone, something. Yet I knew it not, but thought myself in tranquil peace.

Time passed slowly in those infant days as eon succeeded eon; and each day melted into the next causing all to be one continuum of successive sameness. I lay and slept; I awoke to eat; and my body processes went on in spite of all, so that I was not even aware of them. Yet each evening I lay or sat by the fire and perceived its warmth and light while I unknowingly yearned to sleep forever in the womb.

Then one day, as I sat as a child by the fire staring into the flames, I knew who I was; for I was not the fire. It was something I had never thought of before, and from then on I became aware. I knew who and what I was not; however, who and what I was, I still did not fully comprehend.

Of all the things in the universe I was unique—I was me—but I had no idea what this meant. Nor did I care about its meaning; for I was me, and I was happy, and this was all that mattered at the time.

I took my *meness* for granted just as I had taken my unawareness for granted. All that concerned me was that this was *my* mother, *my* father, *my* house, *my* land. I became possessive, and my inward reaching out took on new meaning.

And so time passed, and I sat as a child that evening after returning from being alone on the hill overlooking the bay and thought. Tuac and I, as usual, had had a fight—another fight, there always seemed to be a fight—and this meant we were not talking to each other. In fact he had spent the day with Zhoh, his older brother, and two other boys swimming at the jetty formed by the River Ruha where it flowed into the bay.

I was supposed to have gone with them, but then came the fight; and he went off without me leaving me to spend the day alone since there was not much else to do. My mother had suggested that I clean the shed and my father that I work with him in his shop; but today was supposed to be a free day, and I did not wish to waste it on chores.

That is why I had eventually ended up on the hill. At first I had merely wandered our village looking for something to do, anything to escape going home to my parents and their questioning probes about Tuac and me or their desire to keep me busy around the house. But then I sought out my favorite spot on the hill and spent hours watching the boats come and go through the narrow opening leading out to sea.

It had always been my wish to go to sea, to become a fisherman like my great grandfather. He had served many seasons aboard one of the finest boats in the Thean fleet; but his son, my grandfather, had lacked a desire for the open sea and had become an apprentice blacksmith. After training and serving his master for ten sun cycles, he opened his own shop in Alna. Then, in his turn, my father had followed him in this trade.

Yet I felt little desire to join him. My father knew I hated working in the shop and tried as best he could to interest me in the trade. But my heart longed for the sea since the never ending crash of the waves was somehow familiar to me and stirred in my heart a longing I could not explain.

I decided that evening to tell my parents about my wish to go to sea; for, although my father knew of my dislike for the work of a smith, he had no knowledge of what I secretly desired. He, like my grandfather, lacked any inclination to be at sea; and, to my knowledge, he had never even set foot on a boat in his life—something strange in our land which depended on fishing so heavily.

The question I kept turning over and over in my mind that evening was how to tell them since my mother feared the sea because her own father had also been a fisherman but had drowned when she was a girl of about my own age. In fact, it was only by my father's insistence that I was allowed to learn to swim; for she would have preferred I never went near the water.

At last my father's voice broke the silence startling me and almost causing me to jump, "You're very quiet tonight Idar. Still upset about Tuac?"

"No, nodah. I was just thinking."

"Thinking? You. Don't tell me you are becoming a sage at your young age," he said grinning. "So, what did you and Tuac argue about this time?"

"Nothing really."

"It is always 'nothing really.' You know you really need to stand up to him. After all he is not that much older than you. You should not allow him to push you around like he does."

"Yes, nodah." I paused a moment and then said, "But I really wasn't thinking about Tuac. I...I was up on the hill again today, after I left the house...and I was just thinking."

There was a long pause. "And?" he asked. "Something's bothering you I can tell. Go ahead, you can tell me. You have never been this shy before."

He was right. I had always been able to talk to him. We had a bond, yet as I caught a sideways look at my mother sitting in the corner sewing I was afraid. "I was watching the boats and...thinking. You've never been to sea have you, nodah?"

"And he never will be," snapped my mother.

My heart froze.

"No, I haven't. You know how your mother feels about boats," and he smiled reassuringly at her then turned to me with a quizzical look on his face, almost as if he guessed the truth.

“But when you were a boy like me, didn’t you go fishing…or sailing? Most of the other boys go. Even Tuac and Zhoh have gone with their father on short trips.”

“If Daeo wants to kill his sons, that is no concern of ours.” Again my mother’s voice sounded alarmed. Did she, too, guess what I wanted to say?

“Daeo has no desire to kill his sons, Shahri. Most boys their age go to sea.”

“You didn’t,” she replied.

“And that is why you married me,” again he grinned. “No, I never went to sea. I was always too busy helping my father. It was hard for him to keep the shop going in those early days. I did not have time for overnight trips let alone longer ones. And besides, we had no boat nor any other luxuries when I was growing up.”

“But if you could, you would have gone, wouldn’t you, nodah?”

“Probably. Is this what you have been so sullen about tonight? Does this have anything to do with the fight between you and Tuac?”

“No, nodah. I was just thinking about what it would be like to sail past the point of the bay, to be on the open sea. Tuac says there’s nothing but water, no land anywhere! Wouldn’t that be wonderful!”

“No, it would not!” snapped my mother. “No son of mine is going out to sea. And that is that!”

“Shahri,” began my father, “you know your father’s death was just an unfortunate accident. He slipped and fell from the rigging striking his head on the way down. Anyone could have such a fall. Even I could in the shop as I climb up to the loft for something. Idar could as well, and you do not stop him from going up there.”

“That is different,” she replied.

“But how?”

“It just is, that’s all.” With that the discussion ended. Yet I continued to sit and stare at the fire thinking of the water aflame on the open sea as it surrounded me leaving no land in sight. And I could hear nothing in my head—or my heart—but the sound of the waves.

Chapter III

I awoke to the morning sun and lay beneath the blanket covering my bed. My thoughts turned to the conversation with my parents the previous night, and a sadness began to fill my heart. I longed for the sea; yet I knew my mother would never relent, and I could not apprentice myself to a fishing boat against my parents' wishes.

My mother's voice forced me to drag myself from bed. I washed in the cold water at the pump outside our house then returned to sit at the table in our main room and slowly eat the bread and cheese she handed me.

For a long time we did not speak. Then finally she said, "Your father wants you in the shop right after you eat. He has three nosha to shoe this morning." She paused while I ate in silence, then continued, "I know I worry too much about you. Your father tells me I am too protective, that I do not let you grow up; and maybe he is right…but I love you."

Still chewing silently, I looked at her. "I know, nodeh. I'm sorry I upset you last night. I'll never talk about the sea again."

"No, Idar, I am the one who should apologize. You are a boy, and it is natural that you should be attracted to the sea. But try to understand why I worry so…. Your father is right, I am just being foolish."

"Then, it would be all right if I went with Tuac and Zhoh sometime?"

"I thought you weren't talking to Tuac."

"Well, I'm not. But we always make up. And he has asked me. So, would it be all right?"

"Maybe…I will need to think about it."

"Thank you, nodeh. I'd better go and help nodah. And don't worry, I'll be careful—if you say yes, that is." Then I rose from the table and hurried out to the shop.

My father was at the bellows when I entered, heating the shoes for the nosha. "Tuac came by about an hour ago. I told him you were still asleep, so he left."

"Did he say what he wanted?" I asked a little surprised. Tuac usually was not the one to make the first move after we fought. He felt every fight was always my fault, and I should be the one to come to him.

"No, and I had no interest in asking him," he replied. "Remember what I said last night. You need to stand up to him."

"Yes, nodah."

"Well, enough talk. I need more wood for the furnace." And so for the rest of the morning I worked with my father without speaking again of Tuac.

§ § §

In the afternoon I cleaned the shed like my mother had asked the day before, and it took me much longer than I had thought. By the time I was finished, it was time to eat; and so I had no time to go and see what Tuac wanted.

The next morning I again worked in my father's shop and returned with him after the noon meal to haul wood and water or to sometimes hold the hot metal while he pounded it into the desired shape. It was not until well into the afternoon that I had time to even think of Tuac, and by then I had decided to take my father's advice. I would just wait and see what would happen.

He came by the shop the following day just before we were to stop for the noon meal. When my father saw him he motioned with his head in Tuac's direction, and I turned to see him standing there with the usual smirk on his face. I looked at my father who nodded then took the tongs I was holding and continued hammering the metal as I walked over to where Tuac stood.

"Why didn't you come by my house?" he asked. "I came here two days ago. Didn't your father tell you?" He sounded a little angry.

"Yes," I replied, "my father told me, but I've been busy working; and I still have to work this afternoon."

"When do you think you'll be free?" he asked.

"I don't know, maybe tomorrow. I'll ask my father later. I need to go help him now."

"Sure," he said as I turned to go. He then turned himself and left quietly.

"What was that all about?" my father asked when I took the tongs from him.

"I don't know," I replied. "He wants me to come to his house tomorrow…if I can."

My father said nothing more as he concentrated on the glowing metal in front of us. After a few minutes he stopped, took a couple of deep breaths and said, "Put that in water to cool, and let's have lunch."

I did as he told me, and then followed him to the pump to wash. "I told you he would come around," was all he said at which I merely nodded.

We washed in silence and then went into the house.

§ § §

I did not go to his house the next day nor the day after that. In fact, I did not see Tuac for six days, not until my free day.

I slept late, and after I had eaten went to his house where I found him sitting on the steps watching Zhoh carve. Zhoh had a talent for carving. It was almost magical how he could make animals that looked almost alive; and so I, too, watched for a while without speaking.

"What are you making?" I finally asked.

"An ashka for Leyhah," Zhoh responded.

Leyhah was their baby sister born in the second cycle of the moons the previous winter. Zhoh adored her, but Tuac was a little jealous since so much attention was paid to her.

"When do you think it will be finished?"

"Probably in a couple of days."

"And then he's going to make me a nosha," Tuac broke in.

"Maybe, if you don't pout too much about me making this for Leyhah."

"I don't pout!"

"Yes, you do. All the time. Sometimes I wonder who's the bigger baby, you or Leyhah." He grinned at me, and I started to laugh but stopped when I saw the look on Tuac's face.

To change the subject I asked Zhoh if he had ever seen a real ashka.

"When nodah and I were hunting in the hills above Teuwa last summer I saw lots of them."

"And you can remember how they look just from that?" I asked.

"It's not that hard. I just close my eyes and form a picture in my mind, and when I carve…I don't know, it just takes form."

"I wish I could do that. You make it look so easy," I said.

"Yeah, every time you carve something it always looks the same, a hunk of wood with stick arms and feet," said Tuac.

"You should talk! What can you carve?" I replied.

"Now, children," said Zhoh, "let's not argue."

"We're not arguing," said Tuac, his temper flaring. "Come on Idar, let's go before the old one here wets himself."

"Oh, really grown up," said Zhoh. "I told you, you pout. Go on, play with your little friend. You're distracting me anyway."

Tuac stomped off, and I followed. "He thinks he's so big because nodah told him Miku agreed to let him apprentice on their boat."

"When did this happen?" I asked.

"Last week," he snapped. "If you'd come around more often, you'd know these things."

"Sorry," I told him, "I have to work. Nodah needs me in the shop." I paused then asked, "So, when does he start?"

"The next run, at the changing of the moons cycle," he replied.

"I wish I could go to sea," I said. "My mother told me she would think about letting me go out with you and your father sometime."

"Your mother treats you like such a baby." His voice betrayed the usual hint of bitterness I had grown to accept as just Tuac.

"I know. But she's afraid...because of my grandfather. So, what are we going to do?" I asked, changing the subject. His comment cut to my heart as the talk with my parents flashed through my mind.

"I don't know, what do you want to do?"

"We could go up on the hill and watch the ships," I said.

"I don't need to watch the ships," he replied, "I can sail on one any time I want."

"No you can't. You've only been out a couple of times. And anyway, it's quiet up there. I like it."

"Why don't we go down to the beach. You can watch the ships from there if you want. At least we can walk in the waves and look for eln buried in the sand."

"Fine," I said reluctantly.

Alna lay on the slope of a hill about five and a half leagues from the walls of Theo and a full league from the docks and the beach. The wharf had been built out from the jetty near the mouth of the Ruha on the north side of the river. To reach them, you needed to cross a bridge a few hundred paces outside our village, but Tuac and I headed straight for the beach on the south side of the river since it was quieter and more secluded.

We spent the morning there searching the sand for eln; but since we brought nothing with us in which to carry them, we only amused ourselves by digging them up, letting them go and watching them scurry across the sand to bury themselves in a new hiding place. When we tired of this, we waded out into the water; however, the tide soon began to come in, and this forced us back up the beach where we finally sat in the dry sand and rested.

By noon we were hungry, so we returned to Tuac's house where his mother gave us soup and bread. Zhoh had gone off with some of his friends, and Tuac decided we should stay at his house and play kaylo.

And so we sat as we had so often done and formed the ring of colored stones in the dirt next to the steps of his house. We laughed; we talked; we were friends once more just as we had been since childhood. The afternoon slowly wore on to the click of the stones as we took turns tossing them in an attempt to capture the various colors and earn points. Then, when the sun began to hang low in the western sky, I rose at last—having beaten him for the third time in a row—and told him I needed to go.

As I walked back to my own house following the same familiar path I had traveled so many times, I felt a warm feeling, a feeling Tuac and I would always be friends. Yet it was impossible to know this would not be true, that in a few short cycles of the sun Tuac would be dead—and Alna gone forever.

Chapter IV

I think now of Tuac, my friend from my boyhood; for he lies far from me, his ashes spread upon the soil of Theo. Oh, if these eyes had flesh again they would weep once more, weep for Tuac, for Alna, for Theo and all that I have lost.

But these eyes cannot weep, and there is no heart beating in my chest to feel the pain of loss. Yet I know the loss nonetheless; for loss is naught but emptiness, and death becomes the greatest emptiness of all.

§ § §

I sat naked in the morning sun and played in the coolness of the dust just outside the door of my house. To me, at the time, it was a morning like any other filled with the peace of childhood and the freedom of youth. Time passed in those youthful days such that all seems now like a single moment lived simultaneously. Yet this one morning has been impressed upon my mind and has become one of my earliest recollections; for things are remembered by the impact they make on us and in this way they become distinguishable one from another. Thus, this special morning now stands out in my mind like an island rising from the mists of the sea.

As I sat that morning playing a game, one I had played so many times before, another boy came and stood in front of me and watched. He was a little taller than I, thin with his black hair hanging down over his ears. For a few moments he stood watching as I played with the many colored stones before me; then, without saying a word, he seated himself a few feet in front of me and gathered up the stones then made a kaylo ring.

I had never played the game before, but I learned it quickly from this nameless boy who, in this act of sharing, was to become my life long friend; for I would know him from this day on until his death. Yet even then, I would carry him in my heart as long as it still beat. We played for an unknown time in the morning sun, in the cool greenness of a spring day; and the only words we exchanged were those concerning the game.

Finally, he rose, saying he had to go, and left me sitting in the dust as I had been before he came. Yet in my childhood innocence, I never even asked his name.

He returned the next day and again and again each morning. Gradually, I learned that his name was Tuac; that he was six moons cycles older than me; and that his father, unlike mine, was a fisherman. I discovered he had a brother named Zhoh who was three sun cycles older than the two of us; and that he lived on the edge of the village overlooking the beach.

Each morning we sat and played the kaylo, or we explored the village together. He showed me his house and his family, and together we raced the dusty streets chasing the animals kept as pets by others in our village. We laughed as we ran through days filled with sun or rain and smelled the scents of life which filled the air.

We were light of heart in those youthful days and sang the songs only children sing and cried the tears only children cry when some sudden pain overcomes them from a fall or from a stick or stone hurled carelessly. The sun was in our hearts and the wind in our feet. The blue of the sky shone in our eyes as we lived the life only a child can live. And so time passed for us until that summer when I had reached my tenth sun cycle, and he was nearing his eleventh.

§ § §

I did not get to spend much time with Tuac in the days following our time spent on the beach and playing kaylo, for as it was now high summer my father was very busy which meant I was busy as well helping him in the shop. Harvest would soon be upon us followed by winter, and so there were scythes to sharpen and other farm tools needed to be made in order to prepare for the harvest. Men and boys went into the hills to cut wood in the forests, so axes also had to be sharpened, and nosha needed to be shoed.

My father did try to allow me a free day as often as he could, though these were not as regular as during the winter and spring; for I was becoming more and more indispensable to him, and this caused a sinking feeling to build up in my heart. I began to feel myself doomed to being his apprentice and to spending my life, like him, forever on land.

As the moons cycle came to an end, Tuac showed up at the shop close to the time for our evening meal, and so my father allowed me to leave early in order to talk to him.

"Zhoh will leave in two days," he told me. "And my father says you can come with us when we take him to the camp on Trohan."

"How long would we be gone?" I asked, a strange feeling building up in my stomach.

"Only two days, three at the most. The boat will stay long enough to pick up the dried fish and the men who are returning home," he replied. "But Zhoh will stay on Trohan to learn to dry fish. Miku will bring the boat back to Alna, unload it and then return to Trohan. So we won't be gone very long."

"I'll need to ask my parents," I said as the feeling in my stomach grew, and my heart began to beat a little faster.

"Well, do it tonight, and let me know early tomorrow," he replied. "I need to go, there's lots to do before we go. Don't forget. Ask your parents tonight and come to my house before you start work in the morning," and he was off.

I turned and saw my father standing there. "Ask your parents what?" he said. "So what is Tuac up to now?"

"Zhoh has apprenticed to Miku and is leaving for Trohan in two days," I replied. "Tuac wants me to come with them just for the trip. I would only be gone two days."

My father sighed, "I really need you here."

"I know, nodah," was all I managed to say as I felt I would cry if I said more; and not wanting my father to think me a baby, I turned and walked to the pump.

As I washed, he came over and stood beside me. After a minute or two he said, "Your mother will not like this at all." He spoke quietly, almost as if we shared a secret; and I quickly turned my head to look at him. It could not be possible that he meant…

"No, nodah," I replied. "I won't speak of it."

"Then what will she think when you are gone for two days?" he asked.

"I…I can…I can go?" I gasped.

"It will not be easy to persuade your mother," he said, "but I think you should." Then he walked into the house.

§ § §

The fight between my parents lasted most of the evening, but in the end she relented. My father was calm and never raised his voice; however, my mother was furious. She cried and screamed accusations at him saying he cared not if I lived or died, and all the time I was miserable.

Finally, my father's calm logic prevailed, for she had to agree I was old enough to be careful and should not be treated like I had no respect for the dangers. After all, he had told her, I could be trusted to go to the docks and swim in the bay. To this she had no argument.

I ate quickly the next morning and then was off to Tuac's house to tell him before my mother changed her mind. Although she had said nothing to me while I ate, I could feel a great tension in the room; and I tried not to look at her even as I raced from the room.

Tuac was as surprised as I was when I told him. "I really didn't think they'd let you go," he said. "I really didn't."

"I know what you mean," I replied. "Nodah was the one, though, he talked nodeh into it."

"This is going to be the best thing we've ever done!" Tuac exploded as his excitement burst from him and rushed upon me with a warmth that made me forget the chill of the morning. "Nodah says we can sleep out on deck in hammocks and watch the stars. Wait 'til you see how unbelievable it is, Idar. Just wait." I had never really seen him this excited before, and I was taken back.

"I can hardly wait!" I said as his excitement became contagious. "This really *is* going to be great!"

"What's going to be great?" asked Zhoh coming out of the house.

"Idar can come with us to Trohan," answered Tuac.

"Good," said Zhoh, "You can keep *him* out of my way. I'll have enough to keep me busy without little brother here being under foot. I wouldn't want Miku to think I'm a babysitter."

Tuac started to flare up, but Zhoh just laughed then walked off down the road. "When you see nodah or nodeh tell them I went to Shend's house," he called over his shoulder and continued on without another word.

"I need to go, too," I told him, "Nodah needs me at the shop." I raised my hand in a farewell gesture and began to run down the street toward my house.

Chapter V

The morning we left for Trohan was cold and foggy, and I was a little nervous they would not be able to find the opening to the bay with all the fog. I feared we would crash on the rocks, and my mother would hate my father forever because he talked her into letting me go. But Daeo, Tuac's father, assured me when I asked how they could steer in such fog that the ship had sailed under worse conditions in the past and had never had any problems.

I had been on the *Tok* before, but only when she was tied up at the docks, and it seemed strange to leave the safety of the shore behind and glide out onto the open water. Yet this was only my mother's fears talking, and I quickly put them to rest.

Tuac and I stood at the rail watching the fog slowly swallow up first the docks and then the jetty until we were enveloped in a quiet whiteness which dampened our hands and faces and caused us to shiver.

"If this were a clear day," he said at last, "We could see Theo from here and Alna too."

I grinned at him but said nothing, for my senses ached to take it all in, and words, it seemed, could not begin to explain my feelings. It was all too personal, too overwhelming; and I felt that if I spoke it would be like standing naked before him, so I kept quiet in the joy of the moment.

After about a half hour or so Daeo came and stood behind us. "See, Idar," he said pointing toward the prow of the boat, "the helmsman knows this bay like his own mother's face."

I looked to where he pointed and saw a vague grayness which darkened slowly until the rocky hills forming the entrance to the bay came into view. "We'll sail straight on through the Narrows there and be in open sea in half an hour."

My face, it seemed, became one smile as the joy welling up in my heart tried to escape my body. I was nearing the open sea, and the sound of the waves against the sides of the *Tok* echoed mysteriously within me touching something held in the depths of my being—I was home.

§ § §

After we passed through the Narrows and come out onto the sea, Tuac and I left the rail. We first stored our bags containing what little we had brought with us—a change of clothes and some of my mother's bread, a token she wished me well and was coming to grips with my need to go—and walked around the boat. Yet we were told again and again by the men (and once by Zhoh) that we were in the way, so we returned to the rail to gaze on the open sea.

By midday the fog had lifted, and we were far from the shores of Theo. As we watched, a school of leaping fish swam by about a hundred paces from the *Tok*. Tuac told me they were called kyte and were not really good to eat; and by the tone of his voice, you would have thought he was an experienced fisherman.

Gradually, the glare of the sun on the water and the heat it generated increased forcing us to seek shelter, and so we went below deck into the cool gloom of the hold where we had stored our bags. I took out the bread which my mother had given me and ripped off two large hunks, one for each of us. We talked as we ate, then went to the water keg and each had a drink using the wooden bowl kept next to it.

Having no wish to go back up on deck, we lay on a pile of empty sacks to rest. Soon the rocking of the boat and the stuffiness of the hold caused us to doze.

"So, here you are!" came Zhoh's annoyed voice. "Nodah's been looking for you."

"What's he want?" asked Tuac.

"Not sure," Zhoh snapped, "He just told me to find you. You shouldn't be hiding down here anyway. I told you I can't be looking after you on this trip."

"You don't have to look after us, we're not babies. We can take care of ourselves," Tuac called after him as Zhoh hurriedly climbed the ladder to the deck above. "And we weren't hiding either!"

Tuac jumped up. "He makes me so mad," he said, "I can hardly wait to leave him on Trohan."

We both quickly climbed the ladder, and when we reached the deck we saw Zhoh talking to their father and pointing towards the hatch out of which we were just emerging. Daeo said something to Zhoh and then began walking towards us.

"Been having a little nap I hear," he said, a smile breaking out on his face. I felt relieved, for he did not seem as upset about our disappearance as Zhoh had been.

"It was too hot up here on deck," said Tuac, "so we went down into the hold to eat. Then we…sort of fell asleep."

"That's fine," he replied, "but always let Zhoh or me know were you are going. If you were to slip and fall overboard, we wouldn't know until we were leagues away. You, Idar, should be well aware of such dangers. You know how terrified your mother is of the sea. What could I say to her if we came home without you?"

"I'm sorry, sir," I replied feeling ashamed of myself.

"Sorry, nodah," Tuac responded, his voice almost a whisper.

"I told you this the last time you came out with me, Tuac; so don't let it happen again," his father said sternly.

"Yes, nodah, we won't," Tuac promised.

"That's good," he said, and the smile returned to his face. "It is two hours past midday. We should be at Trohan in another five hours. Try and stay out of trouble until then."

We both nodded, and he ruffled Tuac's hair then returned to his work.

§ § §

Trohan first appeared as a dark mass on the horizon. The sun was low in the sky with about four more hours of daylight remaining, but as we were sailing southwest the glare on the water did not obscure our vision; and this allowed us to watch as the island grew ever larger.

It was not a very large island, only about ten leagues in length and four in width, yet it was the largest of five which were grouped together forming shallow reefs rich in abundant sea life. For generations Thean fishermen had come to these islands from mid spring until early autumn to fish, and several camps had been set up to dry fish during the summer. This dried fish was stored to be eaten in the winter moons cycles when it was impossible to fish beyond the protected enclosure of the bay due to the fierce winter storms.

There were actually five camps on Trohan, and Miku's was located at the southern end where a small cove gave some protection from the sea. A dock had been built out from the beach extending into the cove allowing the *Tok* to anchor in the deeper water and smaller boats, called tarkoi, to ferry men and supplies back and forth. These were raft like vessels with a man on each side and one at the rear who guided the tarrek between the *Tok* and the dock using long poles.

The camp itself was built back from the beach under the shade of the trees. There were five huts, one being nothing more than six posts forming a circle and supporting a thatched roof. This pavilion was where the men cooked their meals and ate in common. Close by was a hut hung with hammocks for sleeping, and off to one side stood two storage sheds. The last hut, located further away from the other four and down wind, was used as a smokehouse and sweat lodge.

When we anchored, there was only an hour of full daylight left until the sun set, and so the men quickly unloaded the supplies they had brought from Theo onto three tarkoi. It took several trips to bring everything ashore, and even Tuac and I were made to help. This we did not mind, for it made us feel grown up.

Tuac, Zhoh and I went ashore on the same tarrek with its second trip, and Zhoh was allowed to help pole it to shore since he was taller than both Tuac and I. After reaching the dock, we helped to unload the tarrek and carry the bags and boxes up to the storage sheds until our arms ached.

By the time everything had been stored away, the sun had already set; and the growing twilight quickly brought a chill to the air. A light breeze blew off the sea, so Tuac and I huddled by the cook fire in the pavilion smelling the aroma of eln bubbling in a huge pot suspended over the fire.

Besides this eln chowder there was hot bread fresh from the oven as well as fruit taken from the island's trees and, because new supplies had just arrived, cheese. The men drank wine, and Tuac and I were each given a mug as well, though ours was mixed with water. My father had let me taste wine from his cup once or twice before; but I had never been given a whole mug of my own to drink, and I felt guilty thinking of what my mother might say if she knew.

Tuac and I sat at the end of a table by ourselves and listened as the men laughed and joked. Zhoh sat with his father and four other men, all from our village, and attempted to fit in by acting as grown up as he knew how. It amused us to watch him, and Tuac's imitations of his brother made me laugh.

Gradually, the men left the pavilion to finish various chores before they slept. Five men were to spend the night on the *Tok* as guards, though there was little fear anything serious would happen to her, and Tuac and I were to join them.

It was not difficult to find our way to the dock because Kohn was full; and

Zayto and Aeto, though both waning, were still bright. This left enough light to see by, and on the dock itself torches had been lit to aid the men still working there.

We rode to the *Tok* on the same tarrek which had brought us to shore. Abdoar, one of the men from our village, tied the boat to a metal ring in the side of the *Tok* then we climbed a rope ladder to the deck. Since Daeo had stayed on shore with Zhoh, who was to sleep with the rest of the men in their cabin, Abdoar found us spare hammocks and helped us to find places to hang them on deck. After showing us how to string up our hammocks and handing us blankets, he went below to sleep in the hold.

Tuac had been right, for despite the brightness of the three moons the stars formed a magnificent canopy above us. Zoar, the red giant, hung with his golden wife, Zheh, in the southern sky both of them jewels amid the other stars sparkling in a rich blackness. We could easily make out the Fisherman, the Warrior, the Hunter and many other familiar constellations; and directly above us was Topa, the Watchman and faithful guardian of the heavens, who never changed his position. It was he the sailors trusted, for he helped them find their way across the dark sea.

"Look!" cried Tuac pointing as a star shot across the sky and fell into the sea. "Wouldn't it be great to find one?"

"Nodah told me the king has one in his palace," I told him.

"Zhoh told me the same thing when I was little," he said. "But I'm not sure I believe it now. They fall all the time. You'd think many others would be found by now. Why should the king be the only one to have one?"

"Because he's the king," I responded. "He can take such wonders if he wants. I'll bet they're found all the time, but those who do keep them hidden so the king won't know about it. I would if I found one."

"I guess you're right, but I'm still not sure," he replied.

We said no more but lay in our hammocks covered by warm blankets and watched the stars. After a while I heard his breathing turn to that of sleep.

"Tuac," I whispered in the darkness, but there was no answer. And so I lay alone watching the sky and listening to the gentle sound of small waves against the side of the *Tok*. It was an oddly familiar sound, and it lulled me at last to sleep.

§ § §

The sun woke us the next morning, that and the sound of klenn calling to each other as they hunted for fish in the cove.

"You sure fell asleep early," I said as Tuac sat up in his hammock, but he made no reply.

There was no sound from the men sleeping in the hold, so we walked to the rail and looked over at the dock and the camp beyond. Nothing stirred, but smoke rose from the cooking fire in the pavilion.

"I'm hungry," said Tuac.

"There's still some of nodeh's bread in my bag," I answered. "But it's in the hold. If we go down there we might wake Abdoar and the others."

"Not if we're really quiet," he replied and started for the hatch.

We descended the ladder as silently as we could, and when we reached the bottom we could hear the snoring of the men coming from a room at the stern of the boat which we had not noticed the day before. There was a dim light in the hold because the hatch was open, and this was enough to allow us to find our bags and take out the bread my mother had given me.

I tore what remained of the bread in half, and we ate silently for a few minutes.

"Now I'm thirsty," whispered Tuac, and he began to grope around in the gloom for the water keg. He found it, for I heard the sound of water pouring into the wooden bowl, then silence, and then more water.

"Here," he said returning and handing me the bowl.

I thanked him, drained the bowl and handed it back. He then groped his way back to the keg and returned to me.

We climbed back up to the deck and stood talking at the rail. About a half hour later Abdoar came up from the hold and told us we would be leaving in a few minutes, and soon the other men came on deck one by one.

The seven of us descended the rope ladder to the tarrek and polled it back to the dock. Abdoar let Tuac and me try using one of the poles, and we quickly learned how difficult they were to operate.

Once on shore, we walked up to the pavilion where we saw most of the men had already gathered. Many were already eating the remains of the eln chowder we had eaten the night before, and Tuac and I helped ourselves to bowls then sat at a table away from the others and ate. We were again given wine mixed with water to drink as well as bread; but as we had already eaten my mother's bread, we satisfied ourselves with the chowder.

After eating, the men began to load the dried and smoked fish onto the tarkoi to be taken to the *Tok*. Tuac and I helped as best we could, but the sacks of fish were heavy. It took both of us to lift one, and we only managed to carry four or five down to the dock. Zhoh, being three cycles older than us, could lift a sack by himself, and each time he passed us struggling down to the dock he laughed and teased us about how slow we were.

"When we were here the last time he couldn't carry a sack by himself either," Tuac hissed. His breathing was heavy from the strain of carrying the sack and sweat poured down his face. I, too, was breathing heavily and kept wiping the sweat from my face with the sleeve of my tunic.

When we had finished and were aboard the *Tok*, Daeo told us we could swim in the cove; so Tuac, Zhoh and I threw our tunics over the rail and dove off the deck of the boat. The water was cool and felt good on our hot skin as it washed the sweat from our bodies.

Strangely, Zhoh acted more like a boy once he was in the water and away from the men who were all too busy getting the *Tok* ready to sail back to Theo to notice us. We swam for about twenty minutes splashing, dunking each other and racing from one end of the *Tok* to the other.

Then Daeo called us, and we reluctantly climbed the ladder back onto the deck. Zhoh put on his old tunic, but Tuac and I went down to the hold and got clean ones from our bags.

When we were back on deck it was time to go. Daeo embraced Zhoh who stiffened and looked embarrassed. "Do what Abdoar tells you," he said. "I'll be back in three days, so don't get into any trouble."

"Don't worry about me, nodah, I'll be fine," was all he said, then turned to Tuac, "Take care of Leyhah, you're the big brother now," and with that he started down the ladder to the tarrek waiting below.

"I will," called Tuac, yet his voice sounded strange.

The three of us went to the rail and watched the tarrek as it returned to the dock, but before it was half way to shore Zhoh turned and raised his hand in farewell. His father returned the gesture, sighed and went to help get the *Tok* under way.

§ § §

The return voyage was much like our trip to Trohan; however, since we had started midmorning and not at dawn as on the previous day, we did not reach Theo until well after dark. Again I worried about passing through the Narrows, but the beacon fires which burned on the hills at the bay's entrance allowed the helmsman to guide us safely through; and we soon saw the docks in the distance lit with torches.

Both Tuac and I were tired from our long day, and so it seemed like far more than a mere league's walk up the hill to Alna. When we arrived at my house in the center of the village, we found both my parents waiting for us. At the sound of our voices, my mother rushed to the door and grabbed me to her in a crushing embrace; and I knew how Zhoh must have felt that morning on the deck of the *Tok*. I looked at Tuac, but he seemed much too tired to care.

My father spoke to Daeo while my mother busied herself getting bread and soup for us. Daeo was glad for the food as he had eaten nothing since midday, and he thanked my mother warmly. However, Tuac and I ate only a little; and, as we could hardly keep our eyes open, we were told to go to bed.

Without argument we went to my room and fell on my bed without even undressing, and in no time at all we were asleep. Yet through the dark hours of the night I dreamt of the sea, of the sound of the waves and the calling of sea birds.

Chapter VI

The next morning Tuac awoke a little disoriented as he had forgotten that he had spent the night at my house. We came out of my room to find my mother waiting with an extra special breakfast including sweetened rolls filled with fruit and boiled klenn eggs. I was greatly surprised as such things were only eaten on special occasions.

She busied herself waiting on us which was itself unusual as Tuac was not considered a guest in our house. Her mood had greatly improved with my safe return, and she joked with us and asked us to tell her about our trip. I was eager to do so, for the excitement of it came flowing back to me; yet in the telling, I failed to mention Daeo's warning to us after we had been found asleep in the hold, nor did I speak of the wine.

After we ate, Tuac went home; and, as my father was waiting in the shop for me, I made a move to go as well. But my mother held me back.

"I am glad you enjoyed yourself," she said. "Your father was right, you should not be kept from doing such things. Of course," she quickly added, "I will always worry when you do, but you are are nearing manhood. You are not a baby anymore."

I hugged her about the waist, and she kissed me on the top of my head.

"Thank you for letting me go, nodeh," I said as I hurried out the door to the shop.

My father was busy sharpening an axe as I entered. He looked up and said, "Well, sleepyhead, about time you were up and about. Was breakfast to your liking? Your mother refused me even a taste."

"You had nothing?" I said in surprise.

"No, my little prince, she wanted you to enjoy it first," he replied with a chuckle. "If any of those sweet rolls are left, I will have one for lunch."

"There's plenty, nodah," I assured him.

"Good, so now we work," he replied, and for the rest of the morning we worked hard to catch up since without me, my father had fallen behind.

§ § §

Ten days past, and I had not had a free day. Tuac came by twice but neither time could I leave my father to go with him. On his third visit Boec, Shend's brother, came with him. Boec was a tall boy, taller than normal for his age of a full eleven sun cycles. We had often gone swimming with him, and a couple of times we had hiked the three leagues to Crayoar to visit his cousins there.

"You're still not free?" Tuac asked entering our yard to find me lugging two buckets of water from the pump to the shop.

"No," I replied putting down the buckets, "I told you last time, nodah is behind because I went to Trohan."

"It's all you do is work," said Boec. "You'd think you were already an apprentice."

"My father needs me," I snapped, for his words had cut to my heart.

"We're going to walk up to those big rocks on the Ruha to swim," Tuac told me. "We'd hoped you could come with us. But since you can't, we'll tell you all about it when we get back."

It was truly an unkind thing for him to say. But that was Tuac, and I had grown used to his ways.

"Fine," was all I could say and picked up the buckets. "Have a great time," and I walked off to the shop.

Boec's words kept eating at me. I *was* like an apprentice. Many boys took up their father's work. Zhoh had become a fisherman like his father, and Tuac would probably do the same. Shend's father kept an inn where the travelers from Arganon and Eltec stayed if their ships were docked at Alna, and Shend now cleaned the inn and served the men their evening meals. Boec would probably join him in another two sun cycles. Even my own father had apprenticed with my grandfather and had then taken over the shop when my grandfather died. So, why should I not end up the same?

Yet Tuac and Boec were off to the Ruha for a free day in the sun, and I was stuck in my father's shop. An apprentice did not start until they were older than I, and this thought made me burn with resentment.

"What took you so long?" my father asked as I entered the gloom of the forge where he stood stoking the fire. "I need that water."

"Tuac came by and asked if I could go with him and Boec to swim in the Ruha," I answered.

"Up by the big rocks?" he asked.

"Yes," I replied.

"And of course you told them you had to work with me."

"Yes."

"So, that is the reason for the long face," he said looking grave.

"I'm sorry, nodah, I know you let me go to Trohan, and it's my fault we are behind…"

"No, it is not your fault we are behind," he cut me off. "We are just behind. But we have almost caught up. I tell you what, tomorrow you can go with Tuac and do something."

"Are you sure, nodah?" I asked in surprise since I knew all that needed yet to be done.

"Yes, I am sure," he replied. "You are still a boy, and I do work you too hard. I remember when I was your age. Your grandfather had me out here every day, and you know what…?"

"What?" I asked now smiling.

"I was really angry with him for not letting me go and have fun with my friends, and I do not want you to feel the same way about me. After all, you are not apprenticed yet."

The smile left my face at his words, and when I looked at him it seemed as if his face reflected mine, for there was an odd look in his eyes.

§ § §

In the afternoon of that day Menlo came by to pick up the scythes he had ordered. My father and I had only finished them the day before which in itself was a good sign, for usually we had a job completed at least two days before the customer was to pick it up. Yet since my trip to Trohan, we were barely finishing on time; so having something done even one day early was a sign of progress.

Menlo was the wealthiest farmer in the region around Alna as it was his custom to buy up the small farms adjacent to him and then hire men to work these new lands. Therefore, it was to my father's credit that he came to our shop to meet his needs; for, since he could afford the best, he could just as easily have gone to the smiths in Theo.

"Well, Kennec, have you had time to finish my order?" he asked as he entered the forge.

"I have," my father replied.

"Good. I had heard you were behind, and I need those scythes today." His voice sounded almost accusing which made me feel a little ashamed for my father and for myself as well, since it had been my trip to Trohan which caused him to fall behind.

"They were ready yesterday," my father responded with a smile. "Idar will get them for you while we settle your account."

I took the metal he was working from him and put it back in the fire to reheat, then went for the scythes. We had made six, but I could only carry two at a time since they were sharp, and I did not want them to slip and cut me. When I brought over the first set, Menlo was just paying my father.

"Put them in the cart outside," was all he said. Menlo's voice was cold and lacked any sense of kindness. My father shot me a glance and smiled, so I turned and carried the scythes out to the waiting cart.

It was one much like any other farmer might use for carrying grain and other such things to market. However, the two nosha harnessed to it were fine animals with hair black as the night sky and two small horns trimmed and neatly rounded. In no way were they like those one usually saw pulling carts through our village which were smaller, hornless and a drab gray. There was no doubt that these nosha were from Arganon and obviously well bred, nosha only one of wealth could afford.

After placing the scythes in the cart, I walked to the one closest to me and patted him gently; and even I could tell that he was a magnificent animal, clean and well groomed.

As I entered the shop for a second load I heard Menlo speaking to my father, his voice sounded slightly angered, "No, he would not sell to me. Sold it to some farmer from Teuwa of all places."

"Teuwa!" my father responded. "Why would any farmer from Teuwa come here?"

"I have no idea. Sounded just as strange to me when I heard," came Menlo's reply. "Paid a good price for it, though I would have given more."

"So, what will Kellnor do now?" asked my father.

"He plans to live with his daughter in Theo. You know, the one married to the cobbler. They live in a fine house, so her husband must be doing well. I even heard he made hunting boots for the king, but that could just be idle talk. Who knows how these stories get started."

"All the same," said my father, "I will be sorry to see Kellnor go. He has always been a good customer and was one of the first farmers to place an order when my father came here from Crayoar to open this shop."

At these words I left the smithy with the second set of scythes, and when I returned they were heading for the door discussing the possibility of an early winter.

"Hurry with those scythes," my father told me, "Menlo needs to be off."

"Yes, nodah," I replied quickening my pace. I rushed to where the two remaining scythes stood then walked as quickly as I dared out to the waiting cart.

Menlo was climbing onto it when I came out, and my father stood beside the nosha I had patted talking to him.

"Come, boy, I have things to do!" he barked at me as I rounded his cart and placed the scythes in the back with the others.

"Good day to you Kennec, and good health to you and family," he said, more as an observance of custom and not as if he truly meant it, and with these words he drove off.

§ § §

That evening I sat with my parents and again watched the fire while I listened as they talked of the strange news Menlo had given my father.

"You say Kellnor refused to sell his farm to Menlo," my mother asked.

"Can you blame him?" he responded. "Most of the farmers see Menlo's greed as a danger to them all. He grows much too wealthy, and they fear he will drive them all to ruin since the grain he produces forces the price down; so they make less while he grows even richer."

"But to sell to someone from Teuwa," she said. "Why, that is unheard of. And why would anyone wish to move here from Teuwa?"

"It is not totally unheard of," he replied. "Remember that Sethel came from Teuwa when he took over the inn."

I looked up surprised. "Boec's father came from Teuwa?" I asked in surprise.

"Yes," my father answered. "Just after he and Anyo married. They say her father bought the inn and gave it to Sethel as a wedding gift."

"He probably wanted to get rid of him," my mother said grinning at her own joke.

"Well, you may be right," he responded, "Sethel can be a bit difficult to get along with at times, but he is a good man nonetheless."

"True," replied my mother, "and I meant no harm by what I said."

"But if Sethel is from Teuwa, how can he run an inn?" I asked. "Those who live in Teuwa are…stupid."

"*You* have been listening to Tuac," replied my father, his voice raised slightly in anger. "Teuwa is far from Theo, and it is true that those who live there are different from us in some ways. But they do not lack intelligence, nor are they the fools many think them to be."

"Tuac should know better," my mother said. "Boec is his friend, and he knows Sethel."

"I don't think Tuac knows Sethel came from Teuwa," I responded. "I didn't."

"That does not matter," she said, "Tuac still should know better. And your father is right, those living in Teuwa may be different from us, but that should not cause us to think less of them for it. They are still Thean just as we are."

"Yes, nodeh," I answered weakly.

"Well then, I do not wish to hear you talk that way again. I remember how many thought I should not marry your father simply because his father was from Crayoar, and Crayoar is only three leagues away."

"Yes, nodeh," I said again.

There was silence in the room for a time as I sat in shame and stared once more into the fire. At last my parents began to talk again of this and that, but I said no more.

Chapter VII

The next day, true to his word, my father gave me a free day; so as soon as I had eaten I went to Tuac's house, but he was gone.

"He's with Boec," his mother told me, and so I walked back through the village to the inn which stood at the very western edge of Alna on the road leading to the bridge over the Ruha.

The inn itself was a two story stone building, the only such building in our village. It was set back from the road with a paved space, a kind of open courtyard, in front of the door. To the side was a wooden stable where Sethel kept the cart he used when going to Theo or Crayoar for supplies as well as Heshel, a small gray nosha.

It was Shend who had named Heshel, and I always thought it a strange name for a nosha since the flowers on the heshel are blue not gray. Once I had said this to Boec, but Tuac had told me I should not be so stupid, which lead to a fight; and I had never mentioned Heshel's name again.

When I arrived at the inn, Shend was dumping a bucket of water onto the stonework of the courtyard. He then picked up the mop standing next to the door, dropped it into the bucket and leaned the handle against the wall.

"To'v," I said.

"If you're looking for Boec, he left with Tuac an hour ago," came his response without so much as a greeting.

"Where did they go?" I asked.

"How should I know?" he answered gruffly, "I have better things to do than to keep track of him and his friends."

"Would your parents know?" I asked.

"They might, but they aren't here. They both went to Theo early this morning."

"So, you have no idea where Boec went?" I asked again.

"I already told you that," he replied and went back into the inn.

I turned and began to walk back to my house but stopped. It was my free day, if I returned now, my father would want me to work, or at least I would feel obliged to work since I knew he was still behind. This made me feel guilty and ashamed for not going straight home.

But it was my free day, and my father had wanted me to have one. He did not want me to resent him, so I should do something I enjoyed. After all, I was not an apprentice. Yet I still felt guilty.

In the end, my boyish nature won out; and I went to the hill overlooking the bay and sat for the morning watching the boats all the while thinking of how it had felt to be out on the sea.

When I grew hungry, I thought of returning home to eat; but if I did, I would be trapped. So I left the hill and went again to Tuac's house and then to the inn.

Not finding them, I asked Shend for soup and paid him with the spare money my father gave me from time to time. I ate quickly, then walked the league to the docks where I searched for them among the boats. When I did not find them there, I checked the jetty before returning to Alna; but they were nowhere to be found.

I thought of walking to the rocks on the Ruha where they had told me they were going the day before, but decided it was too far to walk only to be disappointed again if they were not there. So in the end, I decided to return home.

"You are home early," my mother said as I came into the kitchen.

"I can't find Tuac anywhere," I replied.

"What about Boec?" she asked.

"He's with Tuac."

"Are you hungry? I baked cheshoi." she told me.

"No," I said, "…but I'll have a cheshoh anyway."

She went to the table next to the oven where the cheshoi were cooling and brought me one on a little plate. The scent of the warm crusty pastry reminded my stomach that soup is mostly water, and I began to feel hungry again.

"Gork!" I said, "and cheese. I'll have two."

"I thought you weren't hungry," and her voice betrayed her amusement at my sudden interest in food.

"You know I love gork and cheese," I replied. "Why didn't you tell me what kind they were?"

She returned to the table with the second cheshoh and then sat down with a third one for herself.

"So, what have you been doing all this time if you could not find Tuac?" she asked.

"Looking for him," I replied. "I've been to his house, the inn, down to the docks and the jetty. I even thought of walking up to the big rocks, but it's a long way."

"And you weren't hungry?"

"I bought soup at the inn," I replied. "…Has nodah been busy?"

"Of course, but no more than usual," she replied.

Again I felt guilty. "I should go help him."

"If you wish. He would be glad of the help," she said, "But this is a free day for you."

"I know," I said, "But I should go help him," and made a move to leave.

"Idar." I stopped and looked at her. "Your father and I both know you hate the work of a smith. He has always hoped you would warm to it, that you would grow to at least accept it and someday take over from him as he did from your grandfather."

"I know nodeh," I replied weakly. That clawing at my stomach which I had so often felt of late again returned.

"But…" she paused. "Talk to him is all I ask. Let him know how you feel. If you truly do not wish to be a smith, tell him."

"But how?" The words burst out of my mouth, and my eyes stung, yearning to cry. "He needs me."

"No, Idar, he needs help," she said. "If you are not willing to give it then…"

"I do help him," I interrupted her.

"I know you help him, but he needs more than just your help. He needs your promise to be there always. You are still a boy, I know, but it will not be long until you are a man. Your eleventh sun cycle is almost upon you, and in two more cycles you will reach manhood. That does not leave you much time to decide. Zhoh and Shend are three cycles older than you and have already apprenticed. There are other boys in the village who could apprentice with your father."

The thought tore at me. I did not wish to spend the rest of my life as a smith, this I knew; yet neither did I want another to take my place at my father's side and work with him in the forge.

"Think about it," was all she said, and I left the table.

Chapter VIII

I did not speak to my father. I could not speak to my father, and a river seemed to wind its way between us, one having no bridge across it. He seemed to feel the distance growing and knew not why, but I could not bring myself to tell him and have him choose another to take my place.

Summer had ended and the harvest begun, so the days gradually grew shorter and colder. Soon winter would come, and Zhoh would return from the camp on Trohan. Yet I worked with my father as usual, and we never spoke of my apprenticeship.

In the middle of the last moons cycle of autumn Tuac showed up at my house. My father had given me two free days in a row, and on my previous day off I had told Tuac this would happen. With the onset of autumn came a decrease in business allowing me more time to myself. But now, after all my long summer hours, my father wished to reward me by giving me two days off.

"Kellnor moved to Theo two days ago," Tuac announced as he entered my room.

"I know," I replied, "I saw him go by with his wagon piled high with his things."

"That's surprising, you're always inside working," he said. "But now at least he's starting to give you days to yourself again."

I ignored his comment and changed the subject, "Do you know when the man who bought Kellnor's farm will move in?" I asked.

"Shend told Zhoh he will be here today with his family," he answered. "That's why I came by, I thought maybe we could go out and watch them."

"Watch them?" I asked.

"You know, just see what they're like," he replied. "I've never seen anyone from Teuwa before..."

"Yes, you have," I interrupted, "Sethel's from Teuwa."

"No, he's not!" Tuac said with a tone filled with his usual attitude of superiority as well as surprise.

"He is, my parents told me," I replied, "Ask Boec."

"If his father's from Teuwa, Boec will never admit it," he said. "No, Sethel can't be from Teuwa. He's too much like all the other men in Alna, and besides, Boec has cousins in Crayoar."

I could feel an argument coming on, so again I changed the subject. "Do you think the new family is here yet?"

"I don't know," he replied. "But Kellnor's farm is only a league away. It's a nice day, we could walk there and find out.

§ § §

We walked down the road leading to the farm and stood by the fence watching as the new family unloaded their wagon and carried things into the house. The man was taller than most men of our village, but the woman was about the same height as my own mother, slender with her hair in one long braid running down her back.

There was a boy who seemed to be about my age only a little shorter and a girl about two or three cycles younger than me, and of all things she was leading an ashka on a rope. I watched in wonder as she tethered it to a post near the house, for I had never seen one before.

After about five minutes or so the boy caught sight of us, smiled and raised his hand in greeting. He then said something to his father who nodded, and the boy walked in our direction.

"To'v," he said as he approached the fence.

"To'v," I responded.

"Why the ashka?" Tuac asked.

"He's my sister's. He was the runt of the litter and she's cared for him since he was a baby. She wouldn't leave him behind when we moved and cried so much my father finally gave in and let her bring him."

"Ashka don't do well down in the valley. They don't like the dampness from the sea either," said Tuac, "He probably won't live."

"That's what my father told her, but she insists he'll be fine in the house by the fire."

"You'd keep an ashka in the house? They smell!" Tuac's voice betrayed his distrain for the whole idea.

"They're not that bad if you keep them clean. It's all the dirt that gets in their hair that causes them to smell so bad. Illiad washes him every other day, so he's really not a problem."

"I wouldn't have an ashka in my house," said Tuac.

"I like him," I said. "Could I pet him? They don't bite do they?"

"Of course they don't bite. Don't you know anything," Tuac answered before the boy had time to respond.

"They're really gentle," said the boy ignoring Tuac's comment. "We had a flock of nearly a hundred back in Teuwa." He walked to the gate, which was only a pace or two away, and opened it letting us in then closed it and began walking towards the house as we followed. "I got to sleep out in the hills with them over the summer. Camped out all by myself."

Tuac gave me one of his looks, and I knew he was thinking: "Doesn't he think he's something." Yet I was actually impressed. I was sure I would not be willing to sleep alone in the hills with vood and donect creeping around me in the bushes, but I said nothing.

As we approached the house the boy's father put down a large box he was lifting out of the wagon and walked over to meet us. "And who are your friends, Aarad?"

"Tuac, sir." Tuac extended his hand in greeting and smiled broadly, but I could tell he was faking.

"My name is Idar," I answered also extending my hand in greeting.

"They want to pet Huno," said Aarad.

"He wants to pet Huno," corrected Tuac.

"Well, ask your sister." He smiled, nodded and returned to his box.

"Illiad!" called Aarad.

"Yes," came a reply from the house, and the girl appeared in the door. She looked at us and dropped her eyes shyly.

"Would it be all right if Idar pets Huno?"

"I guess so," was all she said and then disappeared into the house.

I walked over to the ashka as Aarad and Tuac followed. He was much whiter than I thought he would be, but then Aarad said his sister washed him every other day.

When I got close enough I slowly reached out to touch the soft hair. To be truthful I was a little afraid he would bite even though Aarad had said they were gentle. "He's so soft," I exclaimed. "I didn't think their hair was this soft. My mother has a dress made from ashka wool, but it's not as soft as this."

"It's the dyes," said Aarad. "Their hair is really soft, if it's kept clean; yet when the wool is dyed, something happens to it. White wool is the best, but nearly everyone wants it colored."

"Touch him, Tuac!" I said. Then turning to Aarad I added, "You're right about the smell. It's not really that bad, no different than a nosha, actually I don't think it's even as bad."

Tuac reluctantly reached out and touched the ashka. "You're right, he doesn't smell that bad. But I still wouldn't want one living in my house."

"I would," I said.

"We'd better get going," said Tuac.

I stood up, and the three of us started to walk slowly toward the gate. "Would you like to go swimming with us tomorrow?" I asked.

Tuac froze for a second, looked at me a little surprised by my boldness and then smiled one of his fake smiles.

"I don't think so," replied Aarad. "We have a lot to do around here; and besides, I really don't know how to swim."

Both Tuac and I looked at him in surprise. I could not imagine anyone his age not knowing how to swim.

"There's only shallow streams around Teuwa, so I've never really been in deep water. I can splash around and all, but not really swim. At least I'd be afraid in the deep water around here."

"We could teach you," I said without thinking. Somehow I was beginning to like Aarad. He was different from Tuac, for there was something honest about him.

"Right," said Tuac. "We could teach you," but he did not sound at all convincing.

"Well, maybe some other time. I know my father wouldn't let me go tomorrow. We still have a lot to do."

"Sure," said Tuac, "maybe some other time," and opened the gate. We both went through, and Aarad latched it behind us.

"See ya'," said Aarad raising his hand in a gesture of farewell.

"See ya'," I responded.

"Sure, see ya' around," replied Tuac.

"Why did you ask him to go swimming with us?" asked Tuac when we were far enough down the road to prevent Aarad from hearing.

"I like him. He seems nice," I said.

"He's from Teuwa, and he has an ashka living in his house," responded Tuac.

"I don't care. He still seems nice."

Tuac gave me a look of disbelief, and we walked on in silence until we reached his house at the edge of the village where we parted.

Chapter IX

As one would expect, we argued about Aarad. Six days later on my next free day I wanted to ask him along, but Tuac would not hear of it. Even Boec refused, "I'm not going anywhere with someone from Teuwa," he said as soon as I brought up the idea.

"You're father's from Teuwa," I said.

Boec reddened, but said nothing. Tuac either did not notice or thought he was merely angry and insulted.

"I liked him," I continued, "He doesn't know anybody, and we should try to be friends with him."

"You sound like your mother," Tuac said in his usual tone, while Boec continued to be silent.

"What if I do?" I snapped back. "She's right. We're all Thean aren't we? All of us."

"What's that supposed to mean?" Tuac asked sarcastically.

"We're Thean, that's all…I don't know what it means, but I still liked Aarad, and I still think we should ask him along."

"Well, do what you want, but without me," he replied angrily and turned to go. "Coming Boec, or are you going to go make friends with the boy with the ashka?"

Boec still said nothing but turned and walked off with Tuac.

§ § §

When I reached Aarad's farm it looked deserted. Smoke rose from the chimney, but nothing else stirred. I stood for a few minutes trying to decide if I should unlatch the gate and go knock on the door or return home, but before I made up my mind the girl, Illiad, came around from the back of the house leading Huno.

She tethered him to the stake near the door as I had seen her do the day they arrived and turned to go into the house.

"Is Aarad here!" I called, and she spun around with a surprised look on her face.

"Yes," she said, "I'll get him," and ran quickly into the house.

A few moments later Aarad came to the door with a puzzled look on his face. When he saw me he smiled, waved and began to walk toward the fence.

"To'v," I said.

"To'v," he responded. "When Illiad told me there was a boy here asking for me I was surprised. You and your friend are the only ones I've met since I've been here."

"Tuac's busy," I lied, "so I thought I'd come and see if you were free. Maybe we could do something. I could show you around if you'd like."

"That would be great," he said, "I'll need to ask my father first, but I'm sure he won't mind."

He unlatched the gate and stepped aside to let me in, then latched it behind me. As we walked towards the house I noticed little pools of water gathering under Huno who stood in one spot, his hair matted down like mine after swimming.

"You're sister washed him again," I remarked.

"He really hates it," he replied. "All ashka dislike water. That's why they smell, they won't go into a stream or pond by themselves. If you need to move them across water you have to rope them together and pull them."

"How does she wash him then?" I asked.

"We have a big wooden tub behind the house by the pump," he replied. "She has to pick him up and put him in. It's a good thing he's a runt, or she wouldn't be able to do it alone. He's nearly full grown, so I don't think he will get much bigger. If he does, I'll get stuck helping her."

When we reached the house, Aarad opened the door, and I followed him inside. Unlike mine, his house had a second floor which could be reached by a ladder in one corner of the main room, but in all other respects it was very similar to the other houses I knew in Alna. The one main room served them as a cooking, eating and living space and had a large fireplace built into one wall. There was a second door in this kitchen area which led to the back yard where the pump was located. A third door, on the wall directly across from the hearth, led (as I later learned) to his parent's bedroom.

I stood for a few moments staring in amazement at the loft to which the ladder led, for I had never before been in a house having one. In fact the house reminded me of my father's smithy, and for a quick moment I thought of Tuac's comments about the strangeness of those who lived in Teuwa. But this had been Kellnor's house I told myself and dismissed such notions.

"Illiad and I sleep up there," he said pointing. "There are two small rooms, one for each of us, but when Seppan gets here I'll have to share with him."

"Who's Seppan," I asked.

"My older brother," he replied, "He's still in Teuwa helping Morek, our oldest brother. After the ashka are ready for the winter, he'll join us here in Alna. He's the main reason we moved here."

"Why's that?" I asked.

But before he could answer, his mother entered through the back door carrying a bucket of water which she placed on a table by the hearth. She turned, wiping her hands on her apron, and opened her mouth to speak. Then she saw me.

"Oh, who is this?" she asked in surprise.

"This is…" He looked a little embarrassed.

"Idar," I finished for him and nodded politely.

"You are very welcome to our home, Idar." She smiled warmly, and I felt she truly meant what she said.

"Idar wants to show me around Alna," he told her and shot me a look of guilt for not remembering my name.

"I am sure your father won't mind," she replied, "but you had best go ask him. He is out back in the barn feeding the nosha." She started to turn but then asked, "Where is Illiad?"

"In her room," he said and led me through the back door into a garden area filled with the remnants of harvested vegetables. As the door closed behind us we heard his mother calling to his sister.

"Kellnor was kind enough to leave most of the vegetables for us, and my mother and Illiad have been preparing them for winter storage," he told me as we walked towards the barn.

Because of the gloom in the barn, we heard his father before we saw him; for we could hear rustling noises near the stalls where he was feeding the nosha. As Aarad and I walked over to him he looked up from his work and smiled, "Ah, I see your friends have returned."

"Just Idar," Aarad replied. "He wants to show me around Alna. If you don't need me, I'd like to go."

Aarad's father extended a hand to me as he had before on the day I first met him.

"Toev," I said politely.

"You are welcome to our home," he responded, and I thought of Tuac; for though Aarad and his family were from Teuwa, they were well mannered, and their warmth and friendliness made me like them at once.

"How many nosha do you have?" I asked.

"Only the two here, but my son will bring a third when he joins us at the end of the moons cycle," Aarad's father replied.

The nosha were the ordinary gray breed used by all in Alna, except for Menlo, and I reached out and patted the head of one. "Do they have names?" I asked.

"Heshel and Toarak," replied Aarad.

"Are heshel gray in Teuwa?" I asked in surprise.

"No," laughed Aarad. "Why?"

"The innkeeper in Alna is from Teuwa, and he also has a nosha named Heshel," I told him.

"You mean Sethel?" asked Aarad's father.

"Yes," I said, "you know him?"

"His wife, Anyo, and Aarad's mother were best friends when they were growing up in Teuwa," he replied. "He is the one who made arrangements for us to buy this farm."

The news surprised me, but I said nothing.

"So, would it be all right if Idar shows me around Alna?" Aarad broke in.

"Sounds like a good idea to me," his father answered. "Just be back in time to eat. In fact maybe Idar would like to join us."

"Thank you, sir," I replied, "but I'm sure I couldn't. I need to be home before dark since I have to work tomorrow."

"Work? Don't tell me you are apprenticed at your age?" he asked.

"No," I said, fighting away the claws which tore at my stomach, "my father is the blacksmith in Alna, and I help him in the forge."

"Well, maybe some other time then," he replied.

"Thank you, sir," I said with the customary bow of my head.

"Fine, be off now, and mind you, Aarad, be home on time," he warned.

§ § §

I did not want to take Aarad directly into the village, for to do so would mean going past Tuac's house; and so I first brought him to the hill where we could see the bay stretched out before us.

"This is unbelievable," he said, his voice betraying total amazement. "I've never seen the sea before. It just…goes on forever. Nothing but the sky is this big."

"I like to come here and watch the boats on the bay," I told him.

"Have you ever been out there?" he asked.

"Once, during the summer," I replied and told him of my trip to Trohan.

"I'd really be scared to be out on the sea," he said when I had finished, "I don't swim that well."

"I know," I replied, "you told me when I came to your house the last time. I asked if you wanted to go swimming with Tuac and me, remember?"

He nodded.

"I offered to teach you, and I still can if you want; but the water's too cold for swimming now. Maybe next spring."

"Sure," he said, "that would be great."

The hill was on the edge of a steep bluff, but there was a trail that led down to the beach. It was not an easy descent; however, we managed it well enough.

"Now *this* reminds me of Teuwa," he told me when we were half way down. "There are many trails just like this leading up into the hills above the village."

"What was it like camping out with the ashka?" I asked. "I'm not afraid of the sea, but I wouldn't want to be sleeping out on a hill when a vood came creeping by in the dark."

"Vood aren't much of a problem," he told me. "If you keep the fire burning all night they stay away. The hard part is waking yourself up to put wood on it, but after a while you get used to it."

We reached the bottom of the bluff and started walking towards the wet sand on the beach. "Did you ever see a vood?" I asked.

"Once or twice," he replied, "When the moons are full, sometimes you can see them sitting on the hills watching."

"I'd still be scared," I said.

"So was I the first time I saw one, but my father had told me to keep the fire going and they'd stay away. I never slept the whole night," he said laughing, "I must have made the biggest fire in the world. The next day I let the ashka graze while I slept under a tree. I did that for three nights, but I never saw another one."

"What about donect?" I asked.

"They live way up in the hills, far from where we keep the ashka," he replied. "In the winter, when they have trouble finding food, they sometimes come down lower. But by then we've brought the ashka back to our farm and they are penned up at night. That's what Seppan's doing now, helping Morek bring our ashka from the hills and getting their pens ready."

"But if you've sold your farm in Teuwa, where will they bring them?" I asked.

"We didn't sell our farm," he replied. "Morek married last spring, and he will take over the ashka and live at our farm, and Seppan will come here to Alna. He doesn't want to raise ashka, he plans to be apprenticed in Theo. So do I, in four cycles."

"You're only nine cycles," I said as we reached the bay where we stood letting the waves wash over our feet.

"Nine and six moons," he replied.

"Then you're…twelve moons younger than me," I told him.

We walked along the shore until we reached the mouth of the Ruha and stood for a while looking at the docks and the jetty. Then we followed a path up to the village. This was not so well used as the road on the other side of the river, the one leading to the docks, and so it was rocky and overgrown in places. Nor did it follow the banks of the Ruha exactly but veered away from the river and entered the village about half way between the inn and Tuac's house.

By the time we reached the village, it was late morning, and we were hot and thirsty. We walked the winding streets until we reached my house and each had a long drink from the pump and washed our faces, then we went inside.

My mother was at the stove stirring a pot of soup while fresh bread cooled on the table near by. She turned when we entered and smiled warmly.

"This is Aarad, nodeh," I told her, "his family bought Kellnor's farm."

She greeted him kindly, as his mother had greeted me, then offered us soup and bread. While we sat and ate, my father joined us; and he seemed to be pleased to see me with Aarad, for it gladdened him, I think, to know I was no longer listening to Tuac.

"Aarad has two more brothers still in Teuwa," I told my parents, "and a younger sister."

"That is a large family," my mother commented.

"My oldest brother just married," Aarad told her, "so only my brother

Seppan will join us in Alna. However, when he apprentices in Theo, he will live there, and I can have a room to myself. Our house in Teuwa was small, so my brothers and I have always shared a room. My sister, Illiad, had to sleep on a cot in the main room."

"And what will your brother apprentice as?" asked my father.

"He's not sure," replied Aarad. "He only knows he doesn't want to raise ashka, nor do I."

"Your father is not upset by this?" my mother asked and gave me an odd smile.

"Not really," Aarad answered. "We have enough land for Seppan to build his own house and barns if he had wanted. But my father told him he should do what makes him happy."

I looked quickly at my father then turned away, and I think he did not notice. But my mother did, and her eyes told me—tell him.

§ § §

After we ate, my father and I showed Aarad the smithy. He seemed interested in everything especially the many tools we had. Then I walked with him through the village showing him the few shops to be found there: a meat cutter, a bakery, a cobbler and one which sold herbs used for medicine and cooking. Besides the inn, there was also a small tavern; but we did not enter this.

And all the while we talked and laughed which seemed strange, for I was at ease with him. I enjoyed my time with Tuac, yet with Tuac I always felt I needed to be on guard lest we argue; but Aarad was easy to talk to, as Tuac had been when we were younger.

He told me about his life in Teuwa, and I learned that he was not much different from me or from Tuac and Boec, nor were his brothers different from Shend and Zhoh. My mother had been right, we truly were all Thean.

By mid afternoon we headed back to his farm, and I again petted Huno who had dried since his bath in the morning. Illiad stood shyly on the steps of their house and watched.

"Would you like to feed him a krumb?" she asked at last.

"Sure," I replied. So she went over to a basket sitting by the side of the house and brought one to me.

While Huno chewed the yellow leafy vegetable Aarad whispered to me, "You're special. Illiad never lets anyone outside our family feed Huno."

When I looked at him, he was grinning, almost laughing; and for some reason I felt myself redden.

"I'd better be going," I told him at last. "I need to be home early, I'll be working with my father tomorrow."

He again walked me to the gate and as we parted asked, "When's your next free day?"

"Usually about every five or six days," I replied.

"If I can, I'll come to your house," he said.

"Come to the shop first," I told him. "If I'm free we can go up on the Ruha. There's a place there with huge rocks in the water where all the boys from our village and from Crayoar come to swim. I know you don't swim that well, but we could go there and maybe catch fresh water eln."

"Good," he said, "I'll come if I can," and raised his hand as a gesture of farewell. I did the same and began walking home.

Chapter X

"You were in his house!" said Tuac in amazement.

"Yes, and before you ask, it didn't smell like an ashka," I told him.

It was two days after my last free day, and Tuac had come by the shop to see when I would be free again. This surprised me, for I had not expected him to talk to me this quickly. Yet I think he only wanted to know what I had done after he and Boec left me sitting alone in my room.

"So, what did you and Boec do?" I asked.

"We went to the rocks on the Ruha," he replied.

"I asked Aarad to go there on my next free day," I told him.

He said nothing, but I could tell he was not pleased to hear this.

"My father's waiting for me in the forge," I said and started to go back in. When I looked around, he was walking away, and I called to him, "You could come, too, if you want."

He turned his head and looked at me. Then, without saying anything, he walked off.

"Another fight?" my father asked as I entered the forge.

"I'm not sure," I said. "Tuac's not happy I went with Aarad, I can tell; but we didn't fight…not really."

"And this upsets you?" he asked.

"I'm not sure about that either," I replied. "I had fun with Aarad. He's a lot different from Tuac, and not just because he's from Teuwa, it's hard to explain, he's…just different."

My father smiled but said nothing at first. Then, after a minute or two, he spoke, "Give Tuac time, he'll come around. You are doing the right thing, Idar."

§ § §

Aarad came to the shop three days later; and, although it was not my free day, my father let me go with him.

"But we still have the axes to finish," I told him in surprise.

"I can finish them myself," he replied. "And tomorrow you can work twice as hard," but he said this with a grin.

"Thanks, nodah," I said and hurried off with Aarad.

We walked through the village until we reached the Ruha, then followed it eastward along a well trodden path similar to the one which led from the beach to Alna; however, here there were trees, and in the summer we would have seen flowers. This path ran a full three leagues until it met the road running southward out of Crayoar at a point where it crossed a stone bridge much like the one across the Ruha leading to the docks.

The rocks were nearly half way between Alna and Crayoar in a small canyon formed by a waterfall, and for this reason they were frequented by boys from both villages. Yet even so, whenever those from Crayoar came there, we rarely spoke to them unless we were related, or we had somehow become acquainted with them.

From the top of the waterfall, which stood about as tall as five grown men, you could see both villages; yet from the bottom, even Alna was hidden from view. There were three huge rocks jutting out of the pool formed by the falling water, each towering over the height of a man, and five more lay either in the Ruha or along its banks. In addition to these, a series of rapids and pools ran along the course of the river for about a quarter of a league, but after this the water ran smooth and uninterrupted until it met the sea.

When we reached the trail leading from the main path down to the river bank we could hear voices and laughter, and at first I did not recognize either of the two speakers. But as we neared the river I distinctly heard Boec say, "Look, Tuac!"

I froze; and Aarad, who was following me, walked right into me. Why was Tuac here? A fear I had never known before grabbed at me, and many questions raced through my head. I had told Tuac I would bring Aarad to the rocks tomorrow…I had even asked if he wanted to come. Yet here he was now with Boec.

My first thought was to leave since I had no wish to confront Tuac with Aarad and Boec watching. But what could I say to Aarad? He knew nothing of how Tuac felt, and I could not explain it to him. Yet Tuac could be cruel if he wished to be. If we went on…I was unsure of what would happen.

"What?" Aarad said, stepping on the back of my foot; and all thought passed from my mind.

"Tuac and Boec are here," I told him, "I…thought we'd be alone," and continued on down the trail.

As we came out of a grove of trees onto the grassy river bank, Tuac looked up and saw us, and an odd expression came over his face. He quickly said something to Boec who had his back to us, and Boec turned around with a startled look, one mingled slightly with fear.

I thought your free day was tomorrow," Tuac called over the rush of the water.

"It was supposed to be," I replied, "but Aarad came by, and nodah said I could go with him today."

"Your father never let you do that for me," he said with a hint of anger in his voice.

We began walking along the bank toward them, and they continued with whatever it was they had been doing before we arrived.

"Looking for eln?" I asked, but got no reply. In the awkward silence I glanced at Aarad who seemed a little puzzled by what was happening.

I had no idea what to do next, so I walked over to a big rock and sat down. Aarad followed, and when he seated himself on a second rock he said, "Your friend's not happy I'm here, is he?"

I could say nothing. What could I say? I hated Tuac for making me feel this way. Why did he have to be so stubborn? If he would only talk to Aarad as I had, he would see he was just a boy like us.

"I should go," Arad said.

"No," I replied, "Tuac's just being stupid. Let's walk on up further and look for eln."

We both stood up and turned to walk up river, but before we had taken two steps we heard a splash. When we looked back, Tuac was standing on a rock a little way from shore laughing, and Boec's head was just appearing in front of him as he fought to regain his balance.

Aarad and I walked over to them. "What happened?" I called.

"You pushed me!" Boec yelled at Tuac.

"I did not. You fell all by yourself," Tuac replied.

"I felt you push me, Tuac," he said and splashed water at Tuac making him jump back, loose his balance and fall into the river himself.

Aarad and I could not keep from laughing, but Tuac grew angry.

"It's not funny," he snapped.

"It was when you pushed *me* in," replied Boec climbing out of the water.

"I didn't push you," Tuac protested.

But Boec said nothing. Instead, he walked a few steps up onto the bank and sat in the grass.

"My mother's going to kill me if I ruin this tunic," he said.

"It's only water," replied Tuac as he pulled himself back up onto the rock on which he had been standing, "It'll dry."

"That water's cold!" said Boec.

Aarad and I again turned to go, but Boec looked up and said, "What's your name?"

"His name's Aarad," I told him.

"Can't he talk for himself?" asked Tuac joining us on the grassy bank.

"Your mother's Melne," Boec said, "my mother talks about her all the time. I'm Boec," and he offered his hand to Aarad.

The look of surprise on Tuac's face almost made me laugh, and I felt as if a heavy weight had been taken off me.

§ § §

We spent the rest of the morning with Tuac and Boec. When midday came we searched for berries along the bank and were lucky enough to find a palne tree with good sized, well ripened fruit. Boec had brought a sack from the inn with bread and cheese which he shared four ways, cutting the cheese with a small knife he also carried in the sack.

In the afternoon we climbed the rocky trail leading from the lower river to the top of the falls. Then, after a long rest, we took another trail back to the main path leading to Alna and walked the two leagues to the village.

Boec seemed to warm to Aarad, yet Tuac remained sullen and spoke little. The few times he did speak, it was mostly to criticize or grumble and complain about something.

When we reached the village, Tuac and Boec left us and headed for the inn while Aarad and I returned to my house where my mother fed us cheshoi. Then, since the sun was already low in the sky, Aarad left to return home.

As we ate our evening meal that night, and talked over the events of the day, I told my parents what had happened at the river. "And you should have seen the look on Tuac's face when Boec told us his mother and Aarad's mother were friends," I said.

"I would have liked to have been there," my father said grinning.

"What did Tuac say?" my mother asked.

"He never said a thing," I replied. "He just stood there looking…I don't know how to describe it. I almost laughed."

"What about the rest of the day?" my mother asked, "surly he must have said something. It's not like Tuac to keep his feelings about things a secret."

"No," I replied, "he never said anything. He hardly talked at all. In fact I'm not sure if he even spoke to Aarad the whole day."

"That sounds like Tuac," my father said. And our talk turned to other things.

That night, as I lay alone in my room, I felt comforted; for I was sure Tuac would come to accept Aarad. I saw in my mind other days, days like the one I had just spent, days where the four of us would be friends. But in this I was wrong.

Chapter XI

Aarad's brother, Seppan, arrived from Teuwa with the beginning of the next moons cycle; and Zhoh returned from Trohan at about the same time. It was now winter, and it seemed as if the whole world began to change; for it grew colder and storms became more and more frequent. Men could not go out to fish nor did trading ships from Arganon and Eltec came as frequently.

This left me more free time since my father had little to do in his shop, and so I worked mostly in the mornings if at all and had the afternoons free. Even so, I saw little of Tuac.

When he did not come to see me for six days, I decided I should go and talk to him. But his mother told me he was not home, and Boec said he was not at the inn when I went there.

Two days later I again went to his house to find him alone with Leyhah. He told me his parents had gone to Theo to buy a gift for Zhoh, and he had been left to care for his sister until they returned. Since he did not ask me to stay but acted coldly toward me, I left and went to visit Aarad.

Yet this happened again and again for a full cycle of the moons. Boec also seemed puzzled, for Tuac had only come to the inn a couple of times and had not stayed long. Zhoh told me Tuac had become friends with Alnat and Tefnoar who were both in their twelfth cycle. He said Tuac had told him they were more grown up and fun to be with.

And so I spent more and more time with Aarad and Seppan who, unlike Tuac and Zhoh, were close as brothers should be and seldom argued. They came with me to the inn where they were accepted warmly; and soon Seppan, Zhoh and Shend became friends. But Tuac remained cold and aloof, and when I did talk to him, he said little.

§ § §

My eleventh sun cycle came and passed, and still I said nothing to my father about my wish not to apprentice in his shop. As the winter deepened, I spent less time with him in the forge; and in the evenings I sat staring into the fire, dreaming of the sea and wishing I could tell him the truth.

As mothers do, mine prodded me along these lines with subtle hints and knowing looks, but we never had another conversation like the one during the summer. Whenever Seppan came to our house she would ask about his plans to apprentice, but since he was helping his father get the farm ready for the spring planting he always told her the same thing, “Maybe in the spring.” And this became my thought as well: maybe in the spring, when work picked up, I would tell him then—but not now.

Then, as the Winter Guardian gradually disappeared from the night sky, and the world began to show the first signs spring was near, I knew I could not wait; for soon my father would be busy, and I would work for him another season making me as good as apprenticed.

Zhoh returned to Trohan with the first moons cycle of spring to help prepare the camp for the summer season. The winter storms always caused some damage to the huts or the dock, and the tarkoi were also often in need of repair even though they had been dragged up on shore and bound securely to the trees far from the beach.

As the second moons cycle of spring neared its end, Seppan prepared to go to Theo to seek an apprenticeship. Aeshone, his father, was to go with him; and they were to stay at an inn which Sethel had recommended as they expected to be away at least two days maybe more.

Aarad was to do the chores and tend the newly planted fields, and I had begged by parents to let me stay with him and his mother and sister in order to help. My father could have used me in the forge; but he saw that the need of Aarad’s family was greater, and so he agreed as did my mother.

“When will they leave in the morning?” I asked Aarad as we sat on the front steps watching Huno graze in the yard. He had grown used to being in the fenced area in front of the house as well as fat from sleeping by the fire at night, and he made no attempt to wander off.

“With the first light,” Aarad answered. “That means nodah will wake him up well before sunrise…and us too.”

“You’re right, little brother,” came Seppan’s voice as he walked around the corner of the house, “so you two better not keep me awake all night with your talking.”

“Stop doing that!” said Aarad. “You know I hate it when you sneak up on me.”

"I wasn't sneaking up on you," he replied. "Nodah sent me to get you, he needs you in the barn."

"Fine," snapped Aarad, "but you were still sneaking up on me." He got up and started walking around the house while Seppan took his place on the step.

"Are you sure you want to do this?" he asked when Aarad was out of sight. "You've never done farm work before."

"It can't be any harder than working with nodah in the forge," I replied.

"You never know."

"I helped the fishermen on Trohan last summer, and I've been hauling wood and water and carrying lots of heavy stuff for nodah."

To this he only smiled and nodded.

"So, do you have any idea where you want to apprentice?" I asked.

"*You,* sound like your mother," he said with a laugh. "She must have asked me that a hundred times since I've known her."

"She wasn't really asking you…she was asking me," I told him.

He looked at me puzzled. "What do you mean?"

"…I don't want to apprentice with nodah," I told him, "but I just can't bring myself to tell him. She knows, but…it's up to me to say something."

For a long time he said nothing, and we just sat there in silence. Then finally he spoke, "I know what you mean. It took me nine moons before I got up the courage to tell nodah I hated ashka. Well, I don't really hate ashka, but I don't want to spend my life living with them…except for Huno," and we both laughed.

"I know your father," he said, "I'm sure he'll understand…just tell him."

"I know he'll understand," I replied. "He knows I don't really like smith work."

"And…?" asked Seppan. Then, when I did not answer, he grabbed me by the shoulders and playfully shook me causing both of us to laugh. "Come on," he said, "I can tell there's more, so what is it?"

"I…I just don't know how I'd feel having someone else working in the forge with him," I said, and I quickly looked away not wanting him to see my eyes which I knew betrayed me.

Again there was a long pause; and when I felt he wasn't looking, I wiped my eyes on the sleeve of my tunic.

"How would you feel if…I was the one working with him?" he asked at last.

His words hit me in the stomach like a piece of hot iron from the forge, and I glared at him in disbelief.

"You," was all I could say.

"Idar, just say no if you want, but hear me out," he said. "I like your father, and I'd be close to home. I know Theo's not that far away, but your house's even closer. And you could still work with us if you wanted. I'm not trying to replace you or anything."

Again we sat in silence, my mind racing. The idea somehow excited me, but at the same time it terrified me. I felt relief and anger all at once. How could Seppan suggest such a thing after what I had just told him? It was like he had betrayed me. Yet Seppan was my friend, and although I hated the idea of someone else working with my father, it in some way made a difference to me it could be Seppan. I was at a loss for words and could not answer him.

"Last minute orders," came Aarad's voice. "It's not like I don't know all that stuff already." He came over and sat next to me on the step making me bunch up next to Seppan.

The silence almost strangled us, and after a moment Aarad asked, "What's wrong?"

"Nothing," said Seppan and got up to go. "I'm sorry Idar, just forget it."

As he walked up the steps to the house I called to him, "Seppan…it might not be that bad of an idea. I just have to think about it."

"What idea?" asked Aarad.

Seppan came back and sat down again.

"You mean it," he said.

"What idea?" Aarad asked again.

"Yeah…I mean it," I told him.

"What idea!" said Aarad for the third time.

"Seppan wants to ask my father to apprentice with him," I told him.

"You're joking," he said.

"No, I'm not," Seppan told him. "Why should I go all the way to Theo if there's an apprentice job here in Alna?"

"Because there's not," Aarad replied, "Idar works for his father."

"But I don't want to…not really," I said.

"Wait a minute," said Aarad, "you're telling me you don't want to be a blacksmith like your father."

"No, and you don't want to raise ashka like your father," I replied.

"Yeah, but you never told me that," he said. "So, what, you're just going to tell nodah you're not going to Theo tomorrow?" he asked Seppan.

"I don't know," he replied, "I can't really do that. There's nothing sure about Idar's father…and I'm not even sure there is with Idar either."

There was a pause, "Well?" he continued, "is there, Idar?"

"I don't know," I said truthfully and then was silent as all three of us sat and watched Huno.

§ § §

In the end we decided to tell Aeshone since that seemed to be the most urgent need. It would be foolish if Seppan and his father spent two or three days in Theo when an apprenticeship could be had with my father in Alna.

"This is sudden," was all Aeshone could say.

"Not really," Seppan replied, and we all looked at him a little surprised. "Ever since I've known Idar I've been thinking about smith work. To tell the truth I was hoping there'd be a smith apprenticeship in Theo, but I never said anything because I was sure I wouldn't find one."

"All the same," his father replied, "I'm not sure what to do now."

"Just don't go," said Melne.

"That is easy enough to say," Aeshone replied, "but what of Kennec? Idar has told him nothing, and from what you say," and he turned to me, "you are not sure you want to."

"I have to," I told him, "'specially now. What else can I do?"

"Well, we should eat," said Melne, "the food is getting cold, and we can talk more during our meal."

As we ate together that night, I felt a deep sense of peace come over me. For almost a full sun cycle I had faced something like a vood sitting just outside the fire light waiting to devour me; and now, at last, I was finally rid of it. My father knew I did not have the heart to become a blacksmith; and Seppan was right, he would understand if I chose not to become one. And so, as we sat and talked, I resolved to tell him in the morning and to ask him to accept Seppan as his apprentice even though this would mean Seppan could one day become his heir and take over the business my father and his father before him had worked so hard to build and pass on to me.

Chapter XII

At first light the next morning I crept out of Aarad and Seppan's room, being careful not to wake them, and climbed down the ladder from the loft to the main room where Melne was preparing breakfast for us.

"You are up early," she said with a smile, "but I guess I could expect no less. Did you sleep much?"

"Not really," I replied. "Last night I was ready to go home and tell my father, but…now I'm not so sure."

"Well, you will feel better after you eat," she told me. "Sit, I have hot kahl."

She walked to the fireplace and spooned the hot steaming cereal into a wooden bowl then brought it to me at the table. "If you like, we have palne syrup to go with it."

I thanked her and spooned some of the golden liquid into my bowl then slowly mixed it into the kahl watching as it blended in with the coarse brown grains. Yet I did not eat. Instead I sat staring at the bowl allowing the steam to warm my face.

At last she spoke, "Do you know what you will say to your father?"

"I should," I said, "I've told him a hundred times, but I've never said the words aloud." I paused, breathing in the spicy warmth the palne added to the kahl. "I don't want to hurt him," I said at last. "He knows I don't like working as a smith, but telling him…I can never take that back."

"He will understand," she said. "He loves you and only wants you to be happy."

"My mother said that too," I replied. "She's been trying to get me to tell him since last summer."

I heard a noise and looked up to the loft. Illiad was climbing down the ladder, and so I busied myself eating the kahl.

§ § §

Soon everyone was awake, and after we had done chores and eaten, I reluctantly walked back to Alna. It was midmorning by then, and the spring sun warmed the chilled ground under my feet. Yet I barely noticed this since the dread within me radiated a coldness that would not release me. It hugged my chest in a tight embrace and made my feet feel heavy as I trudged along as if I were doomed and the darkest of fates awaited me.

My father stood at the anvil pounding a glowing piece of metal when I entered the smithy, and so he did not hear me as I walked softly toward him. Yet he somehow must have sensed me there, for he looked up; and a puzzled expression came over his face.

"Is something wrong?" he asked, a deep concern in his voice.

"Everything," was all I could say, for tears filled my eyes.

He put the hammer down and quickly came over to me, "What is it?" he said kneeling in front of me.

But I still could not speak, for the words locked within me for so long gripped my throat and would still not come forth.

"Idar," he said gently, "you can tell me."

"I know," I replied, "I know. I just don't want you to be disappointed."

"You are my son, Idar, nothing you could do would ever truly disappoint me."

Again I waited, seeking the strength to say the words which when once spoken would forever change my life. I looked at him across the river that had separated us for so long and saw the concern in his eyes deepen. Then suddenly I could hold it in no longer, for I had to cross over to him no matter what the cost.

"I want to go to sea, nodah. I don't want to be a blacksmith," I cried, then flung my arms around his neck and wept.

He held me, and I felt as if we had been apart for ages.

"I know," he said at last. "I have known for a long time. Why do you think I let you go to Trohan?"

I pulled away looking at him in surprise, and he laughed as he stood up.

"You spend too much time on the hill looking at the ships; and though you work hard, I have always sensed your reluctance to be a smith."

"I'm sorry, nodah," I replied.

"You have no need to be sorry. Sons do not always follow their fathers in the same trade. Look at Seppan."

At the mention of Seppan, I again felt the cold tightness grip me. For a moment I stood in silence, then said, "Seppan wants to apprentice with you as a blacksmith…if you'll have him."

"Seppan," he said in surprise then stood looking down at me unable to say more.

I told him what had happened at Aarad's house the night before and how Seppan had come to tell me of his wish to be a smith. When I finished, he still said nothing for a long time.

At last he walked back to the anvil and placed the metal he had been working back into the fire to reheat.

"Seppan is strong," he said, "and smart, but…"

"We always have trouble keeping up once the work picks up," I told him. "With Seppan here, we would have no trouble finishing the jobs on time."

"And this would meet with your approval," he replied with a grin, "as a business partner of course."

We laughed at this, then he came and stood at my side. "I am glad you told me," he said putting his hand on my shoulder.

§ § §

We told my mother of the arrangement with Seppan, but neither my father nor I spoke of my wish to go to sea; and she was so relieved I had at last told my father how I really felt she asked me nothing. And so, after an early lunch I went back to Aarad's farm to give Seppan the news.

It was nearly midday when I left my house, and the sun shown brightly as it had on my trip into Alna that morning. Yet now I felt its warming rays upon me, for a calming peace had come over me making me glad to be alive.

The vood was gone, and I realized that it had ruled my life in ways I had not known. And so I rejoiced in this new peace, in the confidence I would one day go to sea, and all my dreams would become realities.

Seppan was waiting on the steps as I came down the road; and when he saw me, he ran to the gate to meet me.

"Well," he said.

"He wants you and your father to come this afternoon to make the arrangements," I told him.

Seppan let out a whoop of joy, "Thank you, Idar," he said unlatching the gate, "I owe you."

We found Aeshone in the barn with Aarad and told him my father had agreed to take Seppan as his apprentice. He was pleased with the news, but Aarad did not seem to be as happy as I would have thought. When Aeshone and Seppan went into the house to tell Melne, I asked what was wrong.

"If Seppan works for your father," he replied, "then he'll be coming home at night, and I'll still have to share a room with him. Illiad's so lucky to be the only girl."

His father had told him to clean out the stalls, and since I had promised to help with the chores over the next few days, I started to help him.

"You really don't need to do this," he told me.

"I'm supposed to be helping," I said.

"But only because nodah and Seppan were going to be gone," he replied.

"They'll be going to my house to talk to my father."

"But just for the afternoon."

"Do you want me to help you or not?" I asked getting a little annoyed.

"Yes, but…I just thought that you'd be going home with them, that's all."

"Right, and get stuck in the forge," I replied. "I'd rather be here any day."

"I wouldn't," he told me. "You know, back in Teuwa all my friends were always working on the farm with their fathers. I really felt lucky to be sent out into the hills to tend the ashka alone over the summer. And here you are wanting to do farm work. It doesn't make sense."

"I guess it's what you're used to," I told him. "This isn't a lot of fun, but it's different. It's like last summer on Trohan, I didn't mind helping when we had to unload the boat or carry those heavy sacks of dried fish."

"You're probably right," he said. "So, do you have any idea what you want to do when you're older? I'm still not sure, but whatever it is, I know it will have nothing to do with animals."

"I'd like to go to sea," I answered. "You've never been out there, so it's hard to describe. It's the best place in the whole world. No land, just a blue sky and the sound of the waves. You should see it at night. The stars almost touch you. If I could be at sea, I'd never want to come home."

And so we talked of our futures, as boys so often do, working side by side to clean the stalls and restack the sacks of grain used for feeding the nosha. Yet all the while, we built the friendship which would last until the end, until the day I would leave him forever.

When Aeshone and Seppan returned from Alna, we joined them around the table for the evening meal and listened as they told of the arrangements with my father. Seppan was to be at the forge just after dawn, before full light, and work until dusk. He would share the noon and evening meal with us and then return home to spend the night with his family. If the weather was bad, he was to stay the night at our house sharing my room, and Aarad found this part of the arrangement the best of all.

"With the storms we have around here," he whispered, "he won't be home most of the winter, and you'll be stuck with him."

Since Seppan was to start in the morning, I was to be given the next five days off and could choose from then on if I wished to assist them in the shop or not. For me there would be a new found freedom, and I was not sure what to do with this. Therefore, I decided to stay the next two or three days with Aarad and help on the farm learning the ways of a farm hand.

That night, as I lay with Aarad and Seppan and drifted off to sleep, I thought of what I had said in the barn that afternoon. It was true, if I could be at sea I would never want to come home. Yet now, as I lie so far from all I knew as a child, I know how foolish I was that day; for I long to be on the hill outside of Alna, to be that innocent boy who knew none of what I now know. And I wish these cold and useless bones rested in the land of my birth, in the soil of Theo, near the village of Alna.

END OF BOOK ONE

Book Two
The *Tel*

Chapter I

Warm, I lay warm on a rock by the River Ruha, my skin still moist from swimming, and listened to the sound of water forever falling in one unending motion into the pool at the base of the falls. It was high summer, and in one cycle of the sun I would be approaching manhood and the end of all such days.

Tuac had come to the inn and suggested to Boec that we should all go to the rocks since Alnat and Tefnoar were both starting apprenticeships at the end of the moons cycle, and Boec would be off to Crayoar with the start of the harvest to apprentice as a miller in his cousin's mill. Tuac himself was pledged to apprentice with Abdoar who had saved enough money to buy his own boat and would set up a camp on Kesset the following spring. And so our boyhood days were coming to an end; and I, as the youngest, would then be left alone.

It seemed strange that Tuac would make such a suggestion; for we had seen little of him since the last time we were together at the rocks, and six cycles of the moons had past since then. Yet, as I reasoned, with Alnat and Tefnoar having to work each day, Tuac would soon be alone, and he needed to make friends with us again.

When they came to my house to ask me to join them, Tuac held back and let Boec do the talking. This, too, seemed strange, for never before had I known Tuac to be shy which caused me to wonder if he was ashamed of his actions these past six moons. Yet he gave no true sign of remorse.

"I suppose Ashka Boy will be coming too," Tuac said speaking only after I had agreed to come with them.

"Careful, Tuac," Boec warned him, "Ashka Boy's brother will hear you, and he won't like it."

Tuac reddened, then said, "I forgot he works for your father."

"Aarad hasn't been able to do much of anything since Seppan started working for nodah," I told them ignoring Tuac's usual caustic manner, "so I doubt if we went out to ask him he'd be able to come." To this Tuac made no response, but he looked slightly pleased.

This was true enough; for, with Seppan gone, Aarad was left to help his father with the farm work. It was their hope that they could earn enough from the next two harvests to allow Aeshone to hire a farm hand permitting Aarad the freedom to apprentice where he wished. And so Aarad was willing to do what he could to insure his future.

I told my mother of our plans; and, although I could tell she was not too pleased to see me going off with Tuac again, she packed us a bag of warm cheshoi to go with the fruit and cheese Boec had brought with him. Then we set off to the cobbler's where Alnat and Tefnoar were to meet us.

Alnat's father had inherited the cobbler's shop from his own father as it had been a family business passed on from father to son for generations, and Alnat's apprenticeship would insure this line would not be broken. It was a well known business servicing Alna and the farms around since he made not only shoes and boots but other leather goods such as satchels used to carry seed for planting as well as harnesses for nosha.

Tefnoar, too, was to carry on the family business by apprenticing with his father. Although their butcher's shop was not known outside of Alna it was a thriving business having been started by Tefnoar's grandfather about the time my own grandfather had opened our blacksmith's shop. Yet unlike me, Tefnoar was to become the third generation; for he would not break the line and go against the family tradition.

My father and I had both come to accept my decision not to become a blacksmith, yet neither of us had told my mother of my true desire to go to sea. After Seppan had come to work in the forge with my father, I had spent many days helping Aarad and his father with the plowing and planting on their farm. My mother asked me once if I thought I might wish to be a farmer, for when coming of age I could hire myself out to Aeshone or even to Menlo. Yet I had lied and told her I was not sure what I wanted to do; and she seemed to be resigned, for now, with my uncertainty.

Yet there truly was no doubt in my mind as to what I would do with my life, for daily I grew more and more certain of what my future was to be as the sea called to me in my dreams and haunted me daily whenever I saw the Narrows to the bay from the steps of our house. I knew in my heart that I would one day go out there again; for somehow every fiber of my being told me my destiny lay somewhere far from this bay shrouded in the mists which came in off the sea.

And so, as I lay on the rock allowing the sun to dry my moistened skin, I had no fear of the future as is fitting for boys who have not yet reached the time of manhood. That day belonged to that day alone, and all other days in what was to come lacked meaning to me then. Yet now, as I reflect on what was the last true day of my boyhood, I only wish to recapture the innocence I had then.

"I'm glad we came," said Boec as he pulled himself up out of the water and sat beside me on the rock, "it's almost like old times. I can't believe in just two moons cycles I'll be living in Crayoar, and next summer I'll be working every day and won't have any time to come here."

"And Tuac will be on Kesset," I added.

He nodded, "So, what will you do? If Aarad has to work next summer like this one, there won't be anyone around our age."

"This is really the first free summer I've had in a long time, not since I was about seven. It seems like I've been working with nodah forever. I guess I'll just help Seppan and nodah in the forge or go to Aarad's and help them."

"Doesn't sound like much of a last year before apprenticing," he said.

"You're right," I replied, "but hopefully when I do apprentice I'll be doing what I really want."

"You still want to go to sea?" he asked.

"If I can convince my mother," I told him.

"You know, I always thought your mother babied you too much, but now I'm not too sure. The sea's a dangerous place. I've heard stories from the sailors staying at the inn. I think I'll be glad to live on land for the rest of my life."

"It may be dangerous," I replied, "but I still want to go out there."

"Well, better you than me," he said with a grin, "the sea is definitely not my destiny. There's this girl in Crayoar, a friend of my cousin Kelna, now *she* could be my destiny." With that we both laughed, and he threw himself off the rock into the river.

It seemed strange to hear Boec talk of girls and hint of marriage; yet I, too, had begun to have such thoughts in the past two moons cycles. Even so, it seemed odd; but this, too, I thought, must be what it was to become a man; for men took on a career then later a wife. However, I was still a boy I told myself, and I put all such thoughts out of my mind.

§ § §

When the sun grew too hot for us to swim any longer, we all headed for the shade of some trees which lined the bank of the Ruha and shared the food we had brought. Besides the cheshoi, fruit and cheese Boec and I had brought there were two jugs of palne juice made by Alnat's father after last autumn's harvest and stored in their cellar until they had fermented making them more like wine. These we had left in the river to chill and, with the heat of the day, they were cool and refreshing. Tefnoar had brought fresh baked kinoi topped with honey and nuts; and, even though Tuac came empty handed, there was enough for everyone.

As we ate, we talked and joked laughing far more than we might have if we had not drank the palne juice; and I came to agree with Boec, I was glad I had come. Alnat and Tefnoar had never been friends of mine over the years of our boyhood together in Alna, yet there was still a camaraderie between us; and, though it may have been the effects of the palne juice, we warmed to one another so that in the end a bond had been formed which would last us into manhood.

And so, even now in death I remember them: the casual greetings we exchanged whenever I went into their shops or met them on the street, the evenings spent in later years drinking at the inn and talking over the simple common things of life. They were never friends as Tuac and I had been, nor as Aarad and I were to become, but even so I think of them; for they are a part of the Alna now lost to me forever.

After eating, and a long rest in the shade of the trees, we hiked to the top of the falls as we had done the last time I was there with Aarad. When we finally reached the path leading back to Alna, we turned east and walked the remaining league to Crayoar since Boec wished to show us the mill where he would apprentice.

I had been to Boec's cousins' house before, but neither Tuac nor I had ever been inside the mill which was located on the bank of the Ruha allowing the rushing water to turn the massive wheel. This in turn, through a system of cogs and gears, operated the grinding stone used to mill grain into flour.

As we neared the house, Boec nudged me and said, "That's her, the one in green talking to Kelna."

"Who?" I asked.

"My destiny," he whispered back to me and reddened.

Not knowing what to say, I merely grinned and nodded.

"Well, what do you think?" he asked me, "is she cute or what?"

"She's cute," was all I could manage which was true enough; but I still felt strange talking about girls this way. Nevertheless, this seemed to make Boec happy, for an odd grin spread across his face.

"What's her name?" I asked.

"Mirranu," he replied, his face still covered with an expression I had not seen on a boy's face before but only on the faces of young men just before they married.

"Who's the girl in the blue tunic?" came Tefnoar's voice from behind us.

"That's my cousin Kelna," Boec answered, and the expression on his face changed back to normal.

"Lucky you," came Tefnoar's reply. "Introduce me to her." But there was no need, for at that moment Kelna caught sight of us and came running down the path.

"Boec!" she called, "I was just talking to Mirranu and Sefala about you."

"And what were you telling them?" he asked.

"Nothing, but Mirranu was wondering when you were coming to live with us." At this Mirranu reddened and looked at the ground; and Tuac, Alnat and Tefnoar all laughed.

"I told her she would have to wait 'til the harvest," Kelna continued, ignoring their laughter, "then she can have you all to herself."

With these words Boec, too, reddened; and all of us laughed.

"So who are your friends?" she asked.

"You know Tuac and Idar," he replied.

"To'v," she said smiling at each of us.

"And this is Tefnoar and his friend Alnat, they'll be apprenticing in Alna at the end of the moons cycle. They wanted see the mill."

"Are you from Alna?" Kelna asked.

"My father's the butcher," Tefnoar replied stepping closer to her, "I'll be apprenticing in his shop."

We began to walk along the path toward the mill with Kelna and Tefnoar leading followed by Boec and Mirranu then Alnat and Sefala. This left Tuac and me alone with nothing much to say to each other. Yet I was used to the silence; for, although we had been best friends for many sun cycles, we had not always been on the best of terms having often quarreled.

"Why do you hate Aarad?" I asked at last.

"I don't hate Aarad," he replied with one of his looks of total innocence and fake surprise.

"You call him Ashka Boy all the time, and you haven't spoken to him since the day we first met him last autumn. I'd call that hate."

"I just think he's different, that's all."

"How would you know? You're never around him…or me. You're always off with Tefnoar and Alnat. You haven't even been friends with Boec since he decided to be friends with Aarad," I told him, my voice starting to raise.

"Well, I said he could come today, didn't I?"

"No, you didn't! You just asked if he would have to come with us."

"Keep it down back there, we're trying to talk here," Alnat yelled at us over his shoulder.

"All right, all right," Tuac said in a softer voice, "I'll try and be friends with him if that's what you want."

"I don't want you to do anything. But if you want to be my friend, then you'll have to be his friend as well."

§ § §

I did not speak to Tuac the rest of the day which was easy enough to do as there were so many others around. Kelna and Boec showed us the mill then took us into the house where we had cool drinks before making the long trek back to Alna. Yet through all this, Tefnoar never left Kelna's side, which to me was a little annoying; yet she did not seem to mind.

After about an hour we started for home, and even as we walked the three leagues back to Alna I managed to keep from talking to Tuac. Since all Tefnoar wanted to talk about was Kelna, this was not difficult, and I made an effort to laugh and joke with him and the others so that I would not have to speak directly to Tuac.

When we reached the village, Tuac, as usual, went with Tefnoar and Alnat; and Boec came with me to my house.

"Tuac's not with you?" my mother asked, a tone of relief in her voice.

"He's with Tefnoar and Alnat as usual," I replied showing my disgust.

"Something wrong?" she asked, "Did you have another fight?"

"I asked him why he hates Aarad," I told her.

"So, that's what that was all about," Boec said. "What'd you do that for?"

"I'm tired of his attitude toward Aarad just because he's from Teuwa." I replied, "and the way he's treated you and me this last winter and spring."

"So what did he say?" my mother asked.

"That he really doesn't hate Aarad, and he'll try and make friends with him if that's what I want."

"And what do you want?" she asked.

"For him to grow up."

"I don't think that's ever going to happen," said Boec. "Zhoh told me he doesn't know what Tuac's problem is either. I think he's jealous. We've always been his best friends, and now Aarad's come along and he's jealous."

"I think there's more to it than that," I told him. "I think he doesn't want to admit he's been wrong all this time, but why can't he see it doesn't make any difference where you were born? Zhoh accepts Seppan. I don't know what his problem is."

Chapter II

The next day my boyhood truly ended, though I did not know it at the time. Seppan arrived earlier than usual and crept into my room as the day's first light was breaking through my window.

"Idar," he whispered, "wake up, I need to talk to you."

I rolled over and rubbed my eyes stretching as I did. "What is it?" I asked.

"I probably shouldn't tell you this, but they're having a hard time of it on the farm. You know Aarad and nodah," he added when he saw what must have been a blank look on my face. "They really need help."

"And you can't give it because you have to work for nodah," I replied.

"I really hate to ask you this…"

"But would I go out and help them?" I finished his sentence.

"Well, will you?"

"I was just talking to Boec about that yesterday," I replied. "With all my friends starting their apprenticeships I won't have much to do anyway, so I might as well work. I'll go out there today after breakfast and do what I can to help out."

"You're a real friend, Idar."

"And don't you forget it either," I told him laughing.

"Go back to sleep, you can go out after you eat."

"Thanks for your permission," I told him, "now *you* go to work."

"Sure," he replied, and left my room.

§ § §

I didn't go back to sleep but lay there and thought about the previous day and my argument with Tuac. He had been my best friend since as far back as I could remember, but so many things had changed in the past moons cycles. Aarad and Seppan had become like family to me, and I realized this had never been true of Tuac and Zhoh.

After a while I got up and dressed, then went into the kitchen where my mother was kneading dough. "You're up early," she said.

"I couldn't sleep," I told her.

"I'm surprised, with all you did yesterday," she replied, "If I had walked to Crayoar and back I'd sleep for a whole moons cycle."

I thought of telling her about Seppan and his request I help his family, but I decided to keep it to myself. Instead, I told her I was planning on going out to Aarad's since I hadn't seen him in a while.

"That sounds like a good idea," she told me. "Maybe you could help out a bit while you're there. Farming's a good trade, and if Aarad doesn't want to do it, you could always hire yourself to Aeshone when you reach manhood, or go to work for Menlo."

"You've said that before, nodeh, and I told you I don't think I want to be a farmer."

"Then what do you want to do? You must have some idea. Idar, you are nearing your twelfth sun cycle, most boys your age have already decided on their futures, but all you can tell us is you have no wish to be a smith…or a farmer"

My mind froze. Every fiber of my being wanted to call out the truth to her, to tell her and be done with it. It was like last winter and spring with my father. When I failed to tell him the truth, we drifted apart. Had I learned nothing? Slowly, very slowly, the vood crept back into my life.

"What's for breakfast?" I asked.

"Go wash," she told me, and I went out to the pump to wash my face and hands.

When I returned, there was bread and two boiled gork eggs waiting for me; and my mother was spreading dough onto the baking table by the stove preparing to make cheshoi. Sitting down, I began to slowly eat while the vood sniffed at my inner organs. I had to tell her as I had told my father. It was nearly the same thing.

"Nodeh."

"Yes."

"…can I have some palne juice?"

"There's some in the jug near the sink."

I got up and poured some into a mug, then returned to the table and ate in silence.

"Nodeh."

"Yes."

"…what kind of cheshoi are you making?"

"We have no meat, so I will have to make them with only cheese."

"I could go to the butcher's, if you want."

"There is no time, the cheshoi are nearly ready to go into the oven," she replied, "…but thank you anyway."

Again I ate in silence, and again the vood nudged my stomach.

"Nodeh."

"Why all these questions, Idar?"

"I'm done eating, and I'm going to Aarad's now."

"Be home before dark," she cautioned me.

"I will," I told her and left the house. The vood followed me.

§ § §

"So, you didn't tell her?" Aarad asked after I told him about what had happened at breakfast.

We were in the vegetable garden weeding with Illiad as a hot sun beat down on us. "No, I didn't tell her," I replied. "I wanted to, but I just couldn't bring myself to say, 'Nodeh, I want to go to sea.' You didn't see how angry she was when my father told her he had given me permission to go with Tuac and Zhoh to Trohan. I don't want to face that."

"But you'll have to," said Illiad, "at least some day, won't you?"

I stared at her for a moment, "I know I will," I said at last, "but not for a while anyway. I won't reach my twelfth cycle until this winter, and then I still have ten moons cycles until I'll be expected to apprentice."

"You can't go *that* long without telling her," said Aarad. "Your father knows already. Don't you think your mother suspects something just like he did? I bet that's why she talked to you this morning, she wanted you to tell her the truth."

"Aarad's right," said Illiad. "Somehow I can never keep a secret from nodeh."

"Just make up your mind like you did last spring with your father, and do it," Aarad told me. "Everything worked out all right then. Just do it, and be done with it."

Aarad was right, and the vood told me the same thing. How could I not tell her? How could I go on living with this beast tearing me apart inside, for I would never be free of it until I faced my mother and told her of my desire to go to sea. She had let me go to Trohan last summer even though she feared for my safely, and I remembered what she told me the morning after I had returned: "…you are not a baby anymore. You are reaching manhood."

The memory of those words brought some peace to my heart so that I resolved to tell her as soon as I could; and with that, the vood crept off into the darkness…and watched."

§ § §

But I did not get the opportunity to tell her for some days. Seppan was right, for though Aarad and Illiad did their best to help, there was still much to be done. And so I asked Aeshone if I could stay with them and help for a few days. I told him I liked farming (which was true enough), so he agreed, though I was sure he knew the truth. Maybe Illiad was right, parents always seemed to know when you were not being totally honest with them.

True to my word, I returned home before dark as I had promised my mother and ate the evening meal with my parents. Then I walked back to the farm with Seppan who, as usual, ate with us before going home each night.

"I really appreciate you doing this," he told me for probably the fifth time.

"You don't have to keep thanking me, " I replied, "I told you, I don't mind. To tell the truth, I sort of enjoy working on the farm; and don't start in like my mother, I don't want to be a farm hand some day."

"Has she been asking you about that again?" he asked.

"This morning," I replied and told him what had happened at breakfast.

"So, when *are* you planning on telling her the truth?" he asked when I finished.

"Don't start with that either," I said. "I've already been over this with Aarad and Illiad this morning."

"I'm sorry, I'm sorry, it's just that…you really need to tell her."

"I know, Aarad and Illiad said the same thing. To tell you the truth, I was going to tell her when I got home tonight; but then I saw how much needs to be done on the farm, so I told your father I'd help out…Don't look at me like that, I really mean it."

"All right, I believe you," he said laughing. "Just be sure you tell her."

"*Yes*, big brother, I *will* tell her. Now drop it."

"Fine, *little brother*," he replied and shoved me into the field we were passing, so I picked up a dirt clod and threw it at him.

Chapter III

There are times when fate casts upon us great misfortune only to see it turn out to our benefit, and it was at this point in my life that fate did so for me. I spent five days with Aarad's family working hard in the fields by day and sleeping just as hard at night. We rose each morning with the dawn; and when Aarad and I climbed the ladder to the loft where we slept, my body cried out for nothing but sleep.

After spending that first night cramped three to a bed in the tiny room Aarad and Seppan usually shared, Seppan asked me if I would mind if he took my room at home to which I eagerly agreed. And so, when he did not return that night, we assumed my parents had also agreed to his request.

Then, on the fifth day, as we began the midday meal, Seppan burst into the room hardly able to breathe.

"What's wrong?" his mother cried, and both his parents rushed to his side.

"Idar," he said between breaths, "Idar…your father…you need to come…now."

I rose from the table, knocking over a chair, and stared, "Why?" was all I could say.

"He's hurt…really bad…you've got to come with me now."

"Hurt? How?" asked both Aeshone and Melne at the same time.

"He fell from the loft in the forge…you've got to come now, Idar."

My legs refused to move, my body shook. I looked across the table to where Illiad sat; and she, too, looked pale, a look of deep concern on her face. And for one brief moment, I felt it was for me. Then I began to walk toward the door, slowly at first; but when I reached it, I bolted and ran straight for Alna.

In a few minutes Seppan caught up with me, "Stop!" he cried, "I'm too winded to run any more. Let's walk."

I slowed down, and we both walked at a pace not much below a run; but this gave me a chance to ask questions. "What happened? How did he fall? How badly is he hurt?"

"We were making shoes for Menlo's nosha, and we needed more iron; so your father went up to the loft to get some. I said I'd go, but he told me to feed the fire and work the bellows in order to get the furnace hot enough to complete the job when he returned.

"On his way down, a rung on the ladder broke. The sack of iron was on his shoulder, and he lost his balance. When he landed, his head struck some of the metal that had spilled from the sack onto the floor.

"I ran over to him, but he was unconscious. So I hurried into the house to get your mother who told me to go for help as she ran to the forge.

"When I got to the street, Tefnoar was just coming by—he had been delivering meat—so I told him what happened, and he came to the forge with me. The two of us managed to carry your father into the house and put him on the bed. Your mother had to hold his left leg, it's broken. Then Tefnoar went to get Ujedah, and I came to get you."

"Was he still unconscious when you left?" I asked.

"Yes, but he could have come to by now."

"How bad is the leg?"

"Your mother had to hold it up the whole time we were carrying him. It was really hard to get him into the house without her dropping it. It's bad."

We were nearing the village, so I asked him if he could run yet.

"No," he said, "but you go on ahead, I'll follow."

When I reached our house, the door was open, and I could hear voices coming from my parents room. As I entered, the air was filled with a strong sent of some kind of herb; and Ujedah, the village healing woman, was bending over my father applying wet clothes to his head and chest.

"The smell of these herbs will help bring him back from the realm of the spirits," she told my mother.

I froze in the doorway and stared at my father lying ashen on the bed. This could not be the man I had known all my life. My father was strong. He could not be this broken man lying before me.

"I'm dreaming," I thought, "and I needed to wake up. Aarad, kick me in your sleep! Wake me up!"

Yet though I screamed these words in my mind, nothing happened; for I was not asleep, and I could not wake up.

"Nodeh," I said at last taking two steps into the room. She turned, and I rushed to her flinging my arms around her. "Will he die?" I asked, tears streaming down my cheeks.

"No…no, he will be fine," she replied soothingly.

"He sleeps in the spirit world," Ujedah assured me. "These herbs will awaken him. It was fortunate he was asleep when I set his leg, for he felt no pain."

I looked at his legs, and the left one was bound to wooden poles with strips of cloth tied securely so that it could not move.

"He will be all right," my mother said again, then added, "I'm glad you came so quickly. It will be good for him to see both of us when he awakes."

§ § §

But he did not awake for three days. My mother and I took turns at his bedside keeping watch night and day; and Ujedah came as often as she could since she had others to care for in the village, though none were in as dire a need as was my father. Each time she came, she brought fresh herbs; and I noticed from the smell that she kept changing them trying new ones to see if they would help.

Seppan helped us as well and did not return home until my father had regained consciousness. He worked in the forge trying as best he could to work the iron, and I gave him what help I could; yet even by combining all our skills, we could not finish any of the jobs needing to be done.

Menlo came by the day after my father's fall to ask about the shoes for his nosha, "So, he hadn't finished them before the accident?"

"No, sir," Seppan told him, "he fell while he was bringing a sack of iron down from the loft."

"Then they will not be done any time soon?"

"I'm sorry, sir, but neither Idar nor I have the skills to make them," he replied.

"I know how to do it," I added, "but I'm not strong enough to pound the shoes into shape. Maybe with Seppan's help…"

"I do not want shoddy workmanship," he snapped. "If you cannot do it correctly, I'll take my business to Theo." With that, he turned and stomped out of the shop.

"Keffan," I cursed.

Seppan looked at me in surprise, then he grinned, "Such language from one so young."

"Shut up," I snapped, "Menlo will tell everyone we can't finish nodah's job orders. We're going to loose business."

My eyes stung, and Seppan put his hand on my shoulder. "I'm sorry," he said, "I know it's serious, I shouldn't have joked. It's just I didn't know you could use that kind of language."

"Neither did I," I told him, and we both laughed.

§ § §

The next day Illiad came to our house which surprised me, for she had never been there before. "Aarad told me how to find your house," she said in response to the look of surprise on my face. "He couldn't come. Nodah needs him, but we all wanted to know how your father's doing. When Seppan didn't come home, nodah said it must be serious. How is he?"

"Ujedah says he'll be fine once he wakes up. She says he's in the spirit world, whatever that means."

"Did she say when he would wake up?"

"No, she said sometimes it takes days or even weeks."

"It must be awful," she told me. And I felt from her voice she might cry. "Is there anything I can do? I know how to bake bread, or I could make some soup."

"I…don't know. I'll ask my mother."

"Where's Seppan?" she asked, "nodeh has a message for him."

"He's in the shop behind the house off to the side, there," I told her pointing the way.

"I'll be back to see if you need anything," she said as she left, and for some reason I felt a strangeness in my stomach.

"Who was that?" my mother asked from the doorway of her bedroom.

"Illiad, Seppan's sister," I answered and told her of Illiad's offer.

"That was sweet of her, but we'll manage."

"Nodeh, none of us has really eaten in two days. Maybe we should let her help. You're too tired to cook anything, and Seppan and I don't know how to bake bread. All I can do is boil water in the big pot."

At this she smiled, and it was the first time I had seen her show any sign of happiness since I had been home.

"You might be right," she told me, "but she's so young."

"She helps her mother all the time. I don't think you know what a girl can do since you don't have a daughter."

With these words she even laughed, "and since when have you become an expert on girls?"

I felt myself redden. "I've…just watched her at Aarad's house. I think she can cook. I mean…she helps her mother, and the food's good."

"Well, all right, if you say so," and for some reason the strange feeling in my stomach moved into my chest and made my heart beat a little faster.

§ § §

On the third day, my father woke up. My mother was with him at the time, and she quickly called me and asked me to find Ujedah. "Check Ulanna's house first," she told me, "Ujedah will most likely be there checking the new baby."

"I want to see nodah first," I said.

"Yes, he asked for you. Go in quickly but don't stay long, you need to get Ujedah."

I entered the darkened room and breathed in the scent of the herbs, but I stayed close to the door. "Nodah," I said, my voice almost a whisper.

"Idar," he answered, "come here, it's hard to see you in this light." His voice sounded weak, like someone who is very tired and drifting off to sleep.

"How do you feel?" I asked taking a few steps toward him.

"I've been better. My head hurts…and my leg. Your mother tells me I have been asleep for three days."

"Yes, nodah."

"I don't feel like I've slept that long. I'm still tired."

"I must get Ujedah," I told him. "Nodeh told me not to stay too long. I have to go to Sharn's house. Ujedah said she'd be there."

"Come, give me a hug before you go."

I paused, afraid to touch him, afraid I might wake up and find that this, too, was a dream. The past three days had been like a nightmare from which I had wanted to awake. But now this, too, seemed like a dream, and I was not sure where reality began and ended.

Slowly I walked toward him, and when he took me in his arms I knew the nightmare was over. My father would live. He would be strong again, and life would go on as it always had.

§ § §

That night we ate the last of the soup Illiad had made along with bread my mother had mixed then left for me to knead, make into loaves and bake in the oven. The soup, though not as good as my mother's, was well made; and both my mother and I told Seppan to tell Illiad how good it was and thank her for her kindness in making it.

Seppan ate quickly, then left for home to tell his parents the news of my father's recovery; and after he left, my mother and I went in to sit at my father's bedside and keep him company. I still could not believe fate, which at first had been so cruel, had now turned to favor us. Yet fate was about to show even more favor to me.

"When you fell," my mother told my father, concern still in her voice, "...Oh, Kennec, I truly thought I had lost you. It was like my father all over again."

"But you did not lose me, Shahri. I will be fine, you will see."

"I know...but when I came into the shop, and saw you lying there on the floor, I saw not only you but my father as well. I saw him floating in the water...dead...as I have seen him in my dreams so many times since I was a girl."

"You must not upset yourself, Shahri," he told her soothingly, "it is all over now, it is in the past just like your father's death. I know you see him in your dreams, sometimes you call out for him in your sleep; but it is a thing of the past, and you cannot let the past control the present. Your father died, but I did not...and neither will Idar, unless it is the will of fate.

"Idar," he said, turning to me, "tell her."

"Tell me what?" she asked as the vood bit deeply into my heart causing it to jump in my chest.

I sat in silence, looking at both of them. "It is time she knew the truth, Idar," he told me.

"Nodeh," I began, then, for a moment, my courage failed me. "I...I don't want to be a farm hand or a blacksmith."

"I know, you have told me that again and again."

"Let him finish, Shahri."

"I...want to be a fisherman," I said, "and go to sea." And with these words, the vood died.

"No," she told me; but before she could say more my father stopped her.

"Listen to him, Shahri, you owe him that much."

"You knew of this and said nothing," she said angrily to my father.

"Yes, I have known for a long time. The signs were there, Shahri. You should have seen it yourself, but your fear of the sea blinds you."

"Nodeh," I said softly; then, as I gained courage, my full voice returned, "you said yourself when I returned from Trohan, I'm not a baby. I know how to take care of myself, and I love the sea."

"No," she said again, "I will not have it!"

"Shahri, we talked of this when he went to Trohan. You cannot let your fears of the the past rule Idar's future. In little over a sun cycle he will be a man, and a man cannot be ruled by fear especially if it is his mother's fear. Let him be the man he is to be, Shahri."

My mother sighed, "You are right, both of you. But I will always worry about you and fear for your safety. After all, man or not, I will always be your mother."

Chapter IV

The days passed quickly once my father was awake, and each morning we saw that he grew stronger. Ujedah gave us herbs which we boiled in water and gave to him as a tea. These she said would ease the pain and help him to recover. And so life did gradually returned to normal.

Soon he was up and about, walking with the support of a crutch; and within ten days he was back in the forge doing what he could and overseeing Seppan and myself in finishing orders for his customers. For many days he said his head still hurt, but that the tea helped with the pain. However, soon after he started working in the forge, he stopped drinking it saying he was fine now.

Menlo had gone to Theo as he had said, but none of my father's other regular customers had done so. Each felt they ought to support him in his need as they were sure he would do for them; and so, although money was short for a time, we did not lose business as I had feared.

I did what I could in the forge, and when I was not working there, I went to Aarad's to help him and his father. This left me with no free time as Tuac was quick to point out since, at the end of the moons cycle, he was left alone without Alnat and Tefnoar.

"You could come with me and help," I told him when he and Boec came by to ask me to go with them.

"I'm not spending my summer working on a farm," he replied, "I'll be on Kesset next summer, and this is my last chance to have fun."

"Well, they're my friends, and they need help, so I'm going out there to do what I can.

"I'll go with you tomorrow," Boec told me, and Tuac glared at him.

§ § §

The next day Boec came to my house early, just after Seppan arrived. A few minutes later, we started for the farm; and, as we walked through the village, Boec told me Tuac would be coming with us.

"I talked to him yesterday, and he agreed," Boec said in response to a look of sheer disbelief on my face. "I know, I couldn't believe it either. He didn't even argue. I just told him I thought he was being selfish, and that if he wanted to be friends with us he needed to grow up."

"And he didn't say anything?" I asked.

"No, that surprised me more than anything. He just said, 'All right, I'll come.' and that was the end of it."

We walked to Tuac's house and found him sitting on the steps waiting for us. As we approached, he got up and joined us; and the three of us left Alna and walked through the fields already turning golden in preparation for harvest.

"One more moons cycle and I'll be grinding that stuff for the rest of my life," Boec commented nodding at a field of kalhu.

"One more moons cycle and you'll be spending all your evenings holding Mirranu's hand," Tuac told him. "I can see it now, you and Mirranu sitting by the Ruha under a tree kissing…"

"Shut up, Tuac," Boec said turning red. But this only caused Tuac to laugh and make kissing sounds.

"I told you to shut up," Boec said becoming angry.

"Calm down," Tuac replied as he continued to laugh, "you know you like her."

"I like her, yes; but I don't like you making jokes about her. So drop it."

"So, what are we going to do today?" he asked changing the subject. "I'm not washing that ashka."

"Yesterday we picked krumb," I told him ignoring his comment about Huno, "and tolik. I think today we will have to dig neffan."

"*Dig* neffan? I thought they grew on trees or bushes."

"Oh, don't be so stupid, Tuac," Boec snapped at him. "Everyone knows neffan grow under the ground."

"Well, I didn't. So, how do you dig neffan?"

"I don't know," I said truthfully. "All I know is Aeshone said they should be ready to dig in a few days, and that was about six days ago."

When we arrived at the farm, Aarad was surprised and pleased to see Boec; but I could tell he was a little unsure of Tuac being with us. Yet he said nothing.

As I had predicted, we were to dig neffan and gather them into sacks for storage in the cool cellar beneath the house. We let Tuac do most of the digging since he constantly complained that crawling on his knees to gather the neffan hurt his back. And so he walked along the rows of the browning plants turning the rich black soil with something like a huge fork as the rest of us took turns collecting the neffan then carrying the sacks down to the cellar.

"What a baby," Illiad said to me as we knelt side by side digging in the dirt with our fingers to be sure we had found all the neffan. "Does he always complain like this?"

"Not always," I told her. "It's just that he really didn't want to come today. Boec and I sort of pressured him into it."

"Well, at least he's making the work go a *little* faster," she replied.

"Just ignore him, that's what I do most of the time."

"I'm trying, trust me."

"Did Seppan tell you nodeh thanked you for the soup?" I asked, and for some reason I felt myself redden slightly. But as she was busy with one very large neffan stuck in the dirt, she didn't notice.

"Yes," she said, "and he said you liked it too." These words made me redden even more, and this time she must have noticed since she looked at me as she spoke. "It wasn't really the best soup, but…"

"No, it was really good."

"You don't have to lie, Idar. I know I'm not a good cook like nodeh, and I'm sure I'm not as good as your mother."

"Well, it was really good. And thank you again for helping, it was really nice of you." Again I felt myself redden, and Illiad quickly looked away.

"We're almost done with the neffan," I said to change the subject, "Do we have any other vegetables to pick?"

"Not for a while."

"So what's next then?" I asked.

"Tuac's *really* not going to like this, but the barn needs cleaning out," she told me.

"No," I replied, "he's not going to like that at all."

§ § §

After we finished with the neffan, we all washed up at the pump and went into the house to eat the midday meal. Tuac seemed impressed by the loft, which pleased me until he said quietly to me, "But then Kellnor built this house."

"Don't you ever stop?" I asked.

"Stop what?"

"Never mind, just eat and shut up," I told him.

Then, after eating, the four of us went to the barn and spent the rest of the day cleaning, stacking and straightening up while Illiad helped cook the evening meal. Boec and I were used to this kind of work; for, although we did not have a nosha, I had still spent long hours cleaning our shed as well as the loft above the forge where my father kept his supplies. The inn had a stable, and so Boec had been required to help Shend clean it out about every five to six days. Yet Tuac had never done such work before, and he complained for the first hour until Boec finally said, "Grow up, Tuac, if you complain like this on Kesset, Abdoar will cut you up for fish bait."

At this Aarad and I laughed, and Tuac sulked the rest of the afternoon; but at least his silence made the work go more quickly. When we finished, we again washed up; and Aarad went into the house to see how long it would be before the evening meal would be ready.

"You really enjoy this?" Tuac asked me when Aarad had gone inside.

"It's not that bad," I replied. "You know, you didn't complain this much last summer on Trohan when we had to help load and unload the *Tok*."

"I couldn't," he said, "my father would have killed me."

"Well, if you don't shut up and stop complaining, Idar and I will kill you on the way home," Boec told him. "I start my apprenticeship in about twenty days. You have the autumn and the winter before you go to Kesset, so stop complaining. Like Idar said, they need our help; and a little kindness won't kill you."

To this Tuac said nothing, for Aarad came out and told us we would be eating in a few minutes. "My mother made palnoi as a special thank you for all your help today," he added.

"What are palnoi?" Tuac asked.

"They're little cakes topped with fruit and nuts." he told us. "I don't think they make them around here."

"So, they're like a Teuwa thing," Tuac said.

"I guess you could say that," Aarad replied. "We don't have them very often because they're a lot of work, but nodeh wanted to show you how she appreciates your helping us today."

§ § §

After we ate, we had to leave quickly in order to be home before the sun set; and so Aeshone and Melne again thanked us for our help and bid us farewell. Tuac was actually very gracious and told them he was happy to be of help, and at this Illiad had to turn away so her parents would not see her fighting back laughter. I, too, had to struggle to maintain merely a smile, and Boec coughed.

As usual, Aarad walked to the gate with us and bid us a final farewell. Then, as we walked along the road toward home, Boec turned on Tuac.

"You faker!" he cried. "'It's no problem, I was happy to help.' What a liar!"

"What else could I say," he replied. "I got two good meals from them, and those palnoi were great."

"Is that all you can think of?" I asked him.

"Well, I deserved it," he said with such a straight face that I was sure he meant it. "I worked hard today."

"Worked hard!" bellowed Boec. "Idar and I did most of the work. We had to let you dig because you didn't want to get your hands dirty picking up neffan. I can't believe you, Tuac."

We walked on in silence for a few minutes until we met Seppan coming the other way from Alna.

"How did it go today?" he asked and looked questioningly at Tuac.

"We dug the neffan and cleaned the barn," I told him.

"That's great," he said, "digging those neffan is always a big job. I'm glad it's done, and it's a good thing you had so much help."

"Oh, we had *lots* of help," Boec told him with just a hint of sarcasm, and Seppan gave him an odd look.

"Your father managed to stand all by himself without using his crutch, and we made four shoes for Heshel," Seppan told us. "I was able to do all of the pounding myself, so I'm sure next time there are nosha shoes to make I will be able to do them without any help. That means now I can start earning my own money."

"Why's that?" asked Tuac.

"Part of our agreement is that when I'm ready to do jobs on my own, I get to keep one fourth of what the customer pays us. Kennec gets to keep the rest as payment for teaching me the trade and also for the materials I use. But if I make a mistake, and have to do the job over, I get nothing."

"Who's idea was that?" Tuac asked.

"It's the usual agreement among tradesmen and their apprentices," Seppan told us.

"It'll be the same for me at the mill," Boec added, "but if I ruin any of the grain a farmer gives me, I'll have to pay for it with my own money. So I won't be doing anything on my own for at least a full sun cycle, not until next harvest."

"Poor Mirranu," Tuac said, "no presents for her."

"Don't start, Tuac," Boec warned him, "I'm tired, and I don't want to have to punch you."

At this, Seppan laughed and said, "I'd better be going, and you too. It's getting dark. Thank's again for helping my family today."

He raised his hand in farewell, and we returned the gesture then turned and continued back to Alna and home.

Chapter V

Boec spent the last 20 days of the moons cycle as was befitting a boy about to apprentice while I worked with my father and Seppan in the shop for the next three days then with Aarad, his father and Illiad on their farm for all that remained of the moons cycle then on into the next. Because of this, I saw Boec only twice before he left for Crayoar and both times were when he came out to the farm in order to help bring in the hay. He brought Tuac with him the second time he came, yet this was much like before as Tuac whined about how hard he was made to work.

"Kesset won't be a party," Boec told him. "You need to toughen up. If Abdoar thinks you're a weakling, he'll send you back the first time the *Mer* returns to Theo. This is good practice for you."

"I don't need to practice," Tuac replied angrily, "I know how to work; and besides, when I work for Abdoar, I'll be earning my share from the sale of the catch. Here I only get dinner, and I bet we won't be having palnoi."

At this, I merely shook my head in disgust and asked Boec what they had been doing. If I could not enjoy the summer, I could at least hear how he was enjoying his last days of freedom.

"We've been swimming a lot," he told me, "though mostly in the bay by the jetty. We went fishing a couple of times in the Ruha and spent a morning catching eln at the beach."

"Sounds like fun," I said a little envious.

"You know you really don't have to spend all your time working," Tuac told me.

"I know," I said looking across the field to where Aarad and his sister were stacking sheaves of hay into the wagon pulled by Toarak, "but I can't just leave them and go off and have fun when there's so much work here to be done."

“Of course you can,” Tuac replied sounding a little shocked that I would think such a thing. “You know, its their problem, not yours. They decided to move here from Teuwa, you didn’t ask them to come, did you?”

“I know I didn’t ask them to come,” I told him. “But they’re here, and they’re my friends, and I feel obligated to help them.”

“Obligated?” Tuac asked me.

“If you or Boec needed help, I’d do what I could. It’s the same thing.” And for once Tuac had nothing to say.

§ § §

Seppan and I exchanged bedrooms while I worked to help his family cut, dry and load the hay into the loft of their barn to be used to feed Huno and the nosha during the winter. Then Aarad and I were given a rare three days of freedom, for the kalhu was not quite ready to harvest.

Aarad spent those days with me in Alna, and we went to the beach to gather eln for a chowder my mother prepared. We stopped at Tuac’s house to ask him to join us, but he was with his father on Trohan; and oddly I felt a little relieved, for I really had no desire to put up with Tuac’s attitude.

We swam in the bay near the jetty; and, although Aarad was afraid at first, he quickly took to the deeper water. In fact, he was really quite a good swimmer.

The second day we spent exploring the caves in the hillside along the beach. They were dark and mysterious, and tales of ghosts were associated with some of them; for it was said our ancestors buried their dead in them, though I doubted this was true. However, one cave high in the cliffs about two leagues from Alna was sealed with rocks, and it was said no one could climb up there, for those who had tried had all fallen to their deaths.

The last day we spent just relaxing. Then, after the evening meal, we walked back to the farm leaving Seppan to take my room while I spent almost a full moons cycle helping with the kalhu.

This was a long process, for we first had to cut the kalhu and bind it into sheaves. Then it had to be loaded onto the wagon and unloaded into the barn where we beat the sheaves with wooden poles to knock loose the grains. After this, the stocks needed to be chopped to make straw used as bedding for the nosha during the winter. Finally, the grains had to be sifted to free them from the chaff.

When all this was completed, we gathered the grain into bags and again loaded these onto the wagon to take to Theo where Aeshone sold all but a few sacks. What grain he did not sell was then taken to Crayoar to be milled into flour.

Neither Aarad nor I had ever been to Theo before, and so Aeshone let us ride with him sitting on the bags of grain. Illiad was also allowed to come, which was a rare treat for a girl.

It seemed strange that I had lived nearly twelve cycles of the sun with the walls of Theo in sight, yet during all this time I had only seen it from afar as I walked the road leading from Crayoar to the docks. For Illiad and Aarad this trip was an even greater wonder since Theo had almost been a legend to them as they grew up in Teuwa.

The walls which surrounded the city were massive, as were the gates; and the whole city seemed impregnable. It was the home of the king and the temple where the toha were honored, and to actually enter it filled us with a sense of wonder.

Unfortunately for us, we did not get to go very far into the city since the street running from the South Gate led, after about a half a league, to a market square where produce from the outlying farms was sold. Along this street were houses which Aeshone told us belonged to the gate keepers and the merchants who had shops in the market.

These, unlike the wooden houses I was used to in Alna and Crayoar, were made of brick and were painted different colors. Most were only one story; however, as we neared the market, a few of them had a second floor with balconies; and from one of these a group of children looked down on us as we passed beneath them. The smallest waved to us, but his older brother spit over the railing nearly hitting Aarad who made a rude gesture I had not seen him make before causing both Illiad and I to laugh.

Aarad reddened and looked quickly at his father; but, as Aeshone was facing forward, he had not seen what happened, and said nothing.

"If nodah saw that," Illiad told him in a low voice, "he'd take a stick to you." At these words Aarad motioned for her to be quiet, and we rode on in silence until we reached the market square.

While Aeshone sold the grain, the three of us explored the market and were amazed at all the produce we saw for sale. Fruits, vegetables, eggs as well as cheeses were to be found; and all sorts of meats hung dripping blood from stalls along the sides of the square. There were stacks of grain all of various kinds, and one stall even sold khansh from Shentoar.

I had brought with me a small sack of coins I had managed to save from what my father gave me from time to time as a reward for helping him in the shop, and I bought a khansh for each of us. They were firm yet juicy with a strange kind of sweetness none of us had tasted before.

Both Aarad and Illiad thanked me repeatedly for buying them, and this pleased me greatly since never before had I had an opportunity to share with any of my friends something this wonderful. However, it seemed even more strange to me that Illiad's gratitude pleased me the most.

When we reached the north end of the square, we stood for a while as we ate the savory fruit and stared in wonder at the palace of the king which rose in many tiers above the other buildings right in the very center of Theo. This, we all agreed, if nothing else, was worth the trip to Theo.

Then, before returning to meet Aeshone at the grain stalls near the center of the market square, we all washed our sticky faces and fingers in a fountain and had a drink. This, too, amazed us; for water flowing without the use of a pump was something we had never seen before.

We had left the farm shortly after dawn and had reached Theo in the middle of the morning. Yet by now it was nearly noon, and we were all hungry even though the khansh had been large. Aeshone, therefore, bought bread and cheese which he cut up with his knife; and we ate this while sitting in the wagon. Then we headed for Crayoar with the remaining grain which Hennek was to mill into flour.

Boec was overjoyed to see us; for despite the fact that he could now see Mirranu every day, he missed home, his family and his friends. We helped him unload the grain as Hennek and Aeshone haggled over the price of milling it and then stood talking for a while.

"You haven't seen Tuac since the day he helped us with the hay?" Boec asked somewhat surprised.

"No," I told him. "We went by his house just after you left for Crayoar since we had some free time after the haying was done, but his mother told us he was on Trohan. Since then we've been harvesting the kalhu, and he's never volunteered to help."

"I wouldn't expect he would," said Boec. "But I wonder what he's doing since he's the only one our age in Alna who's not working."

"I've wondered that myself," I told him.

We stayed only an hour or so in Crayoar, and then left for Alna. When we reached the village, Aeshone stopped at my house; for, since the harvest was done, I would no longer be staying with them. It was odd, I thought, to be home; to sleep alone in my own room; to eat my mother's cooking; and to get up in the morning to the familiar sights, sounds and smells that I had known since as long as I could remember. Yet in another way it would be strange to be home, for I had been away for the better part of two moons cycles, and it seemed now that nothing would be the same.

Chapter VI

While I had been gone, Seppan's skills as a smith had improved, and he was now regularly earning a share of the payment my father received. I found his skills impressive, for I had worked in the forge most of my life and had learned much of the craft, though I had never been allowed to practice it as Seppan was now doing because I was much too young. And so I could truly see how much skill he had and appreciate his abilities.

Seppan shared his money with his family as was to be expected, yet he did keep some for himself; and so, as was the custom among the young men of our village, he began to spend time at the inn drinking with those who were apprenticed and unmarried. Therefore, as autumn turned to winter with its storms and biting cold, Seppan spent more and more of his nights sleeping at our house as he had done the previous winter; and on many of these he would first go to the inn for an hour or two.

My parents did not object as he never came home late nor was he ever truly intoxicated; and, though he did wake me up from time to time if I had gone to bed early, he always tried to be as quiet as he could. Therefore, it surprised me when one night he sat on the edge of the bed and shook me.

"Idar," he whispered, "are you awake?"

"I am now," I replied a little angry with him.

"Good, I need to talk to you."

"Can't this wait for the morning?" I asked.

"It could," he replied, "...but I think you'll want to hear this now."

"This better be good," I told him.

"I think you'll be interested," he said as he removed his boots. "There was a man at the inn tonight..."

"Oh, that's really interesting," I said sarcastically.

"Shut up and listen," he told me. "His name is Tenoar, and he's going to build a merchant ship called the *Tel.* It will be built at the docks over in Sefna, and he said it would take about six or seven moons cycles to complete it, but he's looking for a crew."

"He's looking for a crew," I replied not yet realizing what Seppan was getting at.

"Wake up, Idar. He's looking for a crew. You know, men to sail the *Tel* when it's launched."

"And…"

"Oh, really wake up, Idar. Do you want to go to sea or not?"

"Of course I do. Oh…" for I finally understood what he was saying, and I suddenly became wide awake.

"So, you're saying he'd take me on?" I asked.

"Awake at last," he replied. "Maybe. It all depends. You *are* young. In fact by the time the *Tel* is completed you won't be thirteen yet, but I put in a good word for you."

"What did you tell him?" I asked, my voice rising with excitement.

"Keep it down," he told me, "your parents were in bed when I got home, and I don't want to wake them. They might think I came home drunk. So far they've been good about me keeping late hours, and I don't want anything to mess that up."

"Sorry," I said, lowering my voice.

"I told him you're a hard worker and a quick learner, and you've been helping your father and mine at the same time. He was impressed that one so young—that's what he said, 'one so young,' so don't give me that look—that one so young could have such loyalty. He was also impressed you have the skills of a smith."

"I can't do smith work," I told him.

"Sure you can," he replied, "you know how, all you need is practice, and you could get that working in the forge with your father and me. Besides, its not like he'll want you to be the smith aboard ship—at least I don't think he will—but having those skills could come in handy."

He had finished undressing, and as he was getting into bed he told me, "Just think about it, and let me know. The next time I see him, I can tell him you're interested—if you are. You know, being a merchant seaman is a lot less smelly than being a fisherman. And they make good money."

"You're probably right," I told him. "I'll think about it. And thanks for putting in a good word for me."

"No problem. Now shut up and go to sleep."

"You're the one who woke me up," I told him.

"And are you glad I did?"

"Yeah," I replied. "Good night."

§ § §

I did think about it. In fact I even dreamt about it that night and the next as well, for I kept seeing myself on the deck of a great ship—oddly one much like the *Tok*—sailing to strange lands; and this excited me far more than the idea of life on Trohan or Kesset or some other island.

It seemed strange that being a fisherman had been all I ever wanted to be. Yet now the possibility of a new life, one far more exotic, thrilled me in a way I had never known before. I began to long for Eltec, Arganon, Shentoar and all the other places I had only heard of.

I remembered my trip to Theo in the early autumn and the taste of the khansh from Shentoar, and I wondered what other marvels would await me in the far off cities I could visit on the decks of the *Tel*. Theo had truly been a wonder, but Theo was merely five leagues away. Arganon took two days to reach, and a whole moons cycle was needed to sail to Shentoar. My mind was not able to take it all in.

After breakfast a few days later I went into the shop and talked to my father. I told him everything Seppan had said, and Seppan added a few things he had forgotten to say the night he first talked to me.

"Sounds like a good idea to me," my father told me when I had finished.

Seppan's smile broadened at these words, "That's what I thought," he added.

"But what's nodeh going to say?" I asked, for this worried me. She did not like the idea of me living on one of the fishing islands, what would she say to my sailing off to strange lands especially Shentoar so far to the south?

"Your mother will worry, but you cannot let that keep you from living your life. She loves you, as you love her. However, she has to let go, for she cannot live your life any more than you can live hers. Don't worry about your mother, I'll talk to her."

"So, do you want to apprentice on the *Tel*?" Seppan asked.

"I think I do," I told him. "But as you said, I'll still be too young in seven moons to apprentice. I'll be four cycles short."

"I'll talk to him," Seppan replied, "maybe he won't be able to find a full crew, and he'll hold an opening for you…or something."

"Thanks," I told him, "I think we're even."

"No, I owe you a far bigger debt. This doesn't come close to paying you back for all you've done for me and my family."

§ § §

Days passed as did winter's first moons cycle, and with it my childhood neared its close; for each day now drew me closer to my thirteenth cycle of the sun. This seemed strange to me since I would then take on the duties of a man. Yet through it all, Tenoar still had not returned to the inn; and I began to feel my new dream would fade leaving me to find a fishing boat on which to apprentice.

I continued to keep busy, and at Seppan's suggestion my father began to let me do some of the lighter tasks in the forge on my own. This pleased him, for he felt my new interest in smithing might lead me to change my mind about my future. But even though my skills improved, I still had no desire to live my life on land away from the sea.

When weather permitted, I also went out to the farm to do what I could to help Aarad and his father since there were still many things needing to be done in order to prepare for the spring planting. And so one day as Seppan arrived for work, he told me the Toharofa would be held in three days; and I was invited to attend.

Not growing up on a farm, I had no idea what the Toharofa was; and so Seppan explained that it was a special blessing of the fields to prepare them for the spring planting. A priest from the temple in Theo would be coming to perform the rites; and afterward, there would be a party to celebrate.

The party interested me the most; for each family was to bring their own special foods as an offering to the toha, and these would be shared with everyone. He also said there would be music and dancing, but the dancing did not matter to me at all since I did not know how to dance and had no wish to learn.

My father told Seppan he could take the day of the festival off; and so, after working hard for two days in the forge, Seppan and I walked out to the farm on the evening before the feast. Aarad was waiting for us on the front steps of their house and ran to meet us as we came up the road. He seemed beside himself with an excitement I had never seen in him before and went on and on about the party and the fun we would have.

Illiad, too, was in high spirits and insisted Seppan and I each have one of the palnoi she herself had baked. When I told her how good they were, she seemed unusually well pleased; and somehow pleasing her enkindled a feeling in me I had never felt before.

When it was time for bed, Aarad and I agreed that we would sleep in the main room on mats in front of the fire allowing Seppan to sleep alone in their room in the loft. This arrangement seemed to please Huno most of all; for after we had made our beds on the floor, he left his own bed of straw in the corner and lay down between us.

I thought for a moment of what Tuac would say if he saw me sleeping with an ashka but quickly put it out of my mind, for what Tuac thought was no longer of any concern to me. I had changed in these past two sun cycles, and I liked this change; for I was more sure of myself, more independent; and for the first time I wondered if this was what it meant to be a man.

Chapter VII

The morning of the festival was cold but with a bright sun promising a warm and pleasant day would follow. Aarad and I were awakened before the others by Huno's low yet shrill cry at the door, a sound I had come to find so familiar having heard it many times while staying at their house; and after a brief argument about who would get up and let him out, I trudged to the door then quickly returned to my mat on the floor.

"It's cold," I said shivering. "Huno's lucky to have that coat of wool."

"Throw another log on the fire," he told me.

"It's your turn," I replied. "I'm not getting up again."

Neither of us moved but lay snuggled warm under our blankets trying to go back to sleep. But this was not to be, for Huno's whining had awakened Aarad's parents; and after a few minutes his mother entered the room.

"Why didn't one of you boys throw a log on the fire?" she chided, "It is cold in here this morning. Come on, up, up; there is much to be done today."

At this we both reluctantly cast off the warmth of potential sleep and climbed to our feet stretching. While Aarad tended to the fire, I gathered up the blankets and piled them in a corner of the room to be used that night.

By this time Aeshone had entered the room. "Good," he said, "you are up. You can both help feed the nosha while I milk the gamu."

"Why can't Idar and I milk the gamu?" asked Aarad.

"Maybe because you don't do it right," came Seppan's reply as he came down the ladder from the loft. "You know you don't get all the milk."

"That only shows I need the practice," he replied, "and besides, Idar's never milked a gamu before."

"From the look on his face," Seppan told him with a grin, "I don't think he wants to learn."

"Well..." I said, "...I could try...I mean, is it hard?"

"It's easy," Aarad told me. "Please, nodah," he begged, "let me show Idar. We'll even feed the nosha if you let us."

"Oh, that's a deal if I've heard one," said Seppan. "I'd take them up on it if I were you, nodah."

"Yes, you can show Idar," Aeshone replied, "but Seppan can feed the nosha now that he is awake."

"What?" replied Seppan.

"You have no work today," Aeshone told him, and Seppan sighed. Then as we hurried to the door, Aeshone called to us, "Be sure you get all the milk. I will have Seppan checking on you."

We left the house—letting Huno back in as we did—and walked to the barn as quickly as we could because of the chilly morning air.

"Seppan told me you bought gamu," I said as we walked along.

"Nodeh insisted," he replied. "We had some in Teuwa, but Morek got to keep them because he would be having children, at least that's what nodah said. So nodeh insisted we buy two since we made a lot selling the kalhu."

As we entered the barn, the gamu stood nosing the empty manger that stood in front of them. They were huge dark brown animals with shaggy hair; and, though I had seen gamu many times before, their claws looked menacing now that I was about to milk them, an act I was a little reluctant to learn.

"We need to feed them first," Aarad told me, "that calms them down, then they're a lot easier to milk. Go up to the loft and throw down some hay while I get them water."

I nodded and climbed the ladder. "How many?" I called as I reached the loft.

"Two sheaves should be enough," he told me, "but you'd better throw down another two for the nosha and Huno."

As he spoke, Seppan entered the barn. "Where's Idar?" he asked.

"In the loft getting hay," replied Aarad.

"Could you throw down two for the nosha?" he called up to me.

"I already told him to do that," Aarad said as the first sheaf hit the floor of the barn.

"Thank's, Idar," said Seppan grabbing up the sheaf before Aarad could reach it.

"I thought you were getting water?" I called down.

"Yeah, I forgot," he replied, then picked up a bucket and headed for the door.

"Illiad sure was pleased you liked her palnoi," Seppan told me when his brother had gone. "I think she likes you."

At this, I felt my face flush, and I deliberately aimed the next sheaf at his head.

"Watch it," he yelled, "I almost thought you did that on purpose."

"I did," I told him and aimed another at him.

"A little upset?" he asked.

"What makes you think she likes me?" I asked as I picked up the last sheaf.

"Oh, the way she always smiles when you're around," he replied, "I've been thinking maybe she did for a while now, but last night…well, I'm sure now she does."

His words made me feel a little strange, the way I had the night before when she seemed so happy I liked the pallon. I thought about what this could mean as I dropped the last sheaf and headed for the ladder.

"So, what are you going to do about it?" he asked as I neared the floor.

"I don't know," I told him. "What can I do about it? If she likes me, she likes me."

"Well, do you like her back?" he asked, and again I felt myself redden.

"I don't know," I told him again. I was not Boec. I had never thought of a girl this way before.

"Well, she's pretty enough," he replied.

"Who's pretty enough?" Aarad asked as he came back into the barn.

"Illiad," Seppan told him. "She likes Idar."

"I know," he replied. "She told me she does."

"Why didn't you tell me that?" I asked in total surprise, for Aarad had never kept a secret like this from me before.

"She asked me not to say anything," he replied. "She said she'd die if you knew. The only reason she told me was because she wanted to know how you felt," and for some strange reason hearing this brought a faint smile to my face.

"So what did you tell her?" I asked a little unsure I wanted to hear the answer.

"That I didn't know," he replied. "So, do you like her or not?"

"You really think he's going to tell you," said Seppan at last carrying the hay over to the nosha.

"Why not," he protested, "he's my best friend."

"Then why didn't you tell him what she said?" Seppan retorted; and for the next few minutes they argued back and forth. Yet I heard very little, for I stood next to the ladder asking myself how I really did feel about Illiad.

§ § §

After milking the gamu—an act I found a lot easier than it sounded—I returned with Aarad and Seppan to the house to eat the kahl their mother had prepared for breakfast. As usual, there was palne syrup to sweeten the kahl and now cream from the milk we brought from the barn. This added a richness to the kahl I had not tasted before since my mother bought milk to churn into butter or to bake with, and we never used it on cereal.

As we ate, I felt unsure of myself; for now that I knew about Illiad, I did not know how to act around her. I tried not to look at her, yet found myself quickly glancing across the table just to see if she were looking at me; and at times I was almost sure she was watching me, smiling at me and waiting for me to smile back.

When we finished, I went outside with Aarad and Seppan and sat on the front steps.

"Well, that was awkward," Seppan said as he sat down.

"I know," I told him, "I don't think I can be around her without feeling odd."

"Why does it bother you so much?" Aarad asked.

"Oh, little brother," said Seppan, "you do not understand the ways of love."

"Oh, and you do?" Aarad snapped back.

"Far more than you, little brother."

"Stop calling me little brother, I'm not a baby."

"Will you two stop arguing," I said interrupting them before they really got started. "Seppan, what am I going to do now?"

"That all depends on how you feel," he told me. "You never did answer Aarad's question, though I don't blame you. The little traitor might go and tell her."

"I'm not a traitor," he replied, "and I'm not going to tell her anything."

"I don't know," I told them. "I mean, she's your sister, and I've known her for a long time, and...yeah, I like her, but..."

"But if she wasn't our sister," asked Seppan, "would you still like her?"

"If she wasn't your sister, I probably wouldn't even know her," I said.

"But that's not the point," he retorted.

"But that is the point," I told him, "I mean she's pretty but..."

"So," he interrupted me again, "you think she's pretty?"

"You said she was pretty in the barn," I told him.

“But I’m her brother,” he replied, “if I think she’s pretty it’s one thing, but if you thinks she’s pretty it’s another.”

“This is really confusing,” said Aarad.

“That, little brother, is why you do not understand the ways of love.”

“So, if I think she’s pretty it means I like her?” I asked.

“Not necessarily,” he replied, “there’s more to it than that. How does she make you feel? She’s my little sister, and most of the time I find her a bit annoying.”

“Well, I don’t think she’s annoying,” I said.

“So you like being around her?” he asked.

“Yes, but I like being around Aarad too,” I replied.

“But you don’t think Aarad’s pretty.”

“No,” I said with a laugh, “I definitely don’t think Aarad’s pretty.”

“That’s my point,” he told me. “Just think about it for a while.”

§ § §

The blessing of the fields was an important event for Aarad’s family; and so shortly after we had eaten breakfast, Aeshone called to us and told us we needed to change into our best clothes. “Hurry,” he said, “your sister is already up in her room getting ready. You do not want to be late. It would be rude if the priest were to arrive and you were not properly dressed.”

With his warning still ringing in our ears, we climbed the ladder to their room in the loft and changed out of our everyday work clothes. At Seppan’s urging, I had brought my best tunic which was dark green with a black belt. It was woven from klehden fibers, but the belt was of ashka wool. Aarad wore a dark red tunic and Seppan one which was brown almost golden. Both were made of ashka wool as were their matching white belts.

When we returned to the main room, we found Illiad sitting at the table looking nervous, almost tense. “It’s Illiad’s turn to make the offerings to the toha and assist the priest,” Aarad whispered to me.

“She looks scared,” I told him.

“So was I the first time I did it,” he replied, “but don’t tell her that.”

Yet despite her nervousness, I could not help but think of what Seppan had asked me after breakfast, for Illiad seemed to me the prettiest girl I had ever seen. She wore a light blue tunic with a darker blue belt, and her hair, which usually hung loose, had been braided into one long braid that fell down the middle of her back copying the style her mother usually wore, and on her head was a woven crown of heshel with ribbons tied into it forming a colorful pattern.

The sight of her brought on that strange sensation I had felt of late; and again there was an awkwardness, a feeling of almost being embarrassed just to be in her presence. We passed quickly through the room and returned to the front steps where we waited for the priest, and I was glad to be out in the fresh air where I felt my face cool as a slight breeze gently brushed my cheek.

Selyupa, the priest from Theo who was to bless the fields, arrived at their farm in the midmorning. As he came down the road, he was followed by the three farmers whose fields he had already blessed; and when he came to the gate, we all went out to greet him.

"After he blesses our field," Aarad whispered to me, "nodah will join the procession to the next field, and we will take the food to Zhen's farm."

"Quiet," Seppan whispered a bit angrily. "You know we must be silent until after the blessing."

Aeshone opened the gate very solemnly, and Selyupa entered, nodded to Aeshone but said nothing. Illiad then approached the priest, bowed without speaking and silently led him to the field where we had harvested the kalhu.

The rest of Aarad's family followed him as did the three farmers who had come with Selyupa, and Aarad motioned for me to follow as well. At the edge of the field, Illiad stopped, bowed again to the priest, then picked up two small bowls one of which contained seeds. This she presented to the priest. Taking the bowl from her, Selyupa walked out into the field about ten paces all the while chanting words in a strange language I had never heard before.

When he stopped speaking, he took a handful of the seeds, then quietly sprinkled them onto the field and resumed his chanting as Illiad brought him the second bowl which contained water. He passed the seed bowl back to her and, taking the water, he sprinkled it on the field while again chanting a third prayer in the same strange language. At last he turned, handed Illiad the now empty bowl and followed her back to her waiting family.

Aeshone then spoke very formally to the priest thanking him for the bountiful harvest his family would enjoy due to the blessing brought from the temple in Theo by the kindness of the priest. After this, everything became informal, and we walked back to the gate while Aeshone spoke to those who had come with Selyupa.

"What was that all about?" I whispered to Aarad while the adults were busy talking.

"The priest sprinkled seed on the field," he replied, "as a sign that we give the seed to the toha and ask them to allow it to sprout and grow into a rich harvest to feed us in the autumn. Then he asked the toha for rain to water the fields. That's why he sprinkled water, it's a sign of rain falling from the sky."

"But why couldn't we understand what he was saying?" I asked.

"He was speaking to the toha," he told me, "in their language. Only the priests know how to speak it. It's something they learn as an apprentice."

"Why did we have to be so quiet?" I asked.

"We couldn't speak because the priest brought the toha with him," he replied. "Now they're in the field preparing it for the planting. It's very rude to speak without using the language of the toha."

"But why can we talk now?"

"Because now the toha are in the field working," he told me. "Before the priest leaves, he will call them and take them with him to the next farm."

As I stood thinking about everything Aarad had told me, Illiad came up behind me, "Did I do all right?" she asked startling me as she spoke.

"You were fine," Aarad told her. "It's no big deal. All you have to do is carry a couple of bowls. You don't have to say anything."

"You thought it was a big deal when it was your turn," she told him.

"Well I thought you were great," I told her. "I mean I didn't understand what was going on or anything…but you looked very important."

Again I felt myself redden. Yet I could see that she was pleased by my words; and once again I felt that strange sensation deep within me, one I was becoming oddly used to.

§ § §

After Selyupa left for the next farm, we all went into the house and began preparing to take the food to Zhen's farm for the party. When we had placed everything into baskets, we began walking down the road toward Alna being sure Huno was in the yard so that he could graze while we were gone.

"Zhen's farm is the next one over," Aarad told me. "Each farmer takes a turn hosting the feast after the blessing. Next spring it will be our turn."

When we arrived at the farm, we were greeted by Zhen's wife, a rather small woman, and two of their children. The older was a boy about Illiad's age who seemed friendly enough, yet his younger sister acted shyly as had Illiad the day I first met her.

The two families seemed to know one another; for they exchanged no formal introductions, and the two women embraced each other warmly.

"Taya," said Melne, "this is Idar, Aarad's good friend."

"Toev," I said nodding politely.

"You are very welcome to our home, Idar. This is my son, Kron, and my daughter, Narra."

"To'v," I said to each of them, and they responded the same.

"Come," Taya then told us, "follow Kron, and he will show you where to put your offerings." And as I walked away with the basket I was carrying, I heard Taya ask, "Is this the boy who has been of such help to Aeshone this past sun cycle?"

"Yes," I heard Melne reply but heard no more of their conversation; for Kron was walking quickly, and we had to almost run to keep up with him.

He led us to the side of the house where tables had been set out and covered with colorful cloths. One was already piled high with food brought by the first three families whose fields had already been blessed.

"You can put your offerings here at the end of this table," Kron told us indicating an empty table next to the one which was already full. "When the others arrive, they can fill in next to your offerings."

Illiad thanked him, and he smiled at her in a way I did not like at all.

§ § §

One by one the other families arrived until there were fourteen in all. Yet still we waited until early afternoon when Selyupa at last came down the road followed by Aeshone and the other farmers. As they reached the gate leading to the farm, Selyupa again paused and recited a prayer before he and the others entered.

"He's dismissing the toha," Aarad told me, "and sending them back to the temple in Theo." Again Seppan gave him an angry look, but this time he said nothing.

With this final act, the blessing rites were ended, and the party at last began. As we walked informally across the yard toward the tables piled high with food, Seppan came over to us.

"Nodah would be really angry if he knew you had been talking during the blessing," he told Aarad.

"Then don't tell him," Aarad retorted. "Besides, I was only telling Idar what was going on."

"Just don't do it again," Seppan snapped, and walked off.

"He ought to know how mad nodah would get," Aarad told me. "Once, when we were little, the priest came to Teuwa to bless the ashka at mating season, and he talked to me. You should have seen how angry nodah got. He wouldn't let Seppan have anything to eat at the party except raw aldayf, and if you've ever eaten aldayf raw, you know how miserable Seppan was."

At this I laughed, "I don't even like aldayf when its cooked," I told him, "when my mother puts it in soups, I always pick it out, but then she usually catches me and makes me eat it anyway."

When we reached the food tables, the music began; and so Aarad and I each grabbed a pallon and went to watch those wishing to dance. A group of men stood in the back of a wagon playing for the crowd which had gathered around them. One man beat out the rhythm on a large tarrope made from an old water cask with most likely gamu hide for a covering. Another accented the rhythm with small bronze cymbals, and three others piped the melody on zarufoi.

Already another group of men and boys had formed a circle and were doing the kolat, a traditional dance of our village which I had seen many times before. The women, who were not allowed to join this dance, stood watching, many clapping time to the beat of the music.

"Do you know how to do it?" Aarad asked nodding at the dancers.

"No," I replied. "I've seen it done all my life, but I've never been brave enough to join in and learn."

"It looks like fun," he said, "and easy. Come on, let's do it." When I held back, he stuffed the last of the pallon into his mouth and, grabbing my tunic, pulled me into the ring.

He was right. It was easy and fun as well, and I wondered why I had not tried it before; for even Tuac had learned the kolat and teased me because I was too timid to try.

When the music stopped, Aarad and I almost stumbled and fell on the ground because we were laughing so hard.

"You were really good," Illiad told us, suddenly appearing beside us; and the merriment of the moment abruptly stopped as I realized she had been in the crowd watching me.

"Not that good," I replied. "I've never done it before."

"Then you must be a quick learner," she told me. "They're doing the zubah next. Would you like to be my partner?"

"I…don't know," I stammered. "I've never done that before either."

"It's not any harder than the dance you just did with Aarad," she told me.

"Yeah," said Aarad, "I've done the zubah before. It's easy."

I shot him a quick look that said: "You're no help," then said out loud, "Well…"

"If he won't be your partner," said Kron who suddenly appeared out of nowhere, "I will."

"No," I said quickly. "I'll do it." For at that moment I knew there was no way I would ever let Kron dance with Illiad.

"Good," she said. "Aarad, you can dance with Narra."

With that, she took my hand and lead me out into the circle where those wishing to dance the zubah were gathering. At her touch, my heart froze in my chest. I wanted to pull away, but at the same time I felt drawn to her and wanted to feel her hand in mine. I was a little embarrassed, but the feeling quickly went away as she began to explain the steps of the dance.

"We skip three times this way," she told me, "then sort of hop back twice. Then three more skips and hop back twice," but with that the music started, and we began to dance.

"Three skips, hop twice," she chanted, "three skips, hop twice, three skips, hop twice. Now twirl me."

"What?" I said.

"Raise your hand," she told me as she spun in front of me. I did as she said, and she continued to spin now one way and then the other while at the same time holding on to my hand.

"Now three skips, hop twice, three skips, hop twice. I think you've got it," she said laughing.

She was right. The dance was easy, and I began to feel relaxed even though we were in a large crowd.

Aarad and Narra passed us as we skipped and hopped; and I could tell from the look on his face he did not seem to be enjoying himself as much as I was. For I was as happy at that moment as I had ever been in all my life; and if it were possible, and the dance could have never ended, it would not have mattered to me in the least.

But the dance did end; and as we left the circle to join the crowd, we met Seppan who seemed to be seeking us out. "Well, well," he said, "the man can dance like a tuffel looking for eln on the beach."

"Why didn't you do it then?" I said giving him a playful shove.

"No, you were really good," he told me. "I know because I've done it many times, but today no one asked me," and he looked at Illiad. "It seems my little sister's found a new partner for the zubah."

Illiad reddened and looked quickly at the ground. "I'm going with Narra to get something to drink," she said and ran off toward the food tables.

When she was gone, Seppan leaned down and said softly in my ear, "So, do you like her?"

"Yeah," I replied smiling up at him. "I think I do."

Chapter VIII

I spent the night with Aarad and Huno sleeping on the floor in front of the hearth in the main room and then walked back to Alna with Seppan in the morning. When I came into our house, my mother appeared to be upset, but she said nothing. My father was sitting at the table waiting for us which was unusual since he always ate then went out to the shop even if Seppan had not arrived.

"A man came to the house yesterday looking for you," he told me. "He had a message from Tenoar."

"Tenoar?" I asked in surprise.

"Yes," my father said. "I told him where you were, and he asked if you could meet Tenoar at the inn tonight."

"Idar is too young to be going to the inn at night," my mother said in a cold voice, one making no effort to hide her anger.

"Seppan and I will go with him," he told her, "and it will not take long. He will be fine. There is no reason to worry, Shahri."

"But why can't he come here to our house?" she asked. "Why the inn, and at night?"

"Businessmen such as Tenoar do not come to the homes of those they wish to hire," he told her. "They do business in public, and it would be rude if Idar did not go to meet him wherever he wishes. He cannot think of Idar as a boy who needs his parents protection."

"But he is a boy," she said coldly. "He is not a man for six more moons cycles."

"If Tenoar wishes to hire him," he replied, "then Idar must act like a man. It is the only way he can make a good impression. Now stop worrying. He will be fine, Shahri."

§ § §

I had been to the inn many times before yet never at night, for the inn after dark was the realm of men. Even Boec and Shend, when they were still boys, were not allowed downstairs after dark since it was frequented by men who came to drink and talk; and it had an unsavory atmosphere, one parents did not wish their younger sons to experience.

Seamen came to the inn as did tradesmen; for, though Alna was not a large port, it was frequented by those who wished to buy fish, wool or kalhu. The farmers in Teuwa shipped their ashka wool to Crayoar by tarrek where it was unloaded and brought to Alna by cart. Aeshone, as a new farmer, chose to sell his kalhu in Theo. However, many more established farmers, such as Menlo, sold their kalhu directly to the captains of trading ships; and it was at the inn that such deals were made.

And so I was excited, though a little fearful, to go with my father and Seppan to meet Tenoar at the inn. Many questions filled my head that night; for, as my mother had pointed out that morning, I was still a boy and not yet ready to apprentice especially on a trading vessel sailing to exotic ports such as Eltec and Shentoar.

We arrived just after dark as the messenger had said we should, yet Seppan told us he did not see Tenoar anywhere. My father asked us to find a table while he went to talk to Sethel and order drinks, and so we moved off into the crowd while he went to the bar.

"What if he doesn't come?" I asked Seppan as soon as my father left.

"He'll be here," he told me.

"But how do you know?"

"I don't for sure," he replied, "but just be patient. I'm sure he'll come. He's the one who asked you. If he didn't intend to show up, he wouldn't have sent a messenger to your house."

"I guess that makes sense," I told him.

We found a table in a corner were we could watch the door and waited for my father as a pain grew in my stomach.

"I'm really nervous," I told him. "What if he doesn't want me? I know he asked me here, but what if when he sees me he thinks I'm too young or a weakling or…I don't know, there's a million reasons he might not want me to apprentice with him."

"Stop worrying," he said. "When I talked to him, I told him you were young, and he didn't seem to mind; and you're not a weakling, so just relax. Here comes your father."

My father came over to the table carrying three mugs and placed them in the center, then sat down.

"Here," he said sliding one of the mugs toward me, "this will calm your nerves."

"What is it?" I asked.

"Spiced wine," he told me. "And drink it slowly. It is not watered down like it was on Trohan."

I looked at him in surprise and wondered how he knew about Trohan.

"What else would those fishermen on Trohan drink?" he told me as if reading my mind.

I took a drink from my mug and coughed.

"I told you to drink it slowly," he said laughing.

"As you said," Seppan told me with a huge grin on his face, "you don't want Tenoar to think you're a weakling. Just take little sips…like that. It takes some time, but you'll get used to it."

"Did Sethel say anything about Tenoar?" I asked.

"No," my father replied, "he said Tenoar comes in here sometimes, but that he has not seen him for ten to fifteen days."

"Great," I said.

"He'll come," Seppan told me again. "Just relax and sip your wine."

We sat in silence for a few minutes, then Seppan said, "He's here. The man who just walked in," and at these words, my stomach gave an extra jerk so that I thought I would be sick.

Seppan stood up and raised his hand. After a few moments, Tenoar caught sight of him, nodded and began to walk towards us.

My father stood up as Tenoar approached our table and motioned for me to do the same. When he reached us, my father extended his hand in an act of formal greeting as did Seppan.

"Toev, my name is Idar," I told him copying the formal greeting used by my father.

"Toev, I am Tenoar as I am sure Seppan has told you. Please sit."

"Might I buy you a drink?" my father asked.

"Yes, thank you. Kahlmek would be fine," he replied.

"I'll get it while you talk," said Seppan and walked off toward the bar.

"So," he said when the three of us were seated, "you wish a life on the open sea."

"Yes sir," I replied. "Very much, sir."

"Well, you appear sturdy enough. Not like some of the lads I have seen over in Sefna," he told us. "Seppan tells me you have been working with your father in his blacksmith shop."

"Yes sir, for over five sun cycles now."

"And you do not wish to apprentice with your father?" he asked.

"No sir. Seppan has become my father's apprentice," I told him. "I like the sea far more than working in the forge."

"And have you been to sea before?" he asked.

"Once, two summers ago, I went to Trohan with my friend," I told him. "His father is a fisherman on the *Tok*."

"A good ship," he replied. "Then you know Miku?"

"Yes sir, I mean I met him when I sailed on the *Tok*, but I don't really know him."

"And so from this one experience on a fishing boat you have decided to become a seaman aboard a trading ship?"

"No sir…I mean yes…but not really," I stammered. "It's hard to explain. You see, I've always loved the sea. It calls to me…I can't really explain it, but when I went to Trohan aboard the *Tok* I somehow felt I had at last come home. There was this feeling I…I…"

"…was born to have the waves beneath your feet and the salt spray in your face," he said finishing my thought.

"That's it," I told him. "Every time I've heard the waves lapping at the shore I've had this feeling deep inside me that I needed to go with them, that they had somehow come for me and wanted me to follow."

"Seppan also tells me you have been working for his father helping his family to get established on their farm here in Alna."

"Yes sir," I replied.

"And why would one so young wish to give up what free time he has to help work on a farm that isn't even his?" he asked very matter-of-factly.

"They're my friends," I told him. "What else could I do? Seppan works for my father, so I have tried to help his father and brother when I can. His brother, Aarad, is my best friend and wants to apprentice somewhere away from the farm. To do that, their family needs to have the money to pay for extra help, so I've tried to help them."

He sat for a moment and said nothing as Seppan returned to the table and placed a tall mug in front of Tenoar then took his seat next to me. At last he turned to my father and spoke, "As the boy's father, do you consent to his apprenticing as a merchant seaman?"

"If that is his wish," my father replied. "I had hoped he would follow in my profession. But that is not his wish, and I cannot stand in his way. If he is to be happy in life, he must do what truly pleases him."

Tenoar took a drink from his mug. "They serve the best kahlmek in all Theo at this inn," he told us. "That's one of the reasons I have chosen to harbor here instead of in Sefna.

"One thing concerns me, however," he said turning again to me, "and that is your youth. When do you become of age?"

"With the second moons cycle of winter," I told him.

"And by that time I plan to be in Shentoar far to the south," he told us; and these words pierced my heart, for I felt my hopes die.

I wanted to cry, but my father had always told me a man did not waste his tears on small things. This, my mind told me, was a small matter since I could still find a ship and go to sea. Yet my heart told me differently, for the idea of sailing to far off lands had grown in the depths of my being ever since Seppan told me of Tenoar's possible offer.

"Why Shentoar?" Seppan asked.

"The *Tel* will be launched during the first moons cycle of autumn," he replied, "so I intend to sail to Serret and buy melmat—it is the only fish that sells well in Shentoar—then, if no major problems arise, I will sail south and winter there in Kallefandra's warm climate.

"It takes a full moons cycle's journey to reach Shentoar. By the time I trade my cargo and reload the *Tel*, I should be starting my return trip in the third moons cycle of winter. That way I will avoid the major storms on both legs of my voyage. All in all, the round trip should take about a hundred and sixty days or so to make.

"So," he said turning to me, "could you be gone that long? It's a lot to ask of someone on their first voyage away from home."

I was stunned and could say nothing, but my father answered for me, "Is this an offer for my son to apprentice?" he asked.

"If he wishes to sail on my ship, yes," came his reply.

"But I won't reach manhood until after you've sailed," I told him.

"Being a man is far more than counting cycles of the sun," he said. "I have known men who, though well past being of age, are no more than boys with beards. You have shown true manhood in your devotion and your loyalty to your friends. If you give me half as much allegiance, I will be truly pleased to have you as one of my crew."

With that, he extended his hand to me across the table. "Do we have a deal?" he asked.

"Yes, we have a deal," I replied with a grin on my face; and firmly shook his hand.

As was the custom, he and my father then discussed the terms of my apprenticeship while I listened. I was to have the rank of mahlet, which was a kind of general assistant to anyone on board. Since I had some skill working as a smith, I would be assigned directly to the ship's carpenter doing general maintenance; however, I would also assist the cook, stand watch and fetch and carry whatever was needed.

For this I would receive one tenth of a percent of the profit made by the ship on each run; however, after completing one sun cycle, my share was to become one half of a percent provided I did a satisfactory job in my duties and there were no complaints from the rest of the crew. After completing my apprenticeship of four sun cycles, I could choose to stay on with the crew and receive a full one percent of the profits or go elsewhere as I saw fit.

With these terms agreed upon, we again all shook hands; and to further seal the bargain, my father bought another round of drinks. We then sat and talked for what seemed like hours until the effects of the spiced wine made my head light and my eyes begin to droop.

At last my father told Tenoar that we needed to leave as my mother was anxiously waiting at home for news of my apprenticeship; and with that I became wide awake. In my excitement, I had forgotten my mother and what she would say upon learning I was to spend the coming winter in Shentoar so far away from home.

Chapter IX

My mother was not pleased. "What were you thinking, Kennec!" she screamed at my father, "Idar is only a boy. How could you agree to let him go all the way to Shentoar before he comes of age. We will not even be able to celebrate with him when he has reached manhood."

"We can celebrate before he goes," my father told her. "Tenoar has paid Idar a great complement in agreeing to take him before he is formally of age. He respects what he has done and feels he has already proven himself to be a man. And I agree."

These words touched me deeply, and my heart swelled with pride that my own father felt so highly of me.

"Idar has acted like a man these past moons cycles," he continued. "I am proud of him as you should be. I know you are upset, but you cannot keep him from becoming what he is meant to be.

"I, too, will miss him; but since he does not wish to apprentice with me, one way or another he will be gone from us. There is nothing either of us can do to prevent it. In fact, there is nothing I would want to do. Do you, Shahri, wish to keep him as he is now—a boy with no future—or are you willing to let him go, to let him become the man he is destined to be?"

My mother dropped into a chair at the table stunned by what my father had said. "I know," she said crying softly. "I know you are right, but it is so hard to let go. I keep thinking of my own mother, of how hard it was for her when my father died. She had no grave to go to, and it ate away at her until she died of a broken heart.

"You remember how she was, Kennec? You remember how she longed for him every day of her life until she finally died much younger than she was meant to.

"If Idar were not to come back, I don't think I could go on either."

"He will come back," my father told her. "I tell you, Shahri, he is not your father. He will come back."

These words haunt me even now, for I did not fail her. I came back as my father assured her I would. I came back as I promised her at the start of each voyage. I came back.

§ § §

Spring came, and with it the *Mer* joined the fishing fleet at Alna. Tuac then went off with Abdoar to Kesset as he had contracted nearly a sun cycle before, and I stood on the wharf with his mother and Leyhah since he asked me to come to see him off. I was surprised at this, for we had grown apart; yet he was still my friend, and I was saddened to say good-bye knowing that this would be for a long time since in the autumn he would return, and I would be in Shentoar.

Daeo and Zhoh had left for Trohan six days before, the same day the *Mer* set sail on its maiden voyage which was a short five hour trip out into deep water and back again just to test the seaworthiness of the ship. Tuac had not gone out since his duties on Kesset would be primarily on land building the huts and the tarkoi the fishermen would use while on the island. This left him with no real experience on board ship; and he was nervous as he would be now assigned duties when they sailed unlike the times he had gone to Trohan with his father as a mere passenger.

"Now mind yourself," his mother told him, "Remember, Abdoar is your captain now. He's not a friend come over to dinner like in the past."

"I know, nodeh," he replied, "nodah has told me that a hundred times."

"Well, you just keep it in mind," she said, "I don't want him bringing you back and dropping you off at my doorstep in a few days."

"I'll work hard," he told her. "So stop fussing and worrying. I'm a man now. I'm not your little boy. You never made this much of a fuss when Zhoh went to Trohan."

"Zhoh was different," she snapped back at him. "Zhoh was more…responsible. You know I could always trust Zhoh to do his chores. I've always told you to be more like Zhoh."

"Yes, mother, you have," he said with a tone of voice I had never heard him use with his mother before.

"Do not take that tone with me," she told him. "You may be a man, but you are still my son. A son should respect his mother."

"I'm sorry, nodeh" he replied, and I felt a little embarrassed for him.

"Good," she said. "Now give your mother a hug, and Leyhah too, and be on your way."

He reached down and picked up Leyhah, hugged her and kissed her on both cheeks. "Be good for nodeh," he told her. "With Zhoh, nodah and me gone you'll have to help her all you can."

"I will, Tu'c," she told him; and he gave her another hug.

When he put Leyhah down, he hugged his mother and kissed her on the cheek; and I heard her tell him softly, "I love you son. Make me proud of you, and your father too."

"I will," he told her. "I love you too."

Then he turned to me, and I could see there was a tear in the corner of his eye. He extended his hand, an act he had never done before; and I took it. But then he pulled me toward him in a quick embrace.

"Good-bye," he told me and, releasing me, reached into the pocket of his tunic.

"Here," he said placing a red kaylo stone in my hand, "this is for you to remember me by. You always tried to win this one first," he told me. "You were always so predictable. Think of me when you're in Shentoar."

And with that he turned and climbed aboard the *Mer*.

§ § §

The days passed quickly once Tuac was gone, for I was again kept busy helping on the farm and in my father's shop. Yet now there was new purpose to my work, and I did not mind as I had in the past. Whether it was that I was becoming a man or that I had merely grown used to laboring on the farm and in the forge, I do not know. But whatever it was, although I did not truly look forward to getting up each morning and working long hours, I was resigned to it and accepted that this was the way things were to be.

The time I spent in the forge was time spent learning valuable skills in metal working, skills I could put to use on the *Tel* and increase my worth to Tenoar and his crew. Yet the days I spent on the farm became opportunities to be close to Illiad, and I did not know which I preferred the most.

Seppan had told no one of my feelings for Illiad, and I said nothing even to Aarad; for, although he was my best friend, I somehow felt he would not understand. And so it surprised me when one day, as we worked planting the kalhu, that he asked me about my feelings for her.

"You like her, don't you?" and he nodded toward his sister who was in the wagon helping their father fill large bowls of seed which we carried into the field to sprinkle on the ground.

"Yeah, I do," I replied tossing a handful of seed onto the dark soil. "At the Toharofa, when we danced, it was…I just keep thinking about her."

"And you didn't tell *me* because you thought I'd tell *her*," he said. "I'm not a traitor you know, just because Seppan said so."

"Careful," I told him, "you're only supposed to pat the kalhu. If you hit it like that you'll bury it too deep.

"I know you're not a traitor. It's just…I don't know, it's really hard to explain. I just don't like talking about it."

"Does Seppan know?" he asked.

"Yeah, he asked me, so I told him," I replied. "But I told you when you asked. So it's not like I'm trying to be…you know…secretive."

"Well, you still could have told me."

"I know. I'm sorry," I said.

"So when are you going to kiss her?" he asked, and I could feel myself redden.

"I don't know. I haven't thought about it," I lied.

"Well, you really should kiss her."

"Has she said something to you?" I asked.

"No…well…she just keeps asking me how you feel about her," he told me. "So I think you should just tell her…or you could kiss her, then she'd know."

"I don't know," I told him. "Kissing a girl is really serious. I mean, she might think I want to marry her or something."

"Do you want to marry her?"

"Aarad, I just like her. I'm not going to marry her."

"Well, if you married her, then we'd be like brothers."

"We're already like brothers," I told him. "I don't have to marry her for that."

"But if you did want to marry her, and I'm not saying you should, but if you did, it would be all right with me."

"I'm glad I have your permission," I said laughing, "but I just like her and that's all. I'm not going to marry her."

§ § §

The very next day, when my father left the forge to look at a nosha a farmer brought in to be shoed, Seppan told me he, too, thought I should kiss their sister.

"Aarad talked to you last night, didn't he? And then he wonders why I didn't tell him sooner."

"It's not like I didn't already know," he told me.

"I know, but…I told him I didn't like talking about it. So why does he have to talk about it. I mean, is the whole village going to be talking about it next?"

"They will if you don't keep your voice down," he told me. "I just agree with Aarad—and I really can't believe I'm agreeing with my little brother on matters of love—but if you like her, and she likes you, then you should take the next step."

"Have you ever kissed a girl?" I asked.

"Well, I…"

"Oh, come on Seppan, I've never even seen you talking to a girl, except that one at the Toharofa; and you definitely were not kissing her," I told him.

"There were a couple of girls back in Teuwa," he said. "Well, actually there was only one, but I did kiss her; and I was younger than you are."

"And then you left her," I told him. "You came here."

"True, but…"

"Well, I'm going to Shentoar in the autumn."

"But not forever," he retorted. "You'll be back, and if you want her to keep liking you, you have to do something before you go."

"Fine," I said, "I'll think about it."

"Good," he told me, "but don't think too long, you need to do something soon. If you wait too long, she'll start to think there's nothing between you; and you *did* see the way Kron kept smiling at her."

§ § §

I did think about it. In fact that night I dreamt I kissed her, and this confused me even more. I knew I wanted to do it, but I had no idea how to go about it; and I was definitely not going to ask Seppan.

And so the vood was back, at least every time I was around Illiad. I had thought the vood was dead, but it was there biting at my stomach whenever I looked at her. Yet maybe it was a donect which had crept down out of the hill country. Whichever, I did not care, for it made me wish to avoid her; yet this was difficult to do as I often came to their farm, and we worked together in the fields throughout the spring and into the summer.

Yet when I was at home, even while I worked with my father and Seppan in the forge, I longed to be with her; and I often thought of how we danced at the Toharofa and of how her hand felt in mine. These feelings confused me, for I could not understand this conflict within me.

Then one evening in mid summer Tefnoar and Alnat came to our house as we finished our meal to invite Seppan to come to the inn and play kahtore.

"I can't," he told them, "Kennec still needs my help in the forge."

"I can help nodah," I told him.

Both he and my father looked at me in surprise, for I had never before volunteered to help out in the evening. "Are you sure?" Seppan asked.

"I don't mind," I told him. "Go, have fun, if I were older, I'd go to the inn myself…but I'm too young," I quickly added when I saw the look on my mother's face.

"Well, if you really don't mind," he said a little reluctantly.

"Go," my father told him. "If Idar is willing to help, we can manage."

With that, he left; and my father and I finished eating then went out to the forge.

Though I did not look forward to the work, I was glad to volunteer; for I had been looking for an opportunity to be alone with my father as I needed to talk with him without Seppan or my mother being around. But even so, it was difficult at first to speak of what was in my heart; and so we worked for a time in semi silence talking only when it was needed.

At last I found my courage. "Nodah," I said, "…how did you know you liked nodeh, I mean when you first knew her."

"When I first knew your mother," he told me putting down the tongs which held the piece of iron he was working, "I didn't like her at all. In fact, to me she was the ugliest girl I had ever seen."

At this he laughed, for the surprised look on my face must have been something to behold.

"What?" I said, and my mouth hung open.

"But we were only children then," he went on, "and boys usually do not think girls all that interesting…not at first. Then one day, I was not much older than you are now, I saw her walking through the village carrying some laundry that she and your grandmother were forced to do in order to make a living after her father died, and I wondered how she had become so beautiful. After that, well, one thing lead to another and we were married."

"But how did you know you liked her?" I asked again.

"That is a hard question to answer," he replied picking up the tongs and placing the metal back into the fire. Then he walked around from behind the anvil and stood in front of me looking down with an odd smile on his face. "It sort of grew on me until one day I knew being with her made me happy."

"And did you kiss her?" I asked.

"Kiss her?" he said, and his smile broadened. "You're in love."

"I'm not in love," I protested. "I…just…I don't know. There's this girl, and I like being with her like you said."

"And being with her makes you happy?"

"No," I told him, "being with her makes me…scared, nervous, almost sick to my stomach sometimes. But when I'm not around her…"

"And who is she who has such a hold on you?" he asked.

"Illiad, Seppan and Aarad's sister," I answered in almost a whisper.

"Ah, so that's why you spend so much time out there working for her father," he said laughing.

"No!" I told him, "I'm trying to help. I'd go even if she wasn't there."

"I'm sorry," he said, "I was just teasing you."

He put his arm around my shoulder and led me over to the pile of wood we kept at the side of the shop. We each chose a spot among the stacks of logs and sat down.

For a few moments neither of us spoke as I sat staring at the floor of the shop.

"So what can I do?" I asked him at last. "I mean…how can I let her know I like her."

"You could tell her," he replied.

"Is that what you did?" I asked.

"Well, no," he said. "I gave her flowers."

"Flowers? You just gave her flowers? You didn't say anything?"

"If I remember," he told me, "and it was a long time ago, I told her they reminded me of her because they were so pretty."

It may have been the fire, I never knew for sure; but as he spoke, he seemed to redden, and then he, too, stared at the floor.

"So, if I give her flowers, she'll know I like her?" I asked.

"Well," he replied, "she will probably get the idea. After all, boys do not usually give flowers to girls unless they do."

"And I don't have to say anything?"

"Saying something would help," he told me. "You cannot just hand her flowers and walk away. Think of something nice to say."

§ § §

It took me days to think of something nice to say, and even when I did, I still felt it sounded a truly odd thing to say. Nevertheless, as I walked out to the farm with Seppan a few days later, I stopped along the way to pick some heshel.

"What's that for?" Seppan asked slowing up and then stopping to wait for me.

"Illiad," I replied.

"Oh, nice touch," he said. "Where'd you get that idea?"

"I talked to nodah," I told him. "That night you went to the inn to play kahtore. He said that's how he told my mother he liked her."

"You know, that just might work," he said. "But I still think you should kiss her."

"I'll just give her the flowers," I told him. "The kissing can wait. Maybe when I get back from Shentoar."

"That long?" he said.

When we arrived at the farm, I was not at all sure I wanted to give her the heshel, at least not in front of everyone.

"How do I do this?" I asked him. "I don't want everyone watching when I give these to her."

"Leave them by the tree over there and go pet Huno," he told me. "I'll get her to come out to the yard."

"How?" I asked.

"I'll think of something," he replied. "Just do it," and he walked toward the house leaving me by the gate.

I walked over to the tree and put the heshel next to it on the side away from the house so that no one could see it. Then I walked over to Huno who was grazing in the yard. He looked up when I approached but then went back to eating, so I knelt down and patted him.

"Huno," I said, "I sure hope this works," and felt really stupid talking to an ashka. "What am I doing," I thought and stood up; but as I did, Illiad came out onto the steps.

"Is something wrong with Huno?" she asked. "Seppan said you were looking at him and wanted to talk to me."

"No," I told her, "no…there's nothing wrong, I…just…I wanted to give you these," and I hurried back to the tree and picked up the heshel.

“I picked these for you on the way out,” I said. “I remembered how you looked at the Toharofa...you had them in your hair, and you looked nice, so...I just thought maybe...maybe you’d like to have some.”

She walked down the steps smiling and came towards me; and as she did, I felt I wanted the donect to just eat me then and there and get it over with. My hand shock slightly as I raised it, and when she took the heshel, her fingers touched mine causing me to feel again that odd feeling I had felt when we dance in the early spring.

“Thank you,” she said smelling the heshel, “that was really nice of you. Did Seppan tell you that heshel are my favorite flower?”

“No,” I replied. “I didn’t know. I just thought you looked...nice when you wore them in your hair that day...and...”

Without warning it happened. She reached over and kissed me on the cheek, then jumped back. Her face reddened and she looked down. I felt my face burn as the donect leapt at me trying to drag my trembling legs to the ground.

“I need to get water for these,” she said, and ran towards the house.

§ § §

“She kissed you!” said Seppan when I told him and Aarad what happened in the front yard. We were in their room in the loft sitting on their bed, and I had just explained what had happened when I had given Illiad the flowers.

“It wasn’t a big kiss...just on the cheek,” I told him.

“But she *did* kiss you,” he said.

“Yeah,” I replied.

“And you didn’t kiss her back?” asked Aarad.

“No,” I told him, “she just kissed me and ran away. She said she had to get water for the heshel.”

“Well, I’m impressed,” said Seppan standing up and walking the short distance to the wall opposite the bed. He turned and leaned against it with a grin on his face, “I didn’t think my little sister had it in her.”

“I can’t believe she kissed you,” said Aarad. “I really can’t believe she kissed you.”

“So what do I do now?” I asked.

“What’s to do?” Seppan replied. “She knows you like her, and you know she likes you, what’s the problem?”

"The problem is I'm going to Shentoar in about two moons cycles," I told him. "I'll be gone most of the autumn and winter."

"Just tell her you'll bring her something nice from Shentoar," Seppan said. "Tell her you'll be thinking of her all the time you're gone."

"You've really put a lot of thought into this, haven't you?" I asked.

"Do you want my help or not?" he retorted.

"I'm not too sure I do," I told him, but deep inside I truly did.

Chapter X

Summer passed as I worked with Seppan and my father in the forge or on the farm with Aarad and his father. Illiad, it seemed, no longer had the same feelings for me; for she tried to avoid me whenever possible. Yet when I spoke of this to Aarad he assured me that this was not true.

"She still likes you," he told me one day as we weeded the vegetables in the back yard of their house.

"Then why does she keep avoiding me?" I asked.

"I think she's embarrassed about kissing you," he replied.

"So what do you think I should do? And don't say I should kiss her," I told him.

"I don't know," he said. "Girls are so strange. First she likes you; and now, when she knows you like her, she won't talk to you."

"Well, strange or not, I still don't know what to do about it."

And so the final days of my life in Alna and my actual boyhood ticked away, and I gradually grew anxious about what was to come. At the rising of each sun, as I looked upon the bay with the open sea beyond, I thought of how I would soon be out there sailing to new lands. Yet each night, as I lay alone in my own familiar bed, I felt a strange new loneliness; for I realized that I would soon be gone and no longer hear the all too familiar sounds of our house and the village which had surrounded me since I had first drawn breath.

Yet worst of all were the days I spent at the farm; for during the day Illiad's coldness saddened me, and I wished again and again that I could find a way for us to be just friends like we had been before I gave her the flowers. But at night, in Aarad's room, my loneliness deepened; for not being at home enkindled in me a strange foreboding when I realized that even my friendship with Aarad would soon end.

The neffan were ready to harvest at the beginning of the last moons cycle of summer, and the digging would require Illiad to help as well. This meant she would not be able to avoid me which pleased me greatly; for as we worked together, I was sure that things would again be as they once were.

I spent the night before the digging at their farm to allow us to get an early start; and so, as soon as we had eaten, the three of us went straight to work. Yet I was soon disappointed; for, while Aarad and I talked and joked as we gathered the neffan into sacks, Illiad, who did the digging, said nothing.

At last, when Aarad had gone off to store a sack of neffan in the cool cellar of their house, I stopped what I was doing and looked at her.

"Why won't you talk to me?" I asked boldly.

"I…talk to you," she replied without looking up from her digging.

"Only when you have to," I told her. "Aarad thinks it's because you're embarrassed about kissing me."

"You *told* him I kissed you!" she said at last looking up from digging the neffan, and she looked as if she were about to cry.

"You told *him* you liked me. You wanted to know if I liked you, and I do like you. And I'm glad you kissed me, so why can't we just be friends like we were?"

Yet these words had the opposite effect on her as I had intended, for she started to cry; and as Aarad came around the side of the house, she ran off.

"What's wrong with her?" he asked.

"Girls," I said shaking my head. "You do the digging, and I'll gather the neffan."

§ § §

Illiad did not come back to help with the neffan, and Aarad kept asking where she had gone.

"I don't know," I told him. "You gather for a while. When I come back I'll dig," and I got up, hoisted the sack I had just filled onto my shoulder, and headed for the cellar.

When I came up out of the cellar, Illiad was standing by the door waiting for me.

"Are you all right?" I asked, for her eyes were red from crying.

"Yeah," she replied. "…Idar, if you want to be just friends…"

"I want things to be the way they were before," I told her. "Like at the Toharofa. We danced and laughed and had fun.

"I like you. I really like you, and I don't want anything to stop you from liking me."

"I do like you," she said. "Why do you think I kissed you?"

"And why do you think I gave you the heshel?" I asked.

She smiled, "They were really nice. Thank you again, and I'm sorry for how I've acted. Let's try and start over again."

"That's fine with me," I told her, and I began to walk towards the front of the house. "So let's go dig neffan."

"Sure," she said.

Then, without thinking, I reached out and took hand.

"Friends," I said.

"Friends," she replied, and I bent down and kissed her.

§ § §

That night, when all the work was done, Illiad and I went for a walk. The sky was filled with light as all three moons hung together in the summer sky giving us enough light to see by. And so we walked as far as my special place on the hill looking out at the bay.

Since it was early evening, the moons were behind us as we stood in the quiet watching the lights in the harbor and the beacon fires which marked the Narrows. The stars were bright in the western sky, and I held her hand as we talked.

"I can't believe that I won't see this again for a long time," I told her.

"When do you leave for Shentoar?" she asked.

"I'm not sure," I replied. "Tenoar said the *Tel* would be launched in the first moons cycle of autumn. But I haven't heard anything more from him. I think I might have no more than forty days."

"That's not too bad," she said.

"I know," I told her, "but it still sort of scares me. Except for staying at your house or at Tuac's, I've never been away from home. I really want to go to Shentoar, to see new places—like when we went to Theo last autumn to sell the kalhu. But I'll miss everyone and everything. This is my home and always will be."

"I'll miss you too," she said.

"When I come back, I'll bring you something nice from Shentoar," I told her thanking Seppan for giving me the idea of what to say.

"I wonder if they have the same stars in Shentoar?" she asked after a long pause.

"I'm sure they do," I told her. "When I went to Trohan with Tuac two summers ago, the stars were the same there as they are here."

"But Shentoar's so far away. Maybe their stars are different."

"Maybe," I replied after giving it some thought, "but I still think they'll be the same."

"Then we can watch them together," she told me. "Every night while you're gone, I'll look at the stars; and if you do the same thing, then it will be like we're together."

"And if they're not the same?" I asked.

"Even if they're not the same," she said, "at least I'll know you're out there somewhere watching the stars with me. That way we won't really be parted."

"That's a great idea," I told her.

"So promise me that wherever you are you'll watch the stars each night and think of me."

"I promise," I told her, and kissed her again.

§ § §

Five days later, I heard from Tenoar. I was to meet him at the *Pola*, an inn in Sefna, on the seventeenth day of the following moons cycle.

"The *Pola!*" my mother cried, "Why would anyone call an inn the *Pola*?"

"Why?" I asked, "What's a pola?"

"It's a beast that sailors claim lives in the sea," my father told me.

"And drags ships to their doom," my mother added.

"Shahri, those are only stories. No Thean ship has ever really met a pola."

"What about the *Nar*?" she asked.

"No one knows what happened to the *Nar*," he told her, "but I'm sure it was not the doing of a pola. I cannot believe such beasts really exist."

"Why not?" I asked.

"Well, no one has actually seen one," he replied. "And if they did exist, I am sure more than one ship would have been sunk by them. In fact, if they did exist ships would not be able to sail anywhere. No, there is no such thing as a pola."

"You can think what you like," my mother retorted, "but I still think it's no name for an inn, especially an inn where sailors lodge; and I do not like the idea of Idar going there. Will he be sleeping in this place?"

"I don't know," my father told her. "I assume he will only meet Tenoar there, then stay on board the *Tel*."

"He had best," she snapped. "I want no son of mine staying in such a place, and he will not even be a man."

"A mere technicality," my father replied, "Idar will reach legal manhood in three moons that's true; but, as I have said before, he has acted the part of a man since last summer. I think we can trust him. Besides, I will be going with him, so he will not be alone."

"I don't like the idea of you staying in such a place either," she said.

"Come now, Shahri, the *Pola* cannot be any worse than the inn here in Alna," he told her. "You worry far too much."

"That may be," she said in reply, "but you know how I hate the idea of all this, so just let me worry. It's a mother's place to worry. If men weren't so foolhardy, women would not have to worry."

"Yes, my love," he said with a laugh, "but you still worry too much."

§ § §

Tenoar's news meant I would still have time to help with the hay, but I would not be able to finish the kalhu harvest. Yet when I told this to Seppan in the morning, he was not surprised.

"Nodah thought you might not be around to help," he told me. "So he's making plans to hire someone just for the Kalhu, unless you don't feel you will be able help with the hay."

"No," I replied, "the hay's not a problem. I'll be willing to help. But I'll need time to get ready before I leave, and nodah says I should spend lots of time with nodeh before I go—something about mothers and sons."

"I'll tell my father tonight," he told me. "When he picked up the grain last autumn, he talked to Hennek about needing a hand on the farm. Hennek said he'd try and find someone, but nodah didn't think it would be this soon. I hope Hennek knows of someone; but don't feel guilty, it's not your fault. We all think you've done enough already, more than enough, and my parents are truly grateful. Don't worry, it will all work out. We'll find someone."

That night I told Seppan I would go to the farm the next day and spend as much time as I could helping out. And true to my word, I left our house as Seppan was arriving the following morning.

"Nodah told me to tell you how grateful he is for all you've done. He's going to Crayoar today to talk to Hennek. In fact, he gave me a ride in from the farm on the wagon. He should be back by midday with news."

"What needs to be done today?" I asked.

"The barn," he replied; and when I groaned, he added, "I know, the gamu make such a mess. It's too bad we can't milk them in the open field, but we have to bring them into the barn, and then…"

"Don't even talk about it," I said and was off to the farm and a day of cleaning up after gamu.

§ § §

When Aeshone returned from Crayoar in the early afternoon he told us he had made arrangements to hire a boy about my own age named Topek just for the kalhu harvest. Then, if all went well, Topek would return at the time of next spring's Toharofa to become their hired hand; for by then he would have reached his thirteenth cycle. This would allow Aarad to do as he wished and seek whatever apprenticeship he chose upon reaching manhood.

It was agreed that Topek would stay with them while working the kalhu harvest and sleep in Aarad and Seppan's room in the loft. Yet this was not at all to Aarad's liking.

"Why can't he sleep in the barn like any other hired hand?" he asked.

"Because he is only a boy, not a man," Melne told him. "And besides, Idar shares your room and you make no complaint about that."

"Idar's my friend," he replied, "not some stranger I don't even know."

"Well, you will get to know him as you work together," Aeshone said, "so no more talk. If all works out, and he comes back as our hired hand next spring, we will make room for him in the barn; but for now he will be treated like a guest."

"Some guest," said Aarad in a voice his parents could not hear.

"What are you complaining about," I told him. "while he's here, I'll be in a cramped hold with who knows how many other men; and I'll be sleeping in a hammock every night."

"But at least you'll be having some adventures, not harvesting kalhu," he replied.

§ § §

I worked on the farm for the next four days, then returned home to spend time with my family before the hay harvesting began. Since I would be leaving soon, my father insisted that I not work with him and Seppan but use the time to relax and enjoy myself. However, with no one with whom to pass this free time, I quickly became bored; and so I actually looked forward to the harvesting of the hay.

My mother, however, made a great fuss over me. She baked all of my favorite things as treats; and each night we had my favorite foods for our evening meal causing both Seppan and my father to say they would miss the food more than me when I was gone.

"What a thing to say," she scolded, but my father only laughed.

"And what do you expect with all this fuss," he told her. "You'd think the boy was sick and not merely leaving for a few moons cycles."

"I merely want him to be happy," she replied. "I fear even to think of the kind of food he will have aboard that ship. And while he is in Shentoar…why they are not even Kroemaeon. What food can they offer him?"

"I've eaten fruit from Shentoar," I told her. "When I went to Theo last autumn with Aarad and his father. It was very good."

"Fruit," she retorted, "you cannot eat only fruit."

"Well, I am sure the food in Shentoar will be different," my father told her, "but it will not kill him."

"And besides," Seppan added, "it's part of the adventure."

"Adventures!" she said, "he does not need adventures. He needs to eat properly."

My father smiled and winked at me then told her, "With as much as he has been eating lately, he will not need to eat at all while he is gone. He can just live off his fat like a sleeping tegga when it hibernates."

At this, my mother merely shook her head and refilled my bowl.

§ § §

When the hay harvest began, I again spent the nights in Aarad's room. Yet this, I knew, would be my last time there; and a strange sadness came over me each time I thought of this.

Aarad had truly become the brother I had not known before, and this was true of Seppan as well. Tuac and Boec were both my friends with a bond between us that went back to our boyhood together, but with Aarad and his family I felt a kind of closeness experienced only with my own parents.

And so as I ate with them and spent time with them in the evenings, it was as though I was at home. In fact, I almost thought of Aeshone and Melne as my own mother and father.

Yet with Illiad it was different. I had never had a sister, and so I did not know how I should relate to one; but I was sure my feelings for Illiad were far different from what I would have felt if I did have a sister. And as the days of our working and living together passed, I grew more and more fond of her in a way I did not feel towards Aarad or Seppan; and this new feeling was also strange to me.

Strange, too, was Aeshone's treatment of me. He had always acted in a kindly way towards me, and this did not change; but with my return for the harvest, he seemed to sense there was something between Illiad and me that had not been there before. And so when we would go for walks in the evening he always insisted Aarad accompany us which annoyed Aarad since he wished only to stay home and relax by the fire.

Then, at last, the harvest was over; and it was time for me to say my last farewells to them all. I stood on the steps of their house, and Aeshone extended his hand to me thanking me again for all my help and wishing me the best of luck. Melne wept and hugged me, then wept again; and she thanked me as well for everything I had done.

Illiad's eyes were red, though she held back her tears; and it seemed to me that parting from her was the hardest thing I had to do that day. I stood for a few moments not wanting to go yet knowing it was inevitable. Then at last I raised my hand and slowly walked away.

Aarad came with me, for he was to spend the next few days with me in Alna as he had done the previous autumn. Yet this did not detract from the sadness I felt since it seemed to me a part of my life had ended, a part which would be impossible to reclaim.

Chapter XI

I awoke on the morning I was to meet Tenoar and join the crew of the *Tel* with both fear and great excitement. My dream was finally achieved, for by the end of the day I would be setting sail on the greatest adventure of my life; yet I also realized that this would truly be the end of all I had known as a boy.

To make this day even more momentous, my father was to take me to Theo and enroll me as a man in the king's Hall of Records. By rights this was something which should be done only after I had reached my thirteenth cycle of the sun; however, since I would be in Shentoar when this happened, I was to be enrolled early. Then, after the enrollment, my father would take me to Sefna to meet Tenoar at the *Pola*.

Seppan had asked his father if we could borrow their cart so that this long trip would not have to be made on foot, and of course Aeshone agreed saying it was the least he could do after all I had done to help his family. My mother was pleased at this, for she did not like the idea of my father walking all that way and having to spend a night at an inn in Sefna—most likely the Pola—before returning home. Yet in spite of this, she had still not resigned herself to my apprenticing on a ship, and in every way possible she had been making her displeasure known.

When I awoke, I did not at first get up but lay in bed thinking about the day ahead, imagining each event in turn then relishing them again and again. Yet at the same time little fingers of dread crept in, for the knowledge I was leaving my home and all I had known and loved since the earliest moments of my life diminished the joy I felt as these fantasies drifted through my mind.

What roused me was the sound of the cart creaking and rattling down the street then stopping in front of our house. As the cart came to a halt, I threw off my blanket and grabbed my tunic then ran into the main room as I slipped it over my head. There I was met by not only Seppan but Aarad and Illiad as well.

"We wanted to see you off," Aarad told me when he saw the surprised look on my face.

"Great," I said a little embarrassed, for I had not expected to see Illiad again before I left; and I had surly not expected to have her see me running half dressed out of my room. "I'm glad you came."

My mother greeted Illiad quite formally and thanked her again for the soup she had made when my father had been injured, something I had totally forgotten about. She then asked if they had eaten.

"Yes," Illiad replied very politely, "we ate before we left the house. We did not want to be a burden, we only wished to say one last farewell to Idar before he leaves."

"No, no," my mother told her, "you are no burden. You are welcome to our home. I am very glad you came.

"Idar just woke up and has not eaten yet. You are welcome to join him at the table," and she motioned them into the room.

"Thank you," Illiad replied, and her politeness towards my mother gave me a strange feeling of contentment, almost a sense of relief as if I had long dreaded this day and was relieved it had been resolved so favorably.

"What kind of a sailor are you going to make?" Seppan said with a laugh and a punch on my arm. "I would have thought you'd be up well before first light getting ready."

"I have been up—or at least awake—for a while," I told him. "I just felt like staying in bed for a time."

"Well, you won't be doing that for a good long time will you now?" he said.

"That he won't," added my father as he came in from the shop. "Ah, I see we have guests," and he nodded in formal greeting to Illiad, then gave me a quick wink out of the corner of his eye causing me to redden slightly.

"I need to wash," I told them and headed for the pump in front of our house followed by Aarad.

"This is going to be really awkward," I told him as I washed my hands and face in the cold water flowing from the pump.

"What do you mean?" he asked.

"Saying good-bye to Illiad with my parents watching," I told him.

"Why? You didn't have a problem with my parents watching," he said.

"That's different," I told him, "your parents are always around when I'm with her. But…well, nodah knows how I feel about her, but not nodeh. I don't know, it just feels odd, that's all."

"I'm sorry," he replied, "we shouldn't have come."

"No," I said drying my hands and face with the hem of my tunic, "I'm glad you came. It's just going to be awkward that's all."

When we entered the house Illiad was helping my mother by cutting the bread and cheese to be served with the hot soup we would be having. Seppan had gone out to the forge to begin work while my father and I ate together at the table one last time, and so Aarad and I joined him while my mother served the soup and Illiad the bread and cheese.

This, too, seemed awkward; and my father seemed to sense this, for he tried his best to make me laugh. Yet I could not shake the feeling of how odd it was for Illiad to be here in my home serving me with my mother looking on, for it almost seemed unnatural.

I ate quickly, and all too soon we were ready to leave. We all walked out to the cart, my mother weeping as Melne had only a few days before. I had packed what I felt I would need in a sack, and this I placed under the seat of the cart then gave my mother a hug and kissed her on the cheek telling her I loved her and would miss her. She in turn did the same. Finally, I did my best to smile as I climbed up onto the seat next to my father.

Aarad reached up and took my hand, and as with Tuac, I saw a tear in his eye.

"Good-bye," was all he managed to say, then released my hand.

"Good-bye," I told him, and I turned towards Illiad who looked up at me with the same reddened eyes I had seen a few days earlier at their farm. "I'll keep my promise," was all I could manage to say to her.

My father picked up the reins and urged Heshel on as Illiad cried out in a voice struggling to hold back her tears, "I'll be watching the stars."

§ § §

The trip to Theo took us a little over an hour, and so by midmorning we had arrived at the same gate through which I had passed when I came with Aeshone to sell his kalhu. Yet after passing down the same street to arrive at the same open air market, we continued on, heading in the direction of the temple and the palace of the king.

"Will we go into the palace?" I asked my father hoping I might catch a glimpse of the star he had told me was kept there.

"No," he replied, "the Hall of Records is located on a large plaza near the temple with the king's palace at the far end. But we cannot enter it, for only those of great importance are allowed entrance into the palace."

As we rode on, the buildings became more and more impressive as well as massive until we finally came out into a huge open space paved with stone. In the center was an enormous statue of what seemed to be a man yet with strange features making him appear as I had been told the toha looked when they took on mortal form. He was dressed in a long tunic, one that reached to his feet. In one hand he held a sword raised high above his head, and in the other was what appeared to be a lump of stone. His head was crowned with a helmet having three large feathers billowing from its crest, and I was awed to silence by the wonder of him.

"That is Theapan," my father told me, "our first king, and ancestor of Shuman. It is he who found the star and built the temple on the spot where it fell from the sky. The city of Theo then grew up around it."

I stared in amazement and found it hard to believe anything so massive could stand by itself without falling over.

"And the star is kept in the king's palace?" I asked.

"Yes," my father replied, "it is the sign of his authority as king, and it remains close to him at all times."

"What if someone else found a star?" I asked. "Would he become king as well?"

"Many stars fall from the sky each year, you have seen this," he told me, "but they are never found, for only the toha know where they land, and only the toha have the power to touch such things."

"So Theapan was one of the toha," I said in wonder.

"You can see this by his features," he told me, "yet it is said that his mother was mortal, and this is why the kings all die. However, his father was a toha, and this gave him the ability to find and possess the star which fell from the sky.

"But enough of that, we are nearing the Hall of Records. It is there on the right, the building with the two small statues on the steps."

"Are they also toha?" I asked.

"They are Justice and Honor," he replied. "The Hall of Records houses the history of our ancestors, and it is there that one must go to seek justice if they have been dishonored by another. Here I will register you as my son as did my father and his father before me. If ever a question should arise as to your rights as my son and your inheritance, then you must come here and have it arbitrated by the judges appointed by the king."

When we reached the steps of the Hall, my father climbed out of the cart and tied Heshel's reins to a post then motioned for me to join him as we climbed the enormous flight of stairs leading to the massive doors made of polished bronze. Only one stood open, and we walked through it into a hall far bigger than I could have imagined a room to be.

The walls along the sides as well as the far end were lined with columns from which hung lamps to give light to the windowless interior; yet even with this light, I could barley make out the shadow of a ceiling at least three levels above us. Statues stood in the spaces between the pillars, and in a hushed voice my father explained that they were likenesses of former kings of Theo.

"One day," he said, "Shuman's statue will be placed here to join those of his ancestors as our traditions dictate."

When we reached the center of the hall, there was a dais raised above the floor. Here sat two men seated at a stone table while other men waited in silence with boys my own age all looking just as nervous as I felt. We joined them, and soon it was our turn to speak to one of the registrars.

"Name," came a rather bored sounding voice.

"I am Kennec, son of Elem, son of Penepe," my father told him, "I was registered on the twelfth day of the second moons cycle of summer in the twenty-fourth sun cycle of Arman, king of Theo. I have come to register my son as Idar, son of Kennec, son of Elem."

Without saying a word, the man at the desk wrote something on a long sheet of what appeared to be some kind of cloth. Then, without even looking up he told us: "So recorded on this the seventeenth day of the first moons cycle in the thirteenth sun cycle in the reign of Shuman, King of Theo." At this he looked up, and staring intently at me he said: "Remember this, young man, and do not forget it; for as such you are registered, and it is thus your name shall be found if need arises." With that, we left the dais and walked quietly towards the massive doors through which we had come.

When we were outside, my father led me back to the cart and untied Heshel's reins, then he climbed onto the seat, and I joined him. He looked at me with a sense of pride showing in his eyes and on his face.

"The registrar is correct," he told me. "You must remember this day for the rest of your life, for the records are housed in the Hall by date and can only be found again if you know the correct date they were placed there. I am sure you will have no problem remembering since this is also the day you join the *Tel*, but remember it nonetheless; for this day holds the key to your future."

Having said this, he urged Heshel on; and we crossed the plaza and then entered a street which headed in a more westerly direction. Here, too, the buildings were impressive; yet gradually their grandeur diminished giving way to the more common style of shops and dwellings I had seen as we came into the city by the South Gate. As we rode along, I thought about what had been said in the Hall of Records trying to impress everything into my mind so that I would never forget it as my father had told me.

"Nodah," I asked at last, "why were you registered in the summer when you reach your sun cycle in the spring?"

"Because my father was too busy in the spring," he told me. "Spring is one of our busiest times, as you well know; and so my father put off going to Theo until he found time in the summer.

"We did not have a cart, and so we had to walk. I remember it took us hours just to get to the city, and getting through the crowds in the streets was near impossible. Everyone gets out of the way for a cart but not for a man and his son who look bewildered because they are not sure where they are going. By the time I was registered, and we had pushed and shoved our way back to the South Gate, it was late afternoon; and we were truly glad for the extra hours of daylight on our long journey back to Alna.

"If we had no cart, it would have been necessary to leave yesterday to insure we reached Sefna by last night. Then we would have needed to spend the night at the *Pola* so you could meet Tenoar there this afternoon. As it is, I will not be home until after dark; and your mother will be sitting there by the fire worrying about both of us."

We rode on in silence until we had nearly reached the Harbor Gate. As it was time for our noon meal, my father stopped the cart in front of a small tavern. Then, after tethering Heshel to a ring secured to the tavern's wall, I went in with him and waited at a table as he ordered food and drink for us at the bar. When he returned, he carried two mugs one of which he handed to me.

"Here," he said, "you had best get used to this as well."

"What is it?" I asked taking a sip.

"Kahlmek," he replied with a grin, then added after taking a drink from his own mug, "and Tenoar's right, the kahlmek at Sethel's inn is much better than this; but you'll be drinking a lot worse when you are at sea."

"I think I'll stick to the spiced wine," I told him, and he laughed.

"I don't blame you. Ah, here comes our food."

A man approached us and placed a platter of sliced bread and cheese on our table. My father nodded politely to him as did I, and he left telling us to call him if we needed anything else.

There were three different kinds of cheeses on the platter, and the bread was not kalhu bread as I was used to but one made from artet flour which my father told me was imported from Eltec. It was much darker than kalhu bread, almost black, and had a strange taste which I found unpleasant at first, but grew to like after a few bites.

The cheeses, too, were ones I had never eaten before; and I began to wonder what else lay ahead of me as I sailed off to different ports. I thought again of the khansh I had eaten on my last visit to Theo, and I decided that if the food in Shentoar was as good as this, my mother would have nothing to worry about—I would definitely eat well.

After our meal, we left the inn and continued on towards the Harbor Gate which lead to Sefna. It was hard going, for carts were coming into the city laden with cargo off loaded at the docks in Sefna or with produce from the farms around Prion; and we were often forced to pull over so that these heavily loaded carts would have room to pass.

One such cart contained sacks of grain with two wide eyed boys sitting on top, and this reminded me of my trip to Theo the previous autumn. Their laughter and playful banter made me smile yet pained me as well, for I knew that never again would I be that young and innocent.

Then at last we were at the Harbor Gate with a full view of Sefna and the bay before us; and I forgot my youth and became a young man riding off to the greatest adventure of his life, his future stretching out before him in twists and turns like the road winding its way down to Sefna. All thoughts of boyhood left my mind, and I looked only to the future now awaiting me in the harbor town below.

§ § §

We reached the *Pola* in mid afternoon to find Tenoar already inside the inn with a group of men who were to become my crew mates. They each sat with a mug in front of them crowded around two tables which they had pulled together.

"Ah," cried Tenoar, "our mahlet is here at last. Come, join us," and he motioned us towards them.

"This, lads, is Idar and his father Kennec," he told the men sitting at the tables. A general nodding of heads followed these words as well as a few hearty smiles. I, too, nodded to the men trying my best to look as confident and brave as possible; yet the stirring in my stomach and the pounding in my chest told a far different story.

"Here beside me," Tenoar continued placing his hand on the shoulder of the man sitting to his left, "sits Burog, my second in command. You will obey his orders just as if they came from me which they probably will. The man there across from him is Pellonek, our helmsman when Burog is off duty. He also has complete authority when he's at the helm, providing Burog and I are not on deck.

"There, at the end of the table, you will find Benfoar; and it is to him you will be assigned directly. Yet Kebbit there beside him will also have you working for him. He's our cook, and you will assist him whenever Benfoar has no need of you. And if you are ever sick, Kebbit will patch you up in no time, although his remedies may make you wish for death," and this brought on a general round of laughter from the men.

"Have these men served with you before?" I asked.

"These four, yes," he told me. "I stole them from the *Mek*, the ship I was on before I decided to leave and build my own. I was second in command to Keltoar, and he was none too happy when I took his cook and carpenter as well as his two best seamen. But enough of that, he'll find replacements for them, but none as good."

"And the other men?" I asked.

"Never served with them, though I have known some before; yet they all come with good recommendations, as do you," and saying this, he smiled broadly at me.

"So," he continued, "can I buy you both a drink?"

"I was just going to ask you the same thing," my father replied.

"No," said Tenoar, "you bought the last round over in Alna. This round is mine. Sit, and get acquainted. I'll be right back."

As he walked off to the bar, my father and I found chairs and took our places at the table.

"My mother thinks the *Pola* is a terrible name for an inn," I said since I had no other idea of how to get a conversation going.

"She may be right," said a man sitting next to Pellonek, "I don't come here myself. A bit like tempting fate if you ask me."

"Oh, come on Altore," said the man on his other side, "don't tell me a wise man like yourself believes in all that pola nonsense?"

"Don't know for sure," Altore replied, "and don't want to find out. All I want is to get safely to Shentoar and back with money in my pouch. Then I'll be happy."

"Here's to that," said the other man; and the two of them raised their mugs and took a drink.

"So you don't believe the stories about the pola?" I asked.

"Just fables to scare the weak," replied Altore's friend, and with that he jabbed Altore in the ribs with his elbow causing him to spill his drink.

"Who you callin' weak, Torek?" Altore growled. "Just don't like takin' chances myself. I don't say there is a pola, and I don't say there's not; but to be on the safe side, I'll pretend there is," and both men laughed and took another drink from their mugs.

"Been scaring Idar with tales of the pola?" said Tenoar as he placed a mug of kahlmek in front of my father and then one in front of me.

"He's the one who brought it up," Torek told him.

"Yeah, *he's* scarin' *me*," Altore said grinning then took another swig of his drink.

"Well, I agree with Altore," said Tenoar sitting down between my father and me. "I've never had cause to believe in sea monsters. I've not seen one in all my days at sea; but there are plenty of strange things out there, and it's best to be cautious."

"Is this all the crew?" I asked wanting to change the subject.

"No," Tenoar replied, "besides the six men here, there's one more yet to arrive; and then eight on board guarding the ship. It's not safe to leave a ship unmanned. Anyone could come along and take it for themselves."

"But what about the men on board?" my father asked. "I am sure you trust them, but if you do not really know them…well, what's to stop them from sailing off with your ship?"

"A fair question," Tenoar replied. "That's why Jaygore is aboard. He's the one who loaned me the money to build the *Tel*. He's a merchant in Sefna. Half my own profits go to him until I've paid back what he's put into the *Tel*, and then some.

"Ah, here comes our last man now," and he stood up to greet a rather short man approaching us.

After introductions all around, Tenoar sat back down.

"As soon as we've all finished our drinks," he told us, "we can be off, but no hurry. At the interest Jaygore is charging me for the *Tel*, he can wait a bit longer. How about you, Nomlet, will you let me buy you a drink?"

At this the new man smiled broadly, "That I would, captain."

"Fine," said Tenoar, "then be off to the bar and tell Keploh to put your drink on my bill."

We sat in the inn for about a half an hour before Tenoar told us it was time to go. Then we all made our way out to the street where Heshel waited for us.

"Could I offer you a ride to the docks?" my father asked; and his offer was eagerly accepted by the men, some of whom had drank too much inside.

After Tenoar had climbed onto the seat beside my father, and the rest of the men and I had crowded ourselves into the back of the wagon, we set off down the narrow winding street which led to the wharf and the beginnings of my new life.

§ § §

When I first saw the *Tel*, I was overcome with wonderment and awe as I had never seen such a ship before. It was more than twice the size of the *Tok*, a full 120 paces, with two tall masts unlike the merchant ships coming from Arganon that sometimes docked at Alna to take on grain.

It also had two decks, the main deck and a second upper deck 30 paces long which began as the roof of the two forward cabins which served as the officer's quarters. It then continued on to the prow where a lookout stood watch when the weather was bad or we were sailing in strange waters. Two ladders connected these decks, one on either side of the ship, with storage lockers for the ship's equipment built into the walls behind them.

The two masts rose from the main deck with the fore mast being the tallest. This was about ten paces from the cabins. A second shorter mast, or mizzen mast, was located forty paces aft with the hatch leading to the hold and the crew quarters placed midway between them. There was also a small boat lashed to the deck near the aft mast.

A platform ten paces wide ran the entire width of the ship's stern. This platform stood chest high (nearly head high for me the day I joined the *Tel*) and beneath it were additional lockers where among other things two of the ship's anchors were stored. Besides this storage, the platform held the helm which was a tiller, or large lever used to move the ship's rudder. This was located in the center of the platform, and it was here that the helmsman stood for hours holding us on course. At night, however, it was possible to tie the tiller into position giving Burog and Pellonek a chance to sleep; yet this was only done when we were in familiar waters.

The hatch, located mid ship, led to the main hold from which the crew quarters in the stern could be reached. Three other compartments could also be found below deck—all in the prow of the ship—and one of these sometimes housed passengers wishing to sail to other ports.

I thought she was the most beautiful thing I had ever seen. The rail on both sides of the deck was painted a dark red and her sides an equally dark green. This was in keeping with the customs and traditions of Theo, although this striking color combination was a bit unusual.

My father pulled the wagon to a stop on the pier next to the *Tel*, and we all climbed out. I retrieved my sack from under the seat then joined the men as they walked up the plank leading to the main deck. When we boarded the ship, Tenoar offered my father a tour, and I joined them.

"It is a fine ship you have here," my father told Tenoar at the end of the tour. "I am sure Idar will find himself proud to serve on her."

"That she is," replied Tenoar with obvious pride. "I have labored all my life for my own ship, and I couldn't have asked for a better one.

"But I must go now, I need to find Jaygore to tell him I've returned, so I will wish you a safe trip back to Alna and be off."

"And you and your ship," my father said in reply, "I entrust to the toha for a safe journey to Shentoar."

As Tenoar walked away, I realized the time had come for my father to be off for home; and I was suddenly gripped by the realization I soon would be alone in a strange world. I felt the uneasiness first in my stomach and then in my chest as my heart began to beat faster.

As we reached the plank leading to the wharf, my father paused with a look on his face which made me wonder if he, too, would cry; but instead, he reached out and pulled me towards him as Daeo had done to Zhoh the day we left him on Trohan. I hugged him and felt no shame in this, for I saw myself as a man leaving on a long voyage; and it seemed right to me that we should hold each other one last time.

"You have made me proud this day," he told me with tears in his eyes, "and I know you will do your best to make your mother and me proud of you all the days of your life."

With these words, he turned and walked down the ramp; and I stood by the rail watching him, fighting back the tears that I felt would betray me as a mere boy and not the man I wished the crew to think me to be. When he was seated in the cart, he raised his hand in a final farewell which I returned, then slapping the reins on Heshel's back, he drove away.

As I watched him leave, there was a brief moment when I wanted to run after him, to jump in the wagon and go home. But I knew I could not do this, for to do so would forever bind me to a life I did not wish to lead. It was no easy matter to watch him go, but I did find some comfort in knowing that my future lay ahead of me, one shrouded in mystery; and this fact filled me with a mixture of fear and excitement.

Chapter XII

"…and if we do need to make repairs which Benfoar can't handle on his own, then we will return to Sefna; otherwise, we will sail on to Serret."

The sound of Tenoar's voice roused me from my thoughts, and I turned to see him walking towards me accompanied by an elderly man with thinning gray hair. I jumped aside, as it was obvious they wanted access to the ramp, and stood in silence; for I did not know what else to do.

When they reached the rail, Tenoar again spoke to the man, "So, I hope to see you in about five moons cycles and with bags of gold to show for my trip to Shentoar."

"Let us hope," the man replied, "I have put enough into this ship. It is time I got something back to show for my investments. Well, I will be off. I hope you have a safe and prosperous trip." With that, he turned and walked down the ramp to the wharf then off up one of the streets to wherever he was headed.

"That," said Tenoar, "is Jaygore, and I will be glad to be rid of him once I have paid him back."

Then, turning to me he said, "Your father has gone I see."

"Yes, sir," I replied, my voice still a little shaky."

"Five moons are not all that long," he told me. "The time will fly, and before you know it, you'll be home. Trust me, lad, it was the same for each of us here aboard ship. You'll see.

"Now you had best be off. Benfoar won't be needing you until we are well out to sea, so you will start by helping Kebbit prepare our evening meal; but first Kelyan will show you how to raise the plank and push off from the pier. You'll find him down at the stern of the ship by the helm."

"Yes, sir," I replied and quickly walked aft to find Kelyan.

This was not difficult since, besides Burog at the helm, he was the only one at the ship's stern. "I'm Idar," I told him, "Tenoar sent me to help with the plank."

“Ah, so yer the ship’s mahlet,” he said, “and I suppose Tenoar gave ya’ my name.”

“Yes, sir.”

“Now don’t ya’ be callin’ me sir. I’m a mere seaman like yourself. It’s only an officer like Burog there that ya’ call sir.”

“Then what do I call you?” I asked.

“Kelyan, what else,” he replied with a laugh. “I’m only a seaman. Now we best get the plank up so we can be on our way. Don’t want to be late to Shentoar, do we?” and again he laughed.

Raising the plank, or ramp leading from the pier to the ship, was not as difficult as I thought it might be; for we merely pulled it aboard ship, then the two of us carried it to the stern of the ship where we stored it in a locker. It was heavy, yet we managed this easily enough.

“Ya’ve got a lot of strength for a lad yer age,” Kelyan told me, “Not many men o’ thirteen could handle the plank so well. I thought I’d have to do it mostly by myself.”

“I’m not thirteen,” I told him, “I’m only twelve cycles. I don’t reach my thirteenth cycle until this winter.”

“Yet Tenoar hired ya’ on?” he said with obvious surprise.

“I’ve been working in my father’s blacksmith shop,” I told him, “and on my friend’s farm. So Tenoar felt he’d give me a chance to apprentice here on the *Tel*.”

At this he nodded thoughtfully then said, “That’s a lot o’ trust to put in one so young. But ya’ seem like a stout lad, and I’m sure Tenoar knows a bit about pickin’ men for the job. After all, he is the captain.”

With that, he picked up two poles from the deck and handed one to me.

“Now take this,” he told me, “and help me push the ship away from the pier.”

I did as he told me; and this, too, was not as difficult as it had sounded at first, for there were four other men assisting: two mid ship and two more near the ladder leading to the upper deck. Once the *Tel* was away from the pier, we used the poles, which were as tall as three good sized men, to guide the ship out into the water where the sail could catch the breeze which blew across the bay.

“Ya’ve done this before,” he told me. “Ya’ handle the pole too well for a beginner.”

“Yes, I have,” I replied and told him about my trip to Trohan with Tuac and how we had been allowed to help pole the tarrek in from the boat.

"The *Tok*," he said. "A good ship. I apprenticed on her when I was a lad like yourself. So this Tuac be Daeo's son no doubt. I thought I'd seen ya' a time before. Most likely in Alna. I was born there. I'm sure you know Sharn, he's my brother.

I nodded, then asked, "Why don't you live in Alna now?"

"After I served my apprenticeship, I married a girl from Sefna; and we came here to live. Worked as a seaman on a pleasure boat owned by a rich merchant. I made a good living; but now that my kids are all grown, I decided to seek a little adventure, and a little more gold for my old age."

By now the *Tel* was moving slowly into the bay as her sails caught the wind. And so we stored the poles on a shelf just in front of the helm. When the other men had placed their poles with ours, they each hurried off to help with the sails. Then Kelyan latched the long slender door and made a move to go.

"I'm supposed to help Kebbit in the kitchen," I told him, and he turned back towards me. "But I have no idea where it is. When Tenoar gave me the tour of the ship, I didn't see it."

"Kitchen, lad. There's no kitchen on board a ship," he told me. "It's a galley, and ya'll find it down in the hold up in the prow o' the ship. Go through the two forward cabins, and ya'll find Kebbit in the back. Now off with ya'."

"Thank you," I said and hurried off to the hold.

§ § §

Helping Kebbit was less of an adventure than helping get the *Tel* under way, for it was much like helping my mother in the kitchen at home. I hauled water and chopped vegetables, and even kneaded dough for the bread. It was also hot in the galley, and those few times I was sent for water were a relief.

At last Kebbit told me I could take a break, and I went up on deck. But I was disappointed, for we had long since passed through the Narrows, and we were well out to sea. I remembered how I had felt that morning on the deck of the *Tok*, and I wished I could have experienced once again the same feeling of wonderment and awe I had known on that far off day; but this was not to be, for the reality of life aboard ship soon taught me my boyhood days were over.

§ § §

We did not reach Serret until the next day; for though it was not that far from Theo, Tenoar took us on a longer course in order to test the ship's seaworthiness. I, however, saw little of the sea during this time since I was below deck in the galley helping Kebbit to cook and serve the men and then to clean up after.

By the time my duties in the galley were done, the sun had long since set; and so I stood for a few minutes looking at the brightness of the stars wondering if Illiad had kept her pact with me and was now looking up into the night sky at the same stars I beheld. The night air chilled me, and I shivered as I watched Kohn rise slowly to join his brother Aeto in the sky. It would be a few hours before their sister Zayto joined them; and I had no desire to wait that long, for sleep called to me as every muscle of my body began to ache from the rigors of the day.

I returned to the hatch and climbed down into the gloom of the hold lit only by one lamp which hung from a beam in the center of the main storage room. When I reached the bottom, I made my way to the crew quarters and the hammock Tenoar had pointed out as mine during my tour of the ship that afternoon.

At that time, I had merely tossed my bag on the floor next to the wall; so now I retrieved it and sat on my hammock looking through the things I had packed the night before: three extra tunics, a blanket and a warm cloak my mother made just for this trip since she did not wish me to get sick from the cold sea air.

"Is that all ya' have, lad," came Kelyan's voice, and I looked up to see him standing next to me.

"It's all I brought. I didn't know what else I'd need," I told him.

"A mahlet won't need nothing more," he said. "And all ya' got is that bag to store it in?"

"Yes," I replied.

"Well, as soon as we get to a decent port ya' need to get yourself a sea chest to keep yer things in. But for now ya' can share mine."

"Thank you," I said, "but I don't want to be any trouble."

"Oh, it will be no trouble," he told me, "I have plenty o' room in my own chest, so yer things won't be in the way. Besides, we can't get our clothes mixed up 'cause those tunics o' yours are way too small for a man my size."

He dragged his chest out from under his hammock, which was across from mine, and we stowed my clothes away for safe keeping. With this done, he sat on his own hammock, and we talked for a bit.

At last he said, "Well, we both best be getting some sleep. I have the watch at midnight, so I need to get some rest before then; and you will be up early I'm sure helping Kebbit with breakfast."

I had not thought of that since Kebbit had said nothing about helping, but Tenoar had told me I would be working in the galley if Benfoar had no need of me. And so I lay down on my hammock and threw my blanket over me.

"Who sleeps up there?" I asked pointing to the hammocks tied above mine.

"That would be Boaruf and Shaffet," he told me. "Boaruf is on watch now, so he'll be in when he gets off. I don't know where Shaffet's off to, but I should guess he'll be along in a bit. Ya' best get used to the men coming in at all times o' the night and waking each other up to go on duty."

With that, he lay down; and neither of us said anything more.

§ § §

"Stop it Aarad, it's too early to get up," I mumbled and turned over to go back to sleep.

"I don't know who this Aarad fellow is, but ya' best be up now. We got kahl to make for all these men; and they'll be hungry when they wake up."

"Kebbit!" I said, and jumped out of my hammock bumping my head on Boaruf sleeping above me.

"Watch it down there," growled Boaruf.

"Sorry," I told him, but all he did was snore in reply.

"Well, don't dawdle now that yer up," said Kebbit. "I'll meet ya' in the galley in five minutes. Don't be late," and he left the cabin.

I stood in the silence of the room for a few moments more until I heard Kelyan's voice, "Ya' better get on lad, it's best not to keep Kebbit waiting. Ya' need to make a good impression, this being only yer second day."

I nodded, stretched and then walked slowly out of the crew quarters.

When I reached the galley, Kebbit was already hard at work. "Good," he said as soon as he saw me, "I need ya' to fetch two buckets o' water, and be quick about it. Ya've already wasted enough time by sleeping in."

I could not believe what I heard, for when I had passed through the hold, the open hatch had revealed nothing but darkness and a few faint stars. It could not even be first light; yet here I was already at work, and late as well.

And so my second day on the *Tel* was nothing more than a continuation of the first. I helped Kebbit prepare and serve the kahl then helped clean up after the men had eaten. Only when the last dish was put away was I allowed a bowl of what was by then cold cereal.

When breakfast was over, and I had forced down what I considered to be the most repulsive kahl I had ever eaten, we began making eln chowder for the evening meal. I, of course, was given the job of beheading and splitting open the eln in order to clean out the inside. This was a messy job, and even though I had done it many times before, I had never cleaned so many eln in all my life.

After dumping the chopped eln into a huge pot, Kebbit added neffan cut into bite sized pieces as well as minced otlee. While he was doing this, I tried to wash my hands but received a stern reprimanded from Kebbit for wasting fresh water.

"Go dump them eln guts over the side o' the boat. Then ya' can drop the bucket into the sea and pull it up with the line attached to it. Use that to wash in, not our drinkin' water. Fresh water's like gold aboard a ship. Ya' never use it but for cookin' and drinkin'."

Ashamed of myself for not thinking of this, I struggled up the ladder to the deck and did as Kebbit had directed me. Yet the late morning sun blinded me after the gloom of the galley, and I was forced to stand a few moments to allow my eyes to adjust to the light.

When I approached the rail, I could see an island off to the south just resting on the horizon.

"Is that Serret?" I asked a crewman working nearby.

"That it is," he told me. "We should be there in about four hours with the wind blowin' against us like this. Name's Kwellen by the way, and you're our mahlet I take it."

"Yes…my…my name's Idar," I answered almost calling him sir as I had Kelyan the day before."

"Glad to meet ya'," he said. "Got a son about yer age. Apprenticed this last summer with a butcher in Sefna. Said he didn't want no part o' the sea.

"Can't fault him in that. The sea's a rough life.

"So, ya' think ya' got it in ya' to be a sailor?"

"I hope so," I told him. "I've always wanted to go to sea. My mother's father and my father's grandfather were fishermen. I think it's sort of in my blood."

"Well, blood don't make a good sailor," he replied. "It's hard work that does it. Ya' work hard, ya' do what yer told; and ya'll do all right."

"I hope so," I said as I finished washing my hands in the cold sea water. "I better get back to the kitch…the galley," I told him. "Kebbit's waiting for me."

"Right ya' are, lad," he said with a nod. "It's like I said, ya' work hard, and ya'll do all right."

§ § §

I did not see the deck again until it was time for bed, and by then we had anchored as close to Serret as the *Tel* could go. As I stood breathing in the cool night air, I could see the fishing camp with the dock lit by torches; and it reminded me of Trohan.

This made me think of Tuac, of how he was here somewhere in these islands. Yet I was sure I would not see him, and this gave rise to a loneliness I would feel again and again in the days ahead. I wished for home and my own bed, and I wondered if I had made a mistake by going to sea.

Had Boec felt this way when he went to Crayoar? No, he lived with his cousins, and he had Mirranu. All I had was a group of strange men I had never seen before. And Tuac, he had Abdoar and the other men from Alna he had known his entire life. With these thoughts, my loneliness deepened until one lone tear fell on the ship's rail.

I wiped my eyes and took a deep breath as my father's last words filled my head: "I know you will do your best to make your mother and me proud of you all the days of your life." I could not fail him. He had put his trust in me, and I could not fail him.

§ § §

The next day went much like the one before it except that I was also expected to help load the melmat into the ship's hold. However, I took some pride in doing this; for, like Zhoh, I was now able to carry the heavy sacks of fish myself proving to me how much I had grown since I was on Trohan.

Then, in the morning of our fourth day out from Theo, we again set sail and headed south east in order to meet up with the mainland coast. It took us one whole day to sight land, and then we followed the coast veering first out to sea then back towards the shore in order to catch the wind which blew from the south.

On the tenth day out from Serret, we at last sighted Eltec; and I was excited, for I had learned we were going to stop there. This, then, would be the first foreign port I would visit.

By now I had begun to assist Benfoar, although Kebbit kept me busy as well. Helping Benfoar was more to my liking, for I was able to work with my hands building things which was a relief from cooking and cleaning. Benfoar, too, permitted me more leisure time, and working with him often gave me the chance to be above deck and out of the gloom of the hold and galley.

And so I was fortunate to be on deck when the cry came from Kenneb, our lookout, that Eltec was dead ahead. At the word Eltec, I rushed over to the ship's rail to have a look.

"There she is," said Benfoar as he came and stood beside me.

"It looks a lot like Theo," I told him.

"Not much different," he replied, "'cept Eltec's its own port. There are villages off to the east but no smaller ports like Sefna and Alna. In that respect, its much like Arganon."

"I've always wanted to see strange new lands," I told him.

"Then you'll have to wait for Shentoar," he said. "Eltec's a Kroemaeon city same as Theo."

"What do you mean?" I asked.

"They're Kroemaeon, like us," he replied. "Speak the same language, dress the same, not much different than back home. But Shentoar's foreign since it's part of Kallefandra."

"What's Kallefandra?" I asked. "Tenoar mentioned it the night I first talked to him."

"It's a whole big country with over thirty cities and hundreds o' villages and small towns. Stretches for about a thousand leagues inland and a couple o' hundred down the coast. They're not the same as us at all."

"In what way?"

"Oh, lots o' ways," he replied. "They don't talk like us for one nor do they dress the same; and their hair, it's yellow, almost the color of kalhu just before ya' harvest it. Really strange."

"Yellow hair?" I said, "You're joking with me."

"No, I'm not. Ask anyone who's been there. They'll tell ya' the same thing. Sennefen!" he called, "you've been to Shentoar, tell Idar the color o' their hair."

"Kind of a golden yellowish color," he replied.

"That's what I told him, but he don't believe me."

"Don't blame him," Sennefen said, "had a hard time believing it when I saw it for myself."

"Yellow hair," I said with a laugh, "That will be something to see. I can hardly wait."

§ § §

The harbor at Eltec was much smaller than the bay I was used to at home, and this explained why there was only one port, the city of Eltec itself. Nor was this harbor totally enclosed, for only a row of low hills shielded it from the sea on its western side. This left its northern end exposed allowing us to see the city as we approached it from the north.

Benfoar allowed me to watch for a few more minutes, but the need to finish caulking the area around the masts remained, and so I was compelled to returned to work. Yet just as we were finishing, Tenoar came on deck.

"Idar!" he called to me, "when we enter the harbor I want you to assist Kelyan as you did when we cast off from Sefna. He will show you what to do; so as soon as Benfoar can spare you, go to the stern and wait for Kelyan."

"We're just finishing up, captain," Benfoar told him. "All I need is for Idar to help me carry our gear down below."

"Excellent, then be quick about it, and you'll get a good look at the city before we dock," he told me.

"Yes, sir," I replied and hurried off to the hold with Benfoar.

When I came back on deck, Kelyan was nowhere to be seen; so I stood leaning on the rail as I waited. There, I had a perfect view of the city as we grew closer and closer. Then, just as we were passing the first of the hills forming the harbor's protective barrier, Kelyan startled me from behind.

"Impressive isn't she?" he said, and my heart jumped in my chest.

"Yes," I said, "it seems bigger than Theo."

"About twice the size," he told me. "That's because it's like Theo and Sefna combined, and then some."

"Why are we stopping here?" I asked. "Are we going to trade?"

"Water," he replied. "We only have enough on board for twenty days. It takes nearly twice that long to get to Shentoar. So we will refill our water casks and be off. We'll only be here maybe one day. It's late in the day, so we will take on water tomorrow, then leave the morning after."

"Will we be able to go ashore?" I asked.

"If the captain's willin' to let us, we may get a bit o' shore leave," he replied. "Don't know for sure; but if we do, ya' can get that sea chest."

I doubted this since I had very little money, but I said nothing as I stood watching the docks grow nearer.

"Well" he said at last, "we best be gettin' to work," and walked over to the locker where the poles had been stored.

I followed, and he handed me one then explained what I was to do with it when we reached the pier. "Remember how we pushed off when we left the wharf at Sefna?"

I nodded, and he continued, "Well, when we enter the harbor, the crew will lower the sails to reduce our speed. Then, as the ship comes near the dock we will use our poles as we did when we left Sefna. It's our job, and the other men along the rail as well, to ease the ship into her berth while two o' the men jump ashore and tie us up. When they're doing that, we'll bring the plank over to the rail. Then you'll jump to the pier, and I'll slide it out to ya'. We best get it out now, though, so as to be ready," and he placed both of our poles back in the locker and closed the door.

Together we slid the plank out of its locker and lowered it to the deck where it would be easy enough to retrieve when we needed it. Then we stood and waited for the *Tel* to reach the pier.

Gradually the ship slowed as the crew dropped the sails to reduce the amount of wind they caught. Soon we were approaching the pier, and Burog gently maneuvered us along side. Kelyan and I then used our poles to slowly push the *Tel* against the pier as did the other men stationed along the rail.

"You have some skill with the pole," he told me and his praise pleased me greatly.

When we were close enough to the dock, two men holding lines jumped from the *Tel* to the wharf and secured the ship to posts along the pier. At this, Kelyan and I placed our poles in their locker then lifted the heavy plank and carried it over to the rail and laid it on the deck. Kelyan then removed a section of railing with a quick upward jerk, and I stood in the opening waiting to jump to the wharf.

"Now, lad," said Kelyan, and I jumped to the pier then turned and took hold of the plank as he passed it out to me.

"Lower it down and be sure it's secure," he told me.

This I did, and he walked down the ramp to check my work.

"Nice job," he said with a smile and slapped me on the back. "Couldn't o' done it better myself. Now take that section o' railing back to the locker and store it 'til we leave."

I did as he told me, then hurried off to the galley to assist Kebbit with the evening meal.

§ § §

As I helped Kebbit serve the men, Pellonek came up to me and told me to take a tray up the the captain's cabin. This was not an unusual request as I had often done this before, and so I filled a bowl with hot soup and cut a generous hunk of break then left the galley and climbed the ladder leading to the main deck.

Tenoar's cabin was reached by a door on the port side of the ship. On the starboard was a door leading to the cabin shared by Burog and Pellonek. Both of these cabins were accessed from the main deck while their ceilings formed the upper deck where the lookout stood watch.

As was required, I knocked and waited for Tenoar's permission to enter before opening the door. Then, once inside, I took the food over and placed it on the table in the center of the room.

Tenoar was busy at his desk in a corner of the cabin; but as I entered, he moved to the table and sat down. Then, as I turned to go, he spoke, "A moment please, Idar."

I turned and faced him. "I have been told that you are sharing a chest with another seaman."

"Yes, sir," I replied. "He offered because I didn't have one of my own. I hope that's not wrong, sir."

"No, no, that is perfectly all right," he told me, "but I feel it would be a better arrangement if you did have one of your own. Tomorrow you are to go into the city and buy yourself one."

"I'm sorry, sir, but I don't think I have enough money with me to buy a chest," I replied a little fearful.

"I thought as much," he said. "That is why I'm giving you this," and he handed me a money pouch which jingled as I took it. "There's enough in this to buy a decent chest and a little extra."

"Thank you, sir," I told him in astonishment.

"This is not a gift mind you but an advancement on your pay. Kebbit as well as Benfoar both tell me how hard you are working and so does Burog. I feel I made the right choice when I took you on as mahlet. You will do well, so

I am advancing you some of what you will earn when the voyage is over. But tell no one of this. I don't want the other men thinking they will all be treated the same.

"I'm not playing favorites. It's just that you are young, and your needs are greater than theirs. So remember, not a word. Take that down and put it in Kelyan's chest. He's the only one who knows, but don't even speak of it with him."

"Yes, sir," I told him, "I won't say anything. And thank you sir. I won't let you down."

"I'm sure you won't," he replied. "That's why I'm doing it."

§ § §

Eltec was indeed a Kroemaeon city; and though I enjoyed being there, I looked forward to Shentoar and the possibility of something exotic. Before we arrived in Eltec, I was barely aware I was a Kroemaeon; for I had always thought of myself as a Thean. Yet, as Kelyan explained to me, Theo was just one of seven small city states each with its own king who ruled over not only the main city but its surrounding towns and villages.

This, he told me, was the Kroemaeon way as was our manner of dress and even the kinds of foods we ate. We also honored the toha—which those living in Shentoar evidently did not—and shared many of the same customs such as our treatment of women who were given freedoms the women living in Shentoar did not enjoy.

I went into the city after I had helped Kebbit clean up from breakfast. Kelyan came with me as did Altore and another man named Diud. They were to buy eln and other supplies for the galley, and Kelyan was to help me find a shop where I could get an inexpensive sea chest.

"Best to stay close, lad," Diud told me. "The harbor district is not a safe place, especially for one as young as you."

"Why?" I asked.

"Thieves mostly," he replied, "cut you up for only a couple o' coins. A lad like yourself would be eln chowder in no time."

"Or gone missin'," said Altore.

"Missing, how?"

"Slavers," he replied.

"What are they?" I asked.

"They take ya' prisoner then sell ya' to someone," he told me. "Ya' got to work for 'em the rest o' your life."

"You're not serious," I told him, and my voice betrayed my shock and disbelief.

"I know," he said, "it's not our way. But down in Kallefandra it's far different. They do such things, and there are those here in Eltec who make quite a good livin' supplying slaves to the markets in Shentoar."

We walked on in silence for a few minutes, and when I got the chance I quietly asked Kelyan if Altore was just trying to scare me.

"I've never been here myself," he told me, "but I've heard stories back in Sefna of men who never came back from Eltec. So, I'd stay close like Diud told ya'."

We found a shop that sold what Kebbit needed, and the owner told us I could buy a chest at another shop just down the street. So Kelyan and I left Diud and Altore to haggle over the price of eln and went off to buy my chest.

When we returned, Altore and Diud were just leaving the fish market, so we all started back to the *Tel*. The chest was not that heavy, but it was bulky and awkward; and so Kelyan and I each took hold of one of its handles and carried it between us.

"That's a fine lookin' chest," said Altore.

"Yes," I replied, "and it didn't cost all that much either. I'm just glad I had the money for it."

"Still," said Diud, "a mahlet usually don't have that kind o' money, not 'til he's been paid."

"I've been working for my father in his blacksmith shop and saving the money he gives me," I lied.

"Then why'd ya' come to sea?" asked Diud. "If ya' was an apprentice already."

"But I wasn't an apprentice," I told him. "I've helped my father in his shop since I was about seven, but I never really liked it. I always felt like the sea was calling to me. So when I heard Tenoar was looking for a crew, I joined up."

Neither Diud nor Altore said anything more about the money; and I was glad, for I hated having to lie to them. We had spent fifteen days together sharing the same sleeping quarters, eating together, working side by side. It just did not seem right that I should have to be dishonest with them, but I did not want to break the trust Tenoar had put in me.

"What about the eln and the other things you were supposed to get at the market?" I asked as a way of changing the subject.

"They'll be delivered this afternoon," Altore told me. "We couldn't be luggin' that stuff back by ourselves now could we?"

When we reached the ship, Altore and Diud went off to whatever duties they had, and Kelyan and I carried my chest down to the crew quarters where I took my things out of his chest and stowed them in mine. Then with a smile of contentment, I shoved this new symbol of my independence under my own hammock and was off to help Kebbit in the galley.

§ § §

We left Eltec the next morning, and I was again assigned to help Kelyan with the plank and casting off. Then I returned to the galley and cleaned up as usual. And with that, the rhythm of my life aboard the *Tel* resumed, as day followed day, and night followed night for the next twenty-four days until we finally reached Shentoar.

The only break came when we stopped briefly at the River Allubet ten days after leaving Eltec. There we again spent a day taking on water before resuming our course to Shentoar. But since there was no town or place to harbor, the only men who left the ship were those sent in the small boat with our water casks.

Yet here too I learned a bit of seamanship; for I was taught how to drop anchor, a task I had thought would be extremely difficult, but one which again proved to be not all that hard. When we reached the Allubet, Burog ordered all the sails lowered. Then Kelyan and I removed the two stern anchors from their storage locker and carried one of these heavy stones to the port rail using a shorter version of the poles with which we pushed the ship away from the docks. This pole was slid into a hole in the anchor's center allowing us to carry the stone with ease.

When we reached the rail, Kelyan secured the anchor's line to a ring in the deck. We then waited while Diud took soundings to determine the water's depth trying to get us as close to the shore as was safe. With nothing to do, I looked towards the bow of the ship where I saw a third man waiting with an additional anchor which had been stored in a locker located in the ship's prow beneath the platform on which the lookout stood.

Finally Diud gave the signal, and we dropped our anchor over the side.

"It's hit bottom," Kelyan told me. "See, the extra line's floatin' in the water. Pull it up 'til ya' feel the anchor's weight then leave a bit o' slack so the ship can move up and down."

While he talked, he untied the line from the ring, then pulled the length of rope I coiled on the deck through the ring and resecured it. When this was done, we took the second anchor to the starboard side of the *Tel* and went through the same procedure. Then, next day, before we set sail, Kelyan and I reversed this process and stored both anchors in their locker until they were needed again.

After our brief stop at the Allubet, the mundane routine aboard ship resumed as we sailed for another thirteen days. Finally, on the twenty-fifth day of the second moons cycle of autumn, we arrived in Shentoar.

I was in no way disappointed with Shentoar, for it proved to be a city far more wonderful than anything I could have possibly imagined. Unlike the city of Eltec—or Theo for that matter—Shentoar was not situated directly on the sea but on a large river called the Hallucantec. To reach her docks, it was necessary to sail up this river for nearly three leagues to a point where the river made a wide bend. Here, on the curve, Shentoar had been built long ago.

It appeared that the city must once have been a cluster of small towns and villages which grew together with the passage of time since the walled part of the city was located on a hill about two leagues from the river. Yet to reach it, one needed to find their way through an almost endless series of winding streets lined with shops and houses. This massive maze of streets stretched on to the south extending nearly three leagues from the wall as it swallowed up an additional smaller hill.

What I had been told about the residents of this exotic place proved to be true, for they did indeed have yellow hair; and I could not take my eyes off of them as they worked on the docks loading and unloading ships or assisting in casting off. These dock workers were bare chested and wore only a white cloth wrapped around their waists then passed between their legs, and this reminded me of the diapers worn by babies back home in Theo. When I told this to Kelyan as we again helped to bring the *Tel* to its berth, he laughed.

"Yer right," he said, "but I doubt they'd like it much if we told them that."

Yet here and there amidst this sea of golden haired men could be seen one or two who had darker hair, black hair like mine. These, too, were taller; and I could not help but remember what Altore had said about slavers, and I wondered if these men had gone missing and had never returned home to the ones they loved.

End of Book Two

Book Three
Voyages

Chapter I

Warm, I lay warm on my hammock, my body moist with sweat from the heat which had built up in the hold during the day, and I listened to the sound of the water slap against the sides of the *Tel*. It was nearly midnight as far as I could tell, and the men mostly snored or mumbled in their sleep, sounds now as familiar to me as those of our house back in Alna where I had grown up.

I had been in Shentoar for nearly a full moons cycle and had grown used to the heat of the day; yet I still preferred a bit of cool breeze when I slept, and this was something I could never get in this alien land to the south. Much had happened in the past thirty some days, and so I played out the events of my stay in Shentoar over and over again on those nights I could not sleep.

Almost as soon as we had docked, Tenoar had left the ship to seek out buyers for our cargo. He took Pellonek with him leaving Burog in charge. A few hours later, they returned; and Tenoar ordered us to bring the melmat up to the deck, for a buyer would be coming by early in the morning and take it away.

This had taken hours, and I again was made to help whenever Kebbit did not have need of me. And so, between running errands for Kebbit and toting heavy sacks of fish up the ladder to the deck, I was exhausted. But when I tried to sleep that night, I could not; for the excitement of being in a foreign port caused my mind to run wild with fantasies of what I would discover once we were allowed to have shore leave.

As soon as the buyer had arrived at the *Tel* and paid for the melmat, Tenoar again set off to seek additional buyers for the rest of our cargo. We off loaded the fish to the pier while he was gone, letting the buyer's men load it onto carts pulled by brown nosha with spots of gray.

As I needed to assist Kebbit in the galley, I was fortunately relieved of this backbreaking task; yet I did have an opportunity to watch these strange men in diapers as they worked, and I noted none of them looked Kroemaeon.

This, then, became the new rhythm of our day as we waited and waited in port watching our hold empty and then fill back up again with the treasures of Shentoar. There were fine cloths and bronze works, pottery and sacks of exotic foods from the markets, all piled high in our hold or stored safely in the two forward compartments near the galley.

This took us into the first moons cycle of winter; yet it did not seem like winter at all, for it was far warmer than I had known any winter to be. In fact it seemed more like summer, and I wondered what a summer in Shentoar would be like.

"Hot," Diud told me, "very hot. I've been here before in summer, and we couldn't even sleep in the hold. Had to bed down on the deck at night to get any sleep."

"Why is it so hot here," I asked.

"Don't know," he replied. "All I know is the further south ya' go the hotter it gets; and when ya' go north, like to Arganon, it gets colder. Don't make no sense to me, but that's the way it is."

§ § §

Tenoar granted us shore leave soon after the melmat was sold, but we could only go in small groups; for the ship needed to be manned at all times. Even at night two men stood watch to alert the rest of us if anyone tried to come aboard, and during the day we were always on guard against strangers lurking about the ship.

We were divided into parties of four to five men, and each was given a day to explore the city. My group included Diud, who had been to Shentoar before, as well as Nomlet and Kelyan; and we drew the lot for the third day of shore leave.

"Stay close," Diud cautioned me again as we set out, "Shentoar's far worse than Eltec."

"Diud's right," said Nomlet, "never been here myself, but I've heard a few stories that would keep a young one like you up at night," and he laughed.

"What kind of stories?" I asked.

"Oh, stories," he replied.

"Come on, tell me," I coaxed.

"Oh, nothin' a lad like you need know about," he told me.

"I'm not a baby," I told him. "Just because I'm not thirteen doesn't mean anything."

"Oh, yes it does," he replied.

"Fine," I said a little angry, "then you can tell me when I am thirteen."

"Maybe not even then," he replied.

"Come on you two," said Kelyan, "now you're both actin' like babies. We came to have a bit o' fun, not all this squabblin'. Diud, you've been here once or twice before, where should we go first?"

"Well, there's an inn up here a bit that serves drinks that can peel the skin off your tongue, but I don't know if the young'en can handle it," and he too laughed.

"Now don't you start," I told him."

"Just havin' a bit o' fun, lad. Don't be gettin' all mad. Anyway, before we can do anything we need to see the money changers."

"Who are they?" I asked.

"Shentoar has its own money," he told me. "It's different from ours, and they don't accept Kroemaeon coin in the shops. So we need to go to the money changers. They take our money and change it into Kallefandran coins. Then we can spend it here in Shentoar."

Having said this, he led us to the end of the wharf where a large stone building stood. Here three yellow haired men, one of whom spoke Kroemaeon very well, counted our money and exchanged it for odd looking coins. These men were dressed far differently from the dock workers as they wore what looked like dresses or long beltless tunics.

"These coins are really odd looking," I told Kelyan as we waited for Diud and Nomlet to have their money exchanged. "What's this white metal?"

"I think it's called silver," he told me. "I've seen cups made of it when I was a seaman on that pleasure boat back in Sefna."

"Really strange," I said, "but I bet there'll be a lot stranger things here to see."

"That there will, lad," said Diud as he walked over to us from the table where the money changers sat. "This is just the beginnin'."

"What are these holes for in the coins?" I asked.

"No pockets." Diud replied.

"What?"

"Kallefandrans don't have pockets in them loincloths they wear nor in them robes the men back there have on," Diud explained. "So they can't use coin pouches like us. They put their coins on cords made o' twisted threads or on fancy chains then wear them around their necks or on their wrists."

"That's an odd thing to do," I told him.

"To us maybe," he replied, "but not to them. To them it all seems the natural way o' things."

"So how do we know what these coins are worth?" asked Nomlet.

"That's another thing," Diud told us, "they count by sixes."

"Sixes!" I said, "that's confusing."

"Not when you get used to it. This here little coin is a diu and six of them make a tau," and he held up a coin a little larger than the diu.

"So six dioi equal one tau," I said. "What about the tauoi?"

"And that's another thing," he told me, "it's diutem and tautem."

"What do you mean?" I asked totally confused.

"Well, we say *oi* when we mean more than one," he replied, "but they don't. They say *tem*, so it's one diu but six diutem."

"That's even more confusing," I said laughing. "Don't they get mixed up?"

"To them it's all natural, like *oi* is to us."

"If you say so," I replied. "What about this big one?" and I held up the largest coin.

"That's a shen, and it's worth six tautem," he told me.

"I hope I can remember all this," I said, and Kelyan and Nomlet agreed with me.

"You'll get used to it in no time," he assured us.

"So, where is this place with the strong drinks?" Kelyan asked as we at last came out of the money changers' shop.

"Just up here," Diud told him, "not too far."

The inn was called the *Kallumtarra*, and it made the *Pola* seem like the main room of my home back in Alna. I have to admit, though I never told my crew mates, the place really scared me. But all the time I was there I smiled and did my best to put on a brave front.

It was bright and airy, yet only because of the grill work which covered the entire front of the inn. This in fact was typical of Kallefandran buildings because of the heat, especially in summer. Yet in all other respects it was a sinister place.

There were yellow haired Kallefandran some in loincloths and others in long robes. These sat close to the bar talking among themselves and paid no attention to the Kroemaeon sitting in little knots around the room. Nor did they seem to notice the white haired men, some hardly older than I, who had pictures of strange beasts imprinted on their arms as well as rings attached to holes in their ears (one even to his nose). They wore what appeared to be tunics with broad belts, but the bottom half looked more like short dresses.

"How'd ya' like to have your ears pierced like them Shalmarran?" Diud asked as he leaned close to me.

"Not me," I told him.

"Have to do it when they come of age," he explained. "They got to get them pictures on their arms too. Done with needles. Shows the women how brave they are."

"I don't care how brave some woman thinks I am," I told him, "I'd never want to do that."

"Have to if ya' want to be a man," he said with a laugh.

"Come back with one o' those on your arm," said Kelyan, "and that girl back in Alna will really be impressed."

"What's this?" said Diud, "Idar's got himself a girl back home?"

"She's not my girl," I told him and shot Kelyan an angry look for saying anything about Illiad. "She's just the sister of my best friend."

"Oh, just the sister of your best friend," said Nomlet. "That describes my wife, it does," and he, too, laughed while I reddened.

"Well," I said with a smile, "I do like her, but she's not my girl."

"Kissed her yet?" asked Diud.

"Yeah," I said. "a couple of times," and my smile broadened.

"Then she's your girl," and he jabbed me in the ribs with his elbow.

"Fine, if that's the way you see it," I told him taking a sip of the drink I had ordered when we came in. "And if you must know, I did promise to bring her back something from Shentoar. So where are the markets?"

"Bring her back a gift, and she's not your girl," laughed Nomlet. "She has you hooked like a fish on a line."

"After we finish our drinks," said Diud, "we can head up to the walled part of the city. That's were the good markets be."

We sat for a while drinking and talking, and each of the men let me try a sip of their drinks which, as Diud had said, almost did take the skin off my tongue. And so I stuck to wine when we ordered a second round.

At last, we left the *Kallumtarra* and headed towards the market in the walled part of the city. The buildings we passed were much like the inn with intricate grill work covering most of their front walls. This impressed me as I was sure even my father would not have the skill to make such grills.

Yet we soon came to a part of the city where there were only houses, and these were three levels with the top most level having what appeared to be a tent sitting in the middle of a courtyard surrounded by plants. The grills on the houses were on the second level, and only bare walls with a door could be seen along the street.

"They live and cook on that second level," Diud explained, "and sleep up on the roof where they can catch a night breeze from the river even during the summer."

"What about the bottom level?" I asked.

"Storage mostly," he replied.

As we walked along talking and laughing, we came to a place where one narrow street entered the one we were on. Since I was talking to Nomlet, I was not paying attention; and so I walked right into a man coming around the corner.

"I'm sorry," I said instinctively then looked up to see a dark haired man wearing the usual loincloth I was becoming used to seeing.

"Not a problem," he replied; but as soon as the words passed his lips, he stiffened, and a look of terror crossed his face.

I stared into his eyes for a brief moment, then he turned and fled; and an icy chill come over me.

"Wait, friend," called Diud. But in seconds he was gone, swallowed up by the city.

"He was a Kroemaeon," I said. "He spoke to me."

"I heard," Kelyan remarked.

"But why did he run?" I asked still in total disbelief.

"Don't know," he answered, "but he sure looked scared."

"He must be a slave, poor fellow," Diud said. "But there's naught we can do," and we continued on our way.

§ § §

The market was the most wonderful place I had ever seen, surpassing the one in Theo. Since this was not a produce market, it was filled with far more than food. There were clothes, sandals and boots all of a kind I had not seen before. Jewelry—made not only from the white metal that Kelyan had called silver but from gold and copper as well—was to be found everywhere. Bowls and drinking cups made from a material you could actually see through might be had in a nearly endless variety of colors, as could figures of nosha, ashka, tegga and other animals. Some of these I found rather odd since I had not seen them before; yet I was almost sure one was a vood, for it appeared just as Aarad had described them to me.

We spent more than three hours in the market stopping at a vendor when we grew hungry to buy bread and strips of meat which were cold to the touch yet burned our mouths like fire when eaten. Finally, I decided to buy a shawl for Illiad, one made from a material soft and cool to the touch and so light you could almost see through it.

I also bought one for my mother, Illiad's in a shade of blue almost the color of heshel the other in green since this was my mother's favorite color. Though very beautiful, they were not expensive, and so I bought a third shawl in blue for Melne not wishing to slight her as she was like a second mother to me.

"We best be headin' back to the ship," Diud told us when I had paid for the shawls, "It's not a good idea to be walkin' in the harbor district after it's dark."

And so we made our way back to the wharf where the *Tel* was docked, and I stored my gifts in the sea chest under my hammock. I also chose four of the shiniest diutem to be gifts for my father, Aarad, Seppan and Aeshone. These I placed in the coin purse Tenoar had given me then buried it under the shawls.

Since it was my day of shore leave, I had no duties; and so I went up on deck and stood at the rail watching the sun set far to the west. A cool breeze rustled through the strange trees in the forest across the river; and though exhausted from my day in the city, I was wide awake and so filled with excitement I felt I would never sleep again.

This, I thought to myself, had been all I had dreamt it would be; and at that moment, I wanted never to return home.

§ § §

Time passed, and we were given shore leave about every fifteen days; yet these were spent exploring the city as the money Tenoar had advanced me was all but used up. By the middle of the first moons cycle of winter we had sold our cargo and reloaded the *Tel;* yet Tenoar told us the worst of the winter storms would soon be raging in the northern sea, and we could not set sail until this storm season had passed. Therefore, we would remain in port for at least two full cycles of the moons.

In many ways I did not mind this, for the nights were warm with a cool breeze blowing off the river to soothe me as I watched the stars. Yet as day passed into day, I gradually began to long for home and all I had known from my youth. While I still enjoyed the city and discovering wondrous new things to see, it began to grow tiresome causing home to daily seem more and more appealing to me.

Yet I also began to grow anxious in another way, for with the coming of the next moons cycle, I would have lived out my boyhood. In many ways this had happened long ago, for I had not been permitted to enjoy a carefree life typical of boys. However, now that my boyhood was truly coming to an end, I longed to have it back.

This became my first lesson in manhood, for we cannot relive the past. The days we have are fleeting, passing quickly; and once they are gone, they will never return to us again.

And so I spent those last days of boyhood regretting what could not be undone. Yet from this grew a new awareness that it is best to make of each day what you can and to live for the future.

My future, it seemed, had been set in motion the day I joined the *Tel,* for I was sure my destiny lay with the foreign lands I longed to see. I would go home of course, but this would only be for a time; and then I would be off seeking adventure in far off places.

Therefore, it began to seem right to me that I should become a man in a far off land since this was how I would spend my life—looking for what was new and different. Thus, as the three moons rose silently into the night sky over the city of Shentoar, the new moons cycle began; and I became a man.

Chapter II

I sat on the deck with my legs extended over the *Tel's* side watching as men loaded cargo onto a nearby ship. The men on the ship were definitely not Kallefandran; for they, too, had hair as dark as mine. Likewise, the ship was Kroemaeon resembling the *Tel* in many ways. But those who carried the cargo aboard her were all yellow haired and wore the usual diapers I had long since ceased to find amusing.

Again and again my mind came back to the man we had encountered on the street, for I could not forget the look of fear in his eyes; and I wondered what had caused him to run from us. He was obviously a Kroemaeon, for he spoke to us. He must have understood us. If he was a prisoner here, why did he not ask us for help? Why run away?

Suddenly my thoughts were interrupted by a loud call from the wharf, "Adjnee, you want adjnee?"

When I looked in the direction of the voice, I saw a man about my age at the end of the ramp leading to the ship. He was holding something red in his hand, and again he called out, "Kroemaeon man, you want adjnee?"

I stood up and took a few steps towards the plank. Then peering over the side of the ship I asked, "What is it?"

"Adjnee," he replied. "Very good. You try?"

"How much?" I asked him.

"No buy. Just try," he told me. "You like. You buy many adjnee."

"I don't know about that," I said. "I don't have a lot of money."

"You like, you tell captain. He buy for men. Adjnee very good."

"Well," I told him, "if I like it I could tell Kebbit, he's our cook and I help him. Maybe he would buy some."

"Cook, *man?*" he replied with obvious surprise, "and you help. You cook food for other men?"

"Yes," I said.

"Kroemaeon very strange," he laughed. "In Kallefandra only woman cook. Man never."

"Well, I don't really like it," I told him a little angered by his laughter. "I have to because we're on a ship. At home my mother usually cooks."

"Kallefandra ship take woman with," he retorted. "Man never cook."

"We do things differently," I said remembering what Kelyan had told me about how the Kallefandran treated women and started down the plank to the wharf. "I'll try your adjnee, and if I like it, I'll ask Kebbit to buy some."

"Good," he said, "You eat," and he handed me a long slender fruit.

I took it and opened my mouth to take a bite.

"No, no," he cried out, "not eat skin. Here," and he took the adjnee from me and broke open the outer peel with his fingers. "Tear off first," he told me, "then eat."

I did as he said then cautiously took a small bite of the fruit. It truly was wonderful. Far better than the khansh I had eaten back in Theo.

"This *is* good," I told him and took a much bigger bite.

"Tullikan say you like," he said. "Now you buy many adjnee?"

"Well, I will tell Kebbit, but I can't promise anything."

"You tell cook man now?" he asked.

"He's busy now," I told him. "In fact, I need to get back to the galley and help him. I'll take the rest of this and let him try. Can you come back tomorrow?

"Tullikan be back," he replied. "Same time. You be here?"

"Yes," I said, "I'll be here," then raised my hand in a farewell gesture, but he merely bowed his head.

"See tomorrow," he told me, and we parted.

§ § §

The next day, true to his word, Tullikan was back; and I was waiting as I had promised, again sitting on the deck watching the dock workers.

"Cookman buy adjnee?" he asked calling from the pier.

"Yes, he will," I told him. "You wait there by the ramp, and I'll call him."

I hurried down the ladder to the hold and then into the galley.

"Tullikan's here," I told Kebbit.

"Who?" he asked.

"The man selling the adjnee," I replied.

"Oh, right," he said and followed me out of the galley.

When we reached the plank, Tullikan called up in a cheerful voice, "Ah, good day, cookman. You buy adjnee?"

"That I will," Kebbit replied, "if the price is right. How much ya' want for them adjnee?"

"One diu each," Tullikan told him.

"Seems fair," said Kebbit, "I'll take a hundred."

"Ah, very good," replied Tullikan with a look of obvious pleasure. "That one hundred diutem."

"Well," said Kebbit, "since I'm buyin' in bulk, I should get a discount."

"Ah, cookman know how to bargain," he replied, and a look of suspicion came over his face.

"Right, I do," Kebbit told him. "I'll give ya' seventy-five diutem for the lot."

"Seventy-five!" howled Tullikan, "Cookman rob Tullikan. But Tullikan a fair man. He sell for ninety diutem."

"Eighty," came Kebbit's counter offer.

"Eighty-seven."

"Eighty-three," said Kebbit, "and that's as high as I'll go."

"You still rob Tullikan," he told Kebbit, "Tullikan sell for eighty-three, but one hundred adjnee very heavy. Young Kroemaeon man come help carry back."

"Idar's not goin' anywhere," said Kebbit.

"But Tullikan not carry four bags by himself," he replied. "Take many trips."

"You're the one sellin' the adjnee," Kebbit retorted. "A good merchant always delivers."

"Cookman pay eighty-seven."

"Eighty-three, and you have them here by sunset or the deal's off." And with that Kebbit turned and walked away.

§ § §

Tullikan returned well before sunset with the adjnee piled high in a cart having only one wheel. There were two poles sticking out of the cart, and he used these to push the load in front of him.

Nomlet, who was on watch, called into the hold, and I came up with the money Kebbit had given me to pay for the adjnee.

"We need to load them on the ship first," I told him. "Kebbit's orders."

"Cookman very clever," he replied, "but Tullikan not cheat."

"I'm sure you won't," I told him, "but orders are orders," and I picked up a sack of the adjnee and started up the plank.

Tullikan followed with a second sack, and together we carried the fruit aboard the *Tel*.

"Now I'm supposed to count them," and Tullikan sighed.

"Cookman not trust Tullikan," he told me.

"Kebbit's a good business man," I replied, "he just wants to be sure."

I dumped the adjnee in one sack out onto the deck, then counted them as I placed them back.

"So, is this all you sell?" I asked.

"No, Tullikan sell many fruit," he replied. "You want buy more?"

"I was just wondering," I told him. "Do you make enough to support yourself?"

"Support self?" he asked, "What mean?"

"Do you make enough money to buy food and the things you need," I explained.

"Oh, Tullikan not support self," he told me. "Tullikan live with father and three brother. Father buy food."

"So, what do you use this money for?" I asked.

"Well…Tullikan do help father some," he replied. "But Tullikan need save money to buy wife."

"*Buy* a wife!" I asked in surprise.

"Yes," he told me, "no one give wife away free."

"But you buy a wife like a slave?" I asked.

"No, wife not slave," he replied. "Slave you sell to other when you not want. Wife you keep whole life, but buy new one if first wife not please you."

"Well, that's not how we do it," I told him. "We meet a girl and fall in love with her, then we marry her."

"Kroemaeon very strange," he replied. "Why fall in love first? After you live with wife, you love later."

I shook my head and dumped out a second bag of adjnee.

"That's still not how we do it," I told him.

"You have girl you love at home?" he asked.

"Well, I can't say I love her," I replied, and I felt myself redden, "but I do like this one girl. Her name is Illiad."

"Good name," he said, "Tullikan like. So, you marry girl?"

"I haven't really thought about it," I lied. "She's the sister of my best friend. I like her, but I don't know if I'm ready to marry anyone just yet."

"Tullikan like girl too," he told me, "but she cost much money. Father rich man. Want much money for daughter. So Tullikan buy different girl."

"Now that's very strange," I said. "That's just not the way we live."

As I continued to count the adjnee, we talked of other things; and I was surprised how very different our lives were. Yet hearing of his life made my own seem more and more appealing.

When I had thought of strange lands, I had not realized that those who lived there would be any different from those I had grown up with. But now I knew this was not so, and I truly longed to be back home with my own kind.

I finished counting the adjnee and paid Tullikan his money then thanked him for bringing the fruit.

"Tullikan be back," he assured me. "You like, you buy more or other fruit. Soon Tullikan have good wife," and he laughed.

"We'll see," I told him, "but I need to go and help Kebbit. I'll see you soon, then."

"Yes, see Tullikan soon," and he left.

§ § §

I did see Tullikan soon, for he came by the ship almost every other day on his way to sell adjnee and other fruit to those docked in the harbor. He stopped if I was on deck, and we talked. Soon we had become friends, and it was good to have someone my own age to talk to.

Then, one day towards the end of the second moons cycle of winter, he came to the ship in the early afternoon. In the morning, I had gone with Kelyan and Diud to the *Kallumtarra* for a drink since we had been given shore leave that day. Yet the day soon grew hot, hotter than usual; and we had returned to the *Tel* preferring to merely rest and not explore the city as we had done before.

As I sat on the deck of the *Tel* that day, I heard Tullikan's now familiar voice call out, "Kroemaeon man want swim?"

"My name's Idar," I called back, "I've told you that before."

"Tullikan know," he replied, "only make joke."

"Well," I told him, "it's not all that funny."

"Sorry," he said.

"No, I'm sorry. It's hot and I'm just a little irritable that's all."

"What irritable?" he asked as he usually did when I used a new word.

"The heat just makes me get angry easily," I explained.

"Tullikan understand, that why he ask Idar want swim."

"Swim where?" I asked.

"Tullikan know place along river," he replied. "Many trees, cool water. You swim?"

"Yes, I can swim," I told him. "It sounds like a place back home where I used to swim with my friends. I wouldn't mind going there on a day like this."

"You want go?" he asked.

"Yes," I replied, and I crossed the deck to the ramp then joined him on the pier.

"This way," he said then led me through the harbor district and along the river for about a league and a half to a place where bushes and tall trees grew at the edge of the Hallucantec.

"This does remind me of home," I said. "There are even rocks to sit on or dive off of."

"Idar like?" he asked.

"Kroemaeon man like very much," I told him and we both laughed.

We swam and splashed in the cool water for at least an hour. Then at last I climbed out onto a flat rock and lay in the sun to dry off. Tullikan, too, climbed out of the water and lay on a nearby rock. It was quiet and peaceful, a little bit of home in this far off land.

Suddenly there was rustling in the bushes, and I sat up just in time to see three men running towards us. I started to climb to my feet; but before I could, they were on me. Two of them grabbed me and forced me back down onto the rock. The other, the tallest of the three, stood over me with a look of contempt on his face.

Immediately Tullikan was on his feet yelling at the men in words I could not understand. The man standing over me said something to Tullikan then laughed, and the two others pulled me to my feet.

Tullikan rushed at them, his voice filled with rage; but the tall one only pushed him to the ground. As I struggled with my captors, Tullikan continued to speak to them; and though I could not understand what he said, it seemed he was begging and pleading with them.

Finally, the tall man said something to Tullikan in a threatening tone to which Tullikan only nodded. Then the man spoke to the other two and they released me. As they walked away, the tall man turned, pointed his finger at Tullikan and again spoke threateningly to him; but Tullikan said nothing more.

"Who are they?" I asked as I walked over to where I had left my tunic and put it on.

"Brother and friends," he replied sadly.

"*Your* brother?" I asked unable to believe what I was hearing.

Tullikan nodded and looked ashamed.

"What did they want?"

"They want make Idar slave," he replied almost in a whisper.

"Slave?" I asked.

Again Tullikan nodded, "They take Idar and sell in market. Tullikan not know. Idar must believe. Tullikan tell brother he swim with Kroemaeon friend in river, but not know brother do this bad thing. Tullikan not know. Idar must believe."

"I believe you," I told him. "But why did they let me go?"

"Tullikan tell brother let friend go. Tullikan give brother all money save for wife."

"You are going to give him your savings?" I asked in surprise.

"Only way," he told me. "Brother let Idar go. Tullikan must give money or brother be very mad. Friends hurt Tullikan bad.

"Go now. Not safe here. Brother may change mind," and he grabbed my arm.

We talked very little as we walked back to the *Tel*. Then, as I was just about to go up the plank leading to the deck, he spoke, "Tullikan not see Idar again. Say good-bye now."

"Why?" I asked.

"Brother not like Kroemaeon," he said. "Father not like Kroemaeon. They mad Tullikan make friend. Brother try hurt Idar. Tullikan not be friend. Idar safe."

"They can't hurt me if I stay on the ship," I told him.

"Better Tullikan not come back," he replied.

I offered him my hand, but he only bowed his head to me, then turned and walked away.

Silently I walked up the ramp. Yet as I reached the deck, I turned and called after him, "I won't forget you." But if he heard me, I never knew.

Chapter III

It was the fifteenth night of the last moons cycle of winter, and after one more day the *Tel* would set sail for home. I had missed home with the sights and smells of Alna: my mother's cheshoi cooling on a table in our main room, my father hammering red hot iron in the forge, the rustling leaves of a palne tree or merely the familiar sound of Kroemaeon spoken in the streets. But most of all I longed to be home with my parents, to see them once more, to hear their voices so familiar to me yet now strangely forgotten, to laugh at our evening meal.

Being home also meant walking past familiar fields out to the farm and seeing Aarad, joking with Seppan and eating kahl with palne syrup, something I could never get on the *Tel*. Yet home also meant being with Illiad.

I had kept my promise; for each night before I went below deck I stood a few minutes at the ship's rail watching the stars, hoping that at that very moment Illiad, too, was looking at these same familiar stars while thinking of me. It had not been a hard promise to keep, because this time I spent alone and in silent contemplation was time I spent with her.

Then, I would go below deck and try to sleep. But each night, as now, it had been hard for me to fall asleep, for strange new thoughts kept plaguing me; and I did not know how to deal with them.

My coming of age, my reaching true manhood, affected me strangely; and I had spent the past fifty days and nights endeavoring to put my life into perspective. Ever since I boarded the *Tel* I had seen myself as a man doing a man's job, living a man's life. Yet from the moment I saw the three moons rising over the city of Shentoar, I had realized my life was now different; for I was thirteen with all of the honors and the duties this age conferred upon me.

When I returned to my boyhood home, I would have money, my money, earned by me as a man and not given to me by my father. I would be free to come and go as I pleased and could, if I chose, take a room at the inn or live aboard the *Tel* as was the intent of some of my crew mates.

As a man, I could be called to war as the king's need arose and would be required to pay the head tax just as other men must do. Yet I had no fear of war since Theo was at peace with all her neighbors, and I could well afford to pay the tax having only myself to support.

Yet it was this that played most upon my mind, for I was now alone. My life no longer revolved around my parents since becoming a man bestowed on me a new freedom and an independence I had never known before. This new status scared me, for I did not know what to do.

I did plan on living with my parents since the security of my own room was comforting to me; but there was still a longing within me to go off on my own, and I did not know how to deal with this new feeling. Was I disloyal to my parents, or was this but the way all men felt once they attained manhood? I had no way of knowing, and I could not bring myself to ask my crew mates as I feared they would think me weak and but still a boy.

And so I continued to turn these thoughts over and over in my head as I lay awake each night. Yet soon I would be home, and I could talk them over with Seppan, or my father, and come to some understanding of myself.

§ § §

Somehow, as always, I fell asleep that night; for the next thing I knew it was time to get up and help Kebbit prepare the morning meal for the crew. I did not remember sleeping; but when I opened my eyes I was instantly aware it was morning, and that this would be my last day in Shentoar.

Quietly I stood up so as not to awaken anyone, stretched and crept out of the crew quarters to make my way through the jumble that was the hold. When I entered the galley, Kebbit was just taking bread out of the small brick oven built into a space in the prow of the ship where a metal pipe could carry the smoke off into the wind.

"You're up early," said Kebbit. "No need to call ya' then."

"It's our last day here," I told him, "I'm looking forward to going home. It's been too long. I couldn't sleep last night, and…I don't know, I just woke up on my own."

"Know what ya' mean," he said, "I'll be glad to be out of this place as well. Never did like Shentoar, weather's too nice for one thing. Too hot down here in the galley. I'll be glad to be out to sea and get a bit o' breeze runnin' through the ship."

§ § §

That day passed quickly for me since my longing for home made each chore easier knowing it would be my last in Shentoar. I cooked, then served the men and cleaned the galley, then cooked again. In the afternoon, wood to be used in the galley was delivered; and it became my duty to carry it below deck and store it in one of the forward compartments just off the galley.

Finally, the day was nearly done; and Kwellen told me I had been ordered to assist him with the plank, a chore truly signaling the end of our long stay in Shentoar. I followed him up the ladder to the deck for what seemed to be the hundredth time that day and walked over to the rail.

We were just about to pull in the plank when a lone figure jumped from behind a pile of boxes on the wharf, ran to the ship and bounded up the ramp before we could move it. He dropped to his knees in front of me, and at once I recognized him as the man I had bumped into on my first shore leave.

"Mercy," he begged, "please have mercy."

"I know you," I told him.

"Please, take me to your captain," and he began to weep, "please don't send me away, I beg you."

"You know this man?" Kwellen asked.

"I've seen him before, in the city," I told him.

"Well, you better take him to Tenoar," he said, "I can pull in the plank myself. When you come back, we can stow it away."

I nodded and began walking towards Tenoar's cabin. The man stood and followed me nervously.

"Enter," said Tenoar as soon as I knocked.

I opened the door to find him seated at his desk in the corner; and as I entered, he turned to face me.

"Ah, Idar, what is it?"

"I've brought a man to see you, sir," I told him, and at this the strange man pushed his way past me and fell face forward onto the floor.

"Please, captain," he again begged, "take me with you. I ask you out of mercy, don't leave me in this place."

"Who is this man?" Tenoar asked looking at me.

"I don't really know, sir," I replied. "When I went into the city my first time, I bumped into him; but he ran away from us. He looked really scared. I haven't seen him since."

"I was frightened," he said looking up at Tenoar. "If my master knew I spoke Kroemaeon…I would have been beaten and sold into the interior far from the coast and any hope of escape."

"Please come in, Idar, and close the door," then addressing the man on the floor Tenoar asked, "So, you are a slave?"

"Yes," he replied, "but please don't send me back to my master. Take me with you I beg of you."

"You are obviously a Kroemaeon," Tenoar told him. "What city are you from?"

"I was born in Arganon," the man replied. "My name is Naemen, and I was a seaman on a merchant ship. One night I was returning from a tavern in Eltec with three of my crew mates. We drank way too much, and we foolishly stayed way too long. I don't remember everything. We were attacked in the dark. Overpowered. When we woke up, we were chained in the hold of a ship.

"They brought us here to Shentoar and sold us. I never saw my friends again. It's been five sun cycles. Please take me home. I have a wife and two sons. Out of pity for them, take me home," and he began to weep again.

"Get up," Tenoar said kindly. "Idar, get him a chair. Of course we will take you with us…if we can get away safely ourselves."

Naemen got up and sat in the chair I brought him.

"Thank you, sir. Thank you."

"Now," said Tenoar, "is there any possibility you were followed?"

"No," he replied, "I'm sure I wasn't. I snuck out of my master's house a couple of hours ago, and I wandered around the city making sure I was not followed before coming here. I came alone, I'm sure of that. Besides, no one has followed me the other times I came here."

"You've come here before?" Tenoar asked.

"I have been watching your ship for signs you were leaving," he replied.

"And why our ship?"

"The day I met your men on the street," he told us, "one of them used a word I had not heard in a long time, not even in Kallefandran. He called me friend.

"His words touched me. They made me feel I had hope; and so, after I ran from them, I followed them. My master beat me for returning late, but I didn't care. I had made up my mind I would escape on your ship or die trying. You have no idea what it has been like here. I can't live this way any longer."

"Yet if we get caught helping you," Tenoar told him, "you may have to and all of us as well. To help a runaway slave is punishable by enslavement. If I help you, I risk having my ship as well as my crew taken and sold."

"Please, sir. Please."

"I've already told you I will help you," Tenoar went on. "Now, if no one followed you, how long do you think before they start looking for you?"

"That I'm not sure," he said. "But when they do, they won't think of looking for me here. And besides, it's getting dark. No one from the wealthy part of the city will come into the harbor district at night."

"And by the time they do come," said Tenoar, "we will be gone."

"That's how I planned it," he told us, "if I came here at sun set, they wouldn't follow. I could get away if only you would help me."

"Then we must leave at first light," said Tenoar, "and we won't be able to come back for a very long time…if ever.

"Idar, does anyone else know he's here?"

"Kwellen was with me when he came aboard, sir. He's waiting for me to help him with the plank."

"Then go complete your assigned duty," he told me, "but say nothing to anyone. When you finish storing the plank tell Kwellen and Pellonek I want to see them. We must keep this as quiet as we can until we are well out to sea. Hopefully Kwellen has told no one."

"I don't think he has, sir," I said, "we were the only ones on deck."

"Good, then be off with you," and I left his cabin.

§ § §

I had difficulty sleeping again that night, for the fear of being taken as a slave gripped my mind. If I did not return, my mother would not be able to endure such grief. She had lost her father to the sea, and it would kill her if she lost her son as well. Yet as on the previous night, I did fall asleep; for all at once Kelyan was gently shaking me.

"What were you dreamin' about?" he asked. "Ya' kept mumblin' stuff in your sleep. Somethin' about slaves."

"I'll tell you later," I told him. What time is it? Should I be up?"

He nodded and said, "Burog was just here. Said Tenoar wants an early start. We're to be ready to sail at first light.

"I'm as anxious as any to be off for home, but I'd like a bit of food in me first."

"I'd better go help Kebbit," I told him.

"No, lad, you're to help me push off first," and he stood up. "Come on, get a move on."

I climbed out of my hammock and followed him to the ladder leading to the deck, then asked as matter-of-factly as possible, "Did Burog say why we were leaving so early?"

"No. Just told us to be up on deck in ten minutes to start castin' off."

§ § §

The city of Shentoar sat black against the rising sun as we sailed down the Hallucantec towards the sea. I stood on deck for a few minutes watching for any sign of pursuit, fearful that Naemen's master had realized where he was and had sent men to bring him back—to bring us back as well. Yet only the *Tel* made its way westward that morning, and when we reached open sea and headed north, I knew we had escaped.

I was below deck by then, working in the galley. But when Altore came in to eat proclaiming we now had a strong south wind filling our sails and were headed north for home, the tension I had felt in my stomach relaxed. We had escaped. Naemen would return home to his family, and I would not remain in Shentoar forever but would once again see my home and those I loved.

After we had eaten, Tenoar called everyone on deck; and, standing by the helm, he explained to the crew why we had left Shentoar with such haste. The men stood in silence as he explained everything to them, then he ordered Burog to fetch Naemen and introduced him to the crew.

When he was finished speaking, the men stood in little knots around the deck and talked quietly amongst themselves.

"You knew this?" Kelyan asked me, and I nodded. "Yet you didn't say a word."

"Tenoar ordered Kwellen and me not to say anything," I told him.

"And he was wise to do so," he replied. "If even one man had panicked and jumped ship, he could have betrayed all the rest of us. You're one brave lad," he told me putting his hand on my shoulder. "I don't know if I would o' had the courage to keep quiet."

I smiled and felt a deep sense of pride at his words. Yet I had not seen myself as being brave but as merely doing my duty.

§ § §

We again spent a day at the Allubet taking on water and then stopped at Eltec to do the same. While we were docked in Eltec, Naemen was ordered to remain below deck out of fear those who had taken him might by chance recognize him and our crime of aiding a fugitive slave be made known. Eltec, as a Kroemaeon city, did not allow slavery; however, they did sanction it and had an agreement with Kallefandra to return runaway slaves.

Naemen, for his part, became a working member of our crew; and the men soon grew to accept and even respect him for his seamanship as well as for all he had been forced to endure. At first he was timid, fearful after the time he had spent living in fear: beaten for each mistake he made, poorly fed and overworked. Yet he quickly adapted, and by the time we reached Theo, he seemed to be a different person.

And so one day as we neared home, I asked him what he would do once we reached the end of our voyage.

"I'll find a ship heading for Arganon," he told me. "I've got to find my family. My sons were only two and four sun cycles when I left. I'm sure they won't recognize me. And my wife, she will think I returned from the dead."

"There's a ship from Arganon that comes into the harbor at Alna," I told him. "The *Kwel* I think it's called, but I'm not sure"

"That's my ship!" he exclaimed. "I was serving on the *Kwel* when I was taken. How often does she come into port?"

"I don't know," I replied. "I'm not even sure that's the name. I've just seen it when I've been down at the docks with my friends. I've never really paid that much attention."

"Well, it's not that important," he said. "Any ship will do just as long as I get home."

§ § §

Our first night out from Eltec, while I stood on the deck watching the stars and hoping as always that Illiad was doing the same, all three moons rose together to mark the coming of spring; and I thought of Aarad, for this was the beginning of his twelfth sun cycle. In but a short ten moons cycles he, too, would come of age and apprentice with some craftsman; and I wondered what changes had come over him, for I had truly changed since leaving home. Would we still be as we were before? And what of Illiad? Would things be the same between us?

Yet I cast these thoughts from my mind; for I was going home, and this was all that truly mattered. Home would always be home. I was sure of the truth of this, and even now in death, I know it to be true.

§ § §

With a fine south wind at our backs, we made good time on our return voyage; and though we did run into some bad weather, we met nothing major and returned to Theo in a little less than a full moons cycle. As the Narrows drew near, Pellonek sought me out and told me Tenoar wished to see me at once. And so I went to his cabin and knocked.

"Enter," he càlled from within, and I opened the door.

"Ah, Idar, come in."

"You wished to see me, sir?" I asked closing the door.

"Yes," he replied. "When we enter the bay, we will make for Sefna to off load our cargo since I must settle up with Jaygore. And I don't feel your services as a mahlet will be needed after we dock."

"But, sir!" I cried, "what have I done?"

"No, no," he told me in a reassuring voice, "you misunderstand me. I just feel that you have been away from home long enough for a lad your age. You are not being dismissed, far from it. No, I want you to go home to your family and friends while the crew unloads our cargo.

"The other men are from Sefna or Theo and will be able to see those close to them each night if they wish except for when they stand watch on the ship. But Alna is over five leagues from Sefna, far too long a distance to walk each day.

"Go home. Enjoy a good long shore leave, and you can join us when we dock in Alna since I plan on making her my home port…far from Jaygore," and he gave a little chuckle.

"Thank you, sir," I said.

"You have done an excellent job, lad," he continued. "I always expected you would, and you have not disappointed me. I commend you, and I'm sure in the future your service to my ship will not be diminished.

"Now, one more thing."

"Yes, sir."

"Naemen tells me that his old ship, the *Kwel*, sometimes docks in Alna. Is this true?"

"I believe so, sir," I told him. "I mean, a ship from Arganon does dock there, but I'm not sure if it's the *Kwel.*"

"Well, while you are at home, you are to make inquiries. Find out what you can, and get word to me here in Sefna if the *Kwel* is in port or if she is expected in before we dock in Alna, which will be in about eight to ten days if all goes well."

"I will, sir," I told him.

"A good lad," he replied. "Now be off with you. Take only what you will need. You should leave your chest on board. No one will bother it."

"Right, sir, and thank you again."

§ § §

While I assisted Kelyan in poling the *Tel* to the pier in Sefna, I told him about my visit to Tenoar's cabin. He did not seem surprised to hear that I was to go home early and would not be expected to remain with the ship until we reached Alna.

"It's only fair," he told me. "Tenoar's right about family and all, you should go home."

"So, you don't think the men will be angry?" I asked.

"Why should they?" he replied. "They'll be seein' their families right soon enough. You should be able to do the same. Go. And don't give it any thought."

And so, after lowering the plank, I scrambled up the ramp to the deck of the ship and headed straight for the hold to gather my things. I wrapped the gifts I had bought for my mother, Melne and Illiad in my extra tunics and stuffed these into the sack I had used so long ago to carry my things aboard the *Tel.* Then I placed my blanket in my sea chest and hurried off for home.

Chapter IV

All was as it should be as I approached my boyhood home. The sound of my father pounding iron rang out from the forge; and I smiled to hear what, for me, was as comforting and familiar as the song my mother had used to sing me to sleep as a child.

It had taken me a little over three hours to walk the distance from Sefna to Alna, for as soon as I was out of town, I had made my way to the beach. Then I had walked in the all too familiar sand all the way to Alna with the sound of the waves crashing on the shore and the calling of klenn filling my ears.

I was home. That was all I could think of. I was home, and part of me never wanted to leave again.

With each footstep, Alna grew nearer, and my heart beat faster in my chest. I was home. I was home. I was home. I was home.

Then, at last, I had reached the road leading to the docks and made my way along its comfortingly familiar stones to the bridge, the inn, the street where I had played with Tuac, until I was once again standing at the door I had left on an autumn's day in what seemed like another life. I smiled, for I found a deep sense of contentment in the sound of my father at work, the smell of cooking coming from the house, the feel of the latch in my hand and at last the sight of my mother, her back to me, stirring something wonderful in the pot on the stove.

"Nodeh," I said as I dropped my bag by the door, and she spun around dropping the spoon on the floor.

"Idar!" she cried then ran to me and flung her arms around me sobbing as she kissed me on both cheeks. "Idar, I cannot believe it is you. Tohana! I cannot believe you are back, you are home, you are safe, tohana, tohana.

"Oh, you have grown," she said releasing me at last. "Just look at you. You are so tall…but skinny. What did they feed you on that ship?"

"The food was not that bad," I lied, "and there was plenty. I'm not all that skinny," and I patted my stomach.

"Yes, you are," she assured me, "but I will take care of that in no time. Your father and I have missed you so much…you father! He does not know you are home," and she rushed to the door.

"Wait, nodeh, let me surprise him."

"Go, go," she said still weeping, "and bring him back here. We need to celebrate."

"And Seppan too," I said.

"Yes, of course," she told me, "he is in the forge with your father, and he will be just as glad to see you as your father and I are. Now go."

As usual, the door to the forge stood open; and I could hear my father talking to Seppan as they worked together. For a few moments, I stood just outside the door marveling at how well they worked together. It was almost as though they were father and son, and for a moment this pained me. But I had chosen a different life, a decision I did not regret. If anyone was to take my place at my father's side, I was glad it was Seppan.

"Well, you two seem a merry pair," I said as I entered the shop.

The sound of the hammering stopped at once, my father's arm in mid air.

"Well, I'll be a nosha's tail feather," my father said, and he dropped the metal he was working into the bucket of water next to him then set his tongs and hammer on the anvil.

At the same instant, Seppan, who was climbing up to the loft, leaped from the ladder and ran towards me.

"Idar!" he cried then embraced me. When he released me, he led me to my father with his arm still around my shoulder.

"How long have you been home?" my father asked hugging me just as he had done that long ago day on the deck of the *Tel*.

"We docked at Sefna about three or four hours ago," I told him, "but I just got here. I took a short cut along the beach."

"Sefna?" he said, "I thought Alna was to be your home port."

"It will be," I told him. "The ship's docked in Sefna to unload our cargo, then Tenoar will bring her here."

"So why are you not in Sefna with your crew?" he asked with a hint of suspicion in his voice.

"Tenoar told me to go home," I told him. "He said the other men had their families in Sefna and Theo, and that I should go home while they off load the cargo. He feels I've been away too long."

"And I agree," he replied then hugged me again.

"Nodeh wants both of you in the house," I told them. "She thinks I'm too skinny; so I'm sure we're going to eat," and we all laughed.

"I am sure you are right," said my father, and with his arm around my shoulder, he led me out of the forge and toward our house.

§ § §

I awoke the next morning with a start, for it was much too bright, and I was not in my hammock. Then I sank back onto my bed sighing contentedly.

The sound of hammering filled my ears, and I realized both Seppan and my father were in the smithy. I felt a little guilty to have slept so late, for we had all been up well into the night.

Seppan had gone to the inn and returned with a jug of wine; and he, my father and I had finished it off while my mother served everything she could find in the house for us to eat. We talked, laughed and exchanged stories of what had happened to us since I had left for Shentoar the previous autumn.

I gave them their gifts, and my mother was in awe at the beauty of the shawl. Both Seppan and my father also found the small coins amazing since they had never seen such metal before, and they marveled at it. And when I described the intricate beauty of the grillwork in Shentoar, they shook their heads in wonder that such things were possible.

Then, with both of us feeling the effects of the wine, Seppan and I had gone off to bed. Yet he was up early, and I had been allowed to sleep.

I lay on the bed feeling the wonderful joy of its all too familiar softness as I thought about what I wanted to do with my first totally free day in nearly five moons cycles. At last I got up, dressed and went into the main room to find my mother busy as usual cooking at the stove.

Again I smiled contentedly as I stood for a full minute watching her.

"Oh," she said turning around and catching sight of me, "you are up at last. Good, your father and Seppan will be in soon for the noon meal, you can eat with them."

"Noon," I replied unable to believe I had slept so long. "Why didn't you or Seppan wake me?"

"He snuck out of your room quiet as a buk," she told me. "He wanted to let you sleep."

"I can't believe I did. Aboard ship I'm up before first light helping cook breakfast for the crew."

"Well, I will be doing the cooking around here," she told me.

"You sound like Tullikan," I said sitting down at the table.

"That is a strange name," she told me. "Who is he?"

"A man I met in Shentoar," I replied. "He sold fruit at the docks, and do you know what he plans on doing with the money?"

"No, what?"

"Buy a wife," I told her.

"*Buy* a wife!" she cried. "I have never heard of such a thing. You cannot be serious."

"Yes, I am," I replied. "And when I told him that's not our way he said, 'Kroemaeon very strange. After you live with wife, you love later.'"

"Why that is terrible," she said. "But what if he does not come to love her?"

"He'll just buy another one," I told her, and at this she shook her head and made a disapproving noise with her lips.

"So, what plans do you have for the day?" she asked, and I was sure it was to change the subject since I had shocked her by what I said.

"Well, I do need to go to the inn for a bit."

"Why," she asked in a surprised tone.

"Don't worry, nodeh," I said with a chuckle, "I'll not be drinking. I don't have any money for one thing, but I do need to talk to Sethel and Shend."

"Oh, what about?" she asked.

"There's a ship from Arganon that docks here in Alna," I replied, "and Tenoar wants me to find out it's name and when it will be in port. If it's here now—or will be soon—I'll need to go back to Sefna and tell him. Otherwise, I'll just wait until he gets here in a few days."

"So, what is so special about this ship?" she asked.

"Nothing really. Just ship's business," I told her not wanting to speak of Naemen for fear of upsetting her.

"Well, well, well," came my father's voice, "so he is up at last," and I was glad he came in when he did, for I did not wish my mother to press me further about the *Kwel*.

"Sorry I slept so late," I told him again a little ashamed of my laziness.

"It is good for you," my mother replied before my father could speak.

"Well," he said, "that ends the matter," and we laughed.

§ § §

After eating, I went to the inn to speak with Sethel or Shend. When I entered, Shend was behind the bar drying the mugs he had just washed.

"Ah, Idar," he cried, and putting down his towel, he came around from behind the bar and took my hand. "Seppan told us you were back. Said you got in yesterday. It's good to see you."

I grasped his hand, but was a little surprised by his words, for he had never before shown any sign of being pleased to see me.

"How's Boec?" I asked as a way of starting a conversation, for after his greeting it seemed rude to turn immediately to business.

"We've only seen him three times since he left for Crayoar, but he was well and happy. Come, have a drink, and he returned to the bar.

"Sorry," I told him, "I haven't been paid yet, so…"

"Don't worry about that," he replied, "the first one's on me, and your credit is always good here at the inn."

"Thank you," I said, "I'll have a mug of your kahlmek. I hear it's much better than what they serve in Sefna."

"So we've been told," he replied with a little chuckle then filled my mug.

I thanked him for the kahlmek, took a drink then nodded, "This *is* much better than what they serve at the *Pola*.

"Ours is made in Crayoar," he told me, "What they sell in Sefna comes from Prion, and I think they use a different type of kalhu. Everyone who has tried both seems to like the Crayoar made kahlmek better.

"So," he then asked, "your voyage was good I hope?"

"Yes, very good" I told him, "in fact, that's why I'm here. We picked up a man in Shentoar who's trying to get back home to Arganon. I need to know about that ship from Arganon. Does she still dock here?"

"She comes in about every fifteen to twenty days," he told me. "Left here…seven days ago, so she should be back in eight days or so."

"Is she called the *Kwel*?" I asked, and he nodded.

"Yes, I believe that's her name," he replied.

"Eight days," I said. "The *Tel* should be here about that time. How long does she stay?"

"Not long, maybe three to five days," he replied.

"Tenoar wants me to let him know when the *Kwel* comes in. I guess I'll have to walk over there tomorrow and tell him."

"No need," he told me, "I'm going to Sefna tomorrow myself to buy a few barrels of wine. I could stop by the *Tel* and give him the message."

"That would be great," I said.

"Not a problem," he replied. "So, tell me about your trip."

§ § §

I remembered what I had told my mother, so I only had one drink which I sipped slowly as I told him about the wonders of Shentoar. He seemed truly amazed by all I had to say, for no ship docking at Alna went as far south as Kallefandra.

Then I returned home and sat for a few hours in the shop talking to my father and Seppan as they worked. I helped a bit when I could, but they had a rhythm and routine about their work which made me feel a little out of place.

At last the three of us returned to the house for the evening meal, and my mother served all my favorite things. It was a feast for a returning hero not a lowly mahlet from a merchant ship, yet I truly enjoyed the tastes and smells of home.

Finally, when none of us could eat another bite, Seppan rose and took his leave for home.

"Tell your family I'll see them tomorrow," I told him. "I'll come by early in the morning. Well, at least before noon," and we all laughed.

When he had gone, my mother cleared the table while my father and I sat by the fire and talked some more. At last she joined us, sitting in silence sewing as she usually did.

"I made you three new tunics while you were gone," she said during a lull in our conversation, "but I am not sure they will fit you now that you are so tall."

"I'll try them on in the morning," I told her, "before I go to the farm."

"Good," she replied. "Then there will be time to fix them before you go off to this Shentoar place."

"I don't think we will be going back," I said.

"Oh," said my father, "why not?"

"Just something Tenoar said," I replied trying to think of a reason that would not upset my mother. "Probably because it's too far."

My father nodded and my mother said nothing more until it was time to go to bed.

§ § §

I woke up much earlier than the day before, in fact Seppan was still in the main room waiting for my father to finish eating when I came out of my room. When I joined them at the table, my mother quickly brought me a bowl of hot soup and bread warm from the oven.

"You need to hurry out to the farm," Seppan told me as I blew on my soup to cool it. "That little brother of mine may wet himself with excitement waiting for you," and at this my mother slapped him on the shoulder.

"You should not say such things, Seppan."

"Sorry, nodeh," he replied, and my heart jumped in my chest. Yet why should he not call her this; for, though I had never spoken to Melne this way, I did see her as a second mother. It was only natural Seppan had grown close to my family in my absence. Even so, it made me feel almost out of place in my own boyhood home.

"And Illiad," he continued, "she's promising to make you palnoi," and he gave me a wink that my mother did not see.

"What are palnoi?" she asked in a surprisingly cool voice.

"Little cakes," I told her, "they're very good. She made them for the Toharofa last spring."

"That reminds me," said Seppan, the Toharofa will be held in six days. You'll come of course?"

"Since I'm not working for your father, is it permitted?" I asked.

"You're like a member of our family," he replied. "And besides, Illiad would be disappointed if she had to dance the zubah with me and not you." I saw my mother stiffen at this, yet my father merely smiled and encouraged me to go and have fun.

After I had eaten, I went to my room and tried on one of the new tunics which, though a little short, fit fine. Yet my mother insisted on lengthening them, and so I returned to my room, changed, got the presents I had bought for Illiad and Melne as well as the two coins for Aarad and Aeshone then left for the farm.

I truly enjoyed the walk, and along the way I found a patch of heshel by the side of the road. It was just beginning to bloom, so I picked a few as an extra gift for Illiad.

When I arrived at the farm, she was sitting on the front steps waiting for me while Huno grazed in the yard. As soon as she saw me, she leaped to her feet and ran into the house. In a few moments, Aarad flew out the door followed by his mother and sister. He raced across the yard, threw open the gate and flung himself upon me almost knocking me to the ground.

"I've missed you," he cried, "you don't know how boring it's been here without you," and I felt a small pang of guilt; for, though I had missed him and all those I cared about, I had truly enjoyed my time away from home.

He released me then followed me through the gate and closed it behind us. When I reached the steps, Melne, too, embraced me and kissed me on the cheek. And then I stood before Illiad who hugged me as well. Yet it was quick and awkward as we both felt strange to be doing this in front of her mother.

"I watched the stars," I managed to whisper before she released me.

"I did too," she said, and I wanted to kiss her but was too embarrassed to do so with her mother watching.

We went into the house, and Melne insisted I sit at the table. As soon as I was seated, Illiad brought over a plate piled high with palnoi.

"How did you make them so quickly?" I asked, "I know they take a lot of time."

"She stayed up most of the night," Melne told me. "As soon as Seppan told us you were home, she insisted on making them just for you."

"They're wonderful," I told her after I had taken my first bite.

"They better be," said Aarad. "She wouldn't let me have any, 'They're for Idar' she kept saying whenever I asked for one."

"Now you can have one," she told him, "but only one. They're…"

"…for Idar, I know."

"I've got presents for you," I said picking up the sack I had dropped on the floor by my chair. "But maybe we should wait until your father comes in. I have one for him as well."

"Aeshone will be in soon," Melne told me.

"Sooner if I go tell him Idar's here," said Aarad, and he ran to the door.

"He's been like that since Seppan told us you were home," Melne said laughing. "It's been hard for him with you gone and no one to talk to or to do things with. He has a restless spirit, and being penned up on this farm is too much to bear.

"Even with Topek here, he has not been happy."

"He really doesn't like Topek," Illiad told me. "It was terrible when they had to share a room. I think it was because he wasn't you."

"What's Topek like?" I asked.

"He's a good boy," Melne replied, "though I should say man now that he is thirteen."

"I like him," Illiad added, and her words stirred up in me a feeling I had never felt before.

Just then the door opened and Aarad burst into the room, "Nodah will be here in a few minutes with *him*."

"Good," said his mother, "we can eat early."

§ § §

Illiad and her mother loved the shawls I gave them and could hardly wait to wear them to the Toharofa and make the women and girls jealous. Aarad and Aeshone were also pleased with the strange coins, for to them the silver metal was a source of fascination; and their joy at my gifts was a reward far exceeding the palnoi, of which I ate three.

Topek, despite Aarad's dislike of him, was friendly, outgoing and polite. He complemented both Melne and Illiad on how they looked in their shawls (yet his comments to Illiad did cause me to experience again that strange emotion I had felt earlier). The silver coins also fascinated him, but he did not appear envious of their good fortune at being given them.

Nevertheless, Aarad treated Topek coldly; and this I found strange as I had never seen him act this way before. He was sharp with him and critical, and I could see that his behavior displeased both his parents though they said nothing.

At last, with our meal ended, Aeshone stood up and said it was time to return to work; and Topek joined him.

"I will see you at the evening meal," Aeshone said to me.

"Of course you will," Aarad told him, "he's spending the night."

I had not thought of this one way or the other. "I'm not sure I should," I told him, "my parents will be expecting me. Nodeh is obsessed with feeding me and fattening me up."

"Oh please," he begged, "we could stay up most of the night and talk. You must have great stories to tell. Please stay."

"Why don't you go back to Alna with him," his father suggested. "If you think it will be all right with your parents," he added.

"I don't see why it wouldn't," I told him. "Besides, with Seppan coming home, we'd have to sleep out here on the floor and keep everyone awake with our talking."

"Good," Aeshone said, "then we can share our evening meal together, and you two can be off."

Chapter V

"You will never guess who came by while you were gone," my mother said as soon as I came into the house.

"Who?" I asked.

"Tuac and Zhoh," she told me. "They said Shend told them you were home, and they wanted to see you before they left for the fishing islands."

"When do they leave?" I asked.

"They said nothing about that," she replied, "but they did say they would come by in the morning."

"I hope not too early," I said. "Aarad and I plan on staying up all night talking."

We nearly did stay up the whole night since it was well past midnight, almost the time I usually got up to help Kebbit, before we finally fell asleep. I told him everything about my trip, even about Tullikan and Naemen, and he was truly intrigued by all I had to tell him.

"Whatever you do," I told him, "be sure you say nothing about what happened at the river with Tullikan's brother. I don't want my parents to know. Nodeh worries enough. I don't want her thinking I could be taken as a slave."

"But you're not going back to Shentoar," he told me.

"Doesn't matter," I replied. "Naemen was taken in Eltec. After what happened with Tullikan, I'll now be far more cautious; but even so, nodeh will worry, and I don't want that. So just be sure you don't tell Seppan. He could let something slip."

"Don't worry, I won't," he promised. "It will be great having a secret like this to keep from him.

"You know, I really envy you. You've had all these adventures, and seen these strange faraway places. I can hardly wait 'til I can apprentice and go away someplace."

"Do you have any idea what you want to do yet?" I asked.
"Not really," he replied, "but I know it won't be near the farm."

§ § §

Tuac and Zhoh came to my house in the midmorning just as Aarad and I were finishing a late breakfast. To my surprise, they both embraced me, and Tuac pounded me on the back while hugging me. Yet what surprised me even more was the way Tuac greeted Aarad, for he was pleasant, even congenial. Gone was his usual sneering and sarcastic nature, and even my mother was amazed at the change in him.

"Nodeh said you are leaving soon," I told them.

"Day after tomorrow for me," said Tuac. "Zhoh has until the middle of the moons cycle. That's why we thought we could all go over to Crayoar and visit Boec. It's been ages since you've seen him, and the last time he came to visit was in the second winter moons cycle."

"Sounds good to me," I told him. "After being cooped up on that ship for days and days it seems good to stretch my legs."

My mother offered to pack us something to eat on the way, but Tuac and Zhoh refused.

"There's a little tavern in Crayoar," Zhoh told her, "we'll get something to eat there."

"I haven't been paid yet…" I began, but Tuac cut me off.

"Don't worry about that, it'll be my treat, and Ashka Boy too," yet as he said this he smiled broadly and slapped Aarad on the back.

I gave Zhoh a look which said, "What's going on with him?" but he made no response. And so, promising to be back before dark, the four of us set off for Crayoar.

It did indeed feel good to walk, to smell the familiar scents of spring in my homeland, to recognize the trees, the flowers, even the birds. We took the path as we usually did and stopped for a few minutes at the rocks just to skip stones across the water then climbed the familiar path to the top of the falls.

By the time we reached Crayoar, it was just past midday, and Boec and his cousin Hennek were ready to stop for their meal. Boec, of course, was overjoyed to see us; and Hennek willingly gave him the afternoon off to spend with us.

"Nothing much we can do anyway," Boec told us as we walked the short distance to the tavern. "Today's the Toharofa, and the farmers are all off celebrating."

"Ours is in five days," said Aarad.

"I don't know how old Selyupa does it," Boec commented.

"I know," added Aarad, "he must be a hundred cycles at least."

"Well, that is an exaggeration," Boec told him. "But not much of one," and he laughed. "I saw him early this morning as he went past the mill. He was driving a cart with a young apprentice priest sitting next to him."

"Good," said Aarad, "I hope he brings one with him to Alna, that way I won't have to help him."

§ § §

The tavern truly was small. In fact there was hardly any room inside, and so we ordered then went back outside and sat at a table set out in front. The owner brought us our drinks—kahlmek all around—with bread, cheese and sliced palne.

We sat for two or three hours and talked as I shared with them the highlights of my trip to Eltec and Shentoar while Boec and Zhoh each bought a round of drinks. Aarad showed them the silver coin I had given him, and I felt a little odd at not having given one to them.

They in turn told me of their lives on the islands and Boec of his work in Crayoar. Yet this seemed to pale against the backdrop of my adventures.

At last we said good-bye to Boec, who returned to the mill, and began the long trek back to Alna. When we reached the path leading to the rocks, we walked down to the river and swam in the cold water to cool ourselves off then dressed and walked the remaining league and a half back to Alna.

Aarad and I were tired from our long day and sleepless night and Aarad especially so from drinking so much kahlmek, something he had never tried before. And so, we went to bed early, yet not until my mother had feasted us like kings.

§ § §

Aarad stayed the next day, then reluctantly walked back to the farm with Seppan in the evening. The following day I went again to farewell Tuac as he left for Kesset. Then two days later I walked to the farm with Seppan on the night before the Toharofa.

"He is bringing an apprentice," Aarad told me as we were making our beds on the floor in front of the fire.

"Who?" I asked.

"Selyupa," he told me, "so I don't have to help him."

"Well, that's good…I guess," I replied not understanding his aversion to helping the priest.

"That means I'll never have to do it again," he continued, "because by the next Toharofa, I'll be thirteen, and men don't assist the priest."

"What about the apprentice?" I asked.

"That's different," he told me. "It's their job. I mean they're learning to be priests, right, so they have to do it."

"I guess so," I said. "It makes sense."

"No talking you two," came Aeshone's voice from the next room. "We all need to get up early to prepare for the guests."

"I forgot about that," I told Aarad lowering my voice. "It's your turn to host the party."

"And nodah's right," he added, "we'll need to be up extra early to get everything ready."

§ § §

Selyupa arrived early, for he and his apprentice stopped by the gate even before we had finished the morning chores. Aeshone went out to talk to him, and Selyupa assured him there was no hurry.

"He says he will summon the toha when we are ready," Aeshone told us. "In the meantime, he and the novice priest will sample the food we have prepared."

"I bet that's how he planned it in the first place," Aarad whispered to me. "He just wants an excuse to get the good stuff."

"Quiet," snapped Seppan, "it's not polite to talk about a priest that way."

"I'm only telling the truth," Aarad retorted.

"Well, don't let nodah hear you," and he walked off to feed the nosha.

§ § §

After we finished the usual chores, we needed to set up extra tables which had been borrowed from the neighboring farms to be used for the food offerings. This took us an hour or so; but before we did this, Selyupa wished to begin the blessing of the fields. And so we had to quickly change into our best clothes.

With the ceremony over, Selyupa, Aeshone and the novice left for the neighboring farms leaving the rest of us, including Topek, to finish with the preparations. Then, even before we were finished, the first guests arrived; and Melne and her children went to greet them leaving Topek and I to quickly cover the tables with colorful cloths. We then went into the house and began bringing out the food offerings.

Aarad brought Kron and Narra over to the tables each of them loaded down with food. Illiad came with them carrying a big tray of something that smelt delicious. The mouthwatering scent reminded me of the feast we had enjoyed a sun cycle before and filled me with an anticipation for what was to come.

Then we waited as family after family arrived, and the tables became nearly incapable of standing due to the abundance they held. At last Selyupa and the long procession of farmers arrived, and the party began.

We ate; we drank; we danced; and we laughed until night came, and the guests began to leave one by one. Selyupa, as was tradition, was the first to go. Then each family in turn thanked Aeshone and Melne for their hospitality and took their leave. There was no special order to this. They merely left whenever it seemed appropriate for them with those having younger children leaving first.

The last families to leave assisted us with the clean up; but even so, there remained much to do in the morning after chores. When all had gone, Illiad and I lingered for a while by the gate talking of the stars; and I assured her what I had told her before I left was true: the stars in Shentoar were the same, only brighter.

"When will you leave again?" she asked.

"I'm not sure," I told her. "Tenoar said the *Tel* would arrive in Alna today or maybe tomorrow. In fact, I need to leave first thing in the morning to see if she has docked yet. Then I'll find out. So unfortunately, I may not even be back before I go."

"But it's like you only just got here," she told me.

"I only just did," I said. "But it's not as if I'm going back to Shentoar. Eltec is less then half a moons cycle away. I'll be back before you know it," and I leaned down to kiss her.

"Nodah says you two should come in now," Aarad called from the door; and holding her hand, I led her back towards the house.

Aarad and Seppan were in their room in the loft changing out of their party clothes, and I joined them. As I reached the top of the ladder, I could hear them talking.

"So what's her name?" Aarad asked.

"None of you business, little brother," replied Seppan, though his voice betrayed his desire to be coaxed.

"Well, I'd like to know too," I said coming into their room. "You *are* talking about the girl Seppan kept dancing with most of the day."

"Yeah," Aarad told me, "but he won't tell me who she is."

"She's not a girl, she's a young woman," said Seppan with a smile that truly made him appear well pleased with himself.

"Friends have names," I told him.

"Well, if you must know," he said, and I could tell that he was longing to tell us, "her name is Zherna, and she's the daughter of Porel. Their farm's at the end of the road just before it goes up into the hills and the forest."

"So, have you kissed her?" I asked with a grin on my face.

"No, but I really wanted to," he replied.

"Then why didn't you?" Aarad asked.

"Because her father kept watching us," he replied.

"I know what you mean," I said. "I was about to kiss Illiad out by the gate when *he* called us in."

"It's not my fault," whined Aarad. "Nodah told me to."

"Well, your timing was really bad."

§ § §

The *Tel* came into port and docked at Alna the afternoon of the next day, and I was there to meet her. Aeshone insisted I leave right after we ate saying Aarad and Topek could do the final clean up. And so I left with Seppan after thanking his parents and telling everyone I would be back before I left if at all possible.

But it was not possible, for Tenoar had filled our hold at Sefna and was planning on taking on a load of ashka wool from Teuwa then leaving for Eltec as soon as the *Kwel* arrived and Naemen was safely on board.

I was needed to help load the wool yet was allowed to spend my nights at home. However, this gave me no time to return to the farm for a proper good-bye.

At last, just twelve days after I had left the *Tel* in Sefna, we again set sail for Eltec. My mother came to see me off as did my father and Seppan. I sent my best to Aarad, Aeshone, Melne and of course Illiad by way of Seppan then climbed aboard the *Tel* and helped Kelyan with the plank. As I poled the ship away from the dock, I could see my mother standing alone watching as the *Tel* sailed out of sight.

Chapter VI

And so the rhythm of my new life began: twelve to fifteen days sailing to Eltec, eight to ten days in port unloading and reloading the ship, then back again to Alna where we spent another ten to twelve days preparing the *Tel* for its return voyage to Eltec. These cycles of about fifty days very quickly became routine, and my life went on until I reached my fourteenth sun cycle then on into the spring and summer.

My first pay was sparse since Tenoar had advanced me money in Eltec in order to buy my sea chest. Yet from then on I received what for me was a considerable sum. A portion of this I saved at my father's insistence, but I still found myself with more money to spend as I pleased than I had ever had before.

With this I bought gifts in Eltec for those at home or drinks at the inn for Seppan, Alnat, Tefnoar and—when they were at home—Tuac and Zhoh. On these evenings we shared a lasting fellowship recalling our boyhood days to the click of dice while playing kahtore. And I, of course, always recounted my adventures at sea.

In some ways I became almost a hero, for their lives in Alna and on the fishing islands seemed empty compared to mine. They loved to hear me tell of the strange things I saw, and I was sure both Alnat and Tefnoar envied me the most as they would never go to sea.

Eltec was not as strange a place as I had found Shentoar to be since it too was a Kroemaeon city. Yet there were still wonders to see and relay to those at home, for the markets were filled with goods and faces as foreign as in Shentoar.

While the inns and taverns of Eltec were frequented mostly by dark haired men, there were always three or four men with yellow hair and even at times those with white hair and colorful animals dyed into their arms. I tried once or twice to talk with them, for I wished to learn more about the process used to imprint these pictures on flesh; yet they were cold and aloof and in their eyes I saw contempt for those they considered to be weak and inferior.

It took me many trips to explore the city, for I never had as much free time there as I had had in Shentoar. We worked hard to unload the ship and then to fill her hold with cargo. Yet we always received a day or two of shore leave which I loved to spend in the markets and the plazas to be found among Eltec's winding streets.

On the northern side of the city was a market filled with goods for sale mostly from foreign ports. Yet on the southern side was a second produce market where Eltec's farmers came to trade.

It was difficult to go there, for one had to navigate the narrow winding streets to the heart of Eltec then pass on into a second labyrinth to reach this market. But for me it was worth it, for here were sights and sounds not unlike Theo.

Those who lived in Eltec spoke Kroemaeon, though with a strange twist of speech slightly different from what I was used to at home; and the foods found in the markets were also Kroemaeon. Yet a few were special to Eltec, and these I loved to sample. And so this produce market reminded me most of home with a dabbling of the exotic thrown in.

The heart of Eltec was much like the heart of Theo, yet here too there were differences. A temple where the toha were honored dominated Eltec's central core, but unlike Theo there was no plaza with the palace of the king and the Hall of Records forming its sides. Instead, these buildings were both located in separate parts of the city with the Hall of Records located not far from the southern produce market.

Eltec's king lived in the eastern part of the city atop a hill which was walled off at the bottom making it a fortress as well as his official home. It was wondrous to behold; however, one could only see it from afar as the wall surrounding it was well guarded and its gate was opened only on special days when the wealthy citizens of the city were invited in as guests.

All this I told to my friends again and again on those evenings now long gone while we drank to our youth and planned our futures. Thus time passed; and I grew taller, wiser and more the man I was destined to become.

§ § §

Kelyan, Nomlet and Kwellen moved their families to Alna so that they could be with them when in port. Yet they were the only ones who did.

Burog and Kebbit, on the other hand, had no families as both men were bachelors claiming to be married to the sea—an idea I found very difficult to understand—and Pellonek, though unmarried, said he just had not found the right woman. These three spent their nights aboard the *Tel* as did Tenoar, though he sometimes took a room at the inn or spent a night or two in Sefna at Jaygore's home whenever they had lengthy business to discuss. Likewise, Benfoar and Diud remained aboard the *Tel* since both their wives were dead. Benfoar's wife had died in childbirth leaving him with a daughter who had been raised by his sister and had then married a wheelwright in Sefna. Diud's wife had died long ago of an illness, and he remained a widower and childless which I somehow found especially sad.

This left only Altore, Torek, Boaruf and Shaffet to travel between Alna and their homes in Sefna and Theo. And so, after off loading our cargo, they hauled it each day to Jaygore's warehouse in Sefna then came back the next day with cargo to load into the ship's hold. The wagons we used for this were kept in a shed Tenoar rented in Alna, and the nosha which pulled them Tenoar stabled at the inn when not in use.

I, of course, lived at home when in port and spent my shore leave days at the farm with Aarad where I could be close to Illiad. This, however, was never enough, for of each fifty day cycle, I spent merely a day or two on the farm.

Each time I returned from Eltec, I brought Melne, Illiad and my mother a special gift—some little trinket I found in the markets of the city or a bit of fabric from which they could make a dress. Yet I also brought Illiad heshel if I could find it along the road leading to the farm. This, then, became a special bond between us, that and spending a few moments each night watching the stars together no matter where we were.

And so our relationship deepened, at least for my part, as I continued to think of her each evening and dream of her on many nights. In this I was content; for I had the sea, and though I was not able to spend as much time with Illiad as I would have liked, we still managed to be together when I was at the farm.

§ § §

Aarad became more and more restless as he felt trapped on the farm. Thus, since he continued to despise Topek, he developed a friendship of sorts with Kron, though I never understood why. This did, however, allow him to be away from the farm for a while which eased his restlessness. It also led to a relationship with Narra, though this was brief and fleeting.

Yet when I was home, he begged to be allowed to spend time with me in Alna. I would then take him to the *Tel* where he could sit on the wharf, then later on the deck, talking to the men. Gradually, he began to help us, at first doing simple things, then more and more; and Tenoar occasionally gave him a few coins in gratitude for his help.

Therefore, it did not surprise me when Tenoar asked Aarad to become the ship's mahlet when he reached his thirteenth sun cycle in the spring. His acceptance pleased me greatly, for now I could share with him first hand the adventures I could only tell him about after I had returned home.

And so, just before the Toharofa that spring, Aeshone took Aarad to Theo to register him in the Hall of Records. Then, after the festival, we both set sail for Eltec.

Yet with this, my relationship with Illiad began to suffer; for we spent less time together since Aarad stayed with me in Alna when we unloaded and loaded the *Tel*. Then, while he was on shore leave, I felt he should spend time alone with his family; and I came to the farm only to give my gifts then visit for a time before returning home.

Illiad wanted me to stay longer, and grew impatient with me when I did not. This led, by the end of the summer, to her becoming aloof whenever we were together. I still gave her gifts, and of course the heshel, but these she merely accepted politely then left me alone with her parents.

Seppan told me Illiad had developed a friendship with Narra which led to her spending more and more time with Kron. This did not please me at all as I remembered how he looked at her each time they had been together at the Toharofa. The thought of Kron ate at me much as the vood had done when I could not tell my parents how I felt.

Was this the problem I wondered? Was there something I was keeping from Illiad? And I quickly began to realize there was; for, as my feelings for her deepened, I came at last to understand they were those of love. Yet I did not know how to tell her this.

Chapter VII

It was the spring of my fifteenth sun cycle, and Aarad and I would soon be leaving on our first trading voyage of the season. Since Aarad had served ten moons as our ship's mahlet, he had now been promoted to seaman as had I when he came aboard the *Tel*.

Tenoar then felt our crew was sufficient to man the ship, and so he did not taken on a new mahlet. This meant that each of the men took their turn assisting Kebbit in the galley; yet I, due to my knowledge of the art of metal work, continued to aid Benfoar in maintaining the seaworthiness of the *Tel*.

I made nails and links of chain or whatever else was needed to keep the ship sound and in good order; and for this purpose, Tenoar had commissioned a small forge to be built into one of the forward compartments just off the galley. It was here that I labored in both iron and bronze, making all that was needed.

Somehow I felt it ironic that I had never wanted to be a smith yet had become one aboard ship. Even so, this did not in any way bother me as I was still at sea, and my duties on the *Tel* were varied as smithing was only part of what I did.

I, like the other men, stood watch aboard the *Tel* and had also learned to care for the ship's equipment, to take soundings, to raise and lower the sails as well as a variety of other tasks. Thus I had become a true seaman; and now Aarad would perfect these same skills just as I had during my days serving on the *Tel*.

And so we went to the inn with Kelyan, Nomlet, Kwellen and Kebbit to celebrate Aarad's completion of his first sun cycle aboard our ship. Seppan joined us as did Zhoh since he had not yet left for their camp on Trohan.

"To your future as a seaman," cried Kebbit raising his mug to Aarad.

"And to higher pay," Aarad retorted causing us all to laugh. "Now I can finally make some real money."

"For which you'll do some real work," I told him.

"Don't be greedy, little brother," Seppan added. "You may make more, but you'll only spend more as well. You need to save your money like Idar and I have been doing. What if you meet someone who takes your heart? A wife costs more to support than you might think."

"I've only just turned fourteen," he replied, "I can't marry for at least three more sun cycles even if I wanted to, which I don't."

"Who'd he marry anyway?" I said. "No one would have him."

"Narra might," he replied, "that's if I was interested."

"Who's this Narra?" asked Nomlet.

"A girl who lives on a neighboring farm," Aarad told him, "she and my sister are friends."

"And you fancy her?" Kelyan asked.

"Some," he replied, " but not the way Idar does Illiad."

At this I reddened and replied, "I don't think there's much of a future for us despite how I feel. She seems so distant lately."

"You don't spend enough time with her," Seppan told me. Topek's with her more than you."

"Don't even talk about Topek," I said. "I'm beginning to think Aarad's right about him."

"Topek's not a bad sort," Seppan replied. "At least he's better than that Kron."

"I'll take Kron any day over Topek," Aarad told him.

"Don't start you two," I said. "We're here to have fun. I don't want to argue about the likes of those two."

And with that our conversation changed to other matters as we talked of this and that, yet I could not stop thinking of what Seppan said nor of how merely the mention of Kron and Topek made me feel.

§ § §

I continued to think of Seppan's words while we were away on our next few voyages to Eltec. Each night, out of habit, I would spend some time alone on deck watching the stars; and doing this made me realize I did not want my relationship with Illiad to end. Therefore, I finally resolved to talk with her, to let her know how I felt—if only I truly understood what my feelings were.

Again and again I had asked myself how I felt, and the answer had come back the same. I cared deeply for Illiad. She was a part of my life; and I did not want to lose that part, not to Topek, not to Kron, not to anyone.

For some reason I could not share this revelation with Aarad. He was my best friend, but I was sure he would not understand. He had feelings for Narra, but they seemed like a passing fancy; and I remembered how Seppan had once told him he did not understand the ways of love.

Love, was that what I felt for Illiad? Was I truly in love with her? How could I know this for sure? And so I turned to Kelyan, for he had become my mentor aboard ship.

"Sounds to me like love," he told me. "If ya' feel that strongly about her ya' should let her know how ya' feel…and her father too."

"Her father?" I asked. "Why her father?"

"It's only right," came his reply. "If ya' do love her and want to marry her, he has a right to know."

"But I don't know if I do want to marry her," I told him.

"Maybe ya' don't right now," he said, "but if ya' feel ya' don't want yer relationship to end, then what other way is there?"

This scared me, yet I said nothing to him but only nodded and spent the next few days contemplating the meaning of what he told me. I did not want our relationship to end, for the idea of a life without Illiad seemed difficult to comprehend. She had become a part of me, yet marriage seemed a radical step to take as it was a permanent commitment, one I knew I was far from being ready to make.

§ § §

It was early autumn when we returned from Eltec, and the harvest was well under way. This meant there was no opportunity to talk to either Illiad or Aeshone since they both were hard at work with the hay, and all I could do was watch as Illiad laughed and joked with Topek as we once had done—and my heart burned with a deep resentment.

In another fifty days, the kalhu was done. Since Aarad had apprenticed on the *Tel*, Topek's younger brother, Adal, had come to stay on the farm to help with the kalhu; and now that the grain was ready for sale, Adal prepared to return home.

Aeshone was to drop him off in Crayoar when he brought the grain to Hennek to be milled. As he had contracted with Tenoar to sell his kalhu for export to Eltec, there would be no longer trip to Theo; and so I asked Tenoar for a day of shore leave in order to go to Crayoar so that I could see Boec.

It was a warm autumn day with only a few clouds in the sky, and I sat in the back with Adal letting Illiad have the seat in front beside her father. Adal had reached his twelfth cycle just before the harvest, and though I resented his brother, I was drawn to him as he had a friendly and outgoing nature.

We talked at first of the kalhu harvest since we had this in common. Yet after a while he asked me about the sea and my life aboard the *Tel.* I saw from the way he spoke that he, too, wished for a life as a seaman.

When we reached Crayoar, Aeshone dropped Adal off at his house then continued on to the river and the mill. Boec was, as usual, truly glad to see me; and we talked for a bit as I relayed to him what news I could from home. Then, after about an hour, we headed back to Alna.

I climbed into the far back of the wagon and sat propped up against the side. When Illiad made a move to rejoin her father on the seat of the cart, I asked her to sit with me; and to my surprise she did. Yet she merely sat on the edge of the cart with her legs over the side staring off and did not even look at me.

At first we rode along in silence until we reached the road back to Alna. Then, when I could stand the silence no longer, I asked her what had happened between us.

"What do you mean?" she asked.

"You know what I mean," I told her. "We never talk any more. At least not really. We used to have fun together, but now…"

"What do we have to talk about?" she asked. "Your stories of the sea? Your great adventures? They don't really interest me, at least not the way they did."

Her words pained me; for I was sure she had lost interest in me, that she no longer cared about me as she once had.

"I'm sorry you feel that way," I told her with a slight tone of anger in my voice, "but that's my life, that's who I am."

"I know," she said. "but you've changed since you've been at sea. So has Aarad for that matter. I guess that's the way things are when you grow up."

"You've changed as well since I've joined the *Tel*," I told her. "At least towards me. We used to laugh and talk, and now you save you laughter for Topek and probably for Kron as well."

"So what if I laugh with them?" she asked, and for the first time she looked at me. "You're gone all the time. You're never around. Why shouldn't I have friends?"

"I think they're more than friends," I told her.

"Well, what if they are?" she asked, her voice raising slightly. Then, as she glanced quickly at her father, she lowered it. "Why should you care?"

"Because I love you," and the words came easily after so many days of trying to hold them in.

"You…love me?" she asked.

I looked away, then after a few moments I turned towards her, "Yes, I love you," I told her, "and I don't want anything to come between us. I don't want to lose you to Topek or Kron. I want us to be like we were before I went to sea.

"Each night when I'm away I watch the stars and think of you, but when I come home, it's like you don't even care I'm back."

"You don't act like you're glad to be back," she retorted. "At least not towards me. Do you realize how much time we've spent together since the Toharofa?"

"Not very much," I told her. "You're right. I'm sorry. Seppan told me the same thing last spring. He said I should be spending more time with you. So what can I do? I don't want to lose you. I want things to be the way they were."

"I don't know," she said." I liked the boy you were, but I'm not all that sure about the man you've become." And at these words, we both fell silent.

Chapter VIII

The next fifty day cycle brought us into winter, and the *Tel* remained in port because of the storms at sea. This did allow me more free time, yet even so not as much as I would have liked since I was kept busy on board the ship making those repairs which were needed now that we were not at sea.

For two cycles of the sun the wind and the waves had done their best to reduce the *Tel* to ruins, and Benfoar and I had fought back making what repairs we could. Yet we were losing this battle, and now these winter days allowed us the time to thoroughly overhaul the ship.

There were timbers which were cracked and rotting, and all these we replaced. We then pitched the inside of the hull to prevent leaks, patched all the sails and repainted the deck, the rails and the sides of the *Tel* after we had hauled her on shore. Then, as spring approached, we relaunched her and prepared to sail to Eltec.

Yet those winter days were not all work, for Tenoar allowed each of us one free day in every five coming in a rotation which gave four or five men an opportunity to enjoy time off together. As Aarad spent most nights with Seppan and me in Alna because the winter storms kept them from returning home after dark, he spent his free days on the farm. But I continued to be reluctant to join him, for my talk with Illiad had convinced me our relationship would never again be the same. Therefore, I felt even more strongly that it was not right to intrude on Aarad's time alone with his family.

"You should just go," Seppan told me one night. "After all, I'm here a great deal of the time, and so is Aarad. Your parents treat us like sons, and you were always part of the family when you were at our house helping out. Why should things be different now?"

"Seppan's right," said Aarad, "just come with me. It's not like when we were at sea. I'm home a lot more now, and I know Illiad misses you."

"Has she said that?" I asked, and my heart almost stopped beating in my chest.

"Not in so many words," Aarad replied, "but I can tell. When you don't come, she looks disappointed."

"I told you what she said on the way back from Crayoar last autumn. I doubt she's that disappointed."

"Oh, come on Idar," said Seppan as he climbed onto the topmost of the two bunks we had built into my room to accommodate all three of us. "You are about to reach your sixteenth cycle, act like it and stop pouting. I know my sister; and like Aarad said, she misses you. Just go out there tomorrow and spend the day. Talk to here. You'll see."

"Fine," I said, "I'll go."

§ § §

The next day I walked out to the farm with Aarad right after we had eaten. It was a cold and blustery day, and though it had rained over night and showed a promise of more rain to come, it remained dry until we reached the gate leading to the farm. Then the sky broke open, and rain fell in earnest.

"That was lucky," I said as we raced up the steps and into the house, "at least it waited until we got here."

Both Melne and Illiad were working in the kitchen area of the main room when we burst through the door shaking off the water that had managed to nearly drench our hair. Melne came over and hugged both of us, yet Illiad held back giving us only a smile and a cheerful word of welcome.

"To'v," I said and walked over to her. "How have you been?"

"I've been well," she replied, and a coolness came over her which made me want to draw back. But if I was to win her over, I could not.

"What are you making?" I asked as a way of starting a conversation.

But Melne came over and answered for her, "An eln chowder. It should be done by the midday meal."

"I could help," I offered. "I've had a lot of experience aboard the *Tel*. Have you cut up the eln yet?"

"Yes," Illiad replied, "but thank you for your offer."

Not knowing what else to do, I walked over and sat with Aarad giving him a look that said, "I told you." But he only responded by motioning for me to try again. When I said nothing, he gave me a disgusted look.

"Where's nodah?" he asked.

"He and Topek are in the barn with the gamu," Melne replied. "Remember we bred them again, and one is about to give birth."

"That sounds like fun," Aarad told her. "I think I'll stay here and wait for the chowder to be done."

"You are such a baby, Aarad," Melne said with a laugh. "A gamu giving birth is perfectly natural. Why not go out and help your father?"

"I've seen a gamu giving birth, and ashka too," he replied, "I have no desire to see it again. I'll just wait for the chowder."

"What about Idar?" asked Illiad. "I'm sure he's never seen an animal give birth."

"And I'm sure he doesn't want to," which was the beginnings, I was sure, of an argument.

"Illiad's right," I said standing up. "I haven't seen a birth before. Let's go help."

"It's going to be messy," he told me, "but if you want to…"

We left through the back door and entered the all too familiar garden filled with the remnants of a harvest I had not been there to see, then ran to the barn through the steady rain. When we entered it, I stood for a moment letting my eyes adjust to the semidarkness while breathing in the smells I had become used to during my time working on the farm. Yet when my eyes grew accustomed to the light, Aeshone and Topek were nowhere in sight.

"They're probably in that stall," said Aarad leading me across the barn to what appeared to be an empty stall next to Toarak.

"Is that you?" asked Aeshone, his head appearing above the low door blocking our view of the stall. "Ah, I see you have brought Idar with you."

"He wants to see the gamu give birth," Aarad told him.

"Well, he's too late," came the voice of Topek. "She gave birth about twenty minutes ago."

Aarad unlatched the gate to the stall, and we entered to see a gamu lying on her side nursing three tiny little hairless creatures having almost no resemblance to their mother.

"*Those* are baby gamu?" I asked in amazement.

"Yes," laughed Aeshone, "they will not have hair for several days, and it won't be as shaggy as their mother's for nearly two moons cycles. We will need to keep the barn warm until then, but after that they will be fine."

"Do ashka look like that when they're born?" I asked.

"No," Aeshone told me, "they are born with wool, but it's very short and even softer than their mother's."

"It's too bad you missed the birthing," said Topek. "Maybe next time, if you're around, you could help."

"Yeah," I replied, "maybe next time."

§ § §

The eln chowder was as I remembered it from my boyhood days staying with Aarad. Because Melne had grown up in Teuwa far from the sea, she had only learned how the make it after moving to Alna. Yet even so, she was an excellent cook and had come to prepare it in a way uniquely different from all the other women in our village, but it was still well made.

We sat as usual at the familiar table talking, laughing and enjoying one other's company; and I even forgot for a few moments that I disliked Topek. Yet when I saw how Illiad warmed to him and not to me, I quickly changed how I felt about him.

At last, with the meal completed, Topek excused himself to check on the gamu. When Aeshone made a move to join him, Melne reached out a hand and took hold of his arm.

Stay," she told him, "and talk to your son. The work can wait," and he sat back down again.

"I'll clear the table," Illiad told her mother, and I jumped to my feet.

"Let me help you," I said.

"There's no need," she replied.

"I know," I told her, "but I want to help."

She said no more, and I began to carry the dishes across the room to a table near the fireplace. After clearing the table, I helped her to clean and put things away as well as to hang the pot of chowder over the fire to keep it warm.

"Usually, aboard ship, I wouldn't be allowed to eat until all of my chores were done," I told her.

"I know," she replied, "Aarad's told us."

"If the rain lets up," I said as a way of trying to keep the conversation going, "we could maybe go for a walk."

"it's too muddy," she replied.

"Look," I said in a low voice so that no one else could hear, "I did mean what I said last autumn," and I glanced towards the table where Aarad, Melne and Aeshone sat deep in conversation. "I love you, and I'm sorry about how I've acted since I joined the *Tel*. I want things to be different. Don't you?"

She did not look at me directly but merely watched her parents at the table with Aarad; and, for what seemed like an eternity, she said nothing. At last she looked intently at me, and there was a hint of pain in her eyes.

"I don't know," she said. "I'm not sure what I want. There was a time when I thought I loved you; but then you went to Shentoar. When you came back…things were different."

"Different? How?" I asked.

"I'm not sure," she replied. "Just different. I don't know…we just didn't see that much of each other. Before you left you were here almost all the time, and it was easy to talk to you. But not now…

"I've changed too. You said that yourself last autumn. In fact, we've all changed, Aarad and Seppan too. That's what growing up is all about isn't it? It's a time of change. Maybe I've outgrown you."

The pain of her words ripped open my heart, and for a brief moment I thought of how I had almost not come back from Shentoar. If only Tullikan's brother had taken me, I thought, surly a life of slavery could not equal what I now felt.

I turned and walked away. The rain had stopped, and so I went outside and stood on the steps letting the wind blow my hair about my face. Quietly Huno came around the corner of the house, and when he saw me, he walked over to where I stood.

"Where have you been?" I asked, and it again surprised me how easy it had become for me to talk to an animal as if it could truly understand me.

Huno stopped in front of me; so I walked down the steps, and squatting in front of him I reached out to touch his familiar soft white coat of wool.

"Well, at least you're still glad to see me," I told him.

"I'm glad to see you too," came Illiad's voice behind me, and I turned as she came down the steps to stand beside me.

"I really didn't mean what I said in there," she continued. "I mean…yes, we've all changed, but I haven't outgrown you. I don't know what made me say that."

I stood up, put my arms around her and pulled her to me. "It doesn't matter," I said. "I love you, and that's the only thing that truly counts. Even if you never love me back I'll always love you. I don't care where I am. I may be a thousand leagues from Alna, yet I'll always love you—I know I will—until the day I die."

Chapter IX

After reconciling with Illiad that day, I spent all of my shore leave days at the farm. We had stood talking in the yard for nearly a half hour before going back into the house; and when we entered, I was holding her hand, the first outward show of affection I had shown in front of her parents.

"Ah," said Aeshone when he saw us, "it's about time. I have wondered when your two were going to come to your senses."

"Come," Melne beckoned to us with a smile, "sit here at the table," and we walked to where they sat and joined them.

"So," Aeshone continued after a brief pause, "it is as we have felt for a long time, you have feelings for our daughter."

"Yes, sir," I replied.

"Sir?" cried Aeshone, "you have not called me sir since you were but a mere boy."

"I'm sorry," I said.

"No need for that," he told me, "a man will be nervous at such times. But you have no need for concern, Melne and I have long suspected how you two felt about each other—and we are both pleased."

And so I no longer felt awkward going out to the farm on my free days. My mother and father, too, did not object to my going since I was home most evenings during those winter days. My father told me it was only natural a man like myself, one nearing his seventeenth cycle of the sun, should become drawn to a young woman especially one he had known for so long; and to my great surprise, my mother had no objections but seemed truly pleased by the relationship I had with Illiad.

Seppan and Aarad were highly pleased, yet more so, it seemed, with themselves.

"I told you, all you had to do was talk to her," Aarad said as we walked back to Alna that evening.

And when Seppan learned what had happened, I thought he was going to hug me. "You two are meant for each other," he told me. "You'll be glad you took my advice."

"Our advice," Aarad retorted.

"You're right," Seppan replied. "I guess you finally have learned the ways of love. Maybe I *should* stop calling you 'little brother.'"

The only one who did not seem pleased was Topek; for, from the first moment he saw me holding Illiad's hand, he began to act coolly towards me, and it pleased me to know that we had now changed places. He never said a word to betray his feelings, but I knew he was disappointed which was enough for me.

Then, at last, the day arrived when the *Tel* set sail for Eltec; and my mother came, as had been her custom, to bid me farewell. Yet this time she was not alone nor was she from that spring day on; for Illiad joined her on the pier, both of them weeping as I boarded the ship, both standing side by side as I sailed away.

§ § §

The storm season lasted into spring, for we were only five days from Eltec when we were hit by a driving wind which turned into a tempest before we knew it. There was no safe haven where we could ride out this storm; and so we were left to the mercy of the wind and the rain both of which lashed at the ship with a fury that made even the most experienced of our crew fear for their lives.

We headed out to sea and fought the storm as best we could, reefing our sails and attaching a drogue to the prow of the *Tel*. This helped steady the ship and kept her pointed in a general southward direction as we fought to keep the rocky coast in sight while at the same time avoiding being driven aground where we would inevitably break up. Yet the drogue gradually pulled us northward and away form Eltec.

For three days the storm battered us as waves washed over the sides of the ship, and water leaked down into the hold even though the hatch was securely latched shut. We had put out the fires in both the galley and in my small forge, so we had nothing to eat this whole time except for stale bread and raw vegetables.

On the second night of the storm, our mizzen mast broke leaving us a partly crippled ship. I was in our crew quarters attempting to sleep, though the violent rocking of the ship made this close to impossible. Suddenly, there was a cracking sound then a crashing thump as the *Tel* lurched violently to port almost throwing me from my hammock.

I struggled to stand up then made my way as best I could through the hold as the ship continued to list to port. Just as I reached the ladder leading to the deck above, the *Tel* righted herself again throwing me to the floor of the hold. Then, when I regained my footing, I quickly scrambled up the ladder and emerged on deck to the terrible sight of our aft mast floating away into the darkness.

The damage to the ship, however, was not as severe as one might have thought, for the break in the mast had been high enough to allow most of it to fall directly into the sea. A portion of the rail, however, had been broken away where the falling timber hit the deck and had then hung until the rigging had been cut by the men on duty thereby letting the remnants of our former mast break free of the ship.

I was terrified, but Diud quickly assured me we would be able to sail the ship with the two remaining masts—though with greatly reduced speed. Yet fear gripped the crew, for if one mast had broken, our main mast might also be lost as well leaving us to drift at the mercy of the sea.

To our good fortune, this did not happen; and in the evening of the next day the storm abated leaving a calm and tranquil sea. However, although we had been five days from Eltec when the storm began, we had drifted steadily north due to the attached drogue; thus, with the added loss of one mast to contend with, it took us nine additional days to reach safe harbor at Eltec.

Some of the cargo had been damaged by the storm, yet we had enough to sell in the markets of Eltec. Tenoar used a portion of the money to make repairs on the *Tel*, but most of it went to restock our hold with merchandise to sell in Sefna and Theo.

It took us over thirty days before the repairs were completed. First, a suitable mast had to be ordered, and new sails made. The railing Benfoar and I were able to repair ourselves, and fortunately there was extra paint left over from our winter's work to repaint the damaged section of deck and the repaired rail.

To our good fortune, the *Sep* arrived in Eltec from Shentoar ten days after we docked. While they took on water, Tenoar made arrangements with Kuren, her captain, to send messages to Jaygore and Sethel informing those at home we were safe and would return as soon as suitable repairs had been made. Yet even so, I knew my mother would worry until I was safe at home.

And so the extra time I spent in Eltec was some of the loneliest of my life, for I longed to be home with Illiad. I had anticipated being gone no more than forty days, and that would have been long enough; but the extra days of repair, of not knowing when we would sail, of concern for those at home who I knew were worrying about us, ate away at me until I could barely endure what seemed like an eternity spent in port.

§ § §

At last the *Tel* was ready, and we finally set sail for home over fifty days from when we had left Alna. I was glad the *Sep* had arrived when she had; for we would be long overdue by the time we reached our home port; and those who loved us would have been frantic for news of our fate if she had not.

Throughout our voyage home I thought of my mother and of her fear I could be lost at sea. She, I knew, would not take well the news disaster had nearly overcome us; for as soon as she learned of the storm and the damage done to the *Tel*, she would envision all sorts of calamities and would fear for my safety all the more.

Therefore, as the days stretched on, and we sailed further and further north, I was filled with both dread and anticipation. I longed to be home, to be with my parents and Illiad; and even Aarad's companionship could not relieve this longing. Yet I also worried about what my extended absence was doing to both of the women I loved. It was, then, a great relief to me when we at last sighted the Narrows leading to the bay and Alna.

§ § §

We had been gone nearly two full cycles of the moons, and summer was about to begin as I walked up the hill leading from the docks to the village of my boyhood. Just as I had expected, my mother was frantic with worry; and she wept when she saw me, rushing out to me as I neared our house.

Tenoar had given all of the men with families three days of shore leave while he, Kebbit, Burog, Diud and Pellonek remained aboard the ship. Benfoar went in the wagon with those who lived in Sefna and Theo to inform Jaygore of our safe return and then to visit his daughter in Sefna.

Aarad came first to my house then left with Seppan for the farm since my father closed the shop that day in order to celebrate our safe return. Of course my mother insisted on preparing a special meal for me, and we sat at the table, then by the fire, talking long into the night; and I experienced once again the warmth of being home.

The following day I walked out to the farm in order to see Illiad. Since Seppan returned to Alna to work in the forge, I spent the night with Aarad in the loft. Yet before going to bed that evening I went for a walk with Illiad and held her as we watched the sun slide into the cool waters beyond the bay.

We stood there in my special place, alone in the silence of the coming night. She was warmth to me as I held her, and together we watched as the three moons rose on the sixteenth summer of my life.

Chapter X

The first moons cycle of autumn marked the end of my apprenticeship aboard the *Tel*. Yet I chose to stay on and serve indefinitely, a decision which pleased both Tenoar and the rest of the crew. At the same time Tenoar and Jaygore's partnership ended since the *Tel* had been paid for in full due to the success of our voyages over the past four trading seasons.

Tenoar decided to reward the crew by increasing our rate of pay giving each seaman an extra half percent of the profits made on each voyage. This additional money I added to my growing savings which had by then become a considerable amount.

Seppan had already ended his apprenticeship with my father; however, he continued to work in our blacksmith shop as a full partner sharing equally with my father all of the profits from their combined smithing work. Since I was not to become a blacksmith, it was also agreed Seppan would eventually take over the business with the right to pass it on to one of his own sons at the appropriate time. Yet I was not to be completely shut out; for, since the shop and all my father's tools belonged to our family, Seppan agreed he and his descendants would pay me three percent of their income for the rest of my life. And so, although I was just approaching my seventeenth sun cycle, it seemed that my future was secure.

All looked well for me, and my life now appeared laid out in promising prosperity until I grew old with a wife and children around me in the twilight of my days. With this hope in mind, then, I took an additional step and used a portion of my savings to buy a plot of land just outside our village where one day I could build a house looking out upon the bay. There I saw myself coming home to Illiad and the children we would have, for I now realized that I would take her for my wife—if only I could find the courage to ask her.

§ § §

Those winter days when I reached my seventeenth sun cycle were not as busy as the previous winter since we had not only completed a thorough overhaul of the *Tel* one sun cycle before, we had also done major repairs on her just as spring was ending. This left us with merely general maintenance to do so as to keep the ship seaworthy.

Because of this, I had far more free time just as I had had in Shentoar, and I spent as much of this as I could with Illiad. Even so, I did not neglect my other friends and tried to spend some time with Aarad, Seppan and those we met with at the inn while playing kahtore and sharing stories of our lives.

Boec, too, had completed his apprenticeship; and, like Seppan, he had become a partner with his cousin, Hennek. Since Hennek had no sons, Boec was to become the miller in Crayoar once Hennek grew too old to work; and Boec planned on a long and happy life, if only Mirranu would consent to be his wife.

He came more frequently to the inn; for, as a partner, he was allowed to take what time he needed especially as the winter deepened leaving less and less work to be done. With Tuac and Zhoh in port as well, we all became regulars at the inn on those evenings when it was far too cold and blustery to walk out to the farm.

The *Kwel* had been coming regularly into port joined now and then by other ships from Arganon, and it seemed as though our little village was to become a second port supplying Theo with all her needs. The crews of these ships would come to the inn for shore leave, and the men from the *Tel* soon became friends with some of them swapping stories with them of the north for tales of our adventures in Eltec and Shentoar.

One night, in early spring, I was surprised to see Naemen enter the inn; for none of us had seen him since we had sent him on his way nearly four sun cycles before. He looked older, far older than he should have; and at first I did not recognize him as he came through the door.

"Is that who I think it is?" Kebbit asked, and I followed his gaze to see a graying man looking haggard and careworn.

"Naemen?" I replied equally unsure I was right.

"Who's Naemen?" Aarad asked.

"The slave we rescued from Shentoar," I told him. "Remember, I told you about him?"

"He barely looks the same," said Kebbit who then stood up and called his name across the inn.

Naemen turned at the sound of Kebbit's voice, and a faint smile crossed his lips when he saw us. He raised his hand in greeting and came towards our table carrying the drink he had just paid for at the bar.

We all three stood up, and both Kebbit and I extended our hands to him in greeting which he took and clasped heartily. Then, after introducing him to Aarad, the four of us sat down.

"So, tell us," I said cheerfully, "where have you been all this time?"

The smile on his face died, and I could see a deep pain come over him as he told us his story.

"I've been in Pentra for nearly three sun cycles now," he told us.

"Where's Pentra?" I asked. "I've never heard of it before."

"It's up in the far north," he replied, "and not well known. The traders from Arganon like to keep it a secret. It was established to trade with the Draygon. I've been living there trading for furs, mostly tegga and vood but also donect and a few I had never seen before I went there. Then I came to my senses and returned to Arganon where I got my old job back on the *Kwel*."

"But what about your family?" I asked again in surprise. "Were they with you?"

"I have no family," he told us, and the pain deepened.

"But your wife," said Kebbit, "and your two sons."

"Gone," he told us, "at least to me."

"I don't understand," I said.

"My wife…thought I was dead when I failed to come back from Eltec. So she remarried. My sons…they didn't even know me. They now think of her new husband as their father," and with these words, a tear spilled from his eye and landed silently on the table.

"I went to live with my brother," he continued, "but only for a moons cycle or two. Then I signed on with a trading ship and stayed on at the colony of Pentra. I couldn't live in Arganon. I just had to get away."

We all sat in silence for a minute or two, stunned by the news. Then Naemen continued, "It wasn't so bad, Pentra I mean, at least not a first. I was away from Arganon, and I could try and forget. But you can't really you know. When you love someone, truly love them, there's no possible way you can kill the feelings you have for them.

"So I returned to Arganon once I realized I was merely running away. I came to see I had to face the reality of my life.

"It's not so bad now. My boys are older, and my brother had explained to them what happened. They're confused about having two fathers but are beginning to accept me. Maybe there's hope for a relationship. Who knows?"

"So, is this your first trip with the *Kwel*?" I asked.

"Yes," he told us, "the *Kwel's* been making runs when she could most of the winter, but I've been trapped by the harsh winter weather of the far north. When it broke, I took the first trading ship I could out of Pentra and was fortunate enough to reach Arganon about six days before the *Kwel* left for Theo."

"Well, it's good to see ya'," said Kebbit. "We've all wondered about ya' and hoped for the best. Too bad about yer wife and kids though."

"It's fate," he replied. "What can we do against it?"

§ § §

Naemen's story had a sobering effect on me, for it caused me to think about what would happen if, for some reason, Illiad were not part of my life. I had almost lost her once; and I could not bear the thought of not seeing her, not holding her and sharing with her the stories of my days at sea. And so, I resolved to ask her to become my wife.

I told no one of this but merely went out to see her just before I was to leave on our first trading voyage of spring. Everyone assumed I had come to say good-bye before sailing, and I had. Yet there was a deeper reason for my wanting to be alone with her that evening.

We walked to my special place overlooking the sea and sat watching the sun set while we talked of this and that until I finally managed to get control of the conflicting feelings which gripped me. I knew that what I was about to do could never be undone; for if I asked her to marry me, and she should for some reason reject me as she had in the past, then my life would be forever changed. Yet even if she agreed, all would be different; and though I would be happy, nothing would ever again be the same.

"I will be leaving in a few days," I said at last, and my voice and manner took on an almost adult tone.

"I know," she said.

"Well, before I go there is something I need to say."

"You make this sound so serious," and she gave a little laugh.

"It is serious, " I replied. "Probably the most serious thing I have ever done in my life.

For a moment my courage failed me, yet after a brief pause I went on, “You know I love you.”

“Yes,” she began, but I placed a finger over her lips.

“I love you, and I want us to be together,” but at this my courage failed me altogether, and I just sat there looking at her, my mouth open, yet words would not pass my lips.

“If you’re asking me to marry you,” she said at last, pushing my hand away then holding it in hers, “you know I will, so just say it.”

I pulled her towards me and kissed her, yet when I released her, she looked intently at me and said, “Say it.”

“Will you marry me?” I asked at last, and all the anxiety was gone.

“Yes,” she told me, and we kissed again.

§ § §

Her parents were overjoyed as were Aarad and Seppan. Topek was in his room in the barn, and this disappointed me slightly; for I felt a deep need to see the look of total loss on his face. Yet despite this lack of triumph, it was a moment I can never forget.

“We must send word to Morek,” said Melne. “Do you think he will come for the laryat?”

“I doubt he will be willing to make such a long trek with small children,” Aeshone told her. “But maybe for the wedding,” he quickly added at the look of disappointment on her face.

“And when will the laryat be?” Seppan asked. “Idar leaves in just a few days.”

“It would be good if we could hold it before he leaves,” Melne replied. “I know there is not much time…”

“Come now, woman,” Aeshone laughed, “give the man some breathing room. It is not as if he has not known our daughter since boyhood. I do not think he will take back his words. We do not need to rush our plans.”

“I meant nothing like that,” said Melne suddenly becoming very serious. “Of course he won’t. I only meant he will be gone for over a moons cycle, and it seems so long to wait for a laryat. But it will have to do I guess. While he is gone we can plan the laryat and the wedding as well, all in the summer.”

“If that’s all right with the happy couple,” Seppan interjected.

“That’s fine with me,” I replied, and for the first time I kissed Illiad in front of her parents.

§ § §

I spent the night on the floor of the main room with Aarad and Huno, then returned right after breakfast to tell my parents. As soon as we came into my house, Seppan left to work in the forge, and Aarad took his leave for the harbor and the *Tel*.

"You should be going with him," my mother said as my father made a move to join Seppan in the shop.

"In a few minutes," I told her, "but first I need to talk to both of you."

"Sounds serious," said my father with a smile.

"It is," I told him, "but it's nothing bad," I quickly added at the sight of the distress on my mother's face. "Last night, I asked Illiad to marry me."

My mother grabbed her face with both hands, "Tohana!" she cried, then ran to me and hugged me. When she released me, my father took her place.

They were both beside themselves with joy, and my mother wept and hugged me again and again.

"This is the best news I could have asked for," she said. "At last we will have a daughter…and grandchildren."

"Come now, Shahri," my father laughed, "you are getting way ahead of yourself. Idar is not even married yet. Has there been a decision about the laryat?"

"Her parents want to hold it when I return," I replied.

"And the wedding?" asked my mother.

"We don't know yet," I replied. "Probably in the late summer."

"Where will you live?" my father asked.

"We will stay in my room at first," I replied, "…if you don't object."

"Of course there will be no objections," my mother told me and gave my father a look which defied him to say otherwise.

"I have no problem with such arrangements," he said laughing. "I only wondered about the house you plan to build."

"As soon as we're married," I told him, "I will begin building it. I should make enough from the next three runs to Eltec and what I lack both Seppan and Aarad have promised to give me as a wedding present—for taking their sister off their hands."

At this my father laughed, and my mother made a disapproving sound with her lips and shook her head.

"It's only a joke, nodeh," I said.

"That Seppan," she replied, and I saw the faintest of smiles come over her lips, "he never takes things seriously."

Chapter XI

"Nonsense, a proper laryat should be held as soon as possible," Tenoar said when I told him of my plans to marry Illiad. "We can postpone our trip a few days more. It will be no problem. You take the time you need. I am sure the crew will all agree with me, and they will be glad to celebrate with you."

"But..." I began.

"No argument," he told me. "That is an order."

"Yes, sir," I replied. "And thank you, sir."

And so that evening, as soon as I was free, I hurried out to the farm to tell Illiad and her parents what Tenoar had said. They were truly relieved we had been given time to plan a laryat before I left; however, they were equally resolved not to take advantage of Tenoar's generosity and set the laryat to take place six days hence.

Aeshone sent word to Morek in Teuwa by means of a tarrek crew which had brought a load of wool to Alna for export to Eltec. Melne held little hope Morek would be able to make the laryat but continued to hold on to the dream of having all her children present for the marriage of her youngest child and only daughter.

It then fell to me to pick two groom's men. By tradition, they were to be my closest friends. Yet since Aarad was a member of the bride's family, I could not choose him; and so I asked Tuac and Boec to represent me at the laryat.

Boec had no problem accepting my request since, as a full partner with Hennek, he could come to Alna whenever he wished. Tuac, on the other hand, was scheduled to leave with Abdoar before the laryat would take place; yet, Abdoar, out of kindness and sentimentality, permitted him to remain behind saying he could return to Kesset with the first supply run. This pleased Tuac greatly, for not only was he happy to be my groom's man, he was relieved to have extra time at home before resuming life at the fishing camp.

As was also custom, Illiad and I were not permitted to see each other until the day of the laryat which meant Seppan acted as our intermediary and relayed messages between his family and mine. This he did not mind, in fact I was sure it pleased him greatly to have a hand in the preparations since he had invested so much of his time into getting the two of us together.

The days of preparation seemed to go on forever as I longed to be with Illiad but could not. If I were at sea, I would be kept busy, yet Tenoar insisted I take shore leave until the laryat leaving me with very little to do since most of the preparations were the responsibility of the bride's family. Thus, once I had arranged for my groom's men and decided on what I was to wear, there remained almost nothing for me to do. Consequently, I busied myself in the forge with Seppan and my father.

However, I did little work, for each of my father's customers insisted on talking to me and giving me advice on being a good husband. Even Menlo, who had hardly ever spoken a kind word to me, insisted on advising me in the arts of pleasing a wife.

"Do what you can to make her happy at all times," he said, "for when she is pleased, you will be content at home," and at this he chuckled over his own joke.

At last the day of the laryat arrived, and I greeted those who had been invited to join us as they gathered at my boyhood home. When all had come, I walked out to the farm with Boec and Tuac at my side leading the procession of guests. As we approached the gate, I stopped, as was custom, and waited for Illiad's parents to greet me.

"Toev," began Aeshone as he and Melne left the crowd of those invited by their family to witness my betrothal to Illiad. When they reached the gate separating the road from the yard in front to their house, they stopped.

"Toev," I replied, "I am Idar, son of Kennec, son of Elem. I am seeking Aeshone, son of Tellon, son of Morek."

"I am he," came Aeshone's reply. "What is your business here today, Idar son of Kennec?"

"I seek your daughter, Illiad; for I wish to take her for my wife if she is willing to leave her father's home and bind herself to me in marriage."

"And what do you have to offer?" he asked in the prescribed manner. "I will not give my daughter away without assurances she will be provided for. Speak, then, and testify to your good intentions."

"I love your daughter, and will do all I can to make her truly happy," I replied with the customary response. "I am a seaman who has completed his apprenticeship with good report and can earn a living sufficient to provide a happy future for her and such children with which the toha may bless us.

"I have saved money and purchased land on which I will build a house for her, and as the only son of my father I will inherit a portion of his business to be paid out to me by his partner all the days of my life. If your daughter will have me, I will care for her and provide for her while I have breath. What say you Aeshone, son of Tellon?"

"Well said son of Kennec, but who speaks for you in this matter? Who will testify to your good intentions?" Aeshone then asked.

At this, Tuac and Boec both stepped forward.

"I am Boec, son of Sethel, son of Korpel; and I attest to the truth of all Idar son of Kennec has told you."

"I am Tuac, son of Daeo, son of Narren; and I also attest to the ability of Idar, son of Kennec, to provide for your daughter."

"Here are my witnesses," I told him. "What response, then, have you to my request?"

With these words, Aeshone turned to those standing behind him calling out, "Daughter, come here."

Illiad then left the crowd of guests and stood beside her parents.

"Yes, father," she replied.

"Idar, son of Kennec, son of Elem requests to marry you. Your mother and I have questioned him and find him worthy to become your husband. Will you then take him willingly and enter into a bond marriage with him on the day we shall set?"

"Gladly," she replied.

Aeshone then opened the gate, and Melne led their daughter out of the front yard to stand before me on the road. Illiad was dressed in blue and, as was her custom, she again wore a crown of heshel in her hair. When the two women stood before me, Melne placed Illiad's hand in mine.

"She is bone of my bone and flesh of my flesh. I have nourished her as a mother should from the day of her birth. If you will care for my child in the manner of a husband and cherish her as I have, then I will be happy to call you son."

"And I will call you mother all the days of my life," I replied, " for I will truly be a husband of good report to your daughter."

"Then come," she told me, "let us celebrate and plan for the day when your family and mine shall be united."

With this the formal dialogue comprising the laryat came to an end, and my family and friends joined Illiad's to celebrate our future life together.

Chapter XII

I left for Eltec the day after the laryat; and, as had become custom, Illiad and my mother both came to see me off, my mother weeping as usual. I hugged and kissed my mother without a thought; yet when it was Illiad's turn, I redden slightly dreading the teasing I knew I would undergo at the hands of my crew mates.

In this I was not disappointed, for Nomlet was the first to call me lover boy, a name which stuck throughout the entire voyage to Eltec and back but was dropped after our return to Alna.

It was a successful voyage, and the ashka wool brought us a fair price in the markets of Eltec as did the kahlmek we brought from Crayoar to sell to buyers who would then transport it south beyond Shentoar. Thus I felt I could afford the extra money and bought five bowls, all in green, made from the material I had come to know as glass. These would be a wedding present for Illiad.

It had been decided at the laryat that we would wed on the first day of summer, for then the moons would be their brightest. This was a tradition in Theo since it was seen as a promising sign of good fortune to enter into such unions at the beginning of a moons cycle. For this reason I felt an urgency to return home as soon as possible, and I kept track of my time at sea.

The usual fifteen days sailing south against a head wind brought us to Eltec just as the sun was setting on the third day of the second moons cycle of spring, and Kelyan kept assuring me we would have more than enough time to return home before the day appointed for my marriage. Yet, though the wool and kahlmek sold well, we had trouble finding buyers for the remainder of our cargo; and as our days in port stretched far beyond the usual eight, I grew anxious.

"Don't worry, lover boy," Burog told me, "we'll get ya' home on time."

"True enough, lad," said Nomlet. "You just keep your mind on your job and not on that pretty one back home."

But I could not help thinking of Illiad, and I longed to be home with her in my arms pledging my life to her as long as I held breath. Then at last, on the fifteenth day of the moons cycle, we finally sold what remained of our cargo and prepared to sail for home the next day.

Yet fate was still against us, for merely five days out from Eltec, near where we had met the storm that crippled our ship, we lost the wind; and we were set adrift at the mercy of the waves. We drifted in towards shore as far as we dared then dropped anchor to await any wind at all. The next day Tenoar ordered our small boat to be launched with a line secured to the *Tel's* prow, and we each took turns towing the ship northward as others (including Tenoar himself) poled the *Tel* slowly along the coast taking soundings to be sure we had sufficient depth.

We made no more than three or four leagues each day, but at least we were moving closer and closer to home. Yet each night we lay exhausted on our hammocks with only the prospect of repeating this grueling toil the next day.

To make matters worse, Tenoar was force to ration our water as we had no idea how long we would be without wind, and the thickly wooded coast revealed no place where our supply could be replenished. Then, near midday on the sixth day of this ordeal, we sighted a small river, one we could never have seen from our usual position farther out to sea. We anchored near its mouth and sent men in rotation to refill our water casks and bathe in the cool refreshing stream.

We woke the morning of the seventh day to find a breeze blowing from the south and resumed course for home. Yet this was the twenty-seventh day of the moons cycle, and we had been originally scheduled to return home the next day. Our poling of the ship had bought us less than a day, and this left us at least a full nine days of sailing before reaching Alna; and I became concerned, for those at home would fear the worst at our lengthy delay.

By midmorning the light breeze had become a fair wind which continued to blow from the south until we reached home nine days later, just as I had predicted. Yet throughout the trip, I watched the stars each night standing at the rail in silent contemplation; and each time I did, I promised Illiad I would soon be home to take her for my wife.

§ § §

The *Von* and the *Dul* were both in port when we arrived at Alna in the late afternoon on the next to the last day of the moons cycle. At the sight of the *Tel* approaching the docks, men from both fishing boats ran to spread the word of our return. Thus, by the time we docked, the wharf was already crowded with family and friends come from the village to greet us.

My parents were among them, though Seppan was not; for he had gone to the farm to tell his family of our return saying they would all meet us at our house as soon as they could. And so I left the docks with Aarad and my parents after the *Tel* was properly moored to the wharf; for Tenoar—as he had done when we had returned late due of the storm and the damage it had done to the *Tel*—gave those of us with families three days shore leave.

Aarad came with us; and as we walked back to the village, we explained what had caused our delay.

"I was so frightened," my mother told us. "When you failed to return, each day became an agony. I knew you were dead. I even dreamt of you and your grandfather. I saw you both floating in the water, and I kept calling out to you."

"But I'm safe, nodeh," I told her. "I'm back now, and I will always come back; and you will always be here to greet me."

"Not always," she replied.

§ § §

Illiad rushed into my arms as she came into the house while Melne and Aeshone embraced Aarad both at the same time. Then they turned to me, Melne hugging me and kissing me on the cheek, Aeshone taking my hand then pulling me to him in a quick embrace.

"Morek!" Aarad cried as his father released me, and as I turned toward him I caught a quick glimpse of what appeared to be two Seppans standing by the door. Then Aarad threw himself on one of them, locking him in a strong embrace and pounding him on the back. "You came for the wedding! What of Hannee and the children, are they here as well?"

"The girls are too small yet for such a journey," he replied. "I thought about bringing Sepnoar, but decided to leave him at home to help his mother. He was very disappointed, yet maybe when one of you wed," he said putting an arm around each of his brothers, "he will come.

"Ah," he said looking at me, "this must be the young toha who will be marrying our sister," and he moved towards me with his hand extended.

"You should not say such things, Morek," cried Melne. "It will bring bad fortune upon us if you mock the toha."

"I meant no disrespect, nodeh," he replied as he clasped my hand, "but you must admit Illiad has not stopped talking about him since I arrived."

"That is as it should be," Aeshone added, "when a young woman loves a man as your sister does Idar," and at this I felt myself redden slightly.

"I can't believe how much you look like Seppan," I told him as a way of changing the subject.

"We have always looked alike," he replied. "When we were children, you could only tell us apart because I was the the taller. Even nodeh sometimes found it difficult to recognize us."

"I never," his mother cried in shock.

"Well…there was that one time…" Aeshone said with a grin on his face.

"That was an accident," she replied grinning as well, "but let's not talk of that. We have far more important matters at hand…the wedding."

"You're right," I cried, "it's the day after tomorrow."

"That won't be possible," said Illiad taking hold of my arm. "We're not ready. We'll have to postpone it a few days."

"When you did not return on time," my mother added, "…we have all been so worried we stopped making preparations. But now that you are back it will only take a few days more. The moons will still be full if we hold it say, on the third day of the cycle."

"That should be enough time to prepare," said Melne, "and it will still be a good omen."

"The third day will be fine," agreed Illiad.

"Don't I get to have any say?" I asked.

"No," cried all three women at once.

"I think," my father said to Aeshone, "it is time we had a talk with Idar about married life," and they both grinned.

§ § §

The three days of preparation passed quickly; for Aarad and I went to the *Tel* the day after arriving back from Eltec and told Tenoar the plans for my wedding had changed, and he agreed to let us work the next two days so as to have time off when the day for my marriage came. This kept us busy bringing up the cargo from the hold and arranging it on deck for the rest of the crew to off load when they returned from shore leave.

On the first day of the moons cycle, the day that was supposed to be my wedding day, the *Kwel* arrived from Arganon; and Naemen came to see us on the *Tel*.

"So you returned safely then?" he said as he came up the ramp leading to the deck of the ship. "When we left here everyone was worried because you were overdue."

"Had trouble selling our cargo in Eltec," I told him.

"Then we lost the wind on our return voyage," Aarad added. "Had to pole the ship for six days 'til we caught a breeze from the south."

"But you're safe now," he told us, "and that's all that truly counts."

"How are things going with your family?" I asked.

"Not bad," he replied. "My boys are warming up to me somewhat, and their mother has agreed to allow me to register our oldest when he reaches manhood in the winter. Her new husband had planned to take him as his son; but Senyal, that's my oldest, said he wants to be registered as my son. So that's a good start.

"And what's more," he went on, "he says he might want to apprentice as a seamen like me. His mother is not too happy with the idea, but she has agreed to let him sail with me some time this summer, probably in the third cycle of the moons. So if you're in port, you'll get to meet him."

"I hope we are," I told him.

"And what of you?" he asked. "I heard you had your laryat just before you left for Eltec. So when do you wed?"

"It was supposed to be today," I told him, "but it has been postponed three days, so the day after tomorrow. That's why Aarad and I are working. Tenoar gave everyone else shore leave, but we are trading days to have my wedding day off."

"Well, good luck to you," he said clasping my hand. "You're a fine lad, and it's my good fortune to have met you. Fate had something in store when I chanced to run into you that day in Shentoar, and I have a feeling fate has more in store for us in the future."

"We'll see," I told him. "And good luck to you. May all go well with your boys."

§ § §

The day of my wedding dawned bright and sunny—a good omen in my mother's eyes—and I lay on my bed smelling the sea air and taking pleasure in the quiet solitude. Seppan, who had been staying with me to allow his two brothers the room in the loft, had gone home to prepare for the wedding; and so I was alone in my room for the last time. The bunks we had built along the wall to allow the three of us ample sleeping space had been taken down while I was away; and when night came, Illiad and I would share this room, as was our intent, until a house of our own could be built on the piece of land I had bought overlooking the bay.

I lay there in the silence thinking of my boyhood and of how fortune had smiled upon me when Aeshone had decided to move to Alna bringing with him the love of my life as well as two of my best friends. And the words Naemen spoke two days before come back to me, for fate had truly blessed me.

After a while I rose, dressed and went into the main room to find my parents sitting alone at the table talking quietly—a sight I not seen since I was a boy, and one I had all but forgotten. For one fleeting moment I was ten just coming out of my room with a life of mystery ahead of me. Then I was a man of seventeen with my future planned and the mystery gone.

These thoughts warmed me, though the morning was cool; and I stood in silence taking it all in. Then my mother saw me standing there, and as she stood up to greet me, the moment died and was gone forever.

"Good," she said, "I was about to call you, there is much to do before noon."

"How are you this morning?" my father asked. "Nervous?"

"A little," I lied.

"Well, then you are a braver man than I was on my wedding day," and he smiled at me in a way I had seldom seen before. As I looked into his eyes, I remembered saying good-bye to him on the deck of the *Tel*, for I saw on his face the same sense of pride I had seen that day.

I walked over and sat down at the table, and my mother brought me a plate with bread. "Here," she said, "eat this and have a little palne juice. It is not wise to eat too much, for there will be plenty to eat later."

"I think this is all I can eat anyway," I told her. "I'm not really hungry."

"I was almost sick when your grandmother made me eat the morning I married your mother," he told me; and I smiled at the story, one I had never heard before.

"How long before they arrive?" I asked as I nibbled the bread.

"We have maybe three or four hours," she replied. "But even so you must hurry. It is best to be ready well before they come. It will not do to be rushing around at the last moment. All should be done well in advance."

After I ate, my father and I prepared the main room for the wedding as my mother cooked in the kitchen area. We set out the extra tables we had borrowed for the occasion as well as extra chairs, but to do this we first had to carry the furniture out of the main room and store it in our two bedrooms until after the wedding.

When this was done, we covered the tables with colorful cloths as well as flowers in small wooden bowls. Then my father and I went to our rooms to dress leaving my mother to finish some last minute preparations before she, too, went to get ready for our guests.

Finally, all was done, and we waited for Illiad and her family to arrive.

I thought I was nervous when I first got up, but the waiting only made it worse; and when I heard the sound of the wagon pulling to a stop in front of our house, I thought my stomach would fall from my body. Nor did I think my legs would support me any longer. As I walked to the door with my parents, I felt as if I were going to my death and not to the beginning of a new life; and the only thing that kept me going was the joy I had been told I would feel once this was all over and done.

"I greet you Idar, son of Kennec," said Aeshone as we opened the door. "I have brought my daughter to you as we agreed, and now my family comes to share with you and your family that we all may become one."

"I greet you Aeshone, son of Tellon," came my reply, though my voice betrayed the state of my stomach and legs. "You and your family are most welcome."

Then Illiad stepped forward and Melne handed her a tray piled high with bread. This she took and, as was the custom, handed it on to me saying the ancient words of the marriage rite, "Bread from the land I give to you that I might become your wife."

"Bread from the land I receive from you," I responded using the words passed down from generation to generation, "and I pledge that from this day on I will be a good husband to you providing for you as is my duty."

Illiad then took a bowl of cooked fish from her father and again handed it to me with the words, "Fish from the sea I give to you that I might become your wife."

"Fish from the sea I receive from you," came my response, "and I now pledge that as your father has cared for you so now will I care for you all the days of your life."

With these words, Illiad entered my home and became my wife.

§ § §

As was tradition, we feasted together sharing the food her family had brought as well as what mine had provided; and together we became a single family. Then, at the end of the meal, she presented to me a white tunic of a fine ashka wool with heshel flowers embroidered on the collar. With it there was a black belt also of ashka wool, and as I took them, I whispered softly to her, "From Huno?" and she nodded.

I then gave her the bowls I had bought in Eltec; and everyone marveled, for they had never seen glass before. Even Aarad was surprised since I had not shown him the gift I had bought for Illiad but had kept it a secret locked in my sea chest until we returned.

Yet almost before we had finished exchanging these gifts, we heard the sound of music as those who were our friends came to share with us the joy of our marriage. Illiad and I went as a couple for the first time and greeted the many well wishers receiving from them the gifts brought in honor of our union as husband and wife. Then the dancing began.

The party went on well into the night with torches lit in the streets so that the dancing and feasting could continue after dark. It seemed the whole village was there as well as many of the farm families who were friends with Aeshone and Melne. Boec came with Mirranu as did the crew of the *Tel* and Naemen. Ujedah, old as she was, clapped time to the beat of the music while Alnat, Tefnoar and Shend danced with the pretty young women of our village whom I had known all my life. Again, Seppan danced each dance with Zherna though Aarad only danced once or twice with Narra. Even so, Morek watched his brothers with contentment as did their father.

Tuac, Daeo and Zhoh were all on the fishing islands; and this saddened me a little, for I would have liked them to have been with me that night. Yet Leyhah was there with her mother who told me how disappointed Tuac was to be gone and not be able to attend my wedding, but she also assured me that he had been proud to stand with me at the laryat.

Leyhah begged a dance from me which Illiad granted—although not the zubah which she reserved for me alone. As Leyhah and I danced, I remembered Tuac bursting into the forge that morning long ago to tell me his mother had given birth to a sister. Now here she was, a girl of eight, dancing at my wedding and dreaming no doubt, as young girls do, of the day she would stand at her husband's side at a wedding in the far distant future.

Topek and Kron were both at the wedding standing off to the side yet not together. Neither looked as if they were enjoying themselves much, and oddly enough I was not as pleased by this as I would have thought. I had Illiad, and they did not; yet all I could think of at the time was how I wished them to one day be as happy as I was that night.

§ § §

We were granted less than two cycles of the moons together after we wed, for Tenoar was a sentimental man and would not permit me to sail with them the next time the *Tel* went to Eltec. "A groom should spend time with his bride," he told me. "There will be other voyages, lad, you just stay here and get acquainted."

And so I stood with Illiad on the wharf and waved Aarad farewell, then returned home and spent the next fifty days waiting to go to sea. Yet, even though I missed the feel of water beneath me, those were the happiest days of my life; and I treasure them even now.

She went with me to the hill, and there we talked for long hours about our futures together planning the home we would have and the children who would fill it. And at night, as we lay together, I rejoiced at the scent of her hair on the pillow beside me and her soft breath upon my cheek. Even now, in death, it is the memory of those days that gives me comfort.

Then, all too soon, the *Tel* was ready to sail again; and I was to go with her. We went to the docks together, my mother with us; for though I was a man and married, my mother still felt a need to bid me farewell. And as the *Tel* pulled away from the wharf and headed out into the bay, I watched them both from the deck, a picture forever burned into my memory: my wife, my love, my life standing beside my mother who wept as always; for she was sure I would not return, that I would be lost at sea and my body not brought back to Alna to be buried with our ancestors. Yet she was wrong, I did return…I did return.

END OF BOOK THREE

Book Four
The End

Chapter I

We made the run to Eltec in record time with three days to spare, and because of this Tenoar gave us an extra day of shore leave before we sailed for home. Yet in all other respects the trip was basically routine.

I spent the time I had ashore searching the markets seeking a special present for Illiad—a set of ribbons for her hair made of a strange material I had never seen before. I also bought a bottle of maluk for my father and an extra one to keep for myself since it had been an excellent season for maluk, and it was especially dark, sweet and strong.

When I returned to the ship, I stored these in the chest below my bunk, and Aarad did the same with the three bottles of maluk he was bringing home to share with Seppan and Shend at the inn. We then went about our duties in preparation for sailing the next day.

Yet as I worked, I thought of nothing but the look of surprise on Illiad's face when I returned home early as well as the joy I would have in giving her the ribbons. My heart soared while I worked, and in my mind I saw nothing but her smile and heard only her joyful laughter at my return.

"Do you think we'll make good time on the way home?" Aarad asked as we worked.

"I hope so," I replied. "I could do with some extra shore leave at home before sailing back to Eltec."

"We might not be going to Eltec next time," he told me. "Burog says we may be going to Shentoar."

"Shentoar? Why Shentoar?" I asked in surprise. "I would think after what happened on our last voyage there Tenoar would be against it."

"Changed his mind," he replied. "He's heard from Kuren that we can turn quite a profit from importing pottery. Sells like mad in the markets in Sefna and Theo, and the merchants in Shentoar can never get enough ashka wool. Besides, think of how much we'll make on a trip like that."

"True," I replied, "but it will take 'til spring, and I don't want to be gone that long."

"It might not," he told me. "Burog says if we leave now we can be back by late autumn and still avoid the winter storms."

"Even so," I said, "it's a long time to be gone."

"Oh, come on," he chided me, "married life is making you soft. What ever happened to your spirit of adventure?"

"When the right woman comes along," I told him, "you'll understand."

§ § §

It was cold that night before I returned, somehow far colder than it should have been; and the air was filled with an acrid smell which should have warned me of what was to come. But my heart was full of love and longing and the hope of once again seeing everything I held dear.

I stood watch on the deck of the *Tel* with the pale light of but a single moon to give me comfort as it was three nights past the middle of the moons cycle. The helm had been tied off so that the ship sailed on over a calm sea toward home, and I was left with nothing to do but wait and watch for dawn.

Shortly before sunrise, Aarad came on deck which surprised me since I had relieved him not long before and expected him to be asleep in our crew quarters. He walked over and stood beside me, and at first he said nothing.

"I couldn't sleep," he said at last, "I've had a strong feeling of…I'm not sure what…like doom. And then when I finally did get to sleep I dreamt Huno died."

"Huno?" I said in surprise.

"Yeah, he was dead. All covered with blood like a vood or a donect got him. Do you think it means something?"

"My mother would say it did," I told him, "and definitely Ujedah; but I've never believed in dreams. At least they never come true for me."

"I don't know. I still can't shake this feeling. I just feel…scared or nervous, like something bad's going to happen. I can't wait 'til we get home. Has anyone said when they think we should be at the Narrows?"

"Burog came on deck just after you left," I told him. "He said we might see the Narrows about two hours after sunrise."

"I hope he's right. I just want to get home."

§ § §

Dawn rose blood red on the eastern horizon and was filtered through a strange haze that seemed to fill the sky to the north and east. When Burog relieved me and took over the helm, I went below and sat next to Aarad as we ate.

"Kahl again," I whispered, "I'll be glad to be home and have some real food for a change."

"You never minded eating my mother's kahl," he told me with a grin on his face. "In fact I remember you going back for extra helpings."

"But only because she served palne syrup with it," I said. "This stuff is terrible."

"Don't let Kebbit hear you," he warned me, "or you won't eat at all on our next trip."

"That would almost be better than eating his kahl," I said pushing my unfinished bowl away. "I think I'll wait for home."

I left the table and went to our quarters where I took a couple of sips of the maluk to get the taste of the kahl out of my mouth. Then I stood for a few minutes holding the ribbons thinking again of the look of happiness on Illiad's face when I gave them to her. At last I put them back in my sea trunk and went on deck.

By two hours after sunrise the haze had deepened especially where we felt the Narrows should be, and we became alarmed. More and more of the crew come out on deck as even those who were off duty came and stood by the railing watching, waiting, wondering what this meant.

At last the Narrows came in sight, a dark speck against a brown and gray landscape. By then the whole crew was on deck waiting with anticipation as we traversed the waterway between the two rows of hills surrounding the bay.

As we sailed on, it seemed almost like the passageway the priests tell us we must follow to the land of the dead, for the haze cast a deep gloom on the water; and the air was filled with the smell of smoke, of decay, of death.

"I don't like this one bit," Aarad told me as he came over and stood by me at the railing.

"Neither do I," I replied. "What could cause this?"

But even as I spoke, we passed through the Narrows onto the bay; and we could now see Theo, Alna and Sefna dotting the coast with smoke rising from them in faint whispers of a catastrophe of unspeakable horrors.

§ § §

It took us about a half hour to sail across the bay and reach the docks which, as we could see, were unharmed. Yet to us this seemed an eternity as a million thoughts went through our minds; and our hearts, although beating faster and faster, seemed not to beat at all.

At last we reached the docks; and, having hastily moored the *Tel* to the wharf, we all abandoned ship as even Tenoar raced down the pier toward dry land. Aarad and I ran side by side keeping pace with one another even as we ran up the hill leading to the bridge over the Ruha.

Yet as we reached it, we could see that all of the buildings in Alna were in ruins with only the inn—a mere shell of rock and stone—still standing. I was stunned, the shock causing me to cry out, "Tohana, Aarad what went on here?"

"Maybe a house fire that spread," he replied.

"To Theo and Sefna?" I asked in disbelief.

We had reached the inn and were now forced to walk slowly because of the rubble everywhere in the village. The area around the inn was filled with stones which had broken away from the walls, and in the midst of the rubble there was a man lying dead.

As I approached, I recognized him; for he had been a sailor aboard the *Kwel*. He and his mates came to the inn to drink when they were given shore leave. Then they would stagger back to their ship and sleep it off.

I had known him. We were not close, but we had talked; and he had told Aarad and me many tall tales of the sea and of his adventures sailing to the far north and trading with the Draygon.

We left him, both of us stunned and speechless, and moved on through the piles of charred wood that had been the homes of those we knew the day we left Alna less than a moons cycle before. With each step it became more and more difficult to move; for the dread in my heart made my legs tremble, and many times I almost fell to my knees and wept. Yet I went on, for I had to reach my parents and find out what had happened.

The streets, too, were littered with the corpses of men, women and even children I had known, some from my earliest days. I saw Alnat's father and Tefnoar's mother as well as two of Ulanna and Sharn's children, all dead with looks of terror on their faces.

At last we reached the spot where my parents house should have been, the home where I grew up, where I always felt safe and loved. But all I could recognize was the brick furnace which had been my father's forge standing among the charred ashes and the pump where I had washed so many times and drawn water for my mother and father.

Slowly I pushed my way into what should have been the main room and stood by the crumpled hearth beside which I had sat so many nights dreaming of going to sea. When I turned and looked towards my room, I saw a strange grayness lying amongst the bits of blackened wood; and I crossed the room to examine it more closely. Yet to my horror, it turned out to be a skull—all that remained of one of my parents.

§ § §

I do not know how long I stood sobbing, cursing, kicking the rubble that once had been my life. Aarad held me—I remember that—but all else is but a shadow that even now in death I cannot penetrate.

At last I stopped. "Illiad," I cried, and both Aarad and I began to pick our way through the remnants of my life seeking the open fields and the road to the farm where Illiad was staying.

When we reached the edge of the village and the ruins of Tuac's house, we saw him lying face down in the dirt in a stillness I could not comprehend. I walked over to him and gently turned him over, then jumped back; for staring up at me with eyes that even now I cannot forget was the face of Leyhah, his sister, whom he still held clutched in his arms as if trying to protect her.

There was no time to grieve, for I had to find Illiad and see for myself that she was alive; and Aarad, too, was desperate to know his family's fate.

We ran all the way to the farm, then stood in icy stillness as we saw that nothing was left but charred ruins. The gate was broken, and the fence trampled down; and there were nosha tracks everywhere.

Smoke still rose from the barn which smoldered because of the hay and sacks of grain stored there. Yet all else was still with only the leaves on the tree that stood near the gate rustling in a light breeze.

We walked to the house, afraid of what we would find there. Yet as we searched, there was no sign of life, nor that of death either. Illiad and her parents were gone and so was Seppan. But where? For we found no bones in the rubble as a sign that they, too, were dead.

§ § §

After searching for over an hour, after walking the length of the fields I had helped plant so many times, after fruitlessly calling and calling to the emptiness surrounding the house, we sat at last in the dirt under the tree in what had been their front yard and said nothing for a long time. At first my mind raced, then gradually it slowed and became filled with a cold numbness as I wished for death yet hoped life and Illiad would be given to me instead.

"Who could have done this?" I asked at last. "Someone had to, there are nosha tracks everywhere."

When Aarad made no reply, I looked over at him and saw tears falling onto the dirt in front of him. Yet he made no sound. He just sat and wept in an eerie silence; and the sight of him drew me out of my own grief dispelling the emptiness in my heart and made me realize I must go on. I had to know what had happened, I had to find my wife, I had to live.

Chapter II

We made our way back to Alna, and as we walked through the rubble of the ruined village and neared what was left of the inn, I heard a familiar voice calling to us, "Idar! Aarad! Tohana! Tohana!" I turned and saw Boec running towards us followed by Mirranu.

I was speechless, for all we had seen was death; and now someone was alive. Could Illiad, then, be alive as well?

He grabbed me first then embraced Aarad, "Tohana," he kept saying again and again.

"What happened?" I asked at last, "How could you have survived this? Have you seen Illiad?"

"No," he said, "I just got here from Crayoar."

"But how…" and could say no more.

"Three nights ago Mirranu and I went for a walk along the Ruha and stopped under the bridge. Suddenly we heard the sound of many nosha, then screaming and noises like a battle—metal upon metal, cries for help. We climbed the bank and ran toward the village, but as we came out of the trees we saw soldiers on nosha. They were everywhere…they were burning the houses and killing everyone.

"I pulled Mirranu back into the trees, and we ran deep into the woods along the river. We spent the night there listening to the distant sounds of death coming from Crayoar, the scent of smoke from the village all around us. Finally the sounds faded away, and we fell asleep.

"Tennep, Mirranu's cousin, found us just as dawn was breaking. He told us there were survivors hiding in a clearing near by, 15 to 20 men and women with a few children who had escaped the attack on Crayoar, and so we joined them.

"Then Tennep and another man said they were going to warn the farms south of Crayoar. He said the Valnar—that's what he called them, Valnar—

he said they hadn't crossed the bridge but only burned the village and took a few prisoners. He was sure they would return now that there was more light and kill the farmers across the Ruha, so I went with them but only as far as the bridge.

"We got across all right. Then, since I was afraid of leaving Mirranu, I told them I would stay and keep watch while they went to warn the farmers.

"About an hour after they left I heard nosha, so I hid in the brush along the path leading to Alna. The Valnar rode across the bridge and out into the fields; and after a few minutes I began to see smoke rising here and there in the distance, so I crept out and looked south. There were columns of smoke everywhere even down toward Alna.

"I stood watching in disbelief for I don't know how long, and I almost got caught. Fortunately I heard the sound of nosha just in time and ducked back into the brush.

"Five Valnar came up the path from Alna leading Tefnoar, Sharn and his wife Ulanna. Each was tethered to the back of a nosha and forced to run to keep from being dragged."

"We saw two of their children dead in the street near their house" I told him.

"That confirms what we've heard," he replied, "the Valnar don't take children prisoner.

"They stopped right in front of me, just where the path to Alna meets the road crossing the bridge to Crayoar, so I lay quietly for about half an hour. Tefnoar saw me. I know he did. I could see it in his eyes, but he looked quickly away so he wouldn't betray me.

"Then they were joined by a whole column of Valnar leading about 20 nosha and five or six prisoners one of which was Tennep who looked like he had been beaten. One of them said something in their language and struck Tennep so hard he fell to his knees causing Ulanna to cry and pull at the rope binding her, but this only made them laugh.

"They talked for a few minutes, and appeared to be very angry. I got the impression it was because they had not captured many prisoners. Then, in anger, the soldier who had hit Tennep lashed his nosha which took off at a run. Tennep fell, and the nosha dragged him across the bridge. The soldier finally stopped and waited for the others to catch up, and they continued on down the road toward Theo.

"When they had gone, I made my way down the river bank and swam to the other side. Then I found the others and told them about Tennep. So we left the clearing, fearing Tennep might tell them were we were, and made our way down to the falls and then to the rocks below it.

"We've been hiding out there for the past two days living on berries. Then, early this morning, two men went back to Crayoar to see if they could find food. When they came back, they had a man with them who came from Theo. He told us the Valnar had left Theo early this morning with about two thousand prisoners, wagons loaded with treasure taken from the palace and the homes of the rich as well as many nosha.

"Everyone else went back to Crayoar, but I came here with Mirranu to see if I could find any of my family."

"There's no one," I said and told him what we had seen at the inn and throughout Alna. We told him we had been out to Aarad's house and found no one anywhere.

"Could the Valnar have taken my family?" Aarad asked. "There was no sign at the farm that they were killed."

"I don't know," Boec answered, "I only saw those three brought from Alna along the path. But there could have been others after I left, and surly most would have been taken across the bridge to Theo using the main road."

We walked back to the inn, and Boec stood weeping outside for a long time. At last, with my arm around him and his around Mirranu, I lead him out of Alna and down to the docks.

§ § §

Later in the afternoon boats began to arrive from Trohan, Kesset and the other fishing camps. The first to dock was the *Tok*, and we ran to meet Zhoh and Daeo as they jumped onto the pier.

"Idar!" Zhoh cried, "have you seen my family?"

When I told them what we had seen at their house, they were stunned.

"No," was all Zhoh said, then he and his father pushed past us and ran to Alna. The others from the *Tok* all followed except for Miku who stood on the deck of his boat staring at the smoke still rising from Theo.

About an hour later the *Mer* arrived, and its crew also quickly left the docks and headed toward Alna.

"Idar! Aarad!" again I heard a familiar voice and turned to see Abdoar walking quickly toward me.

"She's all right," he told me. "She's on a boat, a merchant ship from Arganon, they took her to Arganon.

"What are you talking about?" I asked, not understanding anything he said.

"Illiad," said Shend coming up behind him. "I was out behind the inn the night those demons came, and so I ran down to the beach, then made my way out to the farm. I warned your family, Aarad, and got them to the docks and aboard the *Kwel* which was loaded and ready to sail the next morning. Then I went with Abdoar to tell the fishing colonies what had happened.

"Illiad's alive!"

"Yes," Shend told me, "she should be in Arganon by now. She's safe."

I hugged him. "Thank you, Shend. How can I ever repay you?"

Then I remembered. "Boec…and Mirranu," I told him, "they're here on the *Tel*, but your parents…"

"I know," he said, "no one escaped the inn. It was the first thing they attacked when they came into Alna. I was lucky I was outside dumping trash on the burn pile. It saved my life. Come on, take me to my brother."

We walked down the wharf to the *Tel* and found Boec below deck with Mirranu who was crying softly on his shoulder, then Aarad and I left Shend and Boec to their grief; for, though my parents were dead, I now had hope of finding Illiad alive in Arganon.

When we reached the pier, two more boats could be seen crossing the bay heading towards the docks; but we turned and walked along the wharf in the direction of the beach where a large group seemed to be gathering. Men were coming from Alna each one carrying something. As we came closer, we saw that some had bodies of loved ones and others carried stacks of wood. Still other men were searching the shore for driftwood, and it soon became obvious what was intended—they were going to cremate the dead.

This shocked me, for it was not our custom; but I had heard stories of this being done among the Shalmarran. What else could we do, I thought, as there was no way we could dig the graves need to bury so many dead.

Aarad and I began to help, and when we returned with a load of wood, I saw Daeo sitting in the sand holding Leyhah in his lap. When I asked, Abdoar told me that Zhoh had guided him back from Alna and had now returned for Tuac.

"He just sits there," Abdoar said, "staring out at the bay. I remember how happy he was when she was born. They thought Tenyata couldn't have any more children after the hard time she had giving birth to Tuac. He told me it was a miracle they had her.

"Now they're both gone, and he has no idea what happened to Tenyata.

Makes me glad my wife and I never had children and that she didn't live to see this day."

Aarad and I went back to Alna to help Zhoh; but when we reached the bridge, he was just crossing it and refused our help. "He's my brother," he told us, "I'll carry him myself."

We followed behind him, and I thought of all the times I had walked this road with Tuac when we were boys. I could not believe this was to be the last time, and I would never see him again.

§ § §

That night we began the burning of the dead, a process which lasted for two days; and it became increasingly difficult to find enough wood. The light from our fire attracted the attention of those still alive in Theo, and in a few hours little knots began to filter into the camp Miku had set up on the beach near the docks.

The next day we sent search parties to Theo, Sefna and Prion to look for survivors. We also sent out scavenging parties to see what food was to be found on the farms around Alna. Boec and Mirranu returned to Crayoar that same day taking Shend with them; and the following day they came back with nearly a hundred survivors, most of these were from the farm families Tennep had warned. They told us that many more had fled into the forested hills to the south and could not be found.

Then, in the evening, Morek arrived from Teuwa with Sepnoar and four other men. Aarad was overjoyed to see them but was greatly saddened upon hearing of the loss of his sister-in-law and two nieces. Morek was relieved to find Aarad still alive and also found comfort in learning the rest of his family was alive and waiting in Arganon.

Soon, news of their arrival spread through the camp; and many sought them out wishing to hear their stories.

"I was in the hills tending the ashka," Morek told us, "and Sepnoar was with me since he had just reached the age when he could help. Seven nights ago we saw a great light down in the valley, and in the morning we returned to Teuwa to see what had happened.

"We found the village in ruins…houses burned…dead everywhere; and my wife and two young daughters were among them. There were nosha tracks leading out of the village toward Theo, and I feared for my family here in Alna.

"When other shepherds came down from the hills, we buried the dead as best we could; and then, on the following day, I left for Alna hoping to find my family alive. Four others, who had family in Crayoar or Theo, joined me. The rest, what few there were, remained behind to search the hills for those who may have survived.

"As we traveled west, we hid from mounted patrols—they seemed to be everywhere—and two days ago we saw a huge army marching east from Theo with a long line of captives. There must have been two thousand at the least maybe more."

"Prisoners," Aarad told him, "taken to be sold as slaves."

"But who are they?" he asked.

"We've only heard the name Valnar," Boec told him. "We know nothing more."

§ § §

On the day after I arrived from Eltec, I returned to Alna bringing with me a cloak my mother had made and wrapped in it the few bones I could find in the ruins of our house. Then I went down to the beach and placed them in a cave in the side of the hill near the path leading to my special place. The remains of others who had died were already waiting there; and, as I left, one of Abdoar's crew could be seen coming from Alna carrying a similar bundle.

I stood with my back to the sea, wishing now that I had never left Alna; for if I had been at home, as my mother wished, I could possibly have saved them. Then I spoke softly the customary funeral prayer commending them to the toha that their spirits might find rest; and as the next mourner came to bury his dead, I turned and walked back to camp.

By the evening of the third day after my return, the cremation fire had gone out, and a strong breeze blowing from the sea had begun to scatter the ashes across the beach and toward the walls of Theo. This we felt was most fitting; for, as was our custom, the dead should return to the soil of Theo.

We sifted through the remains of the fire and removed the bones that had not been consumed. These were placed in bags and taken as well to the cave where I had placed my parents bones. Finally, we filled in the entrance to the cave with rocks so our dead would remain undisturbed. Then Otna, an apprentice priest from the temple in Theo who had survived the pillaging of the city, said a blessing; and we silently returned to camp to morn our dead in our own private way.

Chapter III

From the first day he returned from Trohan, Miku assumed command of those who had survived the devastation of what had once been our way of life. No one ever seemed to object. He simply took control and gave orders; and we all obeyed without question, for it was better that way since it left us no need to think or plan. And so we became like children with Miku guiding us.

He was the son of a merchant in Theo; and when his older brother made the decision to apprentice with their father, Miku became a fisherman. After an apprenticeship on a fishing boat from Alna, his father had bought the *Tok* for him; and he then set up his own camp on Trohan. As time passed, he had become the most respected captain in the fishing fleet.

His father had long since died; and, though his brother was still alive, he did not at first go to Theo to search for him. Instead, he looked to the needs of his crew; and within hours of his arrival this concern was extended to all those who remained alive and in need.

He was not despotic, but kind; and his men were extremely loyal to him. Thus, as those first hours passed, we all knew instinctively that order had to be established; and Miku's reputation allowed him to fill the vacuum the king's death had created.

When we sent out search parties, Miku headed the one which went to Theo. However, when they returned after a day's search with merely forty to fifty survivors, none were from Miku's family.

Yet in spite of this, he carried his loss far better than the rest of us even though the weight of us all was pressed upon him. We mourned, and he also mourned. Nevertheless, he governed as well, and this was taken as the way things should be and never questioned.

Before sunset on his first night back from Trohan, Miku had organized a camp along the road to Alna close to the docks. It began with a few canvas tarps set up on poles, first to protect the dead, and later as shelter for the survivors who began to drift naturally toward the docks at Alna.

We never really knew why Alna's docks had been spared, for those at Sefna, along with the whole town, were burned. Abdoar told us there were only two boats docked there on the night of the attack, and since neither of them displayed lights, they may have gone unnoticed as the Valnar pillaged Alna. Then, in the morning, with both ships gone, it may not have been seen as worth the trouble to destroy the docks.

Whatever the reason, it was fortunate they survived; for without them we would not have had easy access to the shore. The *Tel* was fully loaded with supplies as was the *Ket,* which arrived from Eltec the morning we buried our dead; and Miku ordered rations to be distributed from both these ships as well as from the fishing boats in order to feed those in the camp. If the docks had been lost to us, this would have been very difficult to accomplish.

He also sent parties to search the farms around Alna to see what food may have survived, and Aarad and I volunteered to join them. We had been to the farm and knew that nothing remained standing as the barn and the house had been burned. Yet we also knew some of the vegetables could be salvaged from the garden, and this might be true on the other farms as well. If so, it would help to feed those in the camp who now lacked any source of food. But most of all we wanted to look for Huno.

When we returned with sacks of fresh vegetables and a hope of finding more—though we found no farm animals alive—we were sent out again the following day. This time we came back not only with food but with four men, three women and eight children all survivors who had been hiding in the hills. One of these was Ensoar who had gone with Tennep to warn the farmers near Crayoar.

After Boec told him what he had seen at the bridge, Ensoar recounted what had happened to them after they left Boec.

"We stopped at the three farms closest to Crayoar and told them they needed to get away as quickly as possible. They wanted to pack first, but we told them there wasn't time, that they needed to head for the South Hills and tell everyone along the way.

"They had seen the fires in Crayoar, and though they were confused as to what it all meant, they left quickly enough. One man sent his son on their nosha to warn other farms and another let Tennep and I take his nosha.

"At the fourth house we split up because those there argued with us. So Tennep stayed to convince them to leave while I went on to warn others. I never saw him again.

"About an hour after we left Boec at the bridge I began to see smoke rising behind me in different places. Then, when I was at a house close to the hills, the Valnar caught up with me. I ran into the fields and worked my way toward a forested area near by. A Valnar came looking for me, saw me and chased me almost catching me, but I made it into the woods just in time, and he didn't follow me.

"I hid in the woods until nightfall then made my way under the cover of darkness up into the hills where I hid while working my way toward the west and the sea. Along the way I met up with others, and this morning, because of our hunger, we decided to risk coming down into the valley to find food. It was fortunate that we did, because Idar saw us and brought here."

§ § §

The day after the mass burial, Miku called a meeting of all the captains of the boats and made plans to evacuate the survivors to Arganon. None of us were aware of this at the time as we were in shock mourning our losses; but it was fortunate he did this when he did, as events later proved.

That evening I sat with Boec, Shend and Aarad on the deck of the *Tel* as Mirranu slept in the hold below us. Zhoh, too, had joined us; and we began to talk of what was to come—of our futures, such as they were—as smoke from the cook fires in the camp drifted back towards Theo and Alna.

"We need to get out of here, we need to sail for Arganon as soon as we can," I told them.

"You're right," said Aarad, "there's nothing for us here. We need to join the others who escaped."

The Others, we had been calling them that for days; for they were the nameless ones who had escaped the carnage. Only Aarad and I knew for sure our loved ones were safe; for Shend told us it was dark when he had reached the cave where we had just buried our dead. He said fifteen to twenty men, women and children were hiding in it when he came there with Aarad's family. Yet he had immediately left them, leaving Seppan behind to keep watch at the cave's entrance while he went off to scout out a path to the docks so that they could escape.

When he returned to tell them the Valnar had left Alna, they all ran as fast as they could along the beach, being as quiet as possible. Once across the bridge, they hurried down to the ships at the docks. He remembered only hearing the voices of Alnat and his mother, but they had no living relatives in the camp. This was all he could be sure of, for he had reached the wharf first and alerted the *Kewl's* captain to the danger then boarded the *Mer* to tell Abdoar what had taken place while everyone else rushed aboard the *Kwel*.

Abdoar and two of his crew had also been asleep on the *Mer* and were, therefore, not aware of the Valnar's attack on Alna until Shend woke them. Once Abdoar understood how seriousness the situation was, he went to talk with the *Kwel's* captain to encourage him to leave the harbor as soon as he could and to tell him he would be taking the *Mer* to Kesset. By that time, those who had fled Alna were below deck; and so Abdoar had no idea who they were.

Besides the two ships docked at Alna, Abdoar told us there were about ten which managed to get away from the harbor at Sefna, yet he had no idea how many were on them. All he knew was that one of the ships was a yacht of the royal fleet, for it had hailed him and told him they were heading north to Arganon. He in turn had replied he was going to Kesset and wished them luck. Then the yacht pulled away into the darkness, and Abdoar never saw any of the other boats again.

"There's talk in the camp of staying here and rebuilding," said Zhoh, "but I think Idar's right, we should go."

"I talked to one man who sails on the *Von*," Boec told us. "He thinks we should make for the islands around Trohan and send a ship to Arganon to ask the Others to join us. He feels we'll be safe there since we'll be far from the mainland."

"Safe, yes," Zhoh replied, "but the islands can't support all those we have here. There's plenty of fish and even fruit; but we'd have no grain, and there's no place to plant crops if we did. No, we need to go to Arganon."

"But what if the king of Arganon won't take us in?" Shend asked. "I've talked to sailors from Arganon when they've come to the inn. They complain about him all the time."

"You're right," Aarad added. "I've overheard them myself at the inn many times. They say he's nothing like Shuman. He levies heavy taxes, and even Tenoar won't trade there because of the high tariffs he charges."

"We wouldn't have to stay there," said Boec. "We could leave and find some other place to live, even if we don't go to the fishing islands. But we do need to join the Others. Then we can decide."

Our talk continued on into the night as the stars burned brightly above us and the cook fires on the beach burned lower and lower. Yet I heard little of what was said, for my thoughts turned to Illiad and I wondered if she was watching the night sky as well and was thinking of me. Suddenly, a star shot across the sky landing far to the north in the hills toward Arganon, and I remembered Tuac and our talk that night long ago on the deck of the *Tel* the summer I went with him to Trohan. I wondered if the Valnar had carried away the star held in the king's palace and what they would do with it if they had, and this lead me to think of Tefnoar and those the Valnar had taken whom I was sure we would never see again.

"What do you think, Idar?" Boec's voice broke into my thoughts, and I realized I had no idea what they were talking about.

"I don't know," I said truthfully, "I wasn't listening. My mind wandered. Do you think we will ever see any of those the Valnar took?

"How could we," Aarad answered. "We have no idea where the Valnar came from, but it must be leagues away from here. So even if we stay and rebuild, I'm sure none of them will ever return."

"I can't imagine what their lives will be like," said Boec. "The way they treated Tennep. If they had taken Mirranu, I think I would have gone crazy. I would rather she was dead than to go with them."

This thought shocked me, yet Boec was right, there were fates worse than death. Illiad was safe, and I would be with her soon; but if this were not so, I didn't think I would want to go on living.

§ § §

In the morning, word was put out that there would be a meeting at noon to begin planning what we were to do; and for the rest of the morning no one talked of anything else. Arguments broke out, and tempers flared, as we all began to take sides over the various plans put forth; so that by the time of the meeting I feared nothing would be accomplished.

Miku ordered a platform to be built on the beach using water barrels and spare wooden planking from the ships. This would allow those wishing to speak to be more easily seen and heard; and so as midday approached, we all began gathering around it.

We did not have long to wait; for, as soon as it appeared everyone had made their way to the platform, Miku left the *Tok* with the other captains and walked through the crowd. When he reached the platform, he stood for a few moments greeting some of the newcomers then mounted the platform alone.

He stood in silence for a few minutes waiting until all were silent and all eyes were upon him. Then he began to speak.

"You all know why we're here," he said in a strong voice, one without a hint of the grief we all felt. "The Valnar's attack upon our homeland has left us with but two choices, we can leave Theo and seek a new life elsewhere or we can stay and rebuild what has been destroyed and start anew."

"But is it safe to stay?" came a voice from the crowd.

"That, my friend, I cannot say," he replied. "No one knows if we are safe here or not. The Valnar have left, but they may return. There is still plenty of plunder in Theo, so it is possible they may come back for it."

"And if they do," shouted another voice, "what will become of us?"

"That is the danger we all face," Miku told them. "If the Valnar come back, they will kill us or take us as slaves; for why should we be treated any differently from those we have just buried or those so cruelly taken by the Valnar?

"To stay is to face a constant threat of future invasion, for our lands are now undefended; and the Valnar may wish to use them for purposes of their own. That is why it is my belief we should leave since it will be far safer for all of us if we are not here in the event they do return."

"But what if they don't come back?" and this time it was the voice of Otna. "The land of Theo is sacred to the toha, if we leave, we abandon them; and what will become of us?"

"If Theo is sacred to the toha," asked Ensoar, "then why, priest, did they abandon us to the Valnar?"

"It is not for us to question the will of the toha," Otna replied.

"I think it is," came Ensoar's cold response. "You and the others in the temple served the toha well for hundreds of sun cycles, yet that has made no difference, has it? When the Valnar came, the priests died along with all the rest…except you of course," and at this he bowed feigning reverence to Otna and his office.

Otna flared in anger, "Do not mock the toha…"

"Oh, and what punishment will they inflict on us that the Valnar have not already accomplished?" asked Ensoar.

"Enough!" cried Miku. "We are not here to debate religion but to decide what we are to do about our futures."

"This is our future!" cried Otna. "If we abandon the toha, we will have nothing but sorrow and despair."

"We have that now," replied Ensoar.

At this, the crowd began to murmur general agreement.

"If we decide to leave," said a man I recognized as coming from Theo with his daughter the night the mass cremation began, "we can worship the toha elsewhere; but for now, what is needed is to determine whether we stay or go. And this must be put to a vote."

This was met with cries of assent until many began to chanting, "Vote, vote, vote," again and again.

Miku raised his hands as a sign that we should come to order, and the chanting stopped. Gradually all became quiet, and Miku again spoke: "It was my hope we could discuss this more before putting it to a vote."

"We have been debating this question for five days now," said Daeo, "ever since we came back from Trohan. I think we're ready, Miku. So let's vote and get it over with," and again the chanting began.

With hands again raised to establish order, Miku called out, "We have agreement on one thing at least."

As was our custom, he then called for us to divide ourselves into two groups according to how we wished to vote. "Those who want to stay come to this side of the platform," he said motioning toward Theo, "and any who wish to go should be on that side." This time he pointed to the docks.

Slowly we began moving one way or the other. At first there was some hesitation, for everyone knew this was to be the most important decision we would ever make since leaving meant abandoning all we had known our entire lives. Even Aarad and I were reluctant to walk toward the docks, for what we did affected everyone.

In the end, however, the two groups were about even which meant that nothing had been truly decided.

"What about you?" came a cry from the crowd. "How do you vote?"

"In my heart, I would go," he told us. "But I have lived as a Thean for my entire life; and if there are those who wish to stay, then I will stay and do what I can to rebuild."

And with that, he jumped from the platform and walked over to stand beside Otna.

Chapter IV

There was silence in the entire crowd. Otna smiled triumphantly, and Abdoar, who stood behind me, swore.

I could not believe what I was seeing, for all of us had come to accept Miku as our leader. We had never questioned this, and now we were left with the choice of leaving without him or changing our minds and throwing in our lot with those who wanted to stay in Theo.

Tenoar pushed past me through the crowd and jumped onto the now deserted platform. "This is not what we agreed upon yesterday, Miku. You promised to be with us, to lead us to Arganon."

"I never promised anything," Miku responded. "We all agreed it would be best if we went to Arganon, but I never promised to lead anyone. I truly believe it would be best if we leave here before the Valnar return, but if this many wish to stay, I cannot desert them. I had hoped to discuss this a little more, and that we could persuade the majority to leave with us, but this did not happen."

"And so what are we to do now?" Tenoar asked.

"I am not your king," came Miku's response. "If there are those who wish to leave, then they should go; and you and Abdoar can lead them back to Kesset…or north to Arganon as we decided yesterday."

At these words, the crowd again began to murmur; for we had not known our leaders had made any kind of plan. I wanted to go to Arganon, I desperately needed to go to Arganon; but even I felt betrayed. We had been called here to make decisions, and now it seemed these decisions had already been made for us.

At this, Hebdar also pushed his way forward and mounted the platform.

"Fine," he said. "If these wish to stay, then the rest of us are free to go wherever we please; and I for one do not plan on becoming a slave of the Valnar. So I will take the *Von*, and anyone who wants to go with me, back to

Serret or Kesset or Trohan or any of the other islands you want to settle on. From there we can send word to Arganon, and those who choose to follow us can come and live in peace far from any threat of the Valnar."

"Don't be a fool, Hebdar, we talked about this yesterday," said Tenoar. "There is no way the fishing islands can support any permanent settlements. They do not have the type of soil needed to raise crops. Kalhu will not grow there, so what would we eat?"

"We could trade."

"Trade what? Eltec has its own fishing fleet as well as orchards. They will buy nothing from those living on the islands," said Tenoar. "You need to face the truth, Hebdar, the only hope we have is to sail to Arganon and meet up with those who are already there. Then, with them, we can decide what to do and where to go."

"What do you know, merchant?" cried Hebdar. "Have you ever been on the islands?" Then he looked out on the crowd and said, "I leave tomorrow at first light, and anyone who wishes to go with me should be at the *Von* before then."

§ § §

As morning dawned, I stood on the deck of the *Tel* and watched as the *Von* and the *Nef* sailed out onto the bay heading toward the Narrows with about a hundred passengers and crew who had decided to settle in the fishing islands to the south. Their departure, however, left the nearly five hundred of us who still remained at Theo polarized; for over night those choosing to rebuild Theo and those wishing to leave and go to Arganon became two hostile camps.

All who planned on sailing to Arganon quickly moved to the ships which were making ready to leave within two days. This left the encampment on the shore to those staying behind.

Yet a problem arose immediately since most of the food stores were aboard the ships at the docks. For three days Aarad and I had gone on scavenging parties to gather what we could from the farms to the south of Alna, and these had been deposited in a common stockpile located in the main camp. However, because of the meeting the previous day, we had not gone out nor did we now since we planned on leaving as soon as possible; and the food supply on shore quickly ran low.

Otna came to the *Tel* in the middle of the morning and demanded that Tenoar turn over half of the supplies he held on board, and of course Tenoar refused.

"Everything on board my ship is mine, and I will be taking it to Arganon with me," he told Otna.

"You cannot just desert us here and leave us to starve," Otna replied angrily.

"It is your choice to remain behind, so fend for yourselves. When we leave, what will you do then?"

"If you do not willingly give us the supplies we need," Otna threatened, "we will be forced to take them from you."

"Go ahead and try," Tenoar told him.

"You forget, now that the *Von* and the *Nef* have sailed, we outnumber you."

"And you forget that the supplies you want are aboard a ship. Go, get your little army. Before you get back I will be anchored out in the bay. If you want what is mine, you will have to swim out and take it."

"Be reasonable," said Otna.

"He does not need to be reasonable," Miku said, and we all turned to see him walking toward the *Tel* from the *Tok* which was tied up a few paces down the wharf. "You have the land, and you have chosen to stay here and live off of it. When the fleet sails, they well have to make do with what they take with them."

"Whose side are you on?" asked Otna. "Yesterday you voted with us, yet today you take his side."

"I told you yesterday," Miku replied, "I believe with all my heart that we should leave here, for it is dangerous. I did not vote to stay, but I cannot so readily abandon those in need. Someone must remain as a voice of reason in all this insanity."

With that, Otna turned and walked angrily down the wharf to the camp.

"Should I pull away from the pier?" Tenoar asked.

"Be ready. You might have to," Miku replied. "I will talk to him. If we are going to stay, we will need a plan to feed everyone while we rebuild as will you once you head north."

"Be careful, Miku. Otna is young—too young—and what is worse, he has gained a following giving him too much power for one so young. Watch your back."

"I know," was all Miku said and then followed Otna down the wharf.

§ § §

We watched the shore for any sign that Otna would organize the camp against us, but all seemed calm well into the afternoon. Then, with only three hours of daylight remaining, a great disturbance broke out in the camp; and Tenoar made ready to pull out into deep water as did Elfad, the *Ket's* captain.

We cast off the lines mooring us to the pier and began pushing the ship away from it with our long poles. Yet before we could get far, we heard cries of: "Valnar! Valnar!" as three men raced towards us along the wharf.

Tenoar ordered us to hold, and we stood tensed waiting for the fastest of the group to reach the *Tel*.

"What is it," Tenoar called to the man who reached us first.

"There's a Valnar patrol there on the ridge of that little hill just south of Theo," he said pointing.

We all stared in shock, for we could just make out the dark figures of five or six men mounted on black nosha about a league away from the shore. Our greatest fear had come true. The Valnar had returned.

Chapter V

As we watched, two of the mounted men left the others on the top of the hill and began to ride toward the camp. At this, more and more of those remaining on shore raced down the pier pushing and shoving each other in an attempt to be the first to scramble aboard one of the waiting boats.

We cast a line to those on the pier, and as quickly as possible we again tied up the *Tel* and began taking on as many of those fleeing the camp as we could. Yet within only a few minutes we were forced to halt this crowding of our ship and send the panicking mob on to the ships waiting further on down the pier. We then stood tensely awaiting word to cast off. However, Tenoar held back, for we could now see that one of the approaching Valnar carried a green banner as a sign of truce.

We all watched the two Valnar enter the camp to be met by three men, one of whom we could tell for sure was Miku, but who the others were no one was able to make out.

"Do you think Otna is there with Miku?" I asked.

"Maybe," Aarad replied, "I didn't see him trying to get on board one of the ships."

"Well, if it is him there, he's braver than I thought," Tenoar said with a grin on his face. "I would have guessed the little pup would have run for his life at the first sign of a Valnar."

We waited ten, fifteen, twenty minutes. Finally the Valnar turned and rode quickly back up the hill to join the others waiting for them. The three men who had met with the Valnar also turned and walked through the camp then onto the wharf; and as they came nearer, we could see that Otna was indeed with Miku as was the man who had called for us to vote at the meeting the day before.

"Well, I'm impressed," said Tenoar. "I never thought he had it in him."

"Otna you mean?" I asked.

"Had him pegged as a coward from the first minute I saw him," Tenoar replied.

"Who's the other man with them?" Aarad asked.

"I asked about him after the meeting yesterday," Tenoar told us. "His name is Dennem. Came from Theo with his daughter, Egome, our first night back from Eltec. They say he was a wealthy merchant. Had some kind of a hidden place built into his house where he stored important things. He hid in it with his daughter. Saved their lives."

"What about his wife?" Aarad asked.

"Died two suns ago, so he has no one but his daughter," Tenoar replied. "I guess I better go see what Miku has to say." With that, he swung himself over the side of the ship onto the pier and walked away.

No one left the ships except for the captains who took Tenoar's lead and one by one joined Miku on the wharf. Since the *Tel* had been the first to return from sea, we were moored in the first berth; therefore, Tenoar asked Miku, Dennem, Otna and the other captains to meet on the deck of the *Tel*.

Quietly the crew and passengers made room for them to climb aboard, then everyone stood silently waiting to hear what the Valnar had to say.

"It is as I feared," Miku began, "the Valnar are not planning on leaving Theo. They now consider us a province of their empire and see everything, and everyone, as belonging to their king. If we resist, they will kill us; yet if we go willingly, they will treat us kindly...but sell us as slaves nonetheless. Those are the only choices they gave us."

"They can't be serious," said Abdoar. "There are only five or six of them."

"Eight actually, at least that is what they told us," Miku replied, "but they have weapons, and all we have are a few harpoons and fishing knives."

"I have a sword," Elfad added.

"We all know that will do no good," said Dennem. "Yes, there are only eight now, but they are here as the advance guard to set up a camp for the rest who will be arriving in two days. Our only hope is to be gone before they get here."

"But why did they leave if they were only coming back?" asked a man in the crowd.

"Otna asked that very question," Miku replied looking at Otna who said nothing. "They told us they needed more men to guard the prisoners at first until they weakened from hunger and exhaustion. The group that will return will bring slaves to harvest our fields. Those who surrender will be allowed to help. Then, in the winter, they will be transported elsewhere."

"Don't they realize all we have to do is sail away?" I asked.

"To tell the truth," Dennem replied, "they may not. Ships and sailing do not seem to have any meaning to them.

"You may be right," Tenoar added. "When I was an apprentice seaman, I traveled once to Shalmarra. I have heard of the Valnar. Their kingdom lies far from the sea, so the idea of traveling across water might well be foreign to them."

"Then we need to sail," said Abdoar, "now before any more come."

"I agree," Miku replied. "In fact even Otna now agrees with you."

At these words, Otna looked uncomfortable and stood with eyes cast down toward the deck. "The toha have failed us," he said, "or we have failed them. I do not know which. Maybe both."

"Well, in any event," Dennem told him, "we must leave Theo. The toha can be served elsewhere if need be, but we must be alive to do that."

"And free," added Abdoar.

"And free," said Miku nodding in agreement. "We sail, then, as soon as we can tomorrow…unless anyone objects."

When no one said anything, he added, "Good, then go back to your ships and tell those aboard what we have decided. If anyone wishes to surrender to the Valnar, they are free to do so; but if not, those who have things of value still on shore should retrieve them tonight. I do not think the Valnar will try to prevent us; yet if they do, it will be easy enough to return to the ships before they reach us. However, no one should go too far from the docks, or they could be captured."

§ § §

The last night I spent in Theo was one of the longest of my life. We had only two good hours of daylight left by the time the meeting on the *Tel* was over, and we had to make the best of it. Since there could be no fires lit on the beach that night, those who had personal possessions on shore quickly went back to the camp to gather them. Aarad and I were also sent with the other members of the scavenging parties to retrieve all the stores gathered over the past few days. These we loaded into the hold of the *Tok* as Otna, who planned to sail with Miku, insisted the food from the camp should go with him.

Fortunately, plans had been under way to leave and sail to Arganon, for the water casks were filled aboard all the ships. If this had not been done, it would have been highly dangerous to fill them now that the Valnar were close by, and to sail without fresh water could have been fatal.

At the arrival of the Valnar, everyone had panicked; and so before we could sail, the captains were forced to sort everyone out to be sure families, such as they were, had not been separated. They also needed to balance out the numbers on each ship to ensure none were overloaded.

Since the *Von* and the *Nef* had left for the fishing islands, there were nine fishing boats and two cargo ships. Into these we were forced to crowd almost six hundred men, women and children. Each fishing boat was allotted forty of these—including their own crews—leaving almost two hundred and forty survivors and crew members to be shared between the two merchant ships.

To make room for that many in the hold, we brought much of our cargo on deck and threw it overboard. In this we were aided by those who were to sail with us, and much of this was done well after dark.

Incredibly, everyone was sorted into their ships in little over an hour giving us enough time to cast off and anchor in the middle of the bay. There we spent the night with no lights allowed above deck so that we would not be seen from the shore.

§ § §

I had been given the third watch, a two hour time period in the middle of the night, which meant I did not sleep until I was off duty. Therefore, as soon as we anchored, I had gone below deck to find Boec, Shend and Mirranu in the small corner of the hold where they had been living since their return from Crayoar. It was not much, and afforded little privacy, yet for them it would be home until we found a permanent place ashore where we could live.

Since I was a member of the crew, I was allowed to keep my hammock in our quarters where we were already uncomfortably crowded as usual. This left the passengers—as we called them for lack of a better word—to make do among what was stored in the hold.

"I can't wait to get out of here," said Shend, "ever since I returned I've almost wished I'd gone with Aarad's family and not with Abdoar to Kesset."

"That's a fine thing to say," Boec told him a little angrily.

"I'm sorry, I didn't mean it that way," he replied. "It's just that…I don't know how to express it."

"You feel like there's nothing left," said Mirranu, "like you've no reason to go on, that if you'd died this nightmare would be over."

"Don't say that, Mirranu," Boec told her comfortingly. "We still have each other, and soon we will be out of here. We'll be in Arganon, and life will go on."

"Go on. How? What if they won't take us in? And if they do, how will we live? We've no money, nothing."

"There's always work to be had," Boec answered in a calm voice, "We'll get by."

"Is that all you can say? 'Get by,'" and she fell silent.

"Where's Aarad?" Shend asked in the awkward silence that followed.

"With Morek and Sepnoar," I told him.

"I guess everyone wants to be with family tonight," he replied, then he apologized, "I'm sorry, Idar. I didn't…"

"No…that's all right. I really should be with them I know, but I barely know Morek. Aarad and I have been like brothers since we were boys. Now, with my parents gone, he's the only real family I have. But even so I still feel I'm intruding when I'm around him and Morek."

"And you don't feel that way with us?" asked Boec.

"A little, yes, I think it's maybe because I don't know Morek; and he and Aarad have so much in common. I feel like an outsider at times."

"We're all outsiders," said Mirranu, "or at least we will be once we get to Arganon."

§ § §

The morning dawned cold with a fog on the bay, yet even before I came up from the hold the coldness had already gripped my heart; for I knew that this was to be the last time I would see my homeland again. I stood near the rail of the ship and looked to where Alna should have been, but only the wharf stood out in the hazy dampness.

I was chilled, both from the whiteness surrounding me as well as from the emptiness causing me to feel like the bones which lay in the cave by the shore. My mother had always worried I would not come home, that I would be buried far from Theo. Now it seemed she was right; for before the sun reached its zenith I would be gone, and Theo would be only a memory held in my heart as it is now here in this grave far from my beloved home.

Boec and Aarad came on deck and stood beside me in silence. After a while Aarad spoke, "Tenoar says we are to eat even if we don't feel like it so that we can keep up our strength. He wants no one too weak to sail the ship, but I don't see how I can keep anything down this morning."

"I know what you mean," said Boec.

"Did either of you get much sleep?" I asked.

"No," said Boec. "Mirranu and I stayed awake most of the night talking about our futures. I've said nothing 'til now, but the night the Valnar came I had asked her to marry me."

At this Aarad and I both smiled, something we had not done in days; but at the seriousness of Boec's expression we too grew somber.

"What is it?" I asked.

"She had said yes that night, but now she's not sure," he replied. "She feels we have no future…and I partly agree with her."

"That's foolishness," Aarad broke in. "Theo is dead, that's true, and there is no future for her; but we live on, and wherever we go, we take Theo with us and become her future.

"You must marry. You have to carry on. See how few children the Valnar have left us; and without children we will die out no matter where we go, and our heritage will die with us."

"Aarad's right," I told him. "Just be patient with her. When we reach Arganon and decide what to do, she'll change her mind."

"I hope you're right," he replied.

"I know I'm right, you'll see. Just wait 'til we reach Arganon."

§ § §

Aarad and I forced ourselves to eat some bread and a small kellec as Tenoar asked of us, and then began readying the ship to sail. By midmorning the fog began to lift, and most of those on board came on deck to say one last farewell before we sailed. Tenoar treated them kindly even though from time to time they were in the way, and many times we were forced to work around those who stood along the railing.

The lifting of the fog also allowed the Valnar to see the fleet anchored in the bay, and one of them rode down to the beach and then onto the wharf. From the end of the pier he tried to hail us, but we ignored him. Angered at this, he shot an arrow barely missing the *Son* which was anchored closest to the docks.

After this fruitless attempt, he turned around and rode back to their camp which we could now see pitched before the broken gates of Theo. Yet his actions gave us heart, for in some small way each one felt that what had just taken place was a victory—if only in spirit—against the tyranny of the Valnar.

Then all too soon we were at last ready to sail, and the ships began to raise anchor and move into their prearranged positions. When this had been completed, at a signal from Miku on the *Tok*, we began to move out.

The fleet slowly moved across the bay towards the Narrows and open sea with the *Ket* in the lead followed by the *Tok* and the other fishing boats. Aarad and I stood on the deck of the *Tel*, which was to bring up the rear, and raised the aft anchors. Then, a rare breeze from the shore suddenly blew across us bringing with it the acrid smell of smoke and death, but with it also came the faint yet piercing cry of an ashka.

My eyes quickly scanned the shore, and I sensed Aarad doing the same. At last I saw him, Huno, standing on the hill where I had sat a thousand times watching the boats and dreaming of sailing off to sea. I knew he would never last the winter, for he would sicken with the onset of autumn; yet as long as he lived, Alna lived; and my life, my world, would go on.

I wept. I wept for Huno, for Illiad, for my parents who should have died old and in their beds. I wept for Tuac who would never know the joys a wife can bring, who should have lived to hold grandchildren in his arms. I wept for Theo and those I never knew, and I wept for Aarad standing beside me on the deck of the *Tel* and for the pain I knew he also felt.

Now, in this tomb, I cannot weep. Yet I remember still, and in the very depths of my consciousness I shed the tears of loss only the naked soul can know; for all is gone, and I am alone.

Chapter VI

The passage through the Narrows was strange to me, for ever since I had gone with Tuac and Zhoh to Trohan that summer long ago I always felt an exhilaration, a sense that I was home as I came out onto the sea. But now this feeling was gone, replaced by an emptiness which only being home, being with with Illiad and my parents would ever fill.

We left the Narrows and headed north following the rest of the fleet. However, Torek, who was working in the rigging, sighted a ship far off on the southern horizon; and we quickly changed course to meet up with her. It was the *Sep* returning from Shentoar, and so we hailed her then pulled along side to inform her crew of what had happened.

At first they refused to believe us, for the shock of it all was far too great to comprehend; but Dennem, who was traveling with us and a friend of Kuren, came on deck and persuaded them to accept the truth. After talking for some time, the *Sep's* crew finally agreed their only choice was to join us and sail for Arganon. They also agreed to take thirty-five of our passengers in order to lighten our load.

This transfer took us over two hours; for, although the sea was calm, we had never done anything like this before. Each of the passengers had to be hoisted on ropes then swung from one ship to the next, and since most of them had had no real experience with the sea, they were terrified. In fact, it was difficult to find enough who would volunteer to be transferred, and in the end we had to force seven of them to go.

After making the transfer, we resumed our course to meet up with the rest of the fleet followed by the *Sep*. This took us another five hours, and it was nearly sunset before we were all together at the mouth of a large cove where we anchored for the night so that the *Sep* could take on passengers from the *Ket* as well as spare kegs of water from the other boats.

That evening I sought out Aarad and Morek and sat talking with them as well as with Dennem who had found sleeping space in the same part of the hold as Morek and Sepnoar. I felt comfortable with Dennem and his daughter being there, for I still found it difficult to be alone with Aarad's family even though he, Morek and Sepnoar were now all that I had until I was reunited with Illiad. Yet even after our reunion, they would continue to be part of the only family left to me now that my parents were dead. But as always, I felt I was intruding if I were alone with them.

As we sat and talked, I asked Dennem why he was not on the *Tok* with Miku.

"Because of Otna mostly," he replied. "Miku and I both felt Otna should sail with him so that Miku can keep an eye on him. Otna has gained too much power, far too much power, and it's better that Miku is with him to temper his ego.

"Yet we also felt I should sail elsewhere since I seem to have developed a following myself, and we did not wish it to appear that the three of us were some kind of ruling council, although Otna would wish this to appear so.

"And so, since the *Tel* was to sail last, I decided I would travel aboard her and be as far away from any outward appearance of power as possible. Besides, I have always had an affinity for merchant ships."

"In his youth, nodah was an apprentice on a merchant ship," Egome told us. "On the *Nar*," she added with obvious pride.

"The *Nar*?" I asked in surprise, "I've heard of her. Wasn't she lost at sea?"

"That was obviously after my time," he replied, "but, yes."

"And no one knows what happened to her?"

"The *Sep* last saw her as she left Shentoar," he told us, "but she was never seen again. When the *Sep* sailed three days later, they encountered some bad weather just south of Eltec. It has always been presumed that the *Nar* met a fierce storm and went to the bottom, but this we can never know for sure."

"It's stories like this that scare my mother," I told him. "She's..." I stopped, then continued, "...she was always afraid I would be lost at sea."

"Aarad told us your parents died in the attack on Alna, I'm sorry," and his voice held such warmth I had no doubt he truly meant what he said.

"Better they died than to be taken by the Valnar," I said, "but not the way they died."

All was silent for a time, then Aarad spoke, "I can see how the Valnar could destroy Alna and the other villages, even Sefna, but not Theo. How did they manage to get inside?"

"While I was living in the camp before we sailed," Dennem replied, "I had the chance to talk with two men who served as guards at Theo's east gate. They told me Shuman had allowed security to grow lax, and the Valnar had no trouble in the darkness putting ladders up against the south wall. They then overpowered the sentries and opened the gates allowing their army to simply march in and take the city. After that, we were helpless."

"What you say about Shuman is true," Morek said speaking from the dark corner where he held Sepnoar on his lap. "A man came to Teuwa just as Sepnoar and I were leaving. He had been a friend of mine as we were growing up, you remember him, Aarad, Jefta. He joined the army upon coming of age and was at Trenon, the fort on the head waters of the Ruha.

"He told us the Valnar came upon them unawares the night before the attack on Teuwa. He and his comrades were asleep and had no warning. Yet even with a warning, they still lacked the equipment to defend themselves as Shuman did not feel it necessary to spend money on the additional arms they needed. Jefta said that it was a miracle he managed to get out of the fort alive and into the forest where he hid until the Valnar left.

"Yet from his hiding place, he was able to watch the Valnar divide their army. Part of their cavalry were sent down the Ruha to attack Crayoar and Alna and part went north to Teuwa, and I presume on to Prion, while the main army headed for Theo.

"But why didn't Shuman know of the Valnar?" I asked. "Why wasn't he prepared?"

"After I left the *Nar*," Dennem replied, "I made several trips into the east to trade as I prepared to set up my shop in Theo, and I heard rumors of the Valnar just as I had in Shalmarra. Some said they were moving north, yet others denied this.

"Even after I opened my shop, I continued to hear rumors from those with whom I traded. So you're right, Shuman should have known; but as I said before, he had grown lax."

"But he was our king!" I cried. "It was his duty to protect us. We put out trust in him, and he failed us."

"And now we sail to Arganon and an even worse king," Dennem told us.

"Yet you encouraged us to sail to Arganon," said Morek.

"Not to live," Dennem replied, "we must find the Others and then leave.

There are places to the north where we can settle."

"But what of the Draygon?" I asked.

"The Draygon are peaceable enough," he told us. "We can get along with them."

"I don't know," said Aarad, "Idar and I have heard stories about them. I don't think I'd want to try."

"We may not have much of a choice," was all he said.

§ § §

In the morning, we weighed anchor and continued north, this time with the *Sep* stationed in the middle of the fleet between the *Lot* and the *Dul*. It was a clear day just like the previous one with only a light morning fog to give us a late start. But even though we did not leave the cove until late morning, we made good time; for the winds which blew from the south were fair, and it was felt we would reach Arganon by the next day.

I had never been to Arganon before, and I was intrigued by the coast as it gradually transformed from the rounded hills I had known all my life to the rocky jagged cliffs of the north country. The air also began to feel slightly cooler, though not really noticeable at first; but by the end of the day I felt a chill I had not felt the evening before.

"Colder, isn't it?" said Kebbit as he came on deck to throw a bucket of garbage overboard.

"You feel it too?" I replied.

"Sometimes in the winter," he told me, "if the weather's bad enough, it will snow in these latitudes, especially north o' Arganon."

"What's snow?" I asked.

"It's like rain," he replied, "only white like little pieces o' ashka wool. It stays on the ground like leaves when they fall from the trees in autumn.

"I've never heard of that before," I told him, "I'd like to see it."

"Oh, you'll see that and more if we settle in these parts. Arganon's a strange place that's for sure."

"In what way?" I asked.

"Lot's o' ways," he replied. "Didn't want to come myself. Been here before and didn't like it. Nearly jumped ship and went with Hebdar on the Von but changed my mind at the last minute."

"Why?" I asked.

"Too loyal to Tenoar," he told me.

"No," I said, "Why'd you think about jumping ship?"

"It's just too wild a country up here," he replied. "Too wild for me. I think we should just meet up with the Others and sail south. We can find land some place away from the Valnar besides those fishing islands."

"Well, I hope we stay long enough to see the snow," I told him.

§ § §

Again we stopped for the night since the captains feared sailing in the dark due to the rocks jutting out from the shore into the sea, and it was my good fortune not to have to stand watch; for a light fog set in as night wore on. Aarad, however, was not so lucky and had to do the second watch from sunset until close to midnight. Therefore, I sought out Boec and Shend and sat talking to them until Morek suddenly appeared out of the gloom saying he had been looking for me.

"Is something wrong?" I asked.

"That is for you to tell me," he replied motioning me to one side where we could be alone.

"I don't know what you mean," I told him.

"You are avoiding us," he said. "Aarad senses it. You know, I may be his brother, but we have not really seen each other since he left Teuwa over seven sun cycles ago. He and I were close as boys, but he has grown closer to you since he has lived in Alna; and now that you have married Illiad, you are my family as well."

"I'm sorry. I didn't mean to offend," I told him. "I've just felt a little odd…"

"You should not," he interrupted me. "We simply need to get to know each other. When we reach Arganon, when we are all reunited, we will be one family. I too have lost much. My wife and daughters are dead, but life goes on. It must be so with you as well. You may have lost your parents, but you have a family in us as well; so do not be afraid to join us, to talk with us. We need to get to know each other."

"I will," I told him.

"I must go back to Sepnoar," he said. "He is asleep, and I do not want him to wake up and find me gone. Since his mother and sisters have died he does not sleep well. Just join us when you can is all I ask," and he left.

After he was gone, I stood in the semidarkness of the hold and thought about what he had said. It was true. I had even said this before to Boec and

Shend. Illiad's family had become mine the day we wed; and now more than ever, when I was in need of the companionship of a family, I should be making the effort to get to know Morek and Sepnoar instead of drawing away from them and from Aarad who had grown to be like a brother to me over the past few sun cycles.

Finally, Boec came over to me, "Is something wrong?" he asked.

"He feels I should spend more time with them," I replied, "to try to get to know them and become a family. And he's right…but it's still so hard."

"You know," he told me, "in some ways you're lucky. You have a wife waiting for you in Arganon and in-laws; and all I have left is Shend."

"You have Mirranu."

"She's still so distant," he replied. "I'm not sure I'll ever have her, not really. It's like a part of her will always be in Crayoar, and that part keeps her away from me."

"I remember what my mother once said," I told him. "One night, it was the night I agreed to apprentice with Tenoar, she talked about her mother and how she never got over my grandfather's death, how her grief went on day after day until she died young not being able to overcome it. Is that the way it will be with us? Will we never forget the horror of what's happened?

"My mother always feared I wouldn't come home. That I'd be lost at sea, and she'd never see me again like her father. And now my parents are both lost to me, what's left of them lying in that cave back in Alna, a tomb I will never be able to visit. Yet I'm expected to go on."

"We're all expected to go on," he said. "You and Aarad told me that a couple of days ago, just before we left Alna. If we don't go on, those we left behind won't go on.

"We're their children, we're Theo. It's our duty to survive and build a new life for ourselves and all who will come after us. That's the way things have been since the beginning of time.

"I have to believe that when a thousand cycles of the sun have past, a part of me will be there in the far distant future, that someone will be alive just because I was alive today. And if that comes to pass, then our parents and everything we left behind in that cave back in Alna will live on."

§ § §

The next morning, with only a light fog, we set sail as early as possible hoping to reach Arganon by nightfall. "We have to be inside the harbor 'fore the sun sets," Burog told me, "or they won't let us in."

"Why's that?" I asked.

"'cause ol' Glennoff, their king, is a greedy man," he replied. "He has a huge chain stretched across the entrance of the harbor which his men raise from the bottom each night with a crank. Keeps any ships from leaving and not paying his tolls."

"I've heard stories Glennoff's a cruel man," I told him. "Do you think we should stay in Arganon?"

"No, and neither does Tenoar," he said. "I don't think Glennoff will let us stay neither. All of us showin' up on his door without work and no hope of payin' taxes. He won't like that at all."

"But where should we go?" I asked. "Kebbit thinks we should meet the Others and then go south to the fishing islands, but we don't have to, maybe we could go to Eltec or even Shentoar."

"No," he replied, "that won't do neither. Those who went to the islands is fools. Those islands can't support this many, and we've no idea at all how many more's already there in Arganon. Eltec won't take us in any more than Arganon. And Shentoar, you remember what that was like. Would your really want to live among them?

"No, our only hope is to find a place of our own. But where? I have no idea."

"What if we went north? There's plenty of land north of Arganon. I've heard about it from the Arganese sailors at the inn back in Alna," I told him.

"I've heard them same stories," he replied. "But the land's not free. It may not be civilized, but them that live there won't take to us just comin' in and takin' over their land. We'd have to fight 'em for it most likely. Do ya' think we're ready for that?"

"If that's the only choice we have," I told him, "then I guess we'll have to."

§ § §

As the day progressed, all of us grew more and more nervous with the anticipation of at last finding the Others and learning who had survived. Even Aarad and I, who knew our family was safe, had a deep dread in the depths of our hearts; for we knew for sure that only Alnat and his mother still lived out of all those we had known.

The shoreline remained rocky with high cliffs and no sign of a harbor or any other safe haven. And, even though it was only the end of the last cycle of the summer moons, and autumn was yet to come, the late afternoon air still had a slight chill to it, one unlike what we had been used to at home.

Then, towards evening, with about three hours of good light left to us, we at last rounded a headland jutting out into the sea and caught a glimpse of Arganon crowning a high cliff only a few leagues away. Unlike Theo, which was built on hilly though fertile land, Arganon had been constructed on a bluff overlooking the sea next to a bay which served as its harbor; and as we saw it for the first time, it appeared menacing since it was not only a major city but a fortress as well.

Since the *Tel* was the last ship in the fleet, the rest of the ships were spread out in front of us with the *Ket* as lead nearly two leagues away. As we watched, the *Ket* suddenly turned and headed back towards us followed by the *Tok*, the *Mer*, the *Son* and the *Lot*. When they reached the *Sep*, they stopped and waited for the rest of the fleet to catch up.

We knew something was wrong, but what it was we had no idea until we at last reached the flotilla of ships fighting to stay together. When we did, the *Ket,* which had been along side the *Tok*, maneuvered over to us as Tenoar stood tensely on deck with Dennem at his side waiting to talk with Elfad, the *Ket's* captain.

"What's wrong?" he called as soon as we were within hailing distance.

"It's Arganon," came the grim reply. "She's been sacked. It's just like Theo."

Chapter VII

The news stunned us into silence for a few moments, then the shock of it turned to panic; and outcries could be heard all across the deck of the ship. As I looked across at the *Ket,* and then at the other ships close to us, I could see signs of grief everywhere as women, even men, cried and held one another; yet somehow what I had just heard seemed to have no effect on me, and I stood in a cold dispassionate silence for a few moments.

Gradually, however, the realization of what this could mean touched the inner core of my being, and I had to force myself not to cry out in anguish. I had lived these past ten days with a hope of seeing Illiad again, of holding her in my arms and knowing that in spite of everything life could go on. Yet as I came to accept the truth that this might not be, it seemed to me life truly ended for me; and now, in the true death of the grave, I realize this was true; for at that moment, as a cool breeze gently ruffled my hair, the will to live began to slowly ebb from me.

Aarad swung from the rigging on a line and landed on the deck then ran to my side; and we both stood in silence listening to Tenoar, Dennem and Elfad as they decided what we should do.

"Are you sure of this?" asked Dennem.

"You can't see it from here," Elfad replied, "but the wall at the top of the cliff is charred with part broken away; and there seems to be no sign of life, no smoke rising from any part of the city, no ships coming and going from the harbor. It's nearly nightfall. There should be a lot of traffic trying to get in and out of the bay before that cursed chain is raised."

"Could you see into the harbor?" Tenoar asked.

"We didn't get close enough before we turned about," he replied. "Miku wants to go on. He says there's a small harbor town close to seven leagues north of Arganon. We could stop there if need be."

"Terhal," said Tenoar. "Yes, I know it. The bay would be big enough to hold the fleet if Arganon is truly sacked as you say. But it may not be safe. There could be Valnar close by."

"Are you sure it's the Valnar?" asked Elfad.

"Who else, if the city has been taken," replied Dennem.

"Then we sail on?" asked Elfad.

"We sail on," replied Tenoar, "and stop at Terhal if Arganon is unsafe."

After receiving the order to sail, the *Ket* slowly turned and resumed a northward course toward Arganon; and the rest of the fleet followed. It was an agonizing trip of nearly three quarters of an hour before we saw any signs that something catastrophic had happened to Arganon; yet as we approached the city, we knew Elfad's report was true.

Arganon sat atop the bluff on which it was built as a ghostly shell of all it once had been. We saw her blackened walls partly broken away; and as we watched, one huge chunk of the seaward wall crumbled and sent a cascade of rocks silently into the sea. Elfad was right, there was no sign of life, for the city stood like the Theo we had left behind and became a grim reminder of all we had lost only a few days before.

As we neared the harbor, we could see the chain used to keep ships at dock until morning still in place; and the burned and charred remnants of the port told us none of those who were unlucky enough to be at anchor escaped. If the Others had reached Arganon before the Valnar came, they would have been doomed along with all who lived in the city.

The *Tel* sailed silently past what remained of Arganon with nothing but the sound of the wind in her sails to break the quiet of the moment. I looked away from the harbor and saw the *Ket* maneuvering in dangerously close to the shore, then a small speck left her and headed toward the beach. After a few minutes this dot returned to the ship, and the *Ket* resumed her course for Terhal.

I had no idea what this meant, and looked back at the harbor we were now leaving behind. "Tohana," I said to myself, "let them be alive. Let them be safe somewhere. If only they were late." But the fear within me told me my prayers were of no value, for what had happened had already taken place. If they had been there, I would never see my wife again.

§ § §

We reached Terhal as the sun was setting and anchored just inside the enclosure of the inlet forming Terhal's natural harbor; yet, though Terhal had been a fishing port much like Alna, very little evidence remained standing to tell us this. Here and there blackened chimneys could be seen, and only the stumps of what had been its docks remained above the waterline.

The fishing boats, since they were smaller, had all anchored further in leaving the three merchant ships to guard the entrance to the harbor. When we arrived, we could see two small boats moving among the fishing boats in the process of gathering the captains to a meeting which, it appeared, would be held on the deck of the *Ket*.

This was confirmed almost immediately when Kuren, the captain of the *Sep*, hailed us and instructed us to send Tenoar and Dennem in our small boat to the *Ket* as soon as we could. We lowered our boat as quickly as possible, and Tenoar ordered me to come with him as the oarsman.

When we arrived on the *Ket*, all of the other captains as well as Otna were already on board. These stood near the main mast in a tight group with a man I had never seen before standing in the middle of them. Around them stood a crowd containing most of the *Ket's* passengers all silently pressing in as closely as possible in order to hear everything that went on.

Tenoar and Dennem walked over and joined the group of captains each nodding in quiet greeting to the others present then waited for someone to speak first. This was Elfad, for as captain of the *Ket*, it fell to him to open the meeting.

"You have all seen it for yourselves," he told us. "Arganon has been destroyed, and we have no hope of refuge here; so we need to decide what to do. But before talking of that, I think you should hear from Penepe," and he placed his hand on the shoulder of the stranger standing next to him. "We picked him up off the beach about a league north of Arganon. He and his wife and two daughters were on their way here to Terhal. They lived through the sacking of the city and can tell us what happened." With that, he stepped to one side and waited for Penepe to speak.

"As Elfad told you," the man began, "my name is Penepe; and I am a tailor by trade. My wife and I lived in Arganon with our children, but I grew up here in Terhal. Today we decided to go back to Terhal and see if any of my family were still alive since there was nothing for us in Arganon. It is terrible there in the city. There is little to no food, and the dead lie piled in the streets. We just had to get out..."

"I know how bad it has been for you," said Dennem kindly. "I, too, have lived through the Valnar's sacking of my home city. I am sure Elfad has told you what happened at Theo and why we are here. So could you please tell us about Arganon. When did the Valnar attack?"

"Ten days ago," he replied, "it was the twenty-second day of the cycle of moons. They attacked the harbor in the middle of the night but could not breach the city's defenses...not at first anyway. It took two days, but in the end they managed to get over the wall and open the gates. Then it was killing and burning and..."

"I know," said Dennem. "It was terrible for us as well. I myself had a secret room in my home where my daughter and I hid."

"It was the same for me," Penepe told us, "I had a storeroom under my shop where I could keep my cloth dry. When we saw that the Valnar made it through the walls from the harbor, we hid there."

"Have the Valnar left Arganon or are they still there?" Miku asked.

"Oh, they are gone," Penepe told him. "They left five days ago on the twenty-seventh. My wife and I stayed in the city trying to find her family but left this afternoon. We could stand it no more."

"If the Valnar have been gone five days," said Miku, "then they could be back any day now."

"What?" gasped Penepe.

"Yes, my friend," Miku told him, "the Valnar will most likely come back. They returned to Theo the day before we left, so I am sure they will return here as well; and we must be gone before they do."

"You say the Valnar attacked the harbor on the night of the twenty-second?" Dennem asked turning again to Penepe. "Are you sure?"

"Yes," Penepe replied, "I am sure because we had just celebrated my oldest daughters laryat, though now she cannot wed; for her fiance's family is gone, dead or carried off."

"If the Valnar attacked the harbor here on the night of the twenty-second," Dennem told us ignoring Penepe, "and the Others left Theo on the nineteenth, then it is possible they were in the harbor when it was attacked."

"Did a large fleet arrive in the harbor on the day of the attack?" Miku asked Penepe.

"I don't know," he replied. "I never concern myself with what goes on in the harbor."

"But surely there would have been talk," said Elfad. "If that many ships had arrived at one time and with the story they had to tell, word must have spread. You heard nothing?"

"No," Penepe told us, "I heard nothing. But we were celebrating."

"It took us three days to get here," Otna pointed out. "It should have taken them the same amount of time. They must have been here."

"But it is possible they arrived after the chain was raised," said Poran, captain of the *Bak*. "If they did, they would have spent the night outside the harbor and sailed away when they saw the city was under attack."

"That is true," Miku added. "But as Otna has just said, it took us three days to get here, and on two of those days we started late. Leaving at night on the nineteenth day of the moons cycle would have given them enough time to reach Arganon before sunset."

"Yet, what it all comes down to," Tenoar remarked, "is that we cannot really know this for sure. They could have been in the harbor, and most likely they were; but it is also possible they are still alive somewhere."

"If they are alive," said Sennec who captained the *Lot*, "they didn't go south or we would have sighted them. So they must have headed north."

"Then we should go north," added Abdoar. "If they were captured by the Valnar, then it's done with. But if they are alive and free we'll find them up north somewhere."

"So what you are saying is," said Otna, "we should just sail off into the north country with only a hope of finding the Others. That is insane. Even if they did sail north, they could be anywhere. How can we expect to find them in all that vast territory?"

"Because they will do what we will do," answered Miku. "They will sail along the coast looking for a good place to make landfall, a place where they can settle and build a new life.

"Abdoar, you said the ship that hailed you on the night of the attack told you they were headed for Arganon. They expect us to follow them, so they are not going to hide from us."

"Miku is right," said Poran.

"I agree," added Sennec.

"Then we should put it to a general vote," Dennem suggested. "Each captain can go back to his ship and explain what went on here. After coming to an agreement, we can meet back here in the morning to tally the votes."

"But whatever we do," added Abdoar, "we need to resupply the ships. We must refill the water casks tomorrow and send out parties to look for any supplies that might still be around. Are there farms about?" he asked turning to Penepe.

"Yes," he replied, "the land off to the east is flat and fertile. Some of the best farmland in all Arganon can be found there."

"Then we'll look there tomorrow," said Abdoar.

"Is it then agreed we should vote on what to do?" asked Miku. And a murmur of consent arose from all the captains. "Good," he said, "then we will meet back here tomorrow just after first light."

With that, the meeting broke up; and Tenoar, Dennem and I headed for the boat to return to the *Tel.*

"Tenoar!" came Abdoar's call. "Could ya' take me and Poran back to our ships? Idar here is strong enough to row us all."

Tenoar agreed, and we all climbed down the ship's rope ladder to our awaiting boat. After casting off, we moved silently across the calm waters with each man thinking his own thoughts. No one talked much, and this gave me time to consider what I had heard.

They were right. I had to believe they were right. Somewhere up north the Others had found a place and were waiting for us. But deep inside of me I knew this was not true, and the conflict this caused tore me apart.

It was the thirty-second day of the moons cycle, and all three moons would be full in five days, so there was sufficient light to find both the *Mer* and the *Bak* and then return to the *Tel*. When we climbed onto the deck, the crew and all of the passengers were waiting for us.

"What happened?" Aarad asked as he and Boec walked over to me.

"Tenoar will explain," was all I said; and the second meeting of the night began.

Chapter VIII

A majority of those on board the *Tel* agreed that our only hope was to sail north; and when the captains met the next morning and compiled all the votes, it was decided that we should go north as soon as possible. Since the Others would have hardly any supplies on board, they would be slowed down in trying to scavenge for food along the way. And so, as Abdoar had suggested the night before, we began to stock our ships with everything we could find.

We were fortunate in two ways, for we found a cache of small boats in a little cove of the inlet forming the harbor. All of them had lines with burn marks on them, and it was determined they must have been moored to the pier when it was set afire. As the lines burned, the boats were set free and drifted away from the wharf and into the cove.

Though there were only seven boats, having them allowed us to move supplies more quickly from the shore to the waiting fleet. It also allowed us to transport crewmen and passengers more easily, and Mirranu quickly took advantage of this and left the *Tel* to travel on the *Ket* where many of the survivors from Crayoar were staying.

Boec was heartbroken by this, but helping us search for supplies kept his mind off Mirranu, at least during the day. In fact it was Boec's skills as a miller which provided us with our second good fortune; for when we found the ruins of the village mill, he was able to locate a stone cellar filled with sacks of unmilled kalhu as well as flour. We were glad enough of the flour, but Boec pointed out that the kalhu could be used as seed grain for spring planting in the days ahead, after we found a place to live.

We also found survivors, or rather they found us; for about midday on our second day at Terhal a half-starved young man about my age who told us his name was Telleg walked into our encampment on shore. With him came Marna, an old woman, and her three grandchildren: Topan, Ernoar, and Setlat.

Telleg told us the Valnar had ridden into their valley ten days before using a road which crossed the hills separating Terhal from Arganon twenty leagues east of the village. Unlike at Theo or even at the harbor of Arganon, the Valnar did not at first pillage and burn but rounded up all those who lived on the farms around Terhal and forced them into the village. They then went house to house forcing everyone out of their homes and into the center of the town.

After everyone had been gathered together, the Valnar separated the young from the old, the weak from the strong, roping together all who would be fit to endure the forced march to slavery. They then herded the rest into a storage barn near the wharf; and, when all were inside, they set it afire.

Telleg had been selected for deportation, but somehow his ropes came loose, and he managed to slip away unnoticed. He fled into the fields north of Terhal and made his way into the hills where he found Marna who had gone to pick berries with her three grandchildren in the early morning.

The five of them had lived on what they could find in the hills fearing to come back to the village. But they had seen our fleet sail into the harbor the day before and felt it would now be save to return.

Having told us their stories, and given us the lay of the land, they were taken aboard the *Tel* and given food as well as a place to rest, such as could be found in the hold. Yet their story proved useful; for it not only explained why we found no bodies strewn about the ruins of the village, it also assisted us in finding provisions.

The surrounding farms were a rich source of vegetables, many already being harvested by the villagers; and we were even lucky enough to discover a pasture with a small herd of gamu which had not been taken by the Valnar. These we slaughtered for the meat since we had aboard our ships only dried fish brought back from the islands by the fishing fleet.

That night was very somber, for we were each left to wrestle with our conflicting thoughts. Each of us tried our best to believe the Others were at that moment safe and waiting for us to find them. Yet we also had to face a reality that told us this was not so, that they had been in the harbor and had been killed or taken prisoner by the Valnar.

I remembered Tefnoar, Ulanna, Sharn, and Boec's story of how cruelly the Valnar had treated them and Tennep as well as the story I had heard that day from Telleg. Then I thought of Seppan and Illiad being led away on ropes; starved and beaten; forced to walk leagues in the hot sun to reach a place of slavery; and I tried to put such thoughts out of my mind. But no matter how I tried, I could not clear these horrible pictures from my mind; and that night, when I finally slept, I saw Illiad crying because Huno was dead.

§ § §

The next morning we again went out to gather food. There were six of us this time: Boec, Shend, Aarad and myself, and we were joined by Egome and her friend Lenyana. A farm had been located about a league away from the harbor with a small orchard of palne which were ready to be picked, and so we went there with sacks to gather the fruit.

It was a warm day, warm for that northern climate, one almost like the days we had known at home in Theo; and we talked as we worked, and even laughed, forgetting for a time the uncertainty hanging over us. Then, as we were nearly finished filling our sacks, Lenyana suddenly cried out, "Tohana," and pointed in the opposite direction from the way we had come.

As we looked, we saw two mounted Valnar coming down the road, their black nosha at a slow walk. Quickly, we dropped what we were doing and ran to the side of the orchard where there was a stand of bushes which gave us cover, and we hid there barely breathing for fear we would be discovered.

Panic began to build up in me. The Valnar were heading for the harbor and would find the fleet. But worse, they had cut us off leaving us no way to return to the ships.

Yet our horror increased when the Valnar stopped right in front of the orchard, and one of them dismounted and walked in among the trees about fifty paces away from the road carrying his helmet which he dropped on the ground in order to relieve himself. Watching this simple act enraged me, for I saw no reason why he should be allowed to have this private moment when those he had taken prisoner were denied all dignity and were roped together in packs like animals.

Some form of insanity within me seemed to take over my body, for not realizing what I was doing, I leaped to my feet and ran toward him with all of the hatred and anger I had felt over these past days burning within me. I saw him as the one who had burned my home and killed my parents, slaughtered Tuac and Leyhah on their doorstep, dragged away those I had known, and now had deprived me of my beloved wife.

"Idar, no!" Boec called as soon as I moved, and his cry made the Valnar turn in surprise.

He stood no more than ten paces away, and I was able to reach him just as he drew his sword. Ramming him at full force, I knocking him off balance; and he fell. Instantly Shend, Boec and Aarad were upon him holding him down; and Shend grabbed a large rock lying nearby and brought it down on his head.

We heard movement and jumped up just as the second Valnar came in under the trees, his sword drawn, a look of hatred on his face. He looked at his dead comrade, and said something in his language which must have been a curse. Yet he did not move, and this proved to our advantage.

I quickly grabbed up the dead Valnar's sword lying at my feet and stood there challenging the other one to come to me. At that moment there was no fear in me, and I did not care if I lived or died. If I could only take this man with me, my death would be worth it; for he symbolized to me all we had been forced to endure these past days, and I wanted vengeance.

Shend, Boec and Aarad quickly picked up rocks; and I saw Lenyana and Egome out of the corner of my eye as they emerged from the bushes with a rock in each hand. The Valnar took it all in and took a step backward, a slight look of fear coming onto his face. I advanced one step and stopped. He took another step backward then bolted for his nosha with me in pursuit.

I had no idea how to use the sword in my hand, so I grabbed the hilt like a club and raised it above my head. At that moment, a hail of stones sailed over me, and two of them hit the retreating Valnar. One struck his back and the other his helmet causing him to fall to his knees.

As he tried to get up, I was on him and brought the sword down on his back full force knocking him flat on the ground. He instinctively rolled over, but at that moment a second barrage of stones fell upon him, one hitting him in the face. He cried out in pain; and, quickly turning the sword in my hands to use it like a huge knife, I plunged it into his stomach just where his breast plate ended.

There was blood everywhere; and I turned aside three steps, fell to my knees and emptied the contents of my stomach. Aarad and Boec rushed to my side, "Are you all right?" Aarad asked.

"I'm fine," I replied and was sick again.

At last I stood up and wiped my mouth on the sleeve of my tunic, "We have to get out of here," I said. "We have to warn the fleet."

We quickly retrieved our sacks of palne and stripped the belts from the two dead Valnar placing the swords back into their sheaths. When we reached the road, Shend noticed spears attached to the sides of the saddles on the nosha.

"We could use those," he said and made a move toward the closest of the nosha. But instantly the animal reared up, then lowered its head pointing its horns threateningly at Shend.

"He is definitely not Heshel," he said, and we all laughed.

"Come on, leave them," Boec told his brother. "It's not worth it."

"Boec's right," I said, "Let's get back to the fleet."

§ § §

As we hurried back to the harbor, we warned those we saw along the way; so that by the time we reached Terhal there were about twenty of us in all. The word Valnar brought panic to all on shore, and many began fighting to get into the small boats. Yet Miku, Tenoar, Abdoar and Menepe, the *Zet's* captain, managed to maintain order.

It took us three trips to carry everyone who had been ashore back to the ships, and the first to go were those who were less brave. The captains and those willing to stay and guard the supplies we had gathered remained on shore during the first two runs, with Abdoar and Menepe giving orders. Miku and Tenoar were then free to question us about what had happened, and they seemed very impressed with our tale of how we had overcome and killed the two Valnar.

In fact, as the story of our battle with the Valnar spread through the fleet over the next few days, we all became heroes of sorts; and even Egome and Lenyana were looked upon with great respect. The two swords we had taken from the Valnar were hung with great honor in the hold of the *Tel*, and when we sailed the next morning, Elfad insisted we take the lead position while the *Ket* took up our former spot at the end of the fleet.

Yet that night, as we gathered in the hold to talk over the days events, we felt safe from any attack by the Valnar. The patrol would not come back, and another would be sent out to look for it. But even if the second patrol found the fleet that night, there was nothing the Valnar could do to us; and in the morning we would be gone, sailing north, to be forever free of them.

"The Valnar cannot follow us," Dennem said. "They have no ships, and even if they did, our small numbers would be of little consequence to them."

"But what if we start a settlement someplace and they come later?" Morek asked.

"It is unlikely they will," Dennem replied. "We have questioned Penepe, and he tells us that Terhal is the last outpost of Arganon. Beyond this point there is nothing to the north, at least nothing civilized. Fifteen leagues north of here there is a river, and the territory of Arganon ends there. Those who live on the other side are uncivilized, mere savages.

"The Valnar cannot simply move in at night and surprise them as they did us. There are no cities, no great wealth for the taking. No, they will be stopped here at Arganon, the last Kroemaeon outpost.

"All we need do, then, is settle farther north, and the Valnar will not know of us. There we can live in peace."

"Among the Draygon?" I asked.

"Actually, Penepe called them the Tenyah. He had never heard of the Draygon."

"And you've never heard of the Tenyah?" Shend asked.

"No," Dennem replied. "Have you?

"No," he replied, "the seamen from Arganon never spoke of them. All they ever talked about were the Draygon. Do you think they're the same? I mean, could they just have two different names?"

"That's possible," Dennem told us, "but I doubt it."

"Why's that?" asked Boec.

"Because the Draygon have always been spoken of as peaceable," he replied. "I have never encountered them myself, but being a merchant I have talked with those who have. The Draygon may be primitive, but they have always been willing to get along with those they encounter, at least they are willing to trade.

"Yet from what Penepe tells us—and he was born and raised here in Terhal—the Tenyah are warlike. They fear the military strength of Arganon and keep to their own side of the River Kalnar, yet they will let no one cross over to them and have had no dealings with Arganon."

"So that means the Others would be attacked by them if they tried to make landfall," I said.

"Most likely," Dennem replied, "and us as well, so we must take care in the days ahead."

We talked more of what lay ahead of us to the north until Aarad joined us when he was relieved from watch. Then one by one we excused ourselves and went off to find solitude in sleep.

But again that night I dreamt of Illiad sitting in the main room of the home we planned to build in Alna. She was talking to my parents, yet I heard nothing of what was said. Even so, my mother seemed pleased by her words and laughed and clapped her hands.

It was this laughter which awoke me leaving me to lie in the darkness of our crew quarters waiting for the dawn. As the night passed, I heard nothing but the sound of those sleeping around me and the gentle touch of the waves against the sides of the *Tel;* and all the while I longed for sleep to overtake me, so that I might again dream of Illiad.

Chapter IX

The sun rose on the morning we left Terhal as it had when we left Theo for the last time. It broke through a morning mist to illuminate the ruins of what had been the lives of men, women and children now dead or carried off. And as its warming rays reached the bay and ate away the light fog resting on the water, we silently sailed away.

Aarad and I stood on the deck of the *Tel* raising the anchors as we had done that morning just five days before. Yet this time there was no plaintive ashka cry but only the calling of sea birds which nested in the rocks near the harbor's entrance. There was no acrid smell of death, for time and the late summer rain which Telleg told us had fallen two days after the burning of the village had refreshed the land. It had washed clean this sad and empty place condemning it and all that had taken place here to become lost and forgotten as the ages of the world went on.

We worked in silence, going through the motions we had done so many times before. There was no need to talk, for we knew our duties well; and on the deck as in the rigging all remained in silence save for the sounds the ship made and the wind tugging at her sails.

Once our anchors were on deck and the sails had been raised, we began to move slowly across the tranquil waters forming Terhal's harbor. Aarad and I secured the anchors storing them in their locker at the stern of the *Tel* along with their lines which we coiled next to them. After this we checked to be sure the small boat was lashed securely to the deck then covered it with a tarp.

Then, as we passed through the narrow opening of the inlet, we stood silently for a few moments watching as the other ships got under way. In my mind I saw the two Valnar lying dead in the orchard no more than two leagues away; and even though I felt justice had been served for all they had done to us and to the villagers of Terhal, I could not help but wonder how those they had left at home would feel when these two men did not return.

At last we were out of the harbor, past the silent rocks guarding its entrance, heading north into an unknown world and a future of uncertainty. The rest of the fleet slowly followed us one by one to form a long procession of ships, all that possibly now remained of the Theo we had known but a cycle of the moons before. Our hope, our silent prayer, was to find the Others and together with them rebuild in some quiet corner of these northern lands the lives we once had known. Yet there was a fear filling our souls with agonizing torment that this hope would never come to pass.

Aarad and I went below once we were out to sea since our duties were at an end—he to seek out Morek and I to our crew quarters just to be alone. It was dark in the hold with only a few lamps lit and darker still in our cabin in the stern, yet I still could find my seaman's trunk as well as the ribbons I had bought for Illiad in Eltec.

I took them out and held them in my hands trying to picture her smiling as I gave them to her. Then, in the silence of that room with nothing but the sound of the waves against the *Tel*, I spoke to her and promised that one day these ribbons would be hers; and when she wore them, they would prove my love for her.

§ § §

As midday grew close, we reached the Kalnar, a river about the size of the Ruha, which flowed directly into the sea without the benefit of a bay. It cut the beach in half and had thrown rocks and debris out into the water at its mouth for nearly half a league so that we were forced to head out to sea in order to avoid grounding the ship.

Then, as we turned back towards the coast, and sailed along its rocky shore, we looked for any sign of life, for any indication the Others might have been here. Yet in this we were disappointed; for as the day went on, and as the next day passed as well, we saw nothing to encourage us, to give us hope that those we sought had passed this way.

As the sun set on the third day out from Terhal, the sky ahead of us darkened, yet we sailed on. The coast north of the Kalnar remained just as inhospitable as the coast south of Arganon with high jagged cliffs resting on the shore of the sea; yet here there were no huge rocks jutting out into the water, and so we dared to sail at night with a helmsman to steer assisted by a watchman who scanned for any signs of life along the shore.

Each ship kept watch in this manner with two men constantly on duty throughout the night, and so there were twenty-four sets of eyes surveying the shore at all times looking for any place where the Others could possibly have made landfall. Yet we saw nothing despite the added light given by the moons now waxing full.

It was the last night of the moons cycle, and summer was ending. With dawn would come autumn, and already the night air was far colder than I had known on such nights at any time throughout my life. And so I stood watch wrapped in a sea cloak Illiad had made as a gift for me, and wearing it helped me to feel close to her even though we were apart.

As the moons passed their zenith in the night sky, the stars above the rocky cliffs along the shore seemed to grow brighter; and I remembered my promise to Illiad made on a night like this just before I left on my first voyage on the *Tel*. A warmth filled my heart, for I knew if she were alive somewhere she, too, would be watching the stars and thinking of me.

"Could she be a day's journey up the coast?" I asked myself, "waiting for us to find her. Or did the Valnar take her, and she is leagues away?" But whichever it was, I knew that at that moment she was there with me in the cloak I wore and in the stars I silently watched. And I would have to contend myself to be with her this way until one day I held her in my arms again.

When my watch ended, I went below to the quiet of our crew quarters and fell asleep in my hammock strung above the sea chest where I kept her ribbons; and as I slept, I dreamt of her again. We were dancing the zubah as we had done so many times before; yet we were on Trohan, and for some odd reason I was wearing a Thean military cloak and helmet. Even in my dream it felt odd for me to be dressed this way, and as I danced and laughed with her, the strangeness of it all puzzled me.

§ § §

The first day of autumn dawned cold and overcast, and we could tell a storm was moving in from the west. As I had stood a late watch, I was free of duties that morning; and so, after breakfast, I sought out Morek and told him of my dream while Sepnoar played in the corner with Topan and Ernoar.

"I have no idea what it means, if anything," he told me. "Some believe that dreams come from the spirit world and tell us what will be or what we are to do, but I have never held with such beliefs. Maybe Otna could tell you, if you can trust him."

"You may be right," I said, "but I've had several dreams of Illiad and my parents, too."

"That is only natural," he replied. "I, too, have dreamt of my wife and daughters many nights since their deaths. I think it is only our longing to see them again which makes us dream of them at night."

"All hands on deck!" Burog called through the hatch leading to the hold, "we've sighted what looks like a bay up ahead. Idar, come take soundings."

I jumped to my feet, my heart pounding, and ran to the ladder leading to the deck with Morek close behind me. When I reached the deck, I went to the locker in the fore deck to get the weighted rope we used to measure the depth of the sea when entering or leaving strange waters then stood at the rail awaiting Burog's orders to begin taking soundings.

As we drew closer to the opening of the bay, we dropped our sails to reduce speed. When the *Tok* caught up to us and was within hailing distance, we told them we would approach first then signal for the rest of the fleet to follow us if there was sufficient depth to enter the bay. We then turned and sailed slowly toward the shore as I took soundings.

The first few times I cast the line it did not even touch bottom. But on the seventh throw I felt it barely make contact, and on the eighth and ninth it rested firmly on the bottom; yet the colored ribbons tied to it showed we had plenty of depth to continue on. Throw after throw continued to tell us it was safe to sail on as minute by minute we drew closer to the mouth of the bay.

Each time I threw the line ahead of me I caught a glimpse of the shore and saw that it was rocky yet with no sign of the cliffs we had grown used to these past few days. In fact, it reminded me of the bay at Terhal.

My heart as well as my mind raced, for I hoped that any moment now I would see the masts of ships, a sign we had at last found the Others. If this were so, I would no longer have to dream of Illiad but could once again see her and hold her in my arms.

Yet as we neared the opening to the bay, I could see that this would not come to pass; for no ships lay at rest on the calm waters ahead. Instead, we could just make out what appeared to be a cluster of small rounded huts on the far end of the bay.

"Heave to!" cried Tenoar, and this command was repeated by Burog.

Slowly the ship came to a stop with her starboard side facing the shore allowing me to see full into the bay. The sight which met me, though, caused my blood to run cold, for there were three boats fast approaching us from the mouth of the bay.

"Tenyah!" cried Aarad from the rigging.

"Turn about," came Tenoar's command. "Full sail. Out to sea! Signal the fleet!"

I pulled in the line I was still holding and began to coil the rope when an arrow suddenly struck the side of the ship about five hand's lengths from my foot. When I looked up from what I was doing I saw three Tenyah standing in the boat closest to us ready to fire again.

"Bowman!" I cried. "We're under attack."

"Get the bows and return fire!" Tenoar shouted.

I stepped back from the railing; yet I was unable to take my eyes off the men approaching us, for I had never before seen anything like them. The boats each contained about eight to ten Tenyah warriors all with their faces painted black, red or green. They wore what appeared to be helmets made of the feathers of some kind of bird. Their chests were naked as was the rest of their bodies save for what appeared to be short skirts hanging from their waists; however, the man at the stern of each boat wore some sort of cloak which billowed out behind him.

Arrows began to rain down on the ship, and Burog yelled for us to take cover. I dove for the locker from which I had taken the sounding rope and hid behind the still open door. Yet almost immediately six men came up from the hold with bows and began to return fire.

"I got one!" cried Torek; but having said this, he was hit in the shoulder and fell backwards onto the deck near me.

I ran to his side and pulled him behind the door then, grabbing his bow, I cursed myself for not knowing how to use it properly.

"Give me that," said Dennem, and looking up I handed him the bow.

"Take care of him," he told me then stepped to the railing and began firing arrows at the pursuing Tenyah.

"They're out of range!" he called back after only a few shots, and the order to stand down was given.

"How is he?" Tenoar asked as he approached.

"I don't think it's serious," I replied, "but we need to get him below."

"No, we'll take him to my cabin," he said, "Pellonek, Dennem, give us a hand.

"This is going to hurt," he then told Torek, and he grabbed the shaft of the arrow just above Torek's chest and quickly snapped it in half with his free hand as Torek yelled in pain.

"Help me get him up," he told me as Pellonek and Dennem linked arms to make a support on which to carry him.

I put Torek's uninjured arm around my neck and with Tenoar's help we heaved him up and onto the waiting arms of Dennem and Pellonek. Then, as I gently supported him, we slowly walked to Tenoar's cabin on the port side of the ship.

"Put him on the bunk," Tenoar told us, "and Idar, tell Kebbit to bring us hot water and some bandages."

I nodded and left the cabin. Outside men had gathered awaiting news of Torek.

"He should be fine," said Dennem as he followed me outside. "Even a half a hand lower and it could have killed him. He was lucky."

As I hurried off to the galley to find Kebbit, I noticed we had resumed our course northward away from the Tenyah encampment.

§ § §

The rain began that night and continued on for the next three days. It started as a drizzle and gradually became harder as we moved north, and we were forced to slow our pace since it soon became difficult to see ahead. By the third day it had turned into a mild storm, yet since the winds blew from the southwest we were still able to continue on our course without too much difficulty. However, each night we anchored the fleet as close to the shore as we dared and waited for dawn's light before moving on.

When the storm ended on the fourth day, a fog set in which lasted for another two days; and I was unlucky enough to stand watch on the first of these days. After weighing anchor and getting under way, all those who were not needed on deck went below leaving me in the prow of the ship as lookout to alert Burog at the helm of any approaching dangers while Kellon stood by just below the upper deck ready to take soundings.

Some time in the midmorning I saw a dark mass approaching in the fog and called a warning to Burog who steered hard to port to avoid colliding with it. I thought it strange that any outcrop of rock should be this far out since we were sailing more than a half a league from shore.

"What depth do you have?" I called to Kellon.

"The stone isn't even touching bottom," he called back.

"Looks like we're clearing it," I told him. "Do you think it's an island?"

"Hard to tell in this fog," he replied, "but it could be."

"Did you see that?" I asked suddenly.

"What?" he replied.

"There, on the edge of the rock or island or whatever it is," I told him. "It looks like someone's standing there. Do you see it?"

"I see something," he said, "but your eyes are younger and sharper 'en mine. Can ya' make it out?"

"It looks like a Tenyah warrior," I told him, "like the ones in the boats the other day. I can just make out a helmet and maybe a cloak. I think he's pointing at us."

"Tenyah," Kellon called to Burog, "there on that island. Idar thinks he may have spotted us. Better take us out to sea a bit," and Burog responded by steering us further away from the shore.

Because of the fog, the *Tok* kept within hailing distance as she sailed behind us and likewise the *Mer* behind her; and so my sighting of the Tenyah was relayed quickly from ship to ship, and the whole fleet followed us out to sea. Then, after an hour or so, with no sign of pursuit, we ventured to head back in towards the coast and resumed our course north.

We made no more sightings of Tenyah the rest of that day, nor on the next. But when the fog cleared in the late morning three days later, we were able to make out a village near the mouth of a small river which emptied into the sea. Again we saw the same type of rounded huts I had seen the day the Tenyah attacked us. There were boats in the water close to the shore with men in them whose hair was a reddish orange. These appeared to be fishing; yet, although they stared intently at us as we passed, they made no hostile moves.

Even so, it was now the tenth day since we had left Terhal, and as we had not been able to make landfall in all that time, our water was beginning to run dangerously low. Torek, with his shoulder still bandaged and his arm in a sling, was up and about; but he remained a constant reminder to those on the *Tel* that we did not wish a confrontation with the Tenyah as we were poorly armed. However, if our water supply ran too low, we might be forced to fight the Tenyah in order to save ourselves.

This realization was of little consequence, for the wooded coastline we now passed showed no sign of rivers or small streams emptying into the sea where we could obtain fresh water. And so we sailed on for five more days as the water supply on all the ships grew critical.

At last, on our fifteenth day out from Terhal, we sighted an inlet and cautiously approached it. This time we prepared ourselves for the possibility of an attack by the Tenyah, for Tenoar ordered our bowman to stand at the ready and also signaled for the *Sep* and the *Ket* to come forward and take up positions just outside the entrance to the inlet as a backup.

However, these precautions were not needed; for upon approaching the inlet, we found it unoccupied. Yet our relief and joy at finding a place where we could search for water and possibly take on additional provisions was met with the stark reality that we had not found any sign of the Others; and if we who had been given an opportunity to resupply our ships in Terhal were in dire need, then they who had been less fortunate in this regard must truly be in a grave situation and suffering terribly.

Chapter X

The inlet proved all we had hoped for. It was fed by a small river at its eastern end, and the forest surrounding it was rich in game as well as trees heavy with fruit and edible nuts. The bay itself teemed with fish as did the sea adjacent to it, and here and there along its shores we found patches of berries. And so we spent ten days in this calm and serene place stocking our ships before being forced to move on.

It was past midday before the entire fleet was safely inside the inlet. Yet we did not wait that long to explore the shore, for the first three ships to anchor each sent a small boat to look for signs that either the Others or the Tenyah had recently been there.

By the time all of the fishing boats had anchored, one search party had located a clearing where an on shore camp could be set up; and by nightfall their collective reconnoitering had determined that no one besides our fleet had been inside the inlet in at least a full cycle of the sun. Yet even so, the captains decided we would wait for morning before attempting to establish a land based camp; and we spent our first night in this haven on board ship.

I was fortunate that night not to stand watch as was Aarad, and so we spent this duty free evening together with Morek and Sepnoar, something we had not had the chance to do in several days. Both Boec and Shend joined us, and as usual Dennem and Egome were there with Lenyana since she was alone having no true family among the fleet.

Aarad sat close to Egome, and I had come to sense an intimacy growing between them since Terhal. Lenyana, it seemed, tried whenever she could to catch Boec's eye, but he still felt a deep attachment to Mirranu; and, though he was courteous towards Lenyana, he remained aloof.

"I don't think we're going to find the Others," Boec told us frankly.

"You are probably right," said Dennem.

"How can you say that?" I shouted, then lowered my voice, "they have to be out there somewhere."

"I understand how you feel," Dennem replied, "but the facts speak for themselves. It is fifteen days since we left Terhal and twenty since we left Theo, yet in all that time we have seen no sign of the Others.

"If…" and he raised his hand to silence me as I opened my mouth to speak, "…if the Others were not in the harbor at Arganon, as we all hope, then they must have sailed north. We know they did not enter the harbor at Terhal, for both Telleg and Marna have told us this. Yet we have seen nothing but Tenyah since we left Terhal, and this is the first haven we have come to. Yet they are not here.

"They could not have stopped anywhere along the way to resupply their ships, for we have seen no such place. So, if they are alive and sailing these waters, they must be far more desperate than us, yet they are not here in the only place we have found since leaving Terhal. Nor have the scouts found any sign they were here before us."

The truth of his words stunned me to silence, and I sat there fighting back tears. Yet even so, I refused to believe there was no hope.

"I, too, fear you are right," said Morek, and I looked at him incredulous that he had given up hope of finding those we both loved.

"No, Idar," he said stopping me before I spoke, for I had already opened my mouth, "hear me out. Everything Dennem says is true, you know this. If they were alive we would have found them by now. They were at Arganon on the night the harbor fell and could not get out. My parents, my sister and brother are dead or taken by the Valnar. I can see it no other way, though it grieves me deeply to say this openly in words."

There was silence all around us; and I sat in the semidarkness, a tear running down my cheek, my voice caught in my throat, yet still unwilling to accept what reason told me was the truth. How could I, for to acknowledge what Dennem and Morek had just said would bring my life to an end; and so I hung on to the only thread of existence I had, the hope that one day I would be reunited with Illiad.

"What about that bay," I said at last, "the one we stayed in our first night out from Theo. We only anchored at its entrance and never explored it. What if they stopped there?"

"True," Dennem replied, "they could have. But since then there has been no sign of them. So where are they now?"

"Ahead of us," I told them. "They might not have seen this bay. What if there was fog when they came by."

"True again," said Dennem. "But without food and water, they will be dead before the end of the moons cycle unless there is another haven ahead of us."

"Then we must wait and see," I said.

§ § §

Early the next morning we began to set up a camp on land to act as a collection point for supplies. This was also to serve as a secure place from which to off load those wishing to go ashore and to load food and water onto our ships. We built a small hut where a guard was posted allowing sentries to spend the night watching over the food we collected by day. Each ship took a turn supplying this guard with the *Sep* drawing the lot for the first watch.

Very few of us had extra clothing since most had been forced to flee with nothing but what they were wearing, yet those of us who had extra to spare had done our best to help those without. Even so, all were in need of a wash; and so on the afternoon of our first day ashore the women and small children went to a secluded cove of the inlet to wash their clothing and bathe in the cold water. On the following day half of the men and boys did the same leaving the others to stand guard over the camp. Thus, by the third day, all had been given a chance to refresh themselves.

The men of the *Tok* and the *Tel* drew lots to bathe at the same time, and so we had the chance to talk with Zhoh. He told us Daeo was not well and had not come ashore with him.

"He has all but given up on life," he told us. "He barely eats or sleeps. I begged him to come ashore to bathe, but he wouldn't. I don't know what to do. He misses nodeh and cries out in his sleep for her as well as Leyhah and Tuac. I think he blames himself for not being at home when the Valnar came, but if he had been, he could have done nothing."

"But why should he blame himself?" I asked.

"Miku wanted to return to Alna for supplies, but my father talked him out of it. He told him to wait a few more days. If the *Tok* had left the day Miku planned, my father would have gone with it and would have been at home the night the Valnar came."

"But as you said," Boec told him, "it would have done no good. Tuac was younger and stronger, and he still died."

"My father would have rather died trying to save his family than to live knowing he failed them."

After talking to Zhoh, I went for a short walk in the woods just to be alone; and I thought of how we had spent the extra days in Eltec, of how we, too, could have been home when the Valnar came. Would I now be with Illiad, I wondered, or would we both be dead like my parents? I could never know for certain what the outcome might have been, yet thinking about it caused me to wonder what fate had yet in store for me.

As I walked along, I spotted a patch of heshel at the base of a pahdalla tree. It was the first heshel I had seen since we left Theo, and it surprised me that it grew this far north. Since it was autumn, there were no flowers; yet seeing it was another reminder of Illiad, and so I bent down to pick some from a force of habit.

The berries were almost ripe, for they were just turning a pale yellow and would soon brighten to the golden color I knew so well. Heshel berries are bitter and not good to eat, but I picked a few anyway just to keep as a token of my love for Illiad.

As I stood up, I took my money pouch from my pocket and shook the small square coins it contained onto the palm of my hand next to the berries. They were meaningless, those coins, for they were now without value. I had worked hard to earn them, yet in only a matter of days they had become but worthless tokens. And so I rolled the berries into my pouch. Then I flung the coins off into the forest where they fell among the brush.

I walked back to the cove in the silence of that wooded place, alone with my thoughts, the pouch still in my hand. Somehow it comforted me; for as I held it, I felt strangely close to Illiad as if these small berries were a link—one stronger even than death—which sealed us mystically one to the other in a bond that would never end.

As I neared the shore and the familiar sounds of the men talking, I put the pouch back into my pocket where it remained until the day I died. And as I lie in my grave, it is at my side, an eternal symbol of my love for Illiad.

§ § §

Those foraging in the forest for fruit and nuts sighted a herd of what Morek and the men who had hunted in the hills above Teuwa called zhehpet, but which Penepe and Telleg insisted on calling zehpat. And so we sent out a hunting party to track them. When I first saw these animals, I thought they were small and nearly hairless gamu, yet the tree-like horns protruding from their heads told me I was wrong.

And so gradually we began to replenish our supplies and to feel life was returning to normal, or as normal as it would ever again be for us. In fact to many, the inlet came to be seen as a new home; and talk circulated that we would stay there and build a new life for ourselves in this place of peace and security. Yet this was not to be.

On the fifth day of our stay, Mirranu sought out Boec; and after a long talk she decided to accept his proposal of marriage and return to the *Tel*. It was not possible for us to celebrate a formal laryat for them. Yet even so, their decision to marry was seen as a further sign that life went on.

The sixth and seventh days saw a steady rain, and this hampered our attempt to dry and smoke the meat from the butchered zhehpet. Yet we did complete the process by covering the drying racks with tents made of poles covered with spare sails. Then on the eighth and ninth days we finished the smoking and loaded the cured meat onto our ships.

On the evening of the ninth day a party that had been gathering fruit in the forest returned with news they had sighted six Tenyah warriors heading towards our camp. We quickly called ashore all of our archers and sent the women and children back to the ships. Then we waited.

The Tenyah obviously knew of our presence, for they would have seen the smoke from our fires and the signs in the forest that someone had been hunting and gathering. And so they did not come directly into our camp but hid in the trees and watched us through the night.

We felt that we outnumbered them, but when they did not attack we began to fear they would send for reinforcements. Therefore, we decided to pull back to the ships and prepare to leave before this could happen.

Yet there was danger in this, for the last men on shore would be left to the mercy of the Tenyah and would be vulnerable to attack. Since none of us had any true military experience we were at a disadvantage; and this caused us to make mistakes, the first being we should have left the shore with the cover of darkness and should not have waited until dawn.

At first light we loaded what remained on shore into the small boats and sent these supplies out to the ships. This alerted the Tenyah who would not allow us to escape unharmed. And so they began firing at us from the trees.

The shore itself was out of range, yet our archers were pinned down as they tried to return fire. At last Dennem told them they were wasting their arrows since the Tenyah were well protected in amongst the trees.

"Only shoot if you see one out in the open," he told them, "otherwise, hold your fire."

Yet this, too, proved to be a mistake, for the Tenyah knew the terrain; and before we knew it they had moved to a position closer to us where they could fire at the men on the shore. We were then forced to return fire; but with the Tenyah so well dug in, we were again only wasting arrows.

Aarad, Boec and I were in one boat just shoving off to return to the *Tel* and Zhoh was in another with two men from the *Tok* when an arrow struck him in the back. He fell to the side tumbling into the water, and I leaped from our boat and ran to his side.

As I picked him up, I knew he was dead; for his eyes stared at me just as those of Tuac and Leyhah had that morning not so long ago.

"He's dead," I yelled as an arrow hit the sand next to my foot.

"Leave him," Aarad called to me. "Get in the boat before you get shot as well."

I dropped him in the shallow water, and his body washed back up onto the shore as I jumped into our small boat which then moved slowly out to the *Tel*. After off loading the supplies, I returned in the small boat for those who remained on shore, for I was determined to bring Zhoh's body back with me. Yet as man after man fell, Dennem being one of them, we could not retrieve those who were killed.

As it was, ten men in all were lost and six others were wounded. When we left the shore, the Tenyah hid behind our hut and fired at us as we rowed back to the ships; but they made no move to follow us. Our archers returned fire, yet throughout the battle we did not hit one of their men.

By the time we reached the *Tel*, the fleet was already under way with those ships not waiting for small boats to return weighing anchor and sailing out of the inlet first. As quickly as possible the others followed, for we all feared pursuit by the Tenyah.

When I came on deck, Egome stood with Aarad who had his arm around her; and I knew she was waiting for her father. I had no idea how to tell her he would not return, that he would lie forever in this inlet with Zhoh while we sailed on. Yet words were not needed, for as the small boat was hoisted on deck and the anchors raised, she fell into Aarad's arms; and he held her as I stood by the rail watching the shadowy figures of the Tenyah desecrate our dead.

Chapter XI

For three days after we left the inlet we sailed due north, yet on the fourth day the shoreline began to change and our heading gradually shifted to a more westerly direction. In fact, eight days later, we were sailing due west along a densely wooded coast.

At the same time the weather, too, made a drastic change; for since the storm at the beginning of the moons cycle we had known only two rainy days with the rest being sunny and warm although the nights had been colder than we had known in Theo. But on the first day after leaving the inlet the sky clouded over, and the next morning we awoke to fog which turned to light rain by midday.

The rain continued in a steady continuous drizzle as we sailed north. Then, on the third day, just as we began to veer west, we ran into a bank of fog. At first the rain continued to fall, but within two hours the fog became so dense it hindered even these droplets from following their course through the bone chilling whiteness that had swallowed us. This left us with nothing but the gentle sloshing of the waves against the sides of the *Tel* as we made our way slowly through this dreamlike world while taking soundings to be sure we had sufficient depth.

At last, the lack of light gave us only one choice, to anchor as close to shore as possible with a hope the morning's light would offer us better sailing conditions. It was here that Miku hailed us and told us that Daeo had died two nights before. They had wrapped his body in a piece of torn sail, weighted it down and dropped it into the sea.

The news brought a chill to my heart, for more and more it seemed all I had known and loved was being taken from me. Thus each day, as we sailed on and moved further from the inlet, I accepted more deeply the truth that the Others would not be found.

We sailed on through this fog for two more days stopping each evening as we feared running aground in the dark since, with the setting of the sun, it became impossible to see much beyond the prow of the ship. At first we found the fog merely an inconvenience; yet as it went on and on, and we were forced to remain below deck much of the time because of its bitter cold, we soon grew to hate the very sight of it.

At last, on the sixth day after leaving the inlet, the fog slowly began to lift; and in the morning of the following day the sun broke through the clouds warming the air enough to make us feel that spring, not winter, would soon be upon us. Yet the trees betrayed the bitter truth, for their leaves were all of different colors or lay rotting at their base in preparation for the sleep of winter.

Despite the warmth of the day, the nights continued to become colder and colder, and in the mornings we awoke to find the *Tel* covered in a fog like substance clinging to the ship. This, Marna told us, was called frost; and was a sign the bitter cold of winter would soon be upon us when even the water in the rivers and streams along the shore would become hard like metal making it difficult for us to obtain water.

Six days after this change of weather, I came on deck to watch the sun rise slowly astern; and in the evening, our prow pointed westward towards a setting sun. Then, on the following morning, with only three days remaining in the first moons cycle of autumn, I heard the words every seaman hopes he will never hear.

"Pola! Pola! Pola! Pola!" came Altore's cry from the prow of the ship where he stood watch.

The hearts of all on board became like the frost which still covered the *Tel's* deck and masts. No one moved for a few moments, then panic broke out as all who were below deck scrambled to reach the ladder.

When I emerged from the hatch, I moved aside allowing Aarad, Boec and Shend to follow me. Then the four of us walked towards the prow of the ship in the direction everyone else was staring.

The beast was enormous—a true monster of a creature lying directly in our path. It was fully twice the length of the *Tel* with eyes larger than the head of a grown man, and all any of us could do was to stand silently in utter amazement that such a thing was possible.

"Hard to starboard!" Tenoar called from the top of the ladder just outside his cabin. "Pellonek, get us out of here! Nomlet, hail the *Tok*."

But there was no need; for as I turned to look astern, I could see the *Tok* also turning to the north to avoid meeting up with the pola. Then, when I looked back at the creature, a second, a third, a fourth rose from the sea to join the first. These four massive creatures lay quietly on the surface of the sea like islands of rock the color of tempered steel, yet they showed no sign of hostility towards us.

§ § §

The pola did not attack us but merely swam off to the south in a group first diving below the water then emerging in a spray of awe inspiring beauty as each one leaped from the sea to fall crashing onto the waves, then dove once more to emerge half a league further on until they were out of sight. I stood with the others aboard the *Tel* watching this spectacle until there was nothing more to see.

As soon as the pola began to move off to the south, Tenoar ordered us to sail north towards the coast where the entire fleet anchored close to the shore. Then the captains met on the deck of the *Tok* for nearly an hour to decide what to do next.

When Tenoar returned, he told us we would spend the night waiting to see if the pola had truly gone. If they had, then we could continue our now westward course in the morning. Yet if the pola did return, it was felt that the shallow water near the shore would afford us more protection than the open sea; for beasts of their size were sure to keep their distance as they would be unable to navigate the shallow coastal waters.

That night we again sat as a group in the hold of the ship, for neither Aarad nor I had watches. Though it was not our first time together since the battle at the inlet, the wounds of what had happened there were still fresh in our minds; and I thought of Zhoh and Dennem as well as the others who died because of our foolishness that day. I also thought of Daeo who had given up all hope; and these thoughts caused me to fear for myself since I was at last beginning to lose hope of ever finding the Others, of ever seeing Illiad again.

As always, Aarad and Egome sat close to each other, and now Boec and Mirranu did as well. It saddened me that we could not hold a laryat for them nor, I wondered, how we could celebrate a wedding as neither had any family, save for Shend, to join with them. Our lives seemed totally broken, and hope began to ebb from me leaving in its wake an emptiness that even the pain of loss was not able to penetrate.

Lenyana did not seem to be upset by Boec and Mirranu's reconciliation, but had now turned her attention to Shend, and in this she was not rebuffed. I found it strange that she should so easily change her affections and said so to Morek when it became obvious she wanted Shend's attention.

"She is young and alone," he had told me. "It is understandable, though sad, that she should feel a need to belong to someone. I think many of us will feel this way as time goes on and we finally accept our losses."

"You mean me?" I had asked.

"No, I meant nothing like that," he replied. "It is…we have all lived through a horrible experience. I meant only that as time passes each one of us will come to accept that we must go on, that life still has meaning, that all did not die the night the Valnar came."

"I don't think I'll ever feel that way," I had told him, and the emptiness I had felt then continued even now as I sat with all that remained of my family and friends.

"You're quiet tonight," said Aarad, and his words toppled the wall I had built around me and penetrated my thoughts.

"I was just thinking about everything that's happened to us these past days since we left Alna," I told him. "I think you're right, Morek, we're never going to find the Others. They're dead or gone, so why do we keep sailing on? I wished it had been me and not Zhoh who had taken that Tenyah arrow."

"Don't talk that way," said Egome, and tears began to fill her eyes.

"I'm sorry," I told her. "I meant no…I shouldn't have said that. I'm sorry."

"My parents, Seppan and Illiad are gone," came Aarad's voice in almost a whisper, "and you, Morek and Sepnoar are all I have left." Then in a tone of cold anger he added, "Don't ever say something like that again."

"I'm sorry," I said again, "I just don't think I want to go on," and a tear rolled from my eye. "I can't stop thinking of all we've lost, of those we keep losing. Is it ever going to end?"

"It will end," Morek told me. "I do not know when, maybe it has already ended or maybe we have more to go through, but it will end I promise you."

"How do you know?" I asked. "Can you really promise me this won't go on forever? I just feel there's no hope, there's no future for us; and after all we've been through I think I have a right to feel this way."

"My father didn't think so," Egome replied. "When my mother died he would not give up nor did he when the Valnar came. Of course he had me to care for…but that's my point. Each one of us here has someone to love, and it's our love and concern for each other that will get us through this."

"Egome is right," added Morek. "In time all this will pass, and Sepnoar will grow up to one day have children. Hannee will not be there with me to see this, and I can do nothing about that; yet I will see them, and it is this future I must contend with, not the one I left back in Teuwa.

"You, too, must accept this as your future and live for the day—even if such a day is truly far off in time—when this nightmare will be a thing of the past, nothing more than a bad memory among all those we now hold dear and those we will one day come to cherish."

§ § §

As morning dawned, we weighed anchor and sailed west since there had been no further sightings of the pola. Yet on each ship one pair of eyes was trained on the coast for any sign of a safe haven where we could stop and at last replenish our stores and another watched the sea for the pola.

By now our water was dangerously low, and all of the ships began the rationing of the little that remained as we sailed on day after day for seven more days. The second moons cycle of autumn came, and still we sailed in a westward direction along a coast which offered no river, inlet or bay where we could find water and a place of rest.

We saw no sign of pola in all that time nor, which was also a favorable sign, were Tenyah villages sighted along the shore. Yet since there were no rivers emptying into the sea, we could not expect to see signs of habitation. But even so, we began to hope that the Tenyah were far behind us, and that peace at last would be ours if only we could find a source of fresh water.

Then, just as the wooded coastline began to bend gradually southward, we came upon a bay fed by three large rivers and anchored near the mouth of the most westerly. It was near sunset with only a couple of hours of good light remaining in the day, and so each ship sent a small boat to the bank of the river in order to obtain fresh water before the night set in.

In the morning we then sent out scouts to explore the bay which was almost three times the size of the one we had known in Theo. After a day's search, they reported they had found no sign of settlements along the shore on the western side of the bay, yet they had also not been able to locate any trees or bushes with edible fruits nor had any wildlife been seen save for an unknown variety of bird which nested in the rushes along the shore.

After discussing our options, the captains decided to send the *Tok* up river to see if any sources of food could be located while the *Bak* searched the shore along the eastern side of the bay with the aid of the *Hob*. Thus, on the following day, as the sun rose above the trees on the eastern horizon, we watched Miku's ship disappear into a light fog which hung over the bay leaving us to wait in uncertainty as our supplies now began to run low.

By midmorning the fog had lifted and a sunny, though cool, autumn day followed. I was working on deck with Benfoar making small repairs when the cry of "pola!" was again heard. It started with the *Ket* which was anchored closest to the entrance to the bay but quickly spread to the other ships near us.

As before, all those in the hold clambered on deck; and we all stood in awe of the huge beasts moving across the bay, rising from the water to lie a few moments on the surface then plunge into the depths only to rise again in another place. Our sense of awe was quickly overcome by panic, however, as each of the captains gave orders to move their ship away from all threat of the pola.

"Aarad, Kenneb and Nomlet, raise the anchors," came Tenoar's cry. "Burog at the helm. Idar, prepare to take soundings. The rest of you hoist the sails, and I want all passengers below deck. Now!"

We all moved to obey his orders; and within minutes, we were moving slowly towards the western shore of the bay. As I took soundings, the water grew more and more shallow; however, there was still sufficient depth for a pola to follow. Yet as I stood by the rail holding the rope we used for taking soundings, I could not help watching these strange and wondrous creatures which did not appear to take any notice of us. In fact, as they had done when we first sighted them, they swam away from us in the direction of the most easterly of the three rivers.

At last we reached a place close to the shore where the water's depth was sufficient to keep us afloat yet shallow enough to prevent the pola from attacking us if this became their intent. There we anchored and kept watch, but we again saw no sign of the pola nor of the two fishing boats which were exploring the bay near where those monstrous beasts had headed.

We spent a second night in fear, this time accentuated by the dread we felt because of our uncertainty over the fate of the *Bak* and the *Hob*. When morning came, a small herd of zhehpet was sighted moving among the trees along the shore; yet no one was willing to leave the ships to hunt them. And so we waited well into the afternoon before the two fishing boats were finally sighted moving slowly towards us through the shallow water along the shore.

After they had anchored, a meeting was called on the deck of the *Tel* in order to discuss what had happened. A few of the captains were afraid to leave their ships, but in the end, all agreed to come.

"It's the same 'cross the bay," began Shufec, captain of the *Hob*, "we saw nothin' but those same birds and a few small water animals which didn't look like somethin' we'd want t' eat and wouldn't make much of a meal ifn' we did."

"But what about the pola?" asked Keppoar, the *Son's* captain. "Did ya' see them? Did they try anything?"

"We saw 'em all right," Shufec replied, "but the strange thing is, they seemed as 'fraid o' us as we was o' them. I don't think they're pola t'all."

"What do you mean?" asked Tenoar.

"Well," Shufec told him, "in all the stories, the pola's a fearsome beast that attacks ships without cause. But these creatures seem kind o' shy ifn' ya' ask me."

"I noticed that too," I said. "Yesterday, while I was taking soundings, I watched them; and they acted like they had no interest in us."

"What do you mean?" asked Tenoar.

"Well, like Shufec said," I told him, "they seemed shy. They never even came near us or any of the ships. They just swam away like they did the day we first sighted them."

"That may be," said Poran who captained the *Bak*, "but I'm not willin' t' chance it. I want t' stay as far away from them monsters as I can."

"Same with me," Kuren added. "They may not be pola, but they're too big for me. We should steer clear of them," and the other captains agreed.

§ § §

In the early afternoon five days later, the *Tok* returned with excellent news; for they had found what appeared to be the perfect site for us to build a settlement. They had followed the course of the river for twenty or thirty leagues and found it to be of sufficient depth to allow even the trading ships to sail unhindered. Yet from then on the water was deep enough to let only a fishing boat pass. Then, after five more leagues, the river became too rocky to permit safe sailing for any craft save maybe a tarrek.

But this made little difference, for just twelve leagues up river was a huge clearing in the forest covered only by brush and small trees which could be easily cut down allowing us to build homes and plant the kalhu found in the ruins of Terhal. This news excited everyone attending the meeting again held on the deck of the *Tel*, yet we all still remembered what had happened at the inlet and concern arose about Tenyah.

"We saw no one," Miku told us, "though we sighted plenty of game and edible fruits, nuts and berries as we passed. The water is drinkable, yet we saw no villages along the river the whole time."

"There were no Tenyah at the inlet before we came," said Shufec.

"True," Miku replied, "but we are wiser now. If we anchor off shore in midstream we would have some protection from attack. From there hunting and gathering parties could be sent out, and at the first sign of trouble we now know enough to pull back to the ships where we have a better chance of fending off an attack.

"It would be best if we wintered on the ships, but that doesn't mean we couldn't start clearing the land over the winter. We could even start building a few homes with a protective wall around them. Then, when we determine it is safe to live ashore, we can move from the ships."

"That sounds like a good plan to me," said Elfad. "At least up river we will be far enough away from the pola.

"Pola?" asked Miku, and Tenoar explained what had happened.

"From what you tell me," Miku told us when Tenoar had finished, "I feel I must agree. It is unlikely they are pola. But even so, as Elfad said, it will be best to keep a safe distance from these creatures until we can learn more about them."

"Then let's put it to a vote," said Kuren.

§ § §

As had been our custom since leaving Theo, each of the captains went back to their ships and explained Miku's plan. Then, in the morning, they met again on the *Tel* to tally the votes taken the night before. Nearly everyone felt our only choice was to sail up river and attempt to build a settlement as Miku suggested. And so, as the sun reached its zenith in the sky, we left the bay behind us and began the twelve league voyage up the river which came to bear the name Drevet.

It took us several hours to reach the place Miku had chosen as our new home, and in many ways the trip reminded me of my voyage along the Hallucantec long ago while approaching Shentoar. Here, too, were strange trees—although some were quite familiar—and a deep sense of mystery surrounded the place, one beckoning me once more to a new adventure.

At last, on the fifteenth day of the second moons cycle of autumn, we reached the place that was to become my new home and the place where one day I would be buried far from the village where I was born, far from the cave by the sea that I could never visit. We anchored, as Miku directed us, in the middle of the river as the late afternoon sun blazed brightly on the water and lit up both banks with its warming rays. Yet even so, there was a chill about the place brought on by a breeze which, for the first time since we left Theo, blew from the north bringing with it the threat of an early winter.

Chapter XII

Winter arrived early, for shortly after the last moons cycle of autumn had begun the first snow fell. Yet before winter could cover us with its icy beauty we had sufficient time to glean from the surrounding forest ample provisions to feed us in the coming days.

The forest on the south side of the river was heavy with fruit and nuts as well as game which we hunted, again smoking the meat as we had done at the inlet before the Tenyah attacked. However, this time we saw no sign of enemies, and gradually we came to feel that at last we had found a home.

As Miku suggested, we anchored midstream; and for the first ten days we made sure all those who had been out hunting and gathering were brought safely to the ships each night. Yet gradually our confidence in this new land increased; and, again at Miku's direction, we felled trees in order to build an enclosure thereby securing our drying racks and the supply huts we now felt could be established ashore.

This proved to our advantage; for, although we saw no sign of Tenyah, we did hear vood howling in the darkness each night. Those on duty were able to see, by the light of the waxing moons, shadowy figures prowling the shore; and in the morning we would find vood tracks near the enclosure we had built as well as signs of their attempts to break in.

Then, to our good fortune, I made one of our greatest discoveries just before the snow began to fall. I had gone out on a gathering party with what I now considered to be my family—those with whom I met each night in the hold and with whom I had developed a close bond. We had also brought Topan and Ernoar with us as well as their sister Setlat since the boys had become fast friends with Sepnoar and had little opportunities to go ashore due to Marna's age.

We walked approximately two leagues across the vast clearing where we were building our settlement then stopped to rest at the base of a little hill covered with kellec trees before starting to gather the fruit. As we sat on fallen logs and talked, I by chance picked up a rock which lay at my feet.

"I think the boys could climb high enough in those trees to reach most of the fruit," Aarad was saying when I realized what I was holding.

"This is iron!" I cried, and everyone looked at me in total bewilderment having no idea of the significance of what I was saying.

"This is iron," I said again and stood up to examine a few of the other rocks lying on the ground. "They're all iron. Look, see the reddish color, and even the soil is reddish. We've found a deposit of iron.

"Don't you understand," I told them when I saw the bewildered looks on their faces. "We've found iron. These can be melted and used to make tools and weapons…a plow to till the soil in the spring. We've found iron!"

"But how do we get the metal out?" asked Shend.

"Leave that to me," I replied. "I've never done it, but nodah explained the process to me. We always bought our iron from a merchant in Theo, but I'm sure I can remember how to purify these rocks and get the iron out. It will be a lot of work, but I know we can do it. Besides, we haven't any choice. We have to do it, or we'll never survive in this wilderness if we can't replace the tools that break or wear out."

"You're sure you can do this?" asked Boec.

"Pretty sure," I told him. "But as I said, we've got to try. You start picking the fruit, and I'll look for more ore. Tomorrow we can bring tools and dig up the ground. There's bound to be a lot more rocks buried around here."

§ § §

The snow began to fall the next day, but even so I returned with a few men and began to dig in the now freezing soil for the reddish rocks I was sure held the iron so necessary to our survival in this wild and untamed land. I had spent most of the night at my small forge aboard the *Tel* smelting some of the rocks we had brought back with us, and by the morning I had produced a small quantity of iron to prove that we should be able to make our own tools if only we could obtain a sufficient amount of raw ore.

Miku was impressed and asked for volunteers to brave the winter cold and dig in the now snow covered ground searching for the reddish rocks that were the sign of iron ore. Then, in the evenings, I spent long hours working at my forge until I had finally produced enough metal to make an axe head.

This, everyone agreed, was far too slow of a process; and so we built a crude furnace on shore just outside the north gate to our compound. We dug a large pit and filled it with wood and iron ore. Then we constructed a dome above the hole with boulders and smaller rocks. All of this was sealed with a thick layer of mud leaving only the boulders on the northern side exposed as well as an opening at the top to allow the smoke to vent. Finally, we covered all of this with loose dirt and kindled a fire inside.

The opening at the base drew in the north wind which caused the fire to burn hotter than if left out in the open. This, then, melted the ore; and when all had cooled down we were able to open the pit and extract the smelted ore in far greater quantities than I could produce in my forge aboard ship.

When this proved successful, we fashioned dried mud bricks with which we built a much improved furnace that produced an even larger quantity of iron than could be obtained from the crude pit. Finally, I was able to keep my promise and forge a simple plow to be used to till the soil in preparation for planting the seeds we had salvaged from the ruins of Terhal.

Kellebet, a cobbler from Prion, was able to fashion leather straps from the hides of the zhehpet we killed. These we attached to the plow allowing it to be pulled. Thus, when the snow melted at the end of the first moons cycle of spring, we began planting our first crop.

§ § §

Fortune smiled on us in other ways as well, for a hunting party located a herd of strange animals which we came to call nashcal since they had the appearance of small hornless yet very hairy nosha. These we found to be of no use as food; for, like nosha, they had an unpleasant taste. Yet their hair produced a wool similar to ashka wool and was spun by the women into yarn and woven into much needed cloth for winter clothing.

Marna proved of great assistance in this as she taught the women and girls a skill unknown to us in Theo. This she called killet, a form of weaving done with two sharpened sticks that produced a warm cloth and even caps for our heads all well suited to protect us from the blowing snow of winter.

The nashcal, we soon found, were a docile animal; and it was no problem keeping them inside the enclosed encampment at night then permitting them to forage among the brush during the day. Morek and the other men who had come with him from Teuwa were all experienced with ashka and cared for our small herd. Then, in the spring, we discovered that, like ashka, nashcal could be easily sheared of their wool to produce an abundance of raw material for cloth.

Sepnoar, like Aarad at his age, had no interest in such work preferring to be with me in the forge; and soon Topan and Ernoar joined him which gave me all the assistance I needed and allowed the grown men to busy themselves with other tasks. Topan was ten and, like me, reached his sun cycle at the second winter moons cycle. Ernoar was eight and Sepnoar seven, and both of them reached their sun cycle in mid summer. All three boys were naturals in the forge and were eager to learn everything having to do with the art of metalwork.

I, for my part, missed the sea and the feel of water beneath my feet especially when Tenoar decided that my forge aboard ship was far too small to produce what was needed for our community and ordered me to move to a larger forge built just inside the northern gate of our encampment adjacent to the furnace we used for smelting the ore. With the coming of the second winter moons cycle, we began to feel more comfortable with the idea of living ashore, and so small cabins were built inside the enclosure to allow Morek and the other men who tended the nashcal to spend the night watching over them and to keep fires burning in order to fend off the vood still prowling near our encampment each night. Aarad and I shared one such cabin with Morek, one attached to the forge; yet, as we were still not totally sure we were safe from attack, the three boys were required to spend the night aboard ship with Marna who had became a part of our family. Thus, for the next fifteen cycles of the sun I remained ashore venturing only as far as the bay to fish with the crew of the *Tok* once each summer and never again felt the spray of the open sea upon my face.

§ § §

One day, in mid spring, as we plowed our communal field and prepared to celebrate the Toharofa at which Otna would officiate, two men walked into our encampment. At first panic sprang up as they were seen crossing the clearing in the direction of our settlement, and most of those working in the fields fled to the small boats along the shore attempting to reach the safety of the ships.

Since the strangers appeared to be unarmed and not threatening, Miku, Tenoar and a few others remained ashore yet pulled back to our encampment as a safety precaution. I was one of them and Morek another; however, we entrusted Aarad with the safety of the three boys and sent him reluctantly back to the *Tel*. And so I stood beside Morek at the northern gate ready to close and bar it at the first sign of danger while Tenoar and Miku stood in the gateway to our encampment preparing to meet the approaching strangers.

The men approached us cautiously, and though we now saw they both carried bows strung and ready these were over their shoulders allowing their hands to be held free as a sign of good will. They were tall men with reddish hair yet not the same orange hue I had seen in the Tenyah fishing near their village as we sailed north. The eyes of these men were dark but showed no sign of fear or hostility, and I felt they meant us no harm.

"Ponee du behoowa," said one of the men when they had stopped about fifteen to twenty paces from our encampment.

"I have no idea what he is saying," whispered Tenoar to Miku.

"Nor do I," Miku replied a little louder. "But we need to find some way of communicating with them."

"I could try," I said as I walked out to stand beside Tenoar. "I've had a little experience in Shentoar. Remember Tullikan, the fruit seller?"

"Ah, yes," replied Tenoar. "Well, if you think you can, you surely have my permission. Miku?"

"Anything is worth a try," said Miku. "Just be careful, Idar. If there is any threatening movement at all, you are back here with us and we're behind the wall. Understand?"

I nodded and walked about ten paces forward with my hands in front of me to show them I was unarmed.

"We greet you and mean you no harm," I told them. Then, when I came to a stop, I pointed to myself and said, "I am Idar. Idar," and again motioned to myself.

The man who had spoken to us looked at his companion then stepped forward and pointed to himself, "Adjuwa," he told us then motioned towards the man who had accompanied him saying, "Adayu."

I nodded and motioned to myself and then towards the others behind me saying, "We are Kroemaeon," then pointing first to Adjuwa and then to Adayu asked, "Are you Tenyah?"

Their reaction was swift and a bit unnerving, for they instantly became angry as if offended by my question.

"*Tenyah!*" spat Adayu, "*Kona tay, Tenyah. Tay Draygon,*" and at this he thumped his chest with his right fist.

But Adjuwa raised both his hands and said soothingly, "*Kahnu, aloa. A kandu Adayu.*" Then to me he said, *"Bolo kahlee fah Tenyah. Draygon adun."*

I was unsure of what he had said; but I had made out the word Draygon, and Adayu's reaction to my question led me to believe they were enemies of the Tenyah. So I decided to take a chance and raised my hands as if using a bow and arrow saying, "Tenyah kill Kroemaeon," then I held my heart making a motion as if I had been pierce by an arrow.

Next I pointed to those standing behind me, "Kroemaeon kill Tenyah," I told them, again making a motion as if shooting a bow.

"Kroemaeon no like Tenyah," and I shook my fist in anger.

What I said seemed to please both Adjuwa and Adayu, for they smiled broadly and nodded their heads. And so I continued, making the appropriate motions, "You are Draygon. We are Kroemaeon. Draygon and Kroemaeon be friends?" and I extended my hand.

But at this, Adjuwa merely looked at my hand and then at Adayu, and I could see that what I took for a simple act of friendship was not understood just as it had not been by Tullikan. As soon as I realized this, I walked back to Tenoar and clasping his hand said smiling, "Kroemaeon friends," then, as I returned to the Draygon, I held out my hand and again asked, "Be friends?"

At this, Adjuwa stepped forward and took my hand, "friends," he said.

§ § §

We had found the Draygon and knew that we were at last safe from all threat of the Tenyah. Adjuwa and Adayu entered our encampment; and Miku gave them a grand tour, such as it was. Yet they were truly impressed by all they saw, especially our work with metal; for, as we later learned, their tools and weapons were made only from bone or sharpened stones.

They stayed several hours, and when they saw our ships anchored on the river, they stood for a long time starring at them in awe. Then, before they left, I gave each of them one of the metal knives I had made.

"Friends," I said as I gave them their gifts, and their looks of obvious pleasure told me that they were truly pleased.

A few days later, they came again. This time they brought others of their tribe leading nashcal with baskets strapped to their backs containing a sampling of vegetables. Some of these were strange to us, yet others were well known. They also brought seeds which we planted in our fields after the Toharofa, and for this gift we were truly grateful when the autumn harvest was completed.

As they prepared to leave, Adjuwa and Adayu placed their hands on the shoulders of Miku, Tenoar and myself each in turn.

"Friends," they said adding, "*Mantu*, friends, *mantu*."

"*Mantu*," we each responded raising our hands in a sign of farewell as they turned to go.

End of Book Four

Book V
Beginnings

Chapter I

It was cold in those northern lands far from the hearth I had known all my life and which was now forever lost in the ruins of Alna. Each morning I awoke in the hut which only Aarad and I now shared together to the stillness of the quiet forest clearing that had become my new home. And as I busied myself preparing to meet each new day, there was no familiar smell of the sea to comfort me since the crashing waves I had known all my life were now far from me. Yet I went on.

After the second visit by the Draygon, we felt that we were at last in a place of safety; thus Morek had built a cabin for himself and Sepnoar. Marna and her three grandchildren agreed to share it with him since they, like Morek and Sepnoar, were alone in the world.

The vood had long since disappeared, for they had either left with the melting of the winter snows to hunt elsewhere or the noise of our constant building had frightened them away. This no one knew for sure. Nevertheless, their absence allowed Boec to construct a small cabin along the river not far from the south gate of our protective enclosure, and it was his intention to add a mill onto it before the coming autumn's harvest. Here he and Mirranu made a home for themselves and the child she would bear in the summer.

They had not been able to formalize their marriage in the accustomed way, as Shend was the only true family either of them now had; yet they had recited their wedding vows with the giving of bread and fish in the presence of all on board the *Tel.* This, then, became the new custom among us; and in the future, all weddings reflected this necessary change in tradition.

We discussed sending one of the merchant ships to Eltec for supplies but decided against doing this. It had taken us nearly two moons cycles to reach the bay and the River Drevet, yet each place we had stopped for water and fresh supplies we now knew to be in Valnar or Tenyah hands making such a return trip truly impossible.

By the time of the Toharofa, which was held in late spring, Shend and Lenyana had become close; and everyone expected that soon they, too, would wed despite their great age difference. Likewise, Aarad and Egome spent as much time together as possible. Thus, each evening, he would row out to the *Tel* in order to spend time with her then return to sleep in our cabin, though this was sometimes not until well past midnight.

Both Shend and Aarad were at a loss as to what to do with their lives in this wilderness. All Shend had known was the inn, for he had been born there and grown to manhood assisting his father. Yet now there was no need of an inn, and all he could do was busy himself at odd jobs around the encampment: the planting of our common field, the building of cabins and even the shearing of the nashcal.

In the spring, the *Tok* had returned to the bay seeking a good source of fresh fish. Over the winter we had been able to catch some in the Drevet, yet this had never been enough to supply our needs as a community. When the *Tok* returned ten days later Miku reported they had seen no sign of the pola in the bay nor in the open sea on either side of the bay's entrance since they had spent four days searching the coastal waters for the best fishing grounds. It appeared, however, that only the bay itself held a supply of fish sufficient to meet the needs of our small community.

It was also decided that merely one boat would be needed to provide us with enough fish, yet two additional boats would be kept at the ready as the building of new ships, if they were needed, would be a difficult process. And so the captains of the fishing fleet had drawn lots to determine which would continue to fish and which would see their boat turned into scrap wood to be used in the building of homes for our new settlement. The lots had fallen to the *Tok*, the *Mer* and the *Zet*. These, then, were to take turns in rotation with each fishing for a moons cycle at a time. Thus one by one the remainder of the fleet was scuttled until, as our first summer in this wilderness began, only the *Tel* and these three fishing boats remained of the fleet which had sailed from the harbor at Alna on a morning far off, as it now seemed to us, in our distant past.

Yet the news the *Tel* would never sail again frustrated Aarad since his restless nature was not suited to a settled life. I truly missed the sea, but I had the forge to keep me occupied; and the passing on of my feeble skills as a smith somehow gave me a sense of contentment and inner peace knowing that in this way I would live on in what I taught.

Aarad, however, had only the *Tel;* and the loss of her was hard for him to bear as he found caring for the nashcal and tending the crops something he had spent his whole life trying to escape. And so he became despondent, and only Egome seemed to cheer him and give him cause for hope.

I found this ironic since I had lost the love of my life causing me to wish for death but a few moons cycles before. Aarad, however, had found someone, the one with whom I was sure he would spend the rest of his life; but in spite of it all, he became lost in himself, and there seemed nothing I could do to help him. Yet Morek and Egome had been right that night aboard the *Tel*—life did go on—and I knew one day Aarad would find this to be true as well and would find some new basis for his life.

And so, on one especially chilly morning in the first days of summer, I found Aarad already awake as I crawled out of my bunk along one wall of the only room we had in our cabin. This was strange, for he usually slept later then I due to the late nights he kept, but also because there seemed no real reason for him to get up. I needed to be in the forge before the three boys arrived, yet Aarad found no such urgency.

"You're up early," I commented as I sat on the edge of my bunk having a stretch before meeting the new day.

"Couldn't sleep," he told me. "Besides, I need to be out to the *Tel* as early as I can," then, in a more somber tone he added, "we're going to start tearing her apart today."

"Well, we knew this day would come," I replied as I walked to the table in the center of the room where I poured myself a mug of water. "It's not like we didn't expect it. She's the last of the fleet to go, but I'm really going to miss her."

"Egome has nowhere to go," he continued, "so I'm going to use some of the timber from the *Tel* and build a cabin, then we're going to get married."

For some reason the news stunned me. I had expected it would happen and had long wondered why Aarad had not asked her before, but now that it was happening I suddenly felt alone.

"Married?" was all I could say.

"What else can we do?" he replied. "I mean, I love her. It's not like I'm marrying her because I have to, I want to. But…I just hoped that before I did I'd find something I really wanted to do with my life. I mean…how can I pledge to care for her for the rest of my life when I can't even take care of myself?"

"You'll find your way," I told him. "Maybe you should try your hand at fishing."

"I've already asked Miku, Abdoar and Menepe," he said. "Their crews are full, you know that."

"What about Lenyana and Shend?" I asked somewhat embarrassed, for I had forgotten that he had already attempted to transfer to a fishing boat. "I mean…if the *Tel* is gone, what will they do?"

"Shend's going to help us scuttle the ship," he replied. "Then I guess he'll do the same as me."

"Marry Lenyana you mean?"

"What else," he told me. "At least he doesn't have a problem working in the fields or building cabins. I just don't want to settle down. You were right about the sea. How can you stand knowing that we'll never be out there again?"

"I just live each day as I can," I told him. "That's all any of us can do."

§ § §

With the scuttling of the *Tel*, her crew was forced to find new homes on land as well as work to do within the community. As carpenter on the *Tel*, Benfoar had been asked—as had the carpenters of the *Ket* and the *Sep*—to become a foreman to assist with the construction now going on within the village. These three soon became fast friends and together built a cabin not far from where Morek now lived with Marna.

The rest of the crew followed their lead and shared cabins in groups of two, three or four. Altore and Torek, who had been friends before joining the *Tel*, moved to the mining camp and helped dig for the ore I smelted to make the tools we needed to survive. Diud, Burog and Pellonek joined the men who hunted and shared a cabin with Kebbit who continued cooking for them as he was too old to do any other kind of work.

Boaruf, Shaffet, Kelyan and Nomlet joined those who worked the fields and shared a cabin together on the edge of our growing village not far from the western wall of the stockade. This left Kenneb, Sennefen and Kwellen to build a cabin near Morek's, one with a barn attached; for they had chosen to tend the nashcal as this seemed to them far less labor than plowing, weeding and irrigating the fields.

§ § §

When the *Mer* made its first fishing run in midsummer, Abdoar decided to explore the two remaining rivers which flowed into the bay. The eastern most of these was soon found to be much too shallow to accommodate any of our vessels; yet the middle river, like the Drevet, was easily navigable for more than thirty leagues. Here, along both banks of this river, Abdoar and his crew spotted a total of three Draygon settlements.

Two of these villages were rather small and were both located on the eastern shore of the river. But the third, located on the river's west bank about eighteen leagues from the bay, was much larger and was the home of Adjuwa and Adayu.

The Draygon, Abdoar reported, were excited and seemingly pleased by the arrival of the *Mer;* but Tenoar was even more so, for being a merchant, he immediately saw the possibilities this opened up for future trade with the Draygon. In all of the tales we had heard, the Draygon were eager to obtain Kroemaeon goods in exchange for furs; and Tenoar quickly formed an alliance of sorts with Elfad and Kuren giving him exclusive rights to the trading then persuaded Menepe to take him to see if something could be worked out with Adjuwa and Adayu since they had seemed so pleased to receive the knives I had given them.

When Aarad heard of this, he was elated; for the possibility of trading with the Draygon, of being able to do something with his life besides sheering nashcal and harvesting kalhu, excited him greatly. Therefore, he immediately went to Tenoar and begged to be allowed to go with him to visit the Draygon villages.

"He said yes!" Aarad told me as he came excitedly into the forge. "I can go."

"Go where, edjah?" asked Sepnoar.

"Tenoar is going on the *Zet* to try and trade with the Draygon villages Abdoar found," he said ruffling Sepnoar's hair, "and I will be going with him."

"Can we come?" asked Topan. "I want t' see the Draygon villages too."

"Want to," I corrected him. "You've spent too much time listening to the talk of seamen. It's about time you learned to speak proper Kroemaeon. And no, you can't go. There is too much work here in the forge which needs to be completed. The Draygon will want knives for sure; and being the oldest and strongest, you are my best helper."

"Idar is right," Aarad told him, "we will need as many of those knives as you can make. But I promise you this, if all goes well I will ask Tenoar to let you come on one of our trips some time in the future."

"Me too," cried both Sepnoar and Ernoar at once.

"Yes, both of you as well," Aarad reassured them, "Now do as Idar tells you and get to work on those knives."

"How long will you be gone?" I asked as the three boys scurried off to finish their jobs.

"Tenoar's not sure," he replied. "Abdoar thinks it should take a day or two to get there, and trying to communicate with the Draygon will be a major problem. In all…maybe eight to ten days."

"Well, good luck," I told him. "I'm glad you've finally found something. I hope it all works out…for you and the rest of us."

"I hope so too," he said.

Chapter II

We learned much from the Draygon and they from us as well, and soon we had developed a common language—a mixture of Kroemaeon and Draygon which was used when communicating with each other. Our ability to produce tools and weapons from metal was prized by the Draygon; yet weaving was also a skill unknown to them; for until we came their clothing had been made from the skins of animals. Thus they were willing to trade with us for knives and fabric giving us in return desperately needed food.

The plow I had made had been used to till the soil, and we had planted a field of kalhu as well as the seeds given us by the Draygon. Yet none of this could be harvested until autumn, and over the summer our scant food supply would have dwindled to nothing if it had not been for the trading missions of the *Zet*.

At first Tenoar had been upset the *Tel* had been scuttled, for he felt he could have used her to trade with the Draygon. But this would never have been possible since, as he learned on his first trading voyage, the Adujae—the Draygon name for the river on which their villages were located—would not permit a merchant ship to pass. Therefore, only the fishing boats could reach the Draygon villages; and the *Zet*, then, came to be used solely for this purpose.

Aarad had been correct in his estimation of how long their first trading mission would take, for exactly ten days after the *Zet's* departure she was back with a truly happy Tenoar and an equally elated Aarad. I, too, had made a correct judgment as to the needs of the Draygon since the crew of the *Zet* had traded away nearly every knife, harpoon or metal hook which they could spare aboard ship.

"How quickly can you make more?" was one of the first questions I was asked after Tenoar had related the details of their voyage.

"We've made four knives while you were gone," I told him, but I think it will be possible to forge them faster now that Topan has the practice. He's a quick learner, so together the two of us should be able to turn out on the average one a day."

This was true, for Topan was indeed a quick learner which caused me to wonder what my skills would have been like at his age if I had been as truly motivated as him. Yet at eleven, I had only concerned myself with swimming and fishing or playing kaylo with Tuac. There had been no desire to work, to be penned up with my father in the forge as I saw it. Instead, I had spent my time sitting on the hill overlooking the bay dreaming of being far away from Theo.

This now pained me, for I would give anything to be at my father's side working in our blacksmith shop and eating my mother's cheshoi for our noon meal. But never again would this come to pass, and to dwell on such things was of no use at all.

§ § §

The *Tel* had long since been dismantled, and Aarad had kept his word and built a house—as did Shend—near the mill Boec was constructing along the shore of the river. Egome and Lenyana both moved in with Boec to help Mirranu in the last stages of her pregnancy and then to care for Annaya, the daughter she bore in the late spring and named after her mother.

Yet by mid summer Aarad and Shend were both preparing to wed which destined me to live alone in my little house next to the forge. Topan, who at eleven was eagerly desiring the freedom manhood would bring at reaching his thirteenth sun cycle, offered to move in with me; but Marna said he was far too young for this, and I had to agree. And so, after Aarad's marriage, I was alone each night and often sat in the silent darkness just outside the door to my hut holding the ribbons I had bought for Illiad in Eltec and watching as the stars filled the night sky with the same beauty I had known in Alna. On these nights, I wondered where she was and what her life was like, for I could not let myself believe Illiad had died in the harbor at Arganon.

Even so, I had come to resign myself to never seeing her again, for in my heart of hearts I knew now that when we parted that day on the wharf at Alna, it was for the last time. Nevertheless, as I had promised her long ago, I kept a silent vigil each cloudless night believing that she, too, was with me as together we watched the stars move through their endless rotations of the seasons.

§ § §

One morning in early autumn, Aarad came to visit me as he would be leaving the next day to trade with the Draygon. I had just gotten out of bed and was preparing to eat the last of the stew Egome had made for me when he entered, as usual, without knocking.

"You're up late," he said cheerfully as he came to the table and sat across from me.

"And *you* are up early," I told him a little irritated at his cheerfulness so early in the morning. He had been married now for almost two cycles of the moons, and I had now become accustomed to being alone in the mornings.

"I've got a lot to do today before leaving tomorrow," he replied still far too cheerful for my liking, "and Egome wants me to invite you to eat with us tonight."

"I think I can do that," I told him now becoming less irritated, for I truly enjoyed Egome's cooking which reminded me very much of my mother's.

"Good," he said, "I really didn't think you would have a problem coming. Morek, Marna, Setlat and the boys will be there as well. It's supposed to be a family thing."

"So is this something special?" I asked. "You don't usually have a big dinner before you go."

"Morek asked the same thing," he told me, and a smug look came over his face.

"What?" I asked.

"We'll tell you tonight," he replied. "I promised Egome I wouldn't say a thing to either of you, so just wait until tonight."

"Fine," I said and finished eating my stew.

§ § §

When our work was finished that evening, I left with Topan, Ernoar and Sepnoar. We walked across the enclosed encampment and through the River Gate, as we were now calling it, then along the Drevet to Aarad's cabin which stood near the mill Boec was still laboring to complete by harvest.

As we approached, Boec was standing outside looking at the huge wheel he and Shend had long since attached to the side of the mill.

"Do you think it will be finished by harvest?" I asked.

“I have my doubts,” he replied. “Not enough help for one thing, and we still need to carve all the gears and cogs out of wood.”

“Where are all the men who have been helping you?” I asked, for no one besides Shend could be seen anywhere.

“*That* is a good question,” he replied. “It is becoming harder each day to find help. Not many, it seems, want to work these days.”

“But why?” I asked, “what will we do if we have no way of milling the kalhu we’ve planted, eat kahl for the rest of our lives?”

“No one seems to be thinking that far ahead,” said Shend as he walked towards us.

“Oh, they are thinking ahead,” Boec said, “but they all want to be sure they get their share. When we began building and planting, everyone worked for the common good; but now there are complaints that some do more and others less. Fewer and fewer are willing to help with the mill since it is seen as being to my advantage, that only I will prosper through its use.”

“But that’s nonsense,” I told them.

“That’s what I’ve been saying,” replied Shend. “Miku wants to hold a meeting to talk it all out and come to some understanding.”

“When will that be?” I asked.

“Not sure,” answered Boec, “but it needs to be soon, or we will not be done with the mill by the harvest.”

§ § §

Egome, as I had anticipated, prepared an excellent meal—a stew made of zhehpet and vegetables with herbs taken from the forest. She also prepared kahl which we had been eating in place of bread ever since the milled flour ran out at the beginning of winter. The kahl made a filling hot meal; and, with the stew over it, its usual bland taste was well hidden.

“I will be glad when the mill is completed, and we can have bread again,” said Marna. “I mean nothing against your meal, Egome, as usual everything is very good; but to have fresh warm bread, that will be a treat.”

“You may need to wait a long time for that,” I told her. “Boec tells me that he’s not sure when the mill will be finished. He’s not getting the help he needs.”

“Oh, and why is that?” she asked.

“No one is getting the help they need these days,” Morek answered for me.

"Idar is," Topan remarked in a tone that sounded highly offended.

"True, Idar is," Morek responded. "You boys do a great job, but many others are idle and do nothing. The whole village seems to be falling apart: the fields are not properly tended, those who go out hunting are reluctant to share their kill, and even some of the fishermen feel they need not turn over their catch to the common store.

"To make matters worse, the men tending the nashcal are now talking of leaving, of taking the herd far into the hills away from Mekul. They feel if they withhold the wool from everyone else they will be in a better position to barter for a larger share of the harvest."

"But the herd belongs to all of us," cried Aarad in surprise.

"That is not the way they see it," replied Morek. "They feel they have done the work of caring for the nashcal, and they should reap the benefits."

"Shend told me Miku plans on holding a meeting," I said.

"Well, he needs to hurry," said Morek. "If something is not done soon, I fear there will be trouble once the harvest comes; and we could starve this winter."

"Morek is right," Aarad told us. "The trading had been going well, but now the women who weave woolen cloth are not producing enough to barter with; and the dried meat we get in trade will soon not be enough to feed the whole community."

"Enough of this talk," said Egome, "you are frightening the boys."

"I'm not scared," Topan told us.

"Me neither," said Ernoar, yet his voice quivered just enough to tell us this was not entirely true.

"Edjah will get us the food we need," added Sepnoar in a truly confident voice, "he's the best trader there is."

"I'll surly try," Aarad said smiling at him. "But Egome's right, we didn't invite you all here to talk of the state of the village. We have news," then he looked across the table at Egome. "Go ahead," he told her.

"No, you tell them," she replied.

"Well, somebody tell us," said Topan.

"Be patient, Topan," Morek told him. "And do not interrupt your elders that way. It is rude."

"Sorry, edjah," he replied. But his voice betrayed his true feelings, and we all knew his apology was not sincere.

"Well…" said Aarad ignoring the exchange between Morek and Topan, "Egome will be having a baby in about five moons cycles."

The news stunned me, and I sat in silence while Marna and Morek got to their feet and hugged Egome. At last I, too, stood up, “That’s wonderful,” I said as I came around the table to where she stood and embraced her. Yet in my heart there was a deep sense of loss, a sense of jealousy; for I knew I would never feel the joy Aarad now felt.

Chapter III

The next morning Miku met with all of the captains, and a meeting was then called for the following day to include everyone who lived in Mekul. This meant the *Zet* did not sail as scheduled leaving Aarad with a free day which he spent with me in the forge speculating about what would be decided.

"Somehow we must get everyone to do their share of the work," he said.

"*That* is obvious," I told him, "but we've been over this before."

"I don't see what's the problem," said Topan. "Why's everyone being so lazy?"

"It's a puzzle to me too," I replied. "When we were sailing north looking for the Others, everyone was more than willing to do their share. And even after we started building the village, no one slacked off. Remember how men were willing to volunteer to go with me and dig in the snow just to find ore to smelt in the forge? Now we can barely get enough metal to make a knife or a few nails. Soon we, too, will have to stop work for lack of iron."

"Ernoar and I can go dig, edjah," came Sepnoar's weak voice from the back of the forge.

"I'm sure you would," I told him with a smile, "but I need you both here with me." Then shaking my head I looked at Aarad and said, "These boys act more like men than most of those who have reached the age of manhood."

"It makes no sense," Aarad replied, "to dig the ore or work in the field benefits everyone. Don't they see that? You make knives. I trade with the Draygon. Yet everyone eats the food the *Zet* brings back.

"You made the plow. Kellebet made the reins to pull it, but all will eat the kalhu. If we work together, the entire village can benefit from what each one of us contributes; so why are they being so stupid?"

"Don't ask me," I told him, "ask those at the meeting tomorrow."

§ § §

The meeting began around midday, and was held just outside the River Gate between the stockade and the shore. All who lived in Mekul or who had built homes in the nearby fields came with their women and children, and we stood as we had done on the shore of the bay at Theo not all that long ago to wait for Miku and the captains to call the meeting to order.

"We are here," began Miku when all had become silent, "to decide the fate of our small community; for as you all know harvest is upon us, yet still we lack the will to gather in the crops we planted in the spring nor do we have a plan as to how to divide the fruits of our labors."

He stood on a platform which, like the one we had built on the beach at Theo, was made of old water casks and a few spare boards. Off to the side were the captains of the ships on which we had sailed to reach Mekul, and in front of this platform we had arranged ourselves without intent or purpose in little knots reflecting the friendships and bonds we had forged as we sailed the northern sea seeking a new home.

"Boec has attempted," Miku continued, "to construct a mill so that we can have flour once the harvest is completed. Yet he tells me that he cannot finish it in time to be of use to us unless he has help, and few if any seem to be willing to give him the help he needs.

"And then there are the fields themselves. Idar labored hard to forge a plow for us and Kellebet the reins. Then together many of you were eager to till the soil and plant the kalhu we brought with us from Terhal. But now, at the end of a long summer's work, the fields lie ripe; but few seem willing to harvest what we planted in the spring.

"Tenor tells me the trade with the Draygon now goes poorly since iron is scarce and weavers are few; and though Idar continues to work as best he can in the forge, he can do little without raw ore from the deposit he found for us. Even our hunters, who in the past were eager to supply us with fresh meat, now seem to have lost heart for their work."

"And what of the temple I have asked again and again to be built," cried Otna as he climbed the crude steps to the platform to stand beside Miku. "If the toha are not honored, we cannot expect their aid in the future. This is a further sign our community has lost heart."

"Thank you, Otna," said Miku, "your observation is correct. We have lost heart," yet we could tell he was not pleased to have Otna join him on the platform. "And so my question to all of you is what are we to do about our present situation? We were eager enough to work together on our voyage to our new home, and we all worked together for the common good once we had arrived; but this eagerness has waned, and we need to recapture our former enthusiasm, or we will all perish here in this northern waste."

"It is you who brought us to this place," cried a voice from the crowd; and we all looked around to see who had spoken. But Miku raised his hand as a way of silencing the murmuring which broke out.

"Friend," he replied, "I told you before we left Theo I am not your king. I brought no one here by force. We all voted to sail north from Terhal, and we voted to settle here along the Drevet."

"That, Miku, may be our problem," said Tenoar; and he, too, climbed up onto the platform. "You say you are not our king; but maybe a king is what we need, someone who can command us and not merely suggest what we are to do. We need someone to ensure that plans are carried out, and I think we all feel you are the most likely candidate for the job."

"Tenoar's right," said Elfad. "We've talked of this again and again in the captain's council, and ya' keep telling us the same thing—that yer not our king. Well maybe it's time we gave ya' the job," and with his words a general murmuring of assent began to come from the assembled crowd.

"Yes, Elfad, we have talked of this," replied Miku. "Yet I say now what I have said before in council with the captains, I will not become king and take away the right we have gained for ourselves since the day we left Theo. I will not be king and rule as Shuman did to the ruin of us all."

"There's no need to be cruel or self-seeking," said Menepe. "I think all of us agree we like the freedom we've gained as we've carved out a new life for ourselves in the past sun cycle. But the fact remains, we need someone to lead us, someone to make sure the decisions we make get carried out."

"You served as captain of the *Tok*," Tenoar told him, "and your crew followed your orders both at sea and in your camp on Trohan. If you won't be our king…then be our captain.

"Those who sailed on the *Tel* as both crew and passengers have come to respect me as their captain, and they still come to me if they need help or advice. I think the same is true of all the other captains. This can continue. We can act as a council to solve problems that arise and give you the advice you need, but someone must have authority to carry out whatever decisions we make. Someone needs to be sure the work gets done, the mill is finished on time, the fields harvested and Otna's temple is built—if that be the will of us all. So, what say you? Will you be our captain?"

"That is something that should be put to a vote," Miku replied. "I will serve as captain if it is the wish of all here, but I will not assume the position by force."

"Is there anyone who speaks against the plan?" asked Tenoar. "Then what else is there to say," he added when there was no response.

"No," said Miku, "we must formally vote. That is the way we have done things since the beginning, and that is the way we will do it now. If I am to be in command, I want no one to complain later that they had no say in what we did here today."

"As you think best," said Tenor. Then facing the crowd of assembled villagers he called out, "All who wish to accept Miku as our leader, as captain of us all, move to the east side of the platform. Those who feel differently, come to the west side."

Slowly, as at Theo, everyone moved one way or the other. Then, when all had made their decision, we proclaimed Miku leader of us all.

§ § §

The captains knew those who had sailed on their ships and assigned to them jobs best suited to their abilities, and those who complained were often reassigned. But the Council strictly controlled the food supply, and at Miku's command it was made well known that at the end of each day anyone who did a day's work to the satisfaction of those in charge would receive food. Yet if anyone failed to work, they received nothing.

Some complained at this harsh treatment, but their complaints had no merit in the eyes of those who worked hard and received their due. Thus it was not long before the mill had been completed, the harvest brought in and even the foundation of Otna's temple had been laid out along the east wall of the compound awaiting the spring and the Toharofa to be completed.

Yet the dispensing of food presented a problem; for before the Council took charge and Miku's plan was put into effect, all who wished food would be granted what they needed without question. Now, with a need to work before receiving an allotment came the need to track who had worked and who had remained idle. This was soon solved by introducing a form of money payment throughout the village of Mekul.

The Council ordered wooden chips or tokens to be made. These were thin slices of wood cut from branches and painted with symbols of grain, fish or meat. They were then given to those who worked in accordance with the amount of effort they gave. Soon, however, these "coins," as the villagers began to call them, were regularly traded throughout Mekul acting as a form of money and allowing the villagers to work for one another and still receive payment. This in turn gave way to a sense of normalcy as each of us began to go about our daily lives much as we had before the coming of the Valnar, before our world had been turned upside down.

§ § §

That autumn and winter were the loneliest of my life, for Aarad had married leaving me to live alone in my cabin; and, with the coming of the rain and winter snow, it seemed the sky was always clouded over which made it impossible for me to watch the stars as had been my custom. Each night I slept in the quiet emptiness of my cabin then rose in the morning to work in the forge with Topan who appeared to be obsessed with smithing and never seemed to take time off. Sometimes I would eat an evening meal with Morek and Marna or Aarad and Egome; yet more often than not I was alone in my cabin at the end of each day with only Illiad's ribbons to give me comfort.

Then, one night just after the first snow had fallen in the late autumn, I had another dream of Illiad. It was brief yet haunting, for I saw her alone in a nearly empty room crying; and I knew as I watched her it was because of me that she wept.

I longed to rush to her, to comfort her, to let her know everything was to be all right. Yet I could only watch from a distance.

At last the dream faded. But as it did, she spoke but two words with trembling lips, "forgive me."

"I do, my love," I called out to the darkness and awoke to the silence of my cabin with the echo of my words still ringing in the emptiness of the cold winter night.

Chapter IV

The vood returned that second autumn, but they seemed to shy away from us and our stockade. Instead, they kept to the shadows of the houses outside the main encampment or sniffed around the barns built by Morek and his companions to protect the nashcal at night, yet mostly they merely sat in the meadow near our village and howled. Then, after ten to fifteen days, they were gone never to return again.

True to his word, Aarad took the three boys with him that autumn to see the Draygon villages while he traded. The first to go was Topan since he was eldest, and of course this did not go well with Sepnoar and Ernoar.

"Why does Topan get to go first," whined Sepnoar for the hundredth time, "it's not fair."

"It may not seem fair," Aarad replied with a patience I never knew he had, "but that has always been the way of things. I remember how angry I was when I was your age, and your father or your uncle Seppan were able to do things that I was not allowed to do. But that is the way it will always be; and you must accept this and stop complaining, or next time you will stay at home while Ernoar goes with me by himself."

"Yes, edjah," came Sepnoar's reluctant reply.

"Good," said Aarad, "now work hard for Idar while we are gone and do not make trouble."

"Yes, edjah."

"And do what you can for Egome while I am away," he continued. "This is a hard time for her with a baby coming."

"Yes, edjah."

"You just had to get in that part about Egome and the baby," I said with a chuckle as soon as Sepnoar was far enough away he could not hear me.

"Well, she does need help," Aarad replied. "And the little scamp should be willing to do his part."

"He's her nephew by marriage," I told him, "not her husband."

"He is still family," and to this I could only nod in agreement.

§ § §

As usual, the *Zet* was gone about ten days, and when he returned Topan was beside himself with excitement. We had been sailing and living in these northern lands for well over a cycle of the sun, and we had seen many new and wondrous things; but in Topan's eyes it seemed that the Draygon villages outstripped everything else.

"...and there was a man there with a vood. He kept her on a leash, and she didn't bite or anything," Topan exploded in the midst of telling us of the Draygon villages. We were at dinner in Aarad's house on the evening they had returned, and Topan talked nonstop as his excitement seemed to know no limits.

"Strangest thing I ever saw," Aarad told us confirming Topan's story.

"He said he found her as a cub lost in the forest," continued Topan as if Aarad had not spoken. "He said if you get them really young you can train them, and they're really gentle; and he said he'll give me one of her cubs if I want—if she has cubs that is."

"A vood, living in our house," cried Marna, "not while I am still here."

"Edjah had an ashka in his house when he was young," said Sepnoar.

"That may be," Marna told him a little cautiously, "but a vood would be another thing. I still cannot believe that they are truly as gentle as this man says."

"Well, you may not have anything to worry about anyway," said Aarad. "I have never seen this man before and may not see him again. He is from a village far to the east—over on that river that is too shallow to navigate."

"But didn't Adayu say he wanted to trade with you?" Topan asked.

"He wants to, yes," replied Aarad, "but we cannot reach his village by water, and neither Tenoar nor I are willing to go off into the forest trying to find it. If he wants to trade, he will have to come to us; and who knows if he will."

"Well, if he does," Topan told him, "ask about the vood."

"We will see," said Aarad looking at Marna who was sitting beside Topan and shaking her head.

§ § §

The vood was only part of the news brought back from the Draygon villages that trip, for it seemed that three of the men on the *Zet* had made plans to marry Draygon women. This came as a great shock to all in Mekul as the idea of marrying anyone other than a Kroemaeon seemed unthinkable to most of the villagers. Marna in particular found it impossible to accept the idea no matter what any of us said.

"It is just not natural," she told us, "and no good will come of it. One day you will see that I am right. I may not live to see it, but it will end badly. Mark what I say."

"But who else can they marry?" asked Aarad. "We have so few women of our own. It makes sense that our men should seek wives elsewhere."

"It is still unnatural, and no good will come of it," and that was the end of the discussion. Yet others did not see things as Marna did; and gradually, over the next cycle of the sun, four additional men had taken a Draygon wife.

It was the custom of the Draygon to pledge their daughters in marriage from childhood, and so those women who married Kroemaeon men were older women whose husbands had died leaving them with small children to care for. Such women could sometimes find husbands who had themselves lost a wife; but usually they were left alone and were, therefore, quite willing to take a husband who was Kroemaeon especially since this was seen by the Draygon as an honor.

Yet among the villagers many felt as Marna did, and the three men of the *Zet* chose to live among the Draygon and build a small trading compound where they acted as agents for Tenoar and Aarad. As others entered into these marriages, they also chose to live apart. Two men moved to the small mining camp which had grown up around the deposit of iron I had found; and one, a man from Teuwa, built a cabin a few leagues from Mekul where he lived alone with his new family on the edge of the forest and raised nashcal.

Only one man, Ettak, a crewman on the *Mer*, continued to live within the village of Mekul. He had married Anula, an older woman whose children had all grown and now had families of their own. She was a friendly outgoing woman who quickly won the hearts of many of the villagers. Yet Marna persisted in telling all who would listen that no good would come of such unions.

These Draygon women, however, proved useful in one respect; for they taught us how to harvest and cook narloo, a cereal crop unknown to us until we settled along the Drevet. It grew naturally in the shallows along the river bank as well as in the bay and could be easily cut and harvested with the use of our small boats.

This grain did not mill well into flour. Yet the Draygon boiled it as we did kahl only with meat and vegetables added making a kind of rich thick stew, and we found its flavor preferable to that of kahl in most respects.

Unlike the Draygon, we were farmers; for, though the Draygon planted gardens for their vegetables, they did not have the skills to cultivate whole fields of grain nor those needed to irrigate their crops. And so they had not thought to plant and harvest the narloo as we did kalhu.

When it was found that many in our village desired a greater supply of narloo, some of our farmers began to grow it by building dams around their fields and channeling the water of the Drevet into them to allow the narloo to grow in larger quantities. This, then, added to our food choices. Soon, some of those who knew how to make kahlmek began to use narloo in place of kalhu producing a truly strong drink favored by many men, but one for which I did not develop a liking.

§ § §

It took another cycle of the sun, to the time just before Topan reached the age of manhood at thirteen, before he got his vood; and his grandmother, as could well be expected, was not pleased. She ranted and raved from the day Topan first returned to Mekul from one of Aarad's trading voyages with a small male vood named Andore on a leash, yet nothing Marna said detracted from Topan's happiness.

Andore was, as we had been told, a gentle beast; yet to Marna this was nothing. Since Aarad and I had grown up with Huno living in the house, we did not find Andore a problem; and even Morek had to agree that, though a wild animal, he was indeed gentle even around the nashcal. In fact Morek began to wonder if vood could be trained to act as night guards who would prevent the many creatures that prowled the darkness from sneaking into the barns and eating the grain.

Yet Marna would hear none of this which led Topan to beg me to allow him to become my apprentice so that he might live with me. Since Marna could make no objection to Topan apprenticing once he turned thirteen, she agreed. And the matter died for a time.

However, Topan's coming of age brought with it an additional problem, for he was an orphan with no true male guardian to enroll him. Custom called for him to be listed as Topan, son of Karan, son of Elmel; but it was obvious that he would never have any rights to the heritage of his ancestors. Thus it was decided he would be registered according to the proper format. Yet I was to be his guardian, and all that I owned at my death would fall to him.

Chapter V

In late spring, just after our second Toharofa and the planting of the fields, Egome gave birth to a son whom they named Seppan. Then, as I came into my twenty-second cycle of the sun, she gave birth to a daughter whom they named Tenwa after Egome's own mother as well as Aarad's grandmother.

This was during our fifth winter in Mekul which was the coldest we had seen with snow far deeper than ever before. And so it came as no surprise to those with experience in such things that donect tracks should be found one morning near the barns where we kept the nashcal.

"It is not unusual," said Morek at dinner that evening. "In Teuwa they would come down from the hills almost every winter, but they were more of an annoyance than anything else. They would go after smaller animals, so we had to be sure the ashka were secure; but then they would go away as soon as they found there was no real source of food to be found."

"Did they ever attack anyone?" I asked still a little uneasy about having a donect so close by.

"There were stories," he told us, "but nothing more than that. In my great-grandfather's time there was supposed to have been a small boy killed by a donect, but that may have only been a tale from long ago."

"All the same," I replied, "I don't think I want to be out after dark with one prowling around."

"When you leave," he told me, "take a torch with you. They are afraid of fire just like vood, so you should be safe."

§ § §

But the donect did not go away, and days stretched on into a full cycle of the moons while fresh tracks continued to be found around the barns and in the forest near by. Those who went into the woods to look for firewood often found red patches in the snow and sometimes the remains of an animal half eaten and partially covered.

"They return to their kill and eat it later," Etoar told me one day when he visited the forge to have an axe sharpened.

He had come with Morek and Sepnoar from Teuwa after the Valnar's attack with the vain hope of finding his brother alive in Theo, and so he knew of the behavior of donect. "The snow keeps it fresh," he added. "How they came to know of this, no one knows; but those who hunted high up in the hills during the winter back in Teuwa often saw donect burying the animals they'd killed or digging them out of the snow."

"That's clever of them," I replied. "Too bad this donect isn't clever enough to know it's not wanted around here and leave. I'd sure feel safer if it did."

"All in good time," said Etoar. "Any day now it will realize there is no hope of getting into the barns and having a nice fat nashcal for dinner. Then it will go off to find better prey."

Yet this was not to be, for three days later the donect did manage to break into one of the barns and carry off a nashcal calf. Etoar, Morek and a few others went out with bows to track the beast; but donect are clever, for they do not stay on the ground like vood but climb trees jumping from branch to branch to throw trackers off their trail.

This one was particularly persistent, for over the course of the next twenty days it managed to break into each of the barns in turn and carry off a calf. Yet, though the men who cared for the nashcal were angered by this, and all their efforts to kill the creature were in vain, they knew that soon the snow would melt giving the donect reason to return to its home in the hills.

Then, one evening in the middle of the last moons cycle of winter, both Topan and I were invited to dinner with Aarad and Egome. Morek was also to come as were Marna and the three children, for we were to celebrate the end of Egome's confinement after the birth of Tenwa.

Topan and I broke off work early not wishing to walk to Aarad's in the dark and, as usual, left the compound through the River Gate. As we walked along, Topan made balls with the snow then threw them for Andore to chase which was a game the two of them played whenever they were away from the confines of the stockade.

Soon Topan and Andore lagged behind as Topan was forced to stop and wait for the vood to return to him—his mouth white and frosty from nosing about in the snow—before again throwing another ball. At first I watched the game with amusement but soon tired and decided to go on ahead and let Topan catch up.

As I approached the house, Seppan sat by the door; and when he saw me, he jumped up and ran to greet me.

"Edjah!" he called, but a piercing cry and angry snarl from the roof of the house froze him to where he stood.

The donect lay crouched on the snow covered roof of Aarad's house, a gray and white lump of living flesh almost impossible to see save for its eyes which held a look of hunger and yearning that tore at my heart. There was nothing I could do, for any movement could cause the beast to spring. But to merely do nothing could also doom Seppan to a horrible death, and I was torn by indecision.

"Seppan, don't move," I told him. But my words were meaningless; for he stood with a look of terror on his face, too frightened to even cry.

I cautiously took a step towards him as Aarad appeared at the door. Yet both of us were too late; for as I moved, the donect leaped from the roof with its claws extended and its mouth open as it uttered a cry of hunger and triumph.

"No!" I yelled, and sprang forward as did Aarad; but neither of us could reach Seppan in time. Then, from nowhere, a reddish tan flash flew past me to strike the donect in the side, and Andore and his starving adversary rolled in the snow, a mass of flesh and claws and teeth.

Topan appeared at my side as Aarad reached Seppan and caught him up in his arms then passed him to Egome who had followed him out of the house. I grabbed Topan's arm and spun him around as he leaped forward to rescue his vood almost causing him to fall in the snow.

"Leave me alone," he cried and pushed me away. But before he could move, the two animals broke apart and sat staring at each other in the now reddening snow.

"Andore!" Topan cried, and as the vood turned to look at his master, the donect took the advantage and leapt at its much smaller opponent. But it never reached its target; for as it rose into the air, an arrow struck it in the side, and it fell in the snow a mere pace from Andore.

Shend appeared around the side of the house, the bow still in his hand as he reached for a second arrow. But there was no need, for the donect lay motionless.

Topan rushed to Andore's side and hugged him, but the vood merely collapsed into his arms and lay in his lap breathing heavily. "He's hurt bad," Topan told us stroking the course hair of the vood.

"Bring him into the house," Aarad told him.

"I don't know if I can move him," replied Topan, tears rolling down his creeks. "I think he's dying."

"I will get a blanket," Aarad told him and disappeared into the house.

Shend, who had walked over to the donect to make sure it was dead, knelt down beside Topan and checked Andore's wounds.

"I think he will be all right," he said reassuringly as I reached Topan's side and also knelt down.

"There's a lot of blood," I told Topan, "but it seems to be mainly his leg. I agree with Shend, I think he'll be fine once we clean him up and bandage him."

"Here," said Aarad returning with a blanket, "lay this next to him and we can lift him onto it then carry him into the house."

Topan lay the blanket on the snow then slid it under Andore as Shend and I lifted the vood as gently as we could. When the blanket was in place, we lowered the wounded animal back down. Each of us then took a corner and carried Andore into Aarad's cabin and laid him by the fire.

§ § §

Shend and I were both correct in our assessment of Andore's wounds; for, though his left leg was badly torn, there was no serious damage done to him. He lay trembling by the fire with Topan weeping at his side as Aarad and Shend held him securely while I washed the blood from his fur to assess his wound then applied pressure to stop the bleeding.

"What has happened!" cried Marna as she entered the cabin.

"We saw the donect in the yard," said Morek, "and blood everywhere."

"It tried to attack Seppan," Egome told them still clutching her son in her arms. Yet surprisingly, he remained calm and did not cry though he held tightly to his mother.

"Tohana!" said Marna and rushed to Egome, "is he all right?"

"He is fine," Egome reassured her. "Andore is the one who was hurt."

"Andore?" asked Marna looking at the four of us working on the vood by the fire. "What do you mean?"

"He attacked the donect," Aarad told her. "He saved Seppan's life."

Marna came quickly to the hearth and knelt beside the blanket on which Andore lay. "Here," she said, "let me do that," and she took the bloody cloth from me and examined the wound.

"We need andlen," she told Morek. "The herb I use in soups and stews. It will stop the bleeding. You know," she added when Morek looked puzzled, "the big leaves I crumble into the soup."

"I know what you mean, tolneh," said Setlat. "I'll get it," and she ran from the room.

"Keep the pressure on the wound," Marna told me as she rose slowly to her feet. "I need to boil some water for the andlen.

"We have some already," Egome told her. "I was going to make an herb tea, so there is hot water in the small pot next to the fire."

"Good," Marna replied and took a wooden bowl from the shelf next to the fire. "As soon as Setlat returns with the andlen we can steep it like tea and put it on the wound. It will also help the cuts to heal."

"Thank you, tolneh," said Topan in a weak voice, his lips still trembling.

"I never liked that vood," she told him, "but if he was brave enough to take on a donect…well, maybe it is good to have him around."

§ § §

Andore healed quickly. He spent the next two days on the blanket by the fire in Aarad's house with Topan sleeping next to him. Then, when Marna pronounced him well enough, we moved him to the cabin Topan and I shared; but within twelve days he was up and about walking slowly at first with a limp that never truly went away yet grew less pronounced with time.

He had become a kind of hero within the community at Mekul; and soon it seemed others wished to have a vood as a pet, so that in the spring Aarad and Tenoar added these to what they traded for among the Draygon. Yet it was Andore who seemed prized most, and Topan never ceased to be proud of his pet.

As time passed, nearly twenty vood could be found living in Mekul; and Boec even kept three as it was soon found that Morek had been correct—a vood was an excellent protection against the small animals that got into the grain. Likewise, those who kept the nashcal soon discovered they could be taught to help with the herding as they instinctively pursued the nashcal; but when raised along side of them, they did no more harm than to playfully nip at the nashcal's heals thereby driving them from place to place as directed by the keepers. Nevertheless, what pleased the villagers the most was the fact that no matter how cold the winters became and how deep the snow was that lay about our homes, we were never again visited by a donect in all the days that I lived in Mekul.

Chapter VI

The plane on which Mekul was built ended a few leagues to the north where a series of low hills gradually gave way to the foothills of a mountain chain. These hills marked the course of the Drevet which wound its way in a series of twists and turns along the base of these gently rising bluffs, knolls and hillocks. Then, some forty leagues from Mekul the river was broken by a waterfall a full ten times the height of the one on the Ruha between Crayoar and Alna.

I had seen this waterfall; for Aarad, Boec, Shend and I had twice come to its base and camped just to escape the village and the tedium of daily life. Though a long walk, it was not particularly difficult; for a well worn path lined the bank of the Drevet veering off now and then into the forest to find fords across the little streams which here and there joined the main river along its course. Then, at the base of the falls, this pathway joined another which led to the top of the falls.

Adjuwa had told us that these pathways were all that remained of the Draygon villages which long ago had dotted the course of the Drevet. Then, due to a conflict which arose with the Draygon above the falls, the villages were one by one abandoned leaving only the path now kept open by the many animals which used it to seek water from the river.

Yet this path was useful to our hunters who often hunted zhehpet and other animals along its route all the way to the falls. And so one day, nearly six sun cycles after we had arrived at Mekul, a group of our hunters returned with more than their usual kill; for they brought with them on a stretcher a man wounded by an arrow in his shoulder and near death.

He was obviously not a Draygon; for his hair was as dark as ours, and the remnants of a ragged blood stained tunic betrayed him as a Kroemaeon. The hunters told us they had found him unconscious at the base of the falls; that they had removed the arrow head and cleaned his wound the best they could before beginning the three day trek back to Mekul; but that he had not regained consciousness in all that time.

We had no healer woman, yet Marna served us as best she could since she was skilled to some degree in the use of herbs having raised six children. For this reason the man was brought to Morek's house so that Marna could tend him, and all awaited anxiously to see if he would awake and tell us of the Others.

While the man slept, speculation grew; for if he were truly one of the Others, it made no sense that he should be found so far inland since we had seen no sign of their ships anywhere. The hunters returned to the falls with those willing to accompany them and climbed the path leading to the top then explored the course of the upper river for as far as they dared, yet no sign of an encampment could be found.

Meanwhile Marna ordered Morek and I to bathe the stranger while she prepared a poultice of herbs then dressed his wound with this. Finally, she fed him broth as I sat with her at his side hoping against hope that he would awake and tell us where to find those so dear to us.

The man slept for two more days, and each time Marna changed his dressings she looked grave. "The poison is not spreading," she told us, "but he had been unconscious for a long time." And we all feared he would die at any moment taking his secret with him.

Then, on the third day after his arrival in Mekul, he awoke while I was sitting watch as Marna prepared to feed him more broth.

"Who?" was all he said.

"My name is Idar," I told him. "You're safe. We found you by the falls. What's your name?"

"Almath," he replied, but before I could ask him anything else Marna came into the room.

"He's awake!" she cried. "You should have called me immediately just as I told you. Now go, you must tell Miku and the Council while I feed him."

"I was…"

"You were trying to question him," she cut me off. Then more gently, "I know your concern. But he needs food and rest if he is to get better, not talk. Now go while I care for him."

The whole village was astir with the news that Almath had spoken to me, but this excitement was tempered when he did not again awake all that day. Yet speculation again surged through the village, and a call was made to send an expedition to sail south along the coast as we had not traveled more than a few leagues in that direction searching for the best fishing. Many now felt that the Others could have somehow passed by the bay, maybe in fog, and continued on down the coast. Thus the *Mer,* which was not fishing that cycle of the moons, was to be sent to seek any sign of the Others passing.

With this in mind, when the *Zet* returned from trading, Miku ordered her to return immediately in order to find a Draygon willing to go with the *Mer* and speak with those they might find along the way. This they found not to be a problem, for it seemed the Draygon vied with one another for a chance to sail on one of our great ships.

"You should have seen old Adjuwa," Aarad told us. "You could tell he wanted to go himself; but being chief, he could not leave his tribe, so he sent Adayu instead. I think it nearly killed him."

And so, as Almath slept and tried to recover, the *Mer* sailed down the Drevet and out along the coast in search of the Others.

§ § §

Almath awoke in the evening of the day after I had learned his name; but only Marna was with him, and she did not prod him for information.

"He needs his rest," she kept telling us. "There will be time when he is well to question him. But I can tell you this, he is from Arganon."

"Did he tell you that?" I asked.

"No," she replied, "he said little, but the manner of his speech told me he was raised in the city itself and not in one of the villages round about."

"All this from a few words?" I asked.

"When you are old and have listened much," she told me, "you know."

"Then he is not one of the Others," said Morek.

"He still could be," I replied. "The *Kwel* was from Arganon and was in the harbor at Alna. He could be from the *Kwel.*"

The next time Marna changed Almath's dressing, she was alarmed. "The poison has started to spread," she told us, and even Morek and I knew by his color that he would probably not make it. "If he awakes again, you should ask him what you wish, there might not be another chance."

And so Morek and I took turns sitting by his side through the night and into the next day until he at last awoke in the evening covered in sweat.

"Almath," I said to him, and he looked at me. "Were you on the *Kwel*?" but his eyes registered nothing, and I was not totally sure he had understood my question.

"Marna, he's awake!" I called into the next room then repeated what I had asked in a bit louder voice, "The *Kwel*, did you sail on the *Kwel*? Do you know Naemen?"

"Naemen, you know Naemen?" he replied in a very weak voice as Marna entered the room. "A good man," he said with a smile then fell back asleep.

He never regained consciousness but died two days later, and we buried him in the field next to the south wall of the stockade in the shadow of the temple Otna had built.

§ § §

The *Mer* returned thirty days after she left without finding any sign of the Others. Her crew had sailed south along the coast for over fifteen days and had sighted three large Draygon villages. Yet when questioned by Adayu, the villagers claimed to have never seen Kroemaeon ships before; and from their reaction, Abdoar was sure this was true as they seemed totally amazed at the wonder of all they saw.

And so our hope of finding the Others died again. Yet the mystery of Almath remained very much alive in Mekul; and as the cycles of the sun went on, it was talked about by firelight on dark winter nights when naught much else was left to discuss. Again and again we asked ourselves how he came to be at the falls, and what he could have told us had he lived.

Chapter VII

The discovery of the Draygon villages to the south bought on a flurry of new trade, and Aarad and Tenoar soon divided the business between them. Tenoar wished me to join him on these new expeditions to the south, but I had lost my passion for the sea. It had once been my whole reason for living, but now I desired only what I had left behind in Alna; for my zeal, my ardor, my longing for the open water and the feel of waves beneath me lay in a cave on the side of a hill far away.

With the choice of Miku as leader and the forming of the Council, Mekul had prospered; for the captains encouraged those with skills to put them to use as had I. Soon Penepe opened a tailor's shop and Kellebet one supplying us with shoes and other leather goods. Three men from Sefna, who had once worked in the ship yards, began to build boats—tarkoi at first to ferry men and supplies across the Drevet where the forest had been cleared and farms and orchards now dotted the west side of the river. It was to these three, then, that Tenoar turned when he wished to build another trading ship.

At first he used the *Mer,* just as he had the *Zet;* but Abdoar and the crew of the *Mer* wished only to remain fishermen. This meant that Tenoar needed to build a new ship in order to continue his trading ventures. Thus the *Tellic,* or little *Tel,* set sail on the River Drevet then down the southern coast a mere eight moons cycles after Almath's death.

She was as her namesake, matching the *Tel* as closely as possible, a copy in miniature of the once proud ship. Supporting only a single mast and but sixty paces in length, the *Tellic* did us proud; for she proved that we had finally overcome the wilderness and built a home for ourselves in this land of exile in the far north.

To aid in communicating with the Draygon to the south, Tenoar took as his ship's mallet a young man from the mining camp named Elluel. He was a Draygon, his mother having married a Kroemaeon; and as a boy he had come to live among us and grew up as part of our community. Upon reaching manhood at the age of thirteen, he decided to remain in Mekul, a thing uncommon with the Draygon children whose mothers married Kroemaeon men; and so he had gone to Tenoar and boldly asked to accompany him on his trading voyages to the south.

Tenoar was eager to accept him, for even as a child Elluel had earned a reputation in the mining camp as a hard worker and as one eager to learn the Kroemaeon way of life. I knew him since he often came with his step-father to deliver the raw ore which we smelted into the iron used in the forge, and I added my recommendation when Tenoar asked me about him.

Ernoar and Sepnoar, who by this time had both apprenticed with me, also came to befriend him; for, although Elluel was slightly younger than them, he was an outgoing boy, one hard to dislike. Thus they had admitted him easily into their close knit friendship and eagerly accepted him into the growing band of young men who met together as Aarad and I had once done when we were their age. And this, too, was seen by us as a sign that life went on.

§ § §

I reached my twenty-fifth cycle of the sun as Topan turned eighteen, an age which seemed to bring upon him a renewed restlessness of spirit, one urging him to build a cabin for himself on the edge of the meadow away from the other homes in the community. He had always sought ways to advance his growing desire for independence, and during the sun cycle before turning eighteen Topan increasingly spent more and more time traveling with Aarad to the Draygon villages seemingly on every third or fourth voyage of the *Zet*.

"He has never really had friends his own age," Aarad told me as they were preparing to leave for another trip to the Draygon villages, "not since he came aboard the *Tel* anyway. Marna says he had three good friends back in Terhal, but…

"Anyway, it seems the Draygon like him well enough, for I see little of him during our stays there. Sometimes I almost forget he came with me, and once I nearly left him behind. I think he needs this time."

"I don't begrudge him the time," I replied, "and you're right, he needs friends; yet he still seems to be gone a lot…then he always did want to do things his own way. I guess he's just being Topan."

"Well, one good thing," Aarad continued, "he can almost speak Draygon like one of them, and that could come in handy sometime."

I truly did not begrudge Topan this time away; for with both Ernoar and Sepnoar now apprenticed with me full time, I had plenty of help. And Topan had always been faithful in his work never giving me cause for complaint. Yet something about this new desire of his to be away from Mekul made me feel uneasy, and I could not explain it to myself nor to anyone.

Then, in midsummer, the *Zet* returned from its trading voyage without Topan.

"He told me his friends were going to show him the land route back to Mekul," Aarad told us to ease Marna's concern that he was not aboard ship. "He said he might even make it back to Mekul before the *Zet*, but it seems he was wrong."

"Are you sure nothing happened to him?" asked a concerned Marna.

"He should be all right," Aarad replied, "he has Andore with him, and it is summer. Idar and I have walked nearly as far on our trips to the falls, and we have never had any trouble. He is just taking his time. You know how he is; but if he has not returned by tomorrow, I will ask Elluel to go with me and look for him."

"The *Tellic* left yesterday," I told him.

"Well, one of the other Draygon boys then," he replied. "They all know the way, the older ones at least."

But there was no need to go looking for Topan, for the next morning he walked into the smithy as if nothing had happened.

"Well, well, well," I told him, "the lost one returns at last."

"I wasn't lost," he replied sounding a little defensive, "I knew where I was going. The directions my friends gave me were easy to follow. Besides, there's a trail, not a good one, but a trail anyway; so it's really easy to find your way."

"Well, you're back at last," I said with a chuckle, "and the work's piled up as usual while you've been off having yourself a good time," though this was really not true since Ernoar especially was becoming an excellent smith.

"Idar," and his voice dropped almost to a whisper, "we need to talk."

"We have been," I told him.

"No, I mean yes, we have…I've got something important to tell you, and…"

"What is it?" I asked; for I had never seen him this serious, not since his early days on the *Tel* after we left Terhal. And so I put the piece of iron I was working aside and looked intently at him.

"I've done something," he replied. "Tolneh's not going to be pleased at all when she finds out, but I love her…"

"Love who? What are you talking about?"

"Enuwa," he told me, "I love her, and I brought her with me. I'm taking her as my wife."

The news stunned me. It was impossible that what he was telling me was true.

"*Who* is Enuwa?" I asked cautiously.

"A girl, a young woman," he replied. "She's Draygon, and I met her just after I got Andore. I've come to love her, and we want to get married; so we left together. She's at my cabin now."

"Who knows about this?" I asked.

"Only you, now," he replied.

"The Draygon do not let their young women marry just anyone," I told him. "So what do you mean you want to get married?"

"You're right," he said, "the Draygon don't. She's pledged to someone, a man named Kalleel. But he doesn't love her, and she loves me and wants to marry me. So we left together."

"She just ran away with you?" I asked, my voice beginning to rise.

"Not so loud," he told me. "Yes, she ran away with me, and she's not going back.

"Well, you're right about one thing," I replied, "Marna will not be happy about this. You know how she feels about these kinds of marriages. Why do you always have to be so impulsive? Don't you ever think?"

"Think about what?" asked Ernoar. "What's he done now?"

"Go ahead," I said, "tell him. He'll find out anyway." Then, when Topan made no reply, I added, "Your brother has brought back a Draygon wife."

"Oh, tolneh's going to be *so* mad," Ernoar told his brother as a broad grin spread across his face. "Sepnoar, come here! You have to hear this! Topan's marrying a Draygon."

"No," said Sepnoar as he walked towards us, "he's not that stupid. I mean, not that it's stupid to marry a Draygon; but your grandmother would kill him…" Then he stopped when he saw the look on Topan's face.

"You're doing it!" Sepnoar cried, "you're really going to do it. Oh, I can hardly wait to hear Marna yell at you."

§ § §

Marna did some of her best yelling. In fact, I became concerned as it did not seem a good thing for someone of her advanced age to become that angry. But through it all Topan stood his ground, and nothing Marna said could sway his mind.

Enuwa was truly an attractive young woman, and I could see why Topan might be drawn to her. Yet there was something about her that seemed to put a barrier between her and the rest of the community in Mekul, something that did not endear her to us even beyond Marna's objections.

She was proud for one thing, one might say haughty in her dealings with others especially women; and this gave Marna a new reason to dislike her as her list of objections to Topan's choice of a wife grew almost daily. Nor was Enuwa the hard worker that we had come to expect from a Draygon woman. She was not lazy, yet she lacked the zeal, the energy and drive, we had seen in those who had married Kroemaeon men and come to live among us.

"She is young," Anula told us, "and she is the daughter of Adayu who is second only to Adjuwa, but she will need to change much if she wishes to live here among the Kroemaeon."

Anula had come to the forge with Ettak who needed an axe sharpened in order to begin cutting wood for the winter. As it happened, Aarad was in the forge as well talking with me about Enuwa and how he felt Marna treated her so unfairly.

"Even a change in her attitude will be of little concern to Marna," said Aarad. "No matter what she does, Marna will never accept her."

At this Anula stiffened and looked grave. "Marna is a hard woman to please," she commented. "I know, I have tried my best to appease her; but she has her beliefs and will not change easily. If there is trouble because of this, we will not hear the end of it from Marna."

"Trouble?" I asked, "what trouble?"

"Enuwa's husband," she replied, "I doubt he will accept her running off like this. It is an insult to his honor."

"But Topan says they were never married," said Aarad.

"Not as the Kroemaeon see it," she told us. "But among the Draygon it is different. She was pledged to him, and she is his wife no matter what Topan says. If Kalleel feels his honor has been…how do you say it? I do not remember the word, but he will surly be insulted by her running away and will call for *pallunaroo*."

"*Pallunaroo?*" I asked, "What is that?"

"Oh," she replied, "you ask so many hard questions. *Pallunaroo* is…making things right, justice you might call it. But in this case, I'm sure it will mean death."

Chapter VIII

When pressed, Anula would tell us little more, only that the *pallunaroo* was the Draygon way of seeking vengeance or retribution on those who had wronged them or compromised their honor; and that this usually included the death of the one committing the wrong. She also told us it was a *pallunaroo* that had forced the Draygon living along the Drevet to abandon their homes so long ago and move far to the south and east in order to avoid the endless cycle of killing brought upon them by those who lived in the mountains above the falls. Then, as Sepnoar had finished sharpening the axe Ettak had brought with them, she left at her husband's side.

Yet we did not have long to wait before learning the details of Anula's dire prediction; for a mere three days later—eight days from Topan's return to Mekul—Karnot and Enon, who had married Draygon women and chosen to remain at the trading compound rather than return to Mekul, arrived at the stockade by way of the land route with three nashcal loaded with goods to be traded.

They met with Aarad at his home and told him the reason why they had come. Aarad then found quarters for them in the cabin used to store what was brought back from the Draygon villages then came to the forge.

"It is worse than Anula told us," said Aarad as soon as he entered the forge. "Your wife's *real* husband has put a price on your head," and he gave Topan a look of sheer hatred and anger.

"Seems his honor is worth your life and the lives of four of your male relatives," Aarad continued, speaking now to the silence that filled the room. "But seeing as you only have one male relative, three of us will do; and if we try to trade with the Draygon in Adjuwa's village, or any of the villages along their river, Kalleel will settle the matter by killing five of us in your place."

No one spoke for what seemed like forever, then Aarad exploded with rage, "You foolish little whelp!" he yelled at Topan who stood beside me.

"You never gave a thought to what you were doing, did you? Now look what you've done! You've doomed us all to a war with the Draygon!"

"I…" was all Topan could say.

"Don't speak to me, or I might kill you myself and hand over your head to Kalleel as a token of friendship.

"Miku is calling a meeting of the Council in an hour. Be there. And that…*wife* of yours, bring her with you. She is just as responsible for this as you are—even more so since it is her custom for which we are all expected to die.

"I am going to talk to Anula. She also needs to be at the meeting, and this time she needs to give us answers that make sense." Having said this, he was gone.

"The Draygon are going to *kill* me?" asked Ernoar in almost a whisper as soon as Aarad had left. I turned around and saw him standing at the rear of the forge beside Sepnoar who looked as if he, too, was under a sentence of death.

"No," I told him, "no, I'm sure Miku and the Council will find some way to make the Draygon…"

"No," Topan broke in, "a *pallunaroo* is final. There's no way to take it back."

"You *knew* of this?" I asked him. "Yet you risked your brother's life to get what you wanted."

"My friends among the Draygon talk about *pallunaroo* all the time," he told me. "It can't be taken back. It's a matter of honor, but no one has ever demanded death. They've worked off the debt or given gifts—not a life."

"Aarad's right," said Ernoar walking towards his brother. "You never think of anyone but yourself. You weren't like that back in Terhal, not when nodah and nodeh were alive…but since we've come here you've changed.

"I used to look up to you. You were my big brother," he told Topan with tears in his eyes. "But not any more, you're no brother to me." With that, he left the forge, slamming the door behind him and leaving Topan frozen in silence.

§ § §

The hall in which the Council met had been added on to the house Miku had built for himself along the eastern wall of the stockade and now stood beside the temple we had raised to honor the toha. It was not a large building since the Council usually met alone at a long table set at one end of the hall. Yet there was space for maybe twenty or thirty others to gather and listen as the Council discussed the needs of our community or to present their own concerns to those who governed us.

As soon as Ernoar left I told Sepnoar to bank the fire and prepare to close down the forge for the day. Then I turned to Topan.

"You had best do as Aarad told you," I said. "Get Enuwa and meet us at the Council Hall as soon as you can."

"Idar, I…" he began, but I cut him off.

"There's nothing to say," I told him, "at least not to me and not now. Whatever you have to say, save it for the Council and Miku. Just go."

He looked at me, and I saw a deep pain of regret in his eyes. But there was nothing I could do for him, and after a moment he turned and left.

When I reached the Council Hall nearly a half hour later, it was already full leaving many to stand outside awaiting the start of the meeting even though they would not be able to fit inside the now crowded hall. I was allowed in as was Ernoar though Sepnoar was made to wait outside. Aarad, Morek, Marna and Setlat were already there as was Anula; and so I made my way as best I could across the hall to stand with them in a small group.

Soon Karnot and Enon arrived, and those who guarded the doors were now forced to ask others to leave in order to make room for them. Likewise, when Topan and Enuwa entered the hall others were sent outside; however, this time those who left did so reluctantly, and I could tell that they resented the presence of Topan and his Draygon bride.

At last Miku entered with the Council using a door leading directly from his house into the Council chamber. As they came in, each one took his place at the table, all with somber looks on their faces.

There was no need to wait for silence in order to begin; for as soon as the door opened, what whispered talking there had been died almost instantly as all eyes turned to watch this solemn procession of those we trusted to lead us and make things right again.

When all of the Council members were seated, Miku rose from his chair and addressed the silent crowd.

"I am sure you all understand why we are here," he began, "as it seems news travels quickly in our village, especially news of this kind. But so that all may hear the truth and not rumors, I will ask Karnot and Enon to explain what has happened." Then motioning to the two traders, he sat back down.

As simple seamen, neither Karnot nor Enon were used to speaking to a crowd such as was now assembled before them, and all could tell they were reluctant to begin. Most likely they had thought Miku, or even Aarad, would do the talking; and they would only need to answer a few questions. They stood, therefore, in nervous silence for a few moments before Karnot found the courage to speak.

"It seems Topan here," and he pointed directly at Topan as he spoke, "has decided to take himself a Draygon wife. I guess you all know that, and there's nothing wrong with it, I done it myself. But my wife was a widow, her husband had been dead three sun cycles when I married her; and that's not a problem with the Draygon.

"But Topan, he's decided to marry a young one, someone pledged to an already living husband; and that's somethin' the Draygon don't take to at all. It's dishonorable to them as it would be for us if our wife ran off with some other man. It's just not right."

"But they had never married," said Topan. "And he didn't love her. He was even planning on setting her aside and marrying Abaya."

"Then ya' should have waited 'til he did," said Enon. "Then no one would o' cared. But no, you had to act rashly and run off with her now."

"Well, that now's the problem," Karnot continued. "The Draygon have something they call *pallunaroo*. It's a way of settlin' their differences, but it's nothin' like what we do. It's a kind o' blood feud, like we hear about in the old stories, only worse.

"It seems Kalleel's honor will only be satisfied with the death of Topan and four of his male relatives. Well, we told Kalleel that Topan is an orphan and only has one brother. So Kalleel says Topan can pick three o' his friends to take the place o' the missin' relatives."

At these words, murmuring began to fill the hall, and Miku again stood up this time motioning for silence. "Let Karnot finish," he said. "There will be time for talk afterwards."

"That's about all there is to tell," Karnot told us. "The Draygon are demanding you turn over Topan, his brother and three of Topan's friends to satisfy the honor of Kalleel."

"And if we don't?" I asked.

"If ya' don't, then ya' join in the dishonor Topan's brought upon Kalleel," Enon replied, "and they will just pick five men and kill them themselves."

"But why haven't they killed the two of you?" asked Menepe.

"For one thing they're waiting for us to bring back the prisoners," said Karnot, "but if we don't…well, we don't live in Mekul, so we have nothin' to do with all this. If you don't give them Topan and the others, then Mekul will be just as guilty as he is," and again he pointed at Topan. "Anyone who's not a part o' this village will have no guilt, only those who harbor him."

"And that means we can no longer trade with the Draygon," Aarad told us, "at least the Draygon who live along the Adujae. If we do not give them five men to kill, then they will take the first five who walk off the *Zet* and kill them."

"That's pretty much it," said Enon. "They'll get their blood one way or another."

"What if we just wait them out?" Elfad asked.

"You cannot," Anula told him. "I would suggest you give Kalleel what he asks for. If you don't, he'll take them anyway. Maybe not now, but as long as Kalleel is alive, and his honor is not satisfied, he will pursue you all until he has taken his five lives."

"That, Anula, is not possible," said Miku rising once more to his feet. "You have lived among us for a long time and should know that we cannot kill the innocent along with the guilty. Topan has wronged Kalleel, and though by our laws he has done nothing deserving of death, we could give him over to the justice of the Draygon. But we cannot ask anyone else to die for what he has done."

"But they *will* die for what he has done," Anula replied, "for Kalleel and his friends will pick them off one by one until they have taken five lives; and if you try to stop them, if you kill anyone sent by Kalleel to take his revenge, then more will die. To resist the *pallunaroo* is itself a dishonor. Resist them and you bring more death upon yourselves.

"That is the reason the Draygon who lived here so long ago left. That *pallunaroo* lasted over fifty cycles of the sun. Can you wait that long? This will only be over when Kalleel is dead or his honor is satisfied."

§ § §

Miku was correct, we could not sacrifice the innocent; and as we would accomplish nothing by handing Topan over to the Draygon, the Council voted to send Karnot and Enon back to their homes with the hope they could negotiate a different outcome.

"Try to explain to them that this is not our way," Miku told them. "Tell them that it would violate *our* honor to sacrifice those who are innocent of any wrong doing."

“It will do no good,” Anula cautioned.

“Well,” Miku replied, “we must try.”

As a token of good faith, the goods Karnot and Enon brought with them were exchanged for Kroemaeon made cloth and a few metal tools which could not be used as weapons against us. But the Draygon were to be told that we might not be willing to trade with them in the future if some agreement could not be reached.

In the mean time, the Council decided to expanded the stockade; and Miku ordered all of us to remain within the confines of the village unless we were accompanied by armed bowman for our protection. And so life went on as best it could despite the threat of death, at least for the time being.

Chapter IX

The first death did not come until early spring, just as the snows of winter began to melt. One of the farmers from Mekul had gone out to check the fields foolishly disregarding the order not to leave the compound alone. He left in the early morning; and, when other villagers went out to the forest later in the day to cut fire wood, they discovered his body with two arrows in it lying face down in patch of snow.

His death affected Marna deeply, for she took it personally. She had not really known the man nor any of his family; nevertheless, Marna felt that the blame rested on her because of Topan. Thus she brooded quietly growing into herself and causing her health to suffer. Then, as we were preparing to celebrate the Toharofa, Marna died an old and broken woman.

Topan, too, was affected by the man's death and later by that of his grandmother since he blamed himself as did nearly all of the villagers. And so, as time passed, he grew sullen and quiet, avoiding all contact with anyone in Mekul except for Morek and myself who were the only ones who showed him any compassion.

Aarad would still not speak to him nor would Ernoar and Sepnoar; and, after Marna's death, Setlat joined them in ostracizing her brother. The rest of the village also shunned him. In fact I was forced to obtain food for him and Enuwa since those who dispensed meat, fish, grain and vegetables would not accept the wooden coins he earned for the work he did.

This exclusion of Topan made work in the forge nearly impossible since I alone would speak to him. Yet over time we worked out a schedule, one not mutually agreed upon but an informal arrangement whereby Topan come to the forge in the early morning. Then, in the midmorning, he went off to the furnace where he smelted iron by himself for the remainder of the day. This allowed Sepnoar and Ernoar to avoid Topan's presence while working with me in the forge. No one ever spoke of this arrangement. It just happened and went on moons cycle after moons cycle as summer changed to autumn then to winter and spring, and finally back to summer again.

§ § §

Kebbit had died the winter before Marna's passing, not at the hands of the Draygon but from an illness brought on by the harsh climate of the far north. This meant that I had lost two of those who were dear to me both in the space of three moons cycles.

Since the ground was frozen when Kebbit died due to the harshness of the winter, we buried him in the snow. Then, when spring came and the snow began to melt, we were able to dig a grave for him and formally buried him a short time before Marna passed away.

For this reason, both Aarad and I were especially saddened at Marna's death; for the second burial of Kebbit had torn open the wounds which had just begun to heal. Kebbit had been like a second father to both of us as we worked aboard the *Tel*, and Marna had become for us the grandmother neither Aarad nor I had known. And so we grieved deeply for both of them each in our own way.

After Marna's burial, we all returned to Aarad's house to eat and find what solace we could in one another's company. Topan had not come to the burial, though this was not of his own choosing; and I was grieved at this as well since I knew the pain and guilt he bore and was force to bear alone.

He had spoken of this to me the morning before as we worked alone in the forge before Sepnoar and Ernoar came to work. Yet though I had begged Ernoar to take pity on his brother, it had done no good; and I was forced to tell Topan that it would be best for him to stay away from the burial to avoid an argument which could bring dishonor upon his grandmother's passing.

Boec, Shend and their families had been close to Marna as well, and so they also joined us each bringing something to eat to be shared communally with everyone. Then, as we sat at table, we began talking of Marna, relating our memories of her which was the custom passed down from one generation to the next.

"The thing I will miss most," said Morek, "is her karnel. I had not eaten it before meeting her, yet I have grown to look forward to her making it."

"You should have had it back in Terhal," Ernoar told us. "It was much better. I think it's because she used gamu and not zhehpet, but whatever it was, I used to love to eat at her house because she always made karnel when we did."

"She showed me how to make it," added Setlat, "but no matter how I try, mine is never quite as good as hers. I'll miss her cooking myself. It was something she was always known for."

The talk went on, but I heard little more; for my mind began to wander back to Alna, to Melne's eln chowder which differed so much from that made by the other women of our village, to my mother's cheshoi with cheese and gork, even to the kahlmek which made Sethel's inn so well known Tenoar had come to make Alna his home port so that he might enjoy it. To me it seemed strange how memories came by way of the senses, for the smell of Huno as he lay newly washed drying by the fire was in some way intertwined with that of heshel and the scent of Illiad's hair as she lay beside me on those nights which now seemed to me in a different lifetime.

I remembered the touch of her hand upon mine as we danced the zubah now so long ago; and as I closed my eyes, I pictured both her and my mother standing on the wharf waving me farewell as I left them in a pose now burned forever into my mind. Then I heard once more the laughter Illiad had shared with my mother in a dream I had once had, and her voice came to me clearly from another dream as if spoken only the night before: "Forgive me."

"Idar," Boec's voice broke through my thoughts, "you look a thousand leagues away.

"And more," I told him coming to myself again. "I'm sorry, all this talk of Marna made me think of home, of Alna and…"

"I know," said Egome reaching out a hand from across the table where she sat beside Aarad. "I started thinking of my parents as well. It seems so wrong that we are here so far away from what should be our home; that we, too, will one day rest beside Marna leaving those we left behind in Theo to be forever lost to us."

"Not forever," said Morek. "Marna's body lies here in Mekul, yet she is not truly lost. Her spirit has gone to join her ancestors. She is at peace."

"Do you really think so?" I asked.

"Of course," Aarad replied before Morek could answer. "Don't you?"

"I did once," I told him, "but now, after all that's happened…"

"We go on," said Morek. "This life is only the beginning. We are born, we live, and then we die; but we go on. Our bodies my die, but our spirit does not."

"You're wrong," I told him, "this is all there is, and when you're dead you're dead and nothing more. We find our immortality in our flesh. You will go on. You have Sepnoar. And Aarad, you have Seppan and Tenwa. Both of you will someday have grandchildren, and they will have grandchildren. And a thousand sun cycles from now, even though your names will have long been forgotten, someone will live because you lived today. But I am all that is left of my parents. When I die, they die with me; and my grave will become the final resting place for all three of us."

Chapter X

In the autumn after Marna's death, a second man was killed to satisfy Kalleel's honor. The *Zet* could not safely enter the waters of the Adujae, for to do so would mean death; however, the villages along the Eduin took no part in the *pallunaroo*. Aarad, then, set out to trade with them, though this was difficult as the Eduin was far too shallow to allow the *Zet* to pass.

Yet by anchoring his ship at the far eastern edge of the bay near the mouth of the Eduin, Aarad was able to row up river taking Elluel with him as an interpreter. In this way arrangements were made to meet the *Zet* twice each moons cycle along the shore of the bay where the Draygon could trade for Kroemaeon goods.

This, of course, angered the Draygon along the Adujae since they were no longer welcome to trade with us. As a result, they attacked the *Zet* while she lay at anchor on her second trading voyage that autumn. One crewman on the *Zet* was killed during the fighting, and all trade with the Draygon along both rivers came to an end.

Topan was again deeply affected by what happened, by the death and suffering which had come about because of his rashness; and he grew more and more despondent as there seemed to be nothing he could do. Then one day Elluel came to the forge bringing a message from Tenoar concerning the axes we had agreed to make for the *Tellic's* next voyage south.

After receiving my reply to Tenoar's question, Elluel turned to go. But when he reached the door, he stopped, turned and looked at Topan with the most serious expression on his face I had ever seen.

"You could fight him," he said, and both Topan and I looked up from our work.

"Who?" I asked

"Topan," he replied, "he could fight Kalleel."

"What do you mean?" Topan asked him a little cautiously.

"Kalleel wants you dead," he began, "if he kills you, then that is one life more he has taken to satisfy his honor. But if you kill him, his death will end the *pallunaroo*. The only question is, are you brave enough to risk it, are you willing to offer your life to end the killing and hatred between our villages?"

With that, he turned and left.

§ § §

Three days later, Elluel left on the *Tellic;* but Topan continued to think of what he had said, for several times he talked to me about it during Elluel's absence. I was surprised he even took what had been said seriously since Topan had never been particularly brave as a boy nor now as a man. Besides this, he had told me Enuwa was expecting a baby; so I could not believe that he was actually giving thought to Elluel's suggestion.

"I can't go on like this," he told me. "Even my own family won't speak to me. It's like I'm dead already."

"But you're not a warrior," I argued back. "You have no fighting skills. He'll kill you for sure, and then what will happen to Enuwa and the baby?"

"What will happen to Enuwa and the baby if I don't?" he retorted. "This is not the way I planned things when I asked her to marry me. We were going to be happy, to raise a family, to grow old together. I never thought any of this would happen, Idar, I truly didn't."

"I thought the same thing myself," I told him, "once, long ago. I guess none of us can know for sure what will happen.

"…But that was different. The Valnar came, and changed our lives in an instant. We had no choice. You do."

"Do I really?" he replied. "Do I really have a choice, or did I make that choice already when I acted foolishly?

"I have to live with the consequences of my actions, don't I? All my life you, Morek, tolneh…even Aarad have been telling me this. I guess it's time I did what I've been told."

"But you'll die," I told him.

"Maybe," he replied, "but with a bit of luck, I could end all this."

"Do you really feel that lucky?" I asked.

"Did you, the day you killed the two Valnar soldiers back in Terhal?" he replied. "Don't you see? It makes no difference. I've got to fight Kalleel."

§ § §

The *Tellic* returned to Mekul nearly a moons cycle later and was to be in port until spring since the winter storms would soon be upon us. The day after her arrival, Topan sought out Elluel before he left for the mining camp and shore leave to ask him if he would be willing to talk to Kalleel about a one on one fight to settle the *pallunaroo*.

Elluel seemed surprised at this; for, though it had been his suggestion, he had not truly expected Topan to have the courage to embrace the idea. Yet when asked to act as intermediary, Elluel accepted.

"But are you in any danger?" I asked him when he came to the forge to find Topan before going home to visit his family.

"Not really," he replied. "I have cousins and two uncles who live in the same village as Kalleel, and it is well known I live with my mother in the mining camp and not in Mekul. Since the *pallunaroo* began, we have had no contact with our relatives among the Draygon; so no one will know I sail with Tenoar on the *Tellic*. If they did, I could be seen as an enemy; but as I am a Draygon, I should be safe and not become a victim of Kalleel's honor."

"Still," I told him, "it seems dangerous."

"The most dangerous part," he replied, "will be the trip there and back. If it snows while I'm traveling, I could be in trouble."

When he left, Ernoar asked why he was looking for Topan; and I told him what his brother intended to do. He was shocked as could be expected since none of us thought Topan had the courage to do such a thing.

"He can't take your hatred," I told him, "and now that of Setlat. He's already dead in his own eyes, at least that's what he told me. And now that Enuwa is expecting a baby, he feels he has to do something to prove he's not the cowardly fool everyone thinks him to be.

"You know, he blames himself for all that's happened; and I know you all think he deserves to be blamed. I agree with you that he was a fool. Yet now he only wants to prove he's not a coward as well, one who sits by and waits for others to die in his place."

Ernoar said nothing. He merely nodded and returned to work. Yet I felt I had somehow gotten through to him at last, for he remained unusually quiet the rest of the day.

§ § §

Elluel was gone a long time, and we all feared that he had become the third victim of Kalleel's wrath. But this was not to be, for at the end of the second winter moons cycle he returned to Mekul to inform us that Kalleel had agreed to a one on one combat to the death to be held once spring had come and the snow had melted.

As a sign of his good faith, Kalleel further agreed no one else would die until after he had personally killed Topan; and he challenged Ernoar to fight him as well along with anyone else in Mekul who still defended the stealing of another man's wife. The last part of his message stung Ernoar as it did the rest of us, for no one condoned such an act; but neither did we feel it should cost the lives of four innocent men.

Enon and Karnot returned with Elluel, for the Draygon were anxious to trade with us once more and felt that with a truce in place we should simply overlook the killing of two men and act as if nothing had happened. The men of the *Zet* were especially angered by this seeming lack of feeling for those who had died; yet the Council decided it would be unwise to anger the Draygon further by refusing. And so Enon and Karnot were sent back to their homes with Kroemaeon goods in exchange for those they had brought as well as with a message for Kalleel that Topan would meet him in combat in mid spring when the last of the snow had melted.

§ § §

With the combat arranged for later in the spring, Topan was given time to train, time to prepare himself and learn, as he could, those fighting skills necessary to save his life. There were few in Mekul who could aid him in this as only two guards from Theo had survived and come with us; and neither of these were willing, at first, to assist Topan in training to meet Kalleel. This left only Elluel who, as a boy among the Draygon before he came to live with us, had been taught to fight, first by his father and later by his two uncles. This was the custom among the Draygon; for from time to time the need arose to protect their families, homes and lands from the Tenyah who often raided Draygon territory.

Elluel began to spar with Topan using sections of the poles once used aboard the *Tel* to maneuver the ship in and out of port; for, as Elluel told us, Topan first needed to learn how to defend himself, to fend off an attacker's blows. Only then could he develop the skills he needed to assail another and be victorious on the field of combat.

From time to time I would come to watch them; and as I did, I thought of my battle with the Valnar scouts and how luck had played such a vital part in my victory over them. Yet I also remembered the feeling of horror as well as the nausea that followed my taking of another's life, and I wondered if it were possible that Topan had the ability to strike such a blow.

I had not intended to kill the scouts. They had come upon us without warning, and it was only when my anger boiled over that I had acted. There had been no malice in me, and I could not imagine going up against them on a field of battle, my heart intent on shedding their blood. Yet this was Topan's course, the path he had chosen; and in some small way, each time I watched him spar with Elluel, my respect for him grew.

And this was true of those in Mekul as well, for gradually many came to see Topan differently. Aarad was the first, then others, until Ehnek, one of the Thean guards, offered to train Topan in the art of battle.

At first they, too, practiced with poles using them like swords until I felt Topan was ready to get the feel of a real weapon. Then, one day in the early spring, I brought out the Valnar swords I had kept in my sea chest ever since the *Tel* had been dismantled and offered them to Topan as a sign that I understood his need to fight Kalleel.

Three days later, as Topan and Ehnek sparred with the swords, Ernoar came to watch which surprised me greatly. He stood at a distance and said nothing while his brother struggled in vain to overcome Ehnek. Then, without warning, he walked forward, picked up two practice poles and stopped just outside the area Elluel had marked out as a ring for Topan's training.

"Can't you do any better than that?" he asked with a tone of deepest resentment ringing in his voice.

"Here," he said, "tossing one of the poles to Topan and stepping into the ring, "what you need is to spar with someone who really hates you," then he swung his pole, and Topan barely had time to block him.

Ernoar attacked his brother with a violence I never thought possible as he had always seemed the quieter and more reserved of the two. It was as if all of the anger, hurt and frustration he had kept inside of him came pouring out in one act of rage, a rage directed at Topan who had been the source of all of the pain Ernoar had felt during the past sun cycle.

Topan did the best he could; but all could tell that, despite his brother's violent assault, it was impossible for him to fight back as he should. Ernoar may have felt the deepest hatred possible, but it was obvious Topan did not feel the same; and the compassion he had for his brother would not allow him to strike back as he should.

At last they broke apart and stood panting both trying to catch their breath.

"Had enough?" asked Ernoar with the faintest hint of a snarl.

"I didn't think you had it in you, little brother," Topan replied, "but you are right, Ehnek is too easy on me. Maybe we should do this all the time."

Having said this, he backed over to the side of the ring and reached for the bucket of water sitting on the ground nearby.

As soon as his back was turned, Ernoar struck, bringing his pole down on Topan's back and shoulders with such force it snapped in half. Topan fell to the ground, and Ernoar threw what remained of the pole he was holding at his brother.

"If you don't watch your back," he said with a cold smile on his face, "you're a dead man."

§ § §

Three days before the Toharofa that spring two of Elluel's cousins paid a visit to the mining camp. They came bearing a message from Kalleel saying that he was ready to take his vengeance upon Topan and all else who willingly harbored the one who had dishonored him.

Since Elluel had gone with the *Tellic*, his mother brought the visitors to the forge to see Topan intending to translate for them.

"They say Kalleel will fight Topan just outside the mining camp in the open field," Alleeya told us.

"I know," said Topan. "Remember, I speak Draygon."

Then he turned to the two visitors and spoke to them for a minute or two. When they had finished talking, the two Draygon turned and walked out of the forge without making any sign of formal parting.

"I am sorry for their rudeness," Alleeya told us, "but they are angered that Elluel is not here. They have promised not to speak of his sailing on the *Tellic* when they return home. If they do, there will be much trouble for me and my family."

Then she, too, left after nodding politely to both of us.

"Well?" I asked when we were alone.

"We will meet in ten days," he told me. "Each of us may bring five men to witness the combat, and it is agreed that no one will be harmed before we fight. If I win, his friends have agreed to no longer press for the satisfaction of his honor. That means the *pallunaroo* is over. But if I die…well, those who come to witness the fight will be granted safe conduct to take my body back to Mekul, and we agree to allow Kalleel and his men safe passage back home. But of course the *pallunaroo* will continue on until Kalleel's honor has been satisfied."

§ § §

Since the outcome of the combat concerned all who lived in Mekul, Miku insisted on being one of those who were to witness the combat. I was to be another as was Aarad and Morek. Surprisingly, Ernoar wished to go as well, but Topan would not allow this. And so Menepe was chosen as witness as his crewman had been killed in the Draygon attack upon the *Zet*.

When the appointed day arrived, we all met at the North Gate to walk the nearly two leagues to the field where Topan was to meet Kalleel. Before we left, Ernoar approached, a look of fear and sadness in his eyes. He came up to Topan and stood in silence for nearly a minute before speaking.

"You're my only brother," he said, "and you and Setlat are all I have left. Come back." Then he turned and walked away, and I could see tears in his eyes.

We walked through the gate; but before we had gone more than a few paces, an anguished call was heard behind us.

It was Setlat. She ran towards us; and when she reached her brother, she flung her arms around him.

"I'm sorry," she said crying softly. "I've been so cruel to you."

"I deserved it," he told her. "This is all my fault. That's why I have to make it right.

"Don't cry. I'll be back. I promise. Then we can be a family again. All of us."

"And Enuwa too," she told him.

"Enuwa too," he replied, "and the baby. We'll all be one family just like we were back in Terhal. Now go. Be with Ernoar…and Enuwa. I'll return in the early afternoon, and all of this will be behind us. I promise."

She released him, and we continued on across the open field toward the mining camp.

§ § §

Kalleel stood with his five witnesses just outside the village about a hundred paces from the nearest cabin. When we approached, he called out something in Draygon; and though we did not understand it, his words were obviously contemptuous and filled with malice.

Whatever he said seemed to make no impression on Topan who walked beside me. He said nothing to any of us nor did he respond to Kalleel's taunt but went on in silence, the sword I had given him in its sheath at his side.

Behind the Draygon stood many of the men from the camp; for, since they were not under the *pallunaroo*, they were free to watch with impunity. Among them stood Alleeya, her husband at her side, the only woman among the crowd. This surprised me; yet, I told myself, the *pallunaroo* was a part her life as a Draygon, so of course she would be indifferent to the idea of a fight to the death. Had Anula not suggested without a second thought that we surrender four innocent men in order to settle our differences with the Draygon?

When we were about two hundred paces from the waiting Draygon, one of them stepped forward and shouted something. Topan stopped, and so did the rest of us.

"You are to wait here," he told us, "while I go on to meet Kalleel in the center. All you can do is watch. If I should die," he added after the Draygon spoke a second time, "you will be permitted to take my body back to Mekul. If I win, the Draygon will do the same with Kalleel's body and we must allow this or we risk further dishonor and more killing."

We all nodded that we understood what he had told us. Then each of us in turn clasped hands with Topan—Morek and I embracing him—and stood in silence as he went on alone to face Kalleel.

As Topan advanced, Kalleel left his companions and walked to meet his adversary with a look of contempt and hatred on his face. They seemed to be fairly evenly matched; for though Kalleel was slightly taller than Topan, he also had a more slender build. Topan, who was shorter and stockier, was the more muscular of the two; and so it seemed that what one lacked the other possessed.

When they reached each other at what seemed to be a common middle ground, they both stopped and stood for a few moments in silence. Then Kalleel again spoke to Topan in words we barely heard nor, of course, understood. Topan replied in kind, yet whatever he said caused Kalleel to laugh.

At last Topan drew the Valnar sword from its sheath. Yet at the sight of it, Kalleel again laughed, said something in Draygon, then slashed out with a knife I was sure had been made by Topan himself. There was just time to deflect Kalleel's attack, and Topan did this skillfully then jumped back out of the reach of his enemy.

For the next few minutes they both circled each other looking for some point of weakness which they could use to their own advantage. The Draygon cheered Kalleel on, yet we who had come with Topan said little as we were all fearful of goading him into doing something foolish.

Finally, for whatever reason, Kalleel seemed to find some opening, and he again lunged at his adversary. But his attack did no good as Topan was ready for him and easily deflected the flashing knife once again. Yet this time Topan's skills not only saved him, they allowed him to inflict a wound on his opponent; for blood began to run down Kalleel's upper arm causing him to howl in rage.

At this we cheered and began to call out our encouragements but also cautioned Topan not to take chances. He seemed to take heart from what we said, and for the first time I began to believe that luck would prevail.

Minute by minute the fight went on, and again and again it was Kalleel who was on the attack with Topan skillfully defending himself. At last Topan went on the offensive; for as Kalleel once again lunged at him, Topan not only deflected this assault, he managed trip Kalleel causing him to fall on his back.

In a flash, Topan was on him; and, as I had done in Terhal, he brought his sword down on his adversary with all his might. Yet Kalleel was too quick for him; and in spite of being winded, he was on his feet at once leaving Topan to strike the rocky ground where his enemy had been only a moment before.

Here, luck ran out. As Topan's sword hit the ground, it broke causing him to also lose his balance. Although he did not fall, he became momentarily vulnerable which was just the opening Kalleel needed to fall upon his opponent and bury his knife in Topan's back.

The Draygon cheered streaming into the field to surround the victor as my heart broke. I remembered my father telling me a man did not waste tears uselessly on foolish things but shed them when the need was great, and this seemed to me to be the greatest need. As I turned, I saw Morek, a tear upon his cheek, standing beside me with a look of pain and grief echoing the empty void now within me. Aarad, too, stood motionless for a few moments then slowly walked out to where Topan lay and knelt at his side.

I followed, and when I reached the bleeding body of the boy that I had watched grow to manhood and had come to call my friend, I saw he was still alive, though barely. He looked at me, and a faint smile came across his lips.

"No luck," he said in a voice barely above a whisper. "I tried, but I've failed everyone. Enuwa, the baby…they'll need help, and Andore…"

No more sound came from him. And I wept.

Chapter XI

The villagers in the mining camp brought out the cart they used when bringing ore to Mekul, and we placed Topan's body on it. Then Morek, Aarad and I pulled it back to the North Gate while Menepe and Miku walked on ahead.

When we reached the stockade, a large group awaited our return; and Enuwa, Setlat and Ernoar were among them. The gatekeepers had seen the cart coming along the road that now ran between the two villages; and having assumed the worst, they had raised the alarm throughout Mekul.

Topan's death stunned the villagers; for, though many of them blamed him still for the *pallunaroo* and the deaths associated with it, there had been hope he would put things to right, and peace would be restored. Now all knew this would not happen until two more lives had been lost.

Some had begun to respect Topan for his bravery in agreeing to face Kalleel, and these readily offered their condolences to what now remained of Topan's family. Others felt no real sympathy for him, yet they still took pity upon Setlat and Ernoar in their grief over the loss of their brother. Nevertheless, there were those who felt such a deep resentment towards Topan for what he had done that they could feel no compassion for those he left behind.

And so our village became divided in its sympathies causing factions to appear as the cycles of the sun and moons went on. Yet that day I only felt the pain of loss as we washed Topan's body and dressed him in his best tunic then buried him beside his grandmother.

Enuwa, who had never learned to speak Kroemaeon well, went to stay with Anula who agreed to help her until the baby came. Then, at the start of summer, on the same day Illiad and I had wed so long ago, Enuwa gave birth to a daughter whom she named Topuwa.

Anula acted as midwife with the aid of Setlat. Then, when the baby had passed her first cycle of the moons, Enuwa left Anula's house and returned to the cabin Topan had built. There Setlat joined her in order to help care for the newborn.

Both Ernoar and I provided daily for Enuwa and her child as did Morek; and in this way we honored Topan's memory. To me this seemed only fitting as I had adopted Topan when he came of age, and I made a pledge before Miku and the Council that at my death Topan's daughter should have her share of everything I possessed.

Andore, it seemed, mourned for Topan as well, something I thought an animal would not do. Each day, just after first light, he arrived at the forge to sleep on the steps or if the weather was cold enough, just inside the door. Then, in the midmorning, he went and waited outside the furnace while one of us smelted ore. Finally, in the evening, he would return to Topan's cabin and sleep on the steps or, after Enuwa moved back, by the hearth.

At night he would go and hunt with the other vood for the small animals they caught as food; yet while the cycles of the sun went on, he kept watch faithfully always longing, it seemed, for Topan's return. Sepnoar and Ernoar would often play with him throwing sticks or balls of snow in the winter. Even Seppan and Tenwa would do the same, yet he never seemed to have the same relish for these games as when he had been with Topan.

§ § §

Time goes on, something all of us had learned as we made a new life for ourselves in these cold northern lands. And as time passes, the pain of loss lessens, though it never goes away altogether. So it was with the death of Topan just as it had been with the deaths of Kebbit and Marna and before that the horror of the Valnar's coming.

In that autumn after Topan's death, Karnot and Enon returned to Mekul once again; and this time they brought several Draygon with them. One was a cousin of Elluel, though not one of those who had come the time before on Kalleel's behalf. It was their intent to trade with us, and Karnot encouraged us to do so.

"The Draygon are pretty much fightin' among themselves," Karnot told the Council. "That's why there've been no new killin's in a while. Adjuwa says that since Kalleel killed Topan in open combat, his honor is satisfied, and the *pallunaroo* should end. To tell the truth, he only wants to trade with us, and he's tired of waitin'. But Kalleel and his friends don't agree. They want two more lives.

"So Adjuwa sent us here. He feels that if we open up trade, others'll put pressure on Kalleel; and we can finally have peace."

"What do you think?" asked Miku.

"That Adjuwa knows what he's talkin' about," replied Karnot. "He's a clever man and no fool. That's why he sent them other Draygon with us, to show Kalleel's friends they're on the losin' side."

"Sounds reasonable," said Miku, "yet if we do decide to trade, we can only do it through you, correct?"

"That's true, for now anyway," Karnot told him. "Unless Kalleel feels his honor's been satisfied, the *pallunaroo* goes on; and he and his friends'll kill anyone from Mekul comin' near their village no matter what Adjuwa says. It's a matter o' honor, an ancient tradition, somethin' the chief can't control. All Adjuwa can do is try and talk Kalleel into stoppin' the *pallunaroo*. So he's tryin' to put pressure on him by unitin' the other Draygon against him."

Karnot's words persuaded the Council, and we agreed to resume trade with the Draygon provided there were no more killings. Thus, it appeared Topan might not have died in vain, that the shedding of his blood might still have meaning.

When the trading party left, Enuwa sent a message through them to her father telling him of the birth of Topuwa. This, she believed, would give strength to the cause of all who wished to end the *pallunaroo*.

"Father big man," she told us, "second to Adjuwa. He know he have granddaughter, he want peace. He tell Kalleel stop killing."

§ § §

The winter snows at last set in, yet Elluel did not return home to the mining camp as had been his custom but remained in Mekul sleeping in the hut used by Tenoar and Aarad for storage. In the early evenings he sometimes went to the tavern Shend had opened just as Aarad and I had done when we were his age. Yet more and more he spent time with Setlat at Enuwa's cabin; and by spring, it had been agreed they were to wed in the late summer after Elluel had built a cabin for the two of them.

On the morning of Setlat's wedding, Aarad came to my cabin early since he wished to discuss trading business before the festivities of the day got under way. It had been a clear night, and I had stayed up late watching the stars while holding Illiad's ribbons, for increasingly these gave me even greater comfort—a strange feeling she was close, far closer than ever before. I had then slept in as I would not be working in the smithy that day. And so when Aarad walked in, I had just made kahl to take the place of my usual bread and cold soup.

As I ate my meal, Aarad sat at the table talking and drinking a mug of palne juice. He had again become restless, having little to do now that only the *Tellic* was actively trading. This led him to his latest idea of launching a trading mission to the Draygon living above the falls, and he had come that morning to get my opinion of the venture.

"It is foolish," I told him.

"Because?" he asked.

"For one thing, you have no idea how the Draygon will react to anyone who enters their territory. They killed Almath."

"But who knows what he did to anger them," Aarad retorted.

"Exactly," I replied, "and how are you going to find out? Just walk into their camp and say *'mantu.'"*

"Well, something like that," he told me, "I was expecting to take Elluel with me."

"Elluel is from the villages below the falls," I said. "Who knows if the *pallunaroo* that drove his ancestors away is still in effect? They could easily kill both of you for some ancient point of honor. You know how unpredictable the Draygon are. My advice is not to risk it.

"Besides, even if they were willing to trade, how are you going to get all of your supplies up that trail to the top of the falls? How many men do you really think will be foolish enough to join you on a venture like that?"

"All right, all right," he told me standing up and beginning to pace the room, "it probably is a stupid idea, but right now it is the only idea I have. I cannot keep sailing with Tenoar on the *Tellic*. He tries his best to make me feel a part of the crew; but after having my own ship—I know, it is Menepe's ship not mine—but I am just used to being the one in charge."

When he came to the door, he stopped.

"What are these?" he asked picking up the ribbons I had left lying on a shelf by the door.

"I bought those for Illiad on our last trading voyage," I told him.

"And kept them all this time?"

"They remind me of her," I replied. "I take them out and…I just feel close to her when I hold them."

"She is gone, Idar. You have to face that. I loved her too, but she and Seppan and my parents are all gone."

"She is out there," I told him, "I have always believed that. I knew it as I stood on the deck of the *Tel* and looked into the ruined harbor of Arganon. She did not die there, and I have held onto that belief ever since.

"Maybe the Valnar took her. Maybe her life is one long nightmare, but she is alive somewhere. And at night, when I look at the stars, I think of her; and I know in the depths of my heart that she is thinking of me as well. This is all that keeps me going day after day, the time I spend with her each night watching the stars."

§ § §

Setlat and Elluel were married, as was now the new custom among the villagers of Mekul, without first holding a laryat. It was merely announced in the village that they planned to wed, and all those desiring to attend and wish them well were invited to join them in celebration on the appointed day. And so, after Aarad had left my cabin that morning I turned to preparing myself for the festivities.

Penepe had made a new tunic for me just for the occasion, and for this I had paid him well. It was dark brown with a belt of an orangish gold that had been dyed with the juice of a plant the Draygon called papool.

Then, when I was ready, I walked to the cabin Elluel had built against the wall of the newly extended stockade on the eastern end of the village. Morek was to accompany Setlat as would Egome, one carrying the bread the other the fish. This meant Aarad would arrive later as well, for he would bring the children. Ernoar, too, would come with his sister as would Sepnoar who had been raised in Morek's house as a brother to Setlat. Thus I was alone at first until Boec and Shend arrived with their families.

Mirranu came holding the baby—their fifth child—who was merely six moons cycles old. Then, with the arrival of Shend, Lenyana and their seven children, the cousins intermingled laughing, joking and teasing one another as we waited for the arrival of the bride signaling the beginning of the wedding.

As I made my way across the dusty unpaved street in front of Elluel's cabin, my mind wandered for a moment to that morning on the deck of the *Tel* when Boec had told us he thought he and Mirranu would never wed. Yet that had been but a fleeting moment; and with the passing of time, the pain we had known that day was now all but lost in our memories.

I had once wished for death. Yet now I rejoiced in the happiness of the moment knowing that this day would one day be joined with others, both good and bad, to form the inner core of who I would become in the distant future.

"They have a fine day for their wedding," I told Boec as I approached. "I remember how cold it was aboard the *Tel* the day of your wedding."

"I remember it was cloudy," he replied with a grin spreading across his face, "but I was too nervous to remember much of anything else."

"You men!" scolded Mirranu. "Why do you always talk as if marriage is the end of the world. I remember our wedding; and, yes, it was cold, but the thought of being with you for the rest of my life kept me warm."

Boec shot me a look which said, "I am in trouble now," but said nothing more, for the wedding party had begun to arrive.

Following the new custom, we all allowed Setlat and her wedding party to pass silently then, when she had reached the steps of Elluel's house, we gathered around behind them to watch the exchange of vows. Although I had witnessed this many times before as we made our new lives here in the far north, it still seemed strange to me; for I felt that it should somehow be as it had been for Illiad and me, a private moment, one shared just between our families. Yet now the village was the only family most of us had, and to many it seemed only proper that this was how things were to be done.

Elluel had all but rejected his Draygon heritage, yet his mother insisted an important Draygon custom be observed, one calling for the groom to mark his bride on the forehead with the sign of his clan using a piece of charcoal. Thus after exchanging the bread and fish, Elluel drew a symbol to signify the moon Aeto on the forehead of his bride then kissed her and led her into their new home where they would spend a few moments exchanging gifts in private then rejoin those who had come to celebrate their new lives together.

It was as it had always been. We laughed; we danced; we ate; we drank. Thus it seemed in this respect, nothing had changed since the day I married Illiad; and the joy of Setlat's wedding caused me to live once again the brief time I had spent with the woman who was still so clearly present to me.

As the evening wore on, we one by one left the celebration to return to the solitude of our own homes. Yet while I slept that night, I dreamt what I felt to be the strangest dream I had ever had.

I saw myself as I had looked the day I joined the *Tel*, yet I was dressed in fine clothes and stood on a terrace with a garden surrounding me. There I watched the stars in silence. After a few moments, a man approached me quietly. He bowed his head then smiled warmly.

"Your father bids you come to him," was all he said.

"He's not my father," I replied, "but I have no choice but to obey. Tell him I will come, Laron, and thank you."

The man nodded again and left, and for a few more moments I watched the stars. Then as I turned to leave the terrace, I awoke with the strangest feeling of contentment and peace that I had ever felt in my life.

Chapter XII

There were no killings that cycle of the sun after Elluel and Setlat wed nor on into the next, and we began to feel peace had finally come to us. The men from the villages along the Adujae came regularly to trade with us, and Aarad became a kind of shop keeper as Enon, Karnot and now Shoarnet came at intervals with two or three Draygon to trade for Kroemaeon goods or for those Tenoar brought back from the villages to the south.

At the Toharofa that spring both Egome and Setlat gave birth to sons, Dennem and Topan. Then, two sun cycles later, just as I attained my thirty-second cycle of the sun in the fifteenth since we had come to Mekul, Setlat bore twins to Elluel, a thing rarely heard of in Theo, though Penepe told us it was common among the women of Arganon.

Elluel was overjoyed at the birth of his son and daughter, for births of this kind were also uncommon with the Draygon; and he took great pride in showing them off to his cousins who often visited Mekul as part of the trading missions. He insisted that the twins receive Draygon names, Naleeya for the girl and Idool for the boy. To this Setlat readily agreed since it pleased her to be part of the melding of our two greatly different cultures.

Yet all was not total peace, for rumors of discontent were carried by those of the Draygon who came to trade with us. Thus we all understood the *pallunaroo* was not yet ended, and no one from Mekul—and this now included Elluel—could safely visit the region of the Adujae.

Although no killings had taken place since Topan's death, we continued to be watchful and ever cautious. Yet at the same time most living in Mekul felt Topan had accomplished what he had set out to do; and for this reason, the majority of villagers began to look upon him as a hero though there were still those who had lost loved ones, and these felt differently.

Then, one morning, just as summer began, the eastern sky was dark with smoke causing the sun's light to give an eerie glow, one reminding me of a morning long ago when I returned to Alna from my last trip to Eltec. None of us had any idea what this could mean, yet we had no doubt it did not bode well; and for the next two days we speculated on its meaning.

At last, in the midmorning of the third day, Karnot, Enon and Shoarnet all arrived with their families as well as a great number of Draygon, Elluel's cousins and uncles being among them. They told us the tension the Draygon had experienced the past sun cycles had finally erupted into open conflict as Kalleel and his friends rebelled against Adjuwa's authority.

"There was a council held four days ago," Karnot told us, "and as he always did, Kalleel began his tirade against the Kroemaeon. I wasn't there of course, I not being a Draygon, but my wife's kin told me what went on.

"Ever since Adjuwa began tradin' again with us, Kalleel has turned his hatred for Topan into a dislike for all Kroemaeon, and he's been tellin' anyone who'd listen that we are here to take away their land, that we're worse than Tenyah because we've sneaked in, and soon we'll just take over.

"Adjuwa, of course, argued against Kalleel. He told the council that we were friends and had always been friends. But Kalleel answered sayin' that a friend didn't steal yer wife, and Adjuwa could say nothin' against this.

"Well, they argued some more, a real hot argument, and Kalleel finally stormed out of the lodge where the council was held. But it seems this was some kind of prearranged signal; for no sooner had he left, than some of his friends burst into the lodge and killed Adjuwa."

"So Adjuwa is dead?" asked Miku.

"That's right," Karnot told him, "and a lot of his best supporters too. There was a big fight, as you can imagine. Kalleel's men seemed to have it all planned out in advance because they went for all the important supporters of Adjuwa first.

"They came to the tradin' compound as well, but we had been tipped off by friends of ours and had fled with our families into the forest before they got there. Burned the whole compound and most of the village as well from what we've been told.

"We hid out in the forest 'til mornin' as more and more Draygon joined us. Then, at first light, we headed for Mekul."

"And they didn't follow you?" asked Elfad.

"No," Karnot replied, "we were joined by a few Draygon the first night when we stopped to camp. They told us Kalleel and his party are regroupin'. A lot of Draygon fled east to the villages along the Eduin. Those villages have had nothin' to do with the *pallunaroo* and have not supported Kalleel. So they will be none too happy about Adjuwa's death. That could bring on a civil war, but Kalleel will most likely strike here at Mekul before then."

"Why at us?" asked Miku.

"To finish off the *pallunaroo* for one and to gain status for another. If he defeats us badly enough, he'll win over many of the Draygon who are now lookin' for a new chief. He killed Adjuwa, and if he defeats the invaders, that bein' us, he'll look like a mighty warrior, like someone who should lead all the Draygon."

There was silence for a minute or two in the Council chamber as we all tried to take in everything Karnot had told us. Then Miku rose to his feet to address those fortunate enough to have found room in the crowded hall.

"I told you once that I did not wish to be your king, yet you persuaded me to become your Captain. However, it seems now that what we need is a king, someone to lead us in battle, for there surly will be one if Kalleel and his men make good their threats to our community.

"Neither I nor any other man in our village has experience in battle. We all saw this at the inlet when the Tenyah defeated us so badly, but I am your leader, as this was your wish. And so I will take command unless the Council objects to my having that much authority."

As he sat down, Kuren rose to take his place. "I for one have no wish to lead us into battle. Miku has not failed us in all these cycles of the sun, so I'm sure he won't fail us now. All those who agree with me, take to your feet and show our Captain your support."

At this, the entire Council save for Tenoar and Abdoar, who were with their ships and not present, rose to their feet. When all were standing, Miku joined them.

"I thank you for your confidence, and I hope I do not fail you. My lack of experience in the art of war led to our defeat at the inlet on our way here, but I will do all that I can to ensure our safety. It is my hope the Draygon will be willing to aid me as I am sure they have far more experience in battle than I. And you, Karnot, I hope that you will be willing to translate for them."

"That I will, Captain," came Karnot's reply, "that I will."

§ § §

Our position was desperate. Besides having no army or warriors of any kind except for the Draygon who had taken refuge with us, the south side of our encampment lay exposed to the river. At first we had built an enclosed stockade with a few cabins and my forge inside. Since that time more homes as well as Otna's temple and the Council Hall had been constructed within this enclosure. Yet Boec had needed to build his mill along the river bank; and this encouraged others, including Morek, Aarad and Shend, to followed his lead by building homes outside the stockade. They felt secure in doing this since we had become friends with the Draygon and all fear of attack had long since vanished. Now the village extended for well over half a league along the bank of the Drevet.

When the *pallunaroo* began, Miku had ordered the stockade extended, but this had only been done as a shield to protect the villagers from a sneak attack at night. This new addition was connected to the original stockade on its northern side and stretched east and west then circled back to the river where, on each side, it ended a few paces from the bank. These gaps, which were easy enough to guard, gave us access to the meadow and the communal fields where our crops were planted.

Yet no consideration had been given to the south side of Mekul, for we saw the river as a natural barrier, one which would not allow anyone to enter undetected. This we now saw as a fatal flaw; for in an all-out attack, we would be left totally vulnerable with absolutely no defenses at all along one whole side of our settlement.

To make matters worse, farms and orchards had grown up across the Drevet; and these had no protection at all. When the Draygon came, those who remained there would face certain death.

Miku's first command was to order all those who lived outside of Mekul to move into the village. This meant the farmers across the Drevet, those in the mining camp as well as the men who raised nashcal and had built farms in the hills north of Mekul began to crowd into our small settlement and space needed to be made for them.

At the same time, Miku ordered a trench to be dug on the south side of the village from one end of the stockade to the other. This was to be waist deep, and the dirt taken from it was then piled along its edge adding further height thereby making a barrier behind which we could hide while shooting at those who attacked us.

Weapons also needed to be amassed; and Sepnoar, Ernoar and I were all kept busy making arrow heads some of which were placed atop poles to be used as spears. We were assisted in this by some of the younger men and older boys one of which was Seppan who, at coming of age, had apprenticed himself to Aarad as a merchant trader and now felt proud to help defend his village.

The Draygon, too, were put to work. Elluel's eldest uncle, Atoowa, was chosen as Miku's adviser; and he set his Draygon warriors to making arrows as well as extra bows, for we had far too few of these within our settlement.

Then, five days after our preparations for war had begun, a small band of Draygon were sighted coming down the crude road connecting Mekul with the mining camp. The village was thrown into a panic; yet Atoowa, who was summoned immediately, told us it was Adayu and a few of his warriors.

Since Adayu had been second to Adjuwa, he was the logical successor as chief; and the Draygon staying at Mekul immediately acknowledged him as their new leader as well as Miku's adviser. This change of leadership seemed to be for the best since, before Adayu arrived, the Draygon had appeared leader less; and now even Atoowa followed Adayu's commands without question.

Enuwa was overjoyed to see her father, and he seemed truly happy to see her as well. Yet what appeared to give him the greatest joy was to see his granddaughter and hold he on his lap.

Our preparations continued day after day, yet before we had had time to fully ready ourselves for an all-out Draygon onslaught, a cry arose from those who watched at the Meadow Gate that smoke could be seen rising from the mining camp two leagues away. The Draygon had come.

§ § §

The Draygon were still nowhere in sight when I reached the mill I had been assigned to guard along with Boec, Aarad, Morek and Shend. Even so, I felt the same sickening fear I had experienced that day at Terhal when I saw the Valnar patrol riding slowly down the road towards the orchard where we had been picking fruit.

Oddly, when the alarm was raised at the first indication the Draygon were near, there had been no panic; and everyone had taken their assigned stations in a surprisingly orderly manner. The women and children went quickly to the enclosed stockade where they could find shelter in one of the buildings while the boys of ten sun cycles and older met at the Council Hall to be used as runners carrying messages, arrows or other weapons wherever they were needed.

The Draygon insisted on being our first line of defense; for, as Adayu told us, they had more experience on the field of battle than any of us. Yet there was also the matter of Adjuwa's death and the question of who was to become chief, for Adayu needed to assert his rights and prove himself the rightful leader of the Draygon.

To this we made no objection since he was correct. We were fishermen, shopkeepers, farmers and laborers. None of us were warriors, and we had seen this in the death of Topan as well as in the disaster we had experienced at the inlet so long ago when we had lost so many who were dear to us.

And so I stood on a rock near the mill and watched as a group of about forty Draygon warriors led by Adayu moved quickly along the western wall of the stockade and prepared to meet the opposing Draygon who were now just coming into view along the road leading from the smoking ruins of the mining camp. Adayu had sent a second group of men out along the eastern wall of the stockade; and these, of course, I could not see. Yet as I watched those closest to me positioning themselves in front of the stockade, I knew that the rest of the Draygon were doing the same thing on the other side.

The Draygon had left their bows behind for those who would defended the village to use, and so they stood, almost like Tenyah, stripped to the waste of all that would encumber them, each holding a knife or an axe, each waiting as their kinsmen approached slowly from the north. The silence surprised me; for, since I had been in a battle before, I assumed there would be far more noise than there was. Yet it was early on, and the fighting had not yet begun. Thus each of us stood in the quietness of our own individual solitude awaiting what was to come.

Kalleel and his men advanced slowly, and when they were less than half a league from Mekul they also began forming a line. Yet as they grew near, the stockade began to partially block my view; and Kalleel, as well as most of his men, were soon outside my line of vision.

While I watched, tensely waiting for the battle to begin, cries arose in the village; and I turned my attention to what was happening along the river. The rock on which I stood was just ten paces outside the stockade, a mere twenty from the mill. This meant that my view of Mekul was almost totally restricted, allowing me to see practically nothing. Yet Boec, who stood near the door to the mill, called out and told us what had happened.

"A group of about twenty Draygon attacked from the river," he told us, "but our men in the trench seem to have driven them back, at least for now. I think the Draygon expected us to be totally defenseless because they seemed surprised to find a trench with bowmen at the ready, but I bet they will be back."

I had no time to think on this; for at that moment cries went up from the Draygon in the meadow. When I turned, I saw both lines were now running towards each other, each man with a weapon raised ready to kill whomever came within his reach.

Then shouting again rose from the village, and I could see arrows in the sky arching over the stockade and falling into the compound. It seemed that not all of the attacking Draygon were engaged in one on one combat, for some were free to fire upon our village; and volley after volley fell relentlessly into the crowd of men and boys now scurrying to take cover.

"They are back," cried Boec, "the ones who attacked from the river; and they have bows with them this time. Our men are now pinned down in the trench, but fortunately they are out of range of the arrows coming over the stockade."

"Those have stopped," I told him. "I can't see from here, but Adayu's men are somehow keeping Kalleel's bowman from firing at us."

"Well they haven't stopped the ones firing at our men in the trench," he said, "but at least now they are getting reinforcements. Those who had been pinned down are now up and helping drive the Draygon back towards the river."

I turned and scanned the river to the west looking for any sign in the forest that Draygon were advancing upon us from that direction as well, but I saw nothing. Then, when I looked back toward the meadow, I saw Kalleel. He had been fighting alongside his men on the eastern end of the stockade which meant I had not been able to see him before. But now he ran towards Adayu; and as he did, he raised his knife high in the air preparing to strike the final blow and ensure his own victory in the struggle for leadership of the Draygon.

As I watched, a cold sickness came over me; for this, I was sure, was the knife Kalleel had used to kill Topan.

Adayu was an experienced warrior; and though he was already engaged in hand to hand combat with another Draygon, he was able to deflect this new assault from the side. As luck would have it, one of Adayu's men rushed to his chief's side and leaped upon the man Adayu had been fighting. This meant Adayu was now free to contend with Kalleel who again lunged at his opponent.

This new assault threw Adayu off balance, and he fell backward with Kalleel on top. But the older man knew a few tricks, for he quickly managed to throw Kalleel to the side and was on his feet in an instant.

Again and again the two men lunged at each other knives flashing in the light of the sun. Yet they were both able to skillfully avoid the weapon held in the other's hand.

I could not take my eyes off the sight, and everything else seemed to vanish completely from my mind. The battle in the village also went on, yet I could barely hear the sound of it. Shend and Aarad both yelled something to me, but it seemed like a shadow in my mind.

Then Kalleel lunged at Adayu once more, but this time Adayu managed to grab hold of the hand in which Kalleel held his knife and twist it behind his oponent's back. Kalleel dropped his knife, and Adayu threw him to the ground leaping upon him as he did.

When he arose, Adayu shouted a cry of victory as he stood over the lifeless body of the man who had brought such suffering upon us all. Kalleel was dead, and the *pallunaroo* was ended. Adayu would become leader of the Draygon, and our lives could once again return to what normalcy there was in this cold northern world.

I leapt from the rock to the grass along the shore; and as I did it hit me, a Draygon arrow just above my heart, and I fell. The pain radiated out in a sudden shock wave touching every nerve of my body, and I could not move. Another Draygon was suddenly upon me with a spear upraised to strike, but Aarad struck him a blow to the head causing him to fall into the river. At the same moment Boec fired an arrow and killed the Draygon who had shot me.

"Idar," Aarad shouted and dropped to his knees at my side. "No, Idar, no."

He held me; and I lay warm in his arms, my body moist with sweat, the pain almost too great to bear; and I heard nothing but the sound of the water rushing against the wheel of the mill, a wheel which would grind the flour for the village in seasons yet to come, yet seasons I would never see. Somehow I was at peace with this; for I knew death was near, and I longed for the total nothingness I knew awaited me.

"You know it's strange," I said, my voice weak, all my strength fighting against the pain.

"Don't talk, Idar," he told me.

"It's strange, Aarad, I can see Huno standing on the hill outside of Alna calling to us…and we couldn't go back. We couldn't take him with us. He was afraid, Aarad, he was alone and afraid…and we just sailed out of the bay. We couldn't go back for him."

"Don't talk, Idar, save your strength," he pleaded.

"He's gone. And now, so am I."

"Don't say that, you're going to be fine."

"And with me dies my little part of Alna...my mother, my father, all gone."

"No, Idar, not gone, not yet."

"Yes, Aarad, we're all gone...we're all gone." And with these words I left him. A darkness crept over me, and the pain was no more as I floated in a quiet aloneness while time itself stood still; and I could only ponder all that life had given me.

Then, he was there, standing by my grave weeping, Aarad at his side holding him, consoling him for the loss death brought to both of us. I saw him from beyond the grave, from the timeless realm of the infinite; and though my heart no longer beat, it still reached out to him—my son.

END OF BOOK FIVE

To be continued in

The Kroemaeon League:
The Book of Idaric

Epilogue

Here ends *The Book of Idar*. Yet with the arrival of Idar's son at Mekul—a son he was not able to know in life—the seed was planted which, when it sprouted, became the Kroemaeon League, the union of a remnant of a once flourishing culture crushed by the Valnar.

This vestige of Kroemaeon civilization, transplanted far to the north of its native soil, survived long after the empire which absorbed its homeland had crumbled under both the weight of its own tyranny and the military might of Kallefandra, the only kingdom the Valnar were never able to conquer. The League thrived in its new homeland for well over two millennia eventually senting off into space a second remnant which arrived here on our planet in the early stages of human history.

Then, once again, disaster struck bringing the League to its final end. Yet the Kroemaeon League lives on in the records it left behind. Thus it is my hope that in the future I will be able to pass on to our world the complete record of this alien race, for the tale of the Kroemaeon League has much to tell us about ourselves as a people.

Pronunciation Guide

a = a	as in and	kh = c	as in Christmas
ae = i	as in island	ô = o	as in on
ah = a	as in father	o = o	as in old
au = ou/ow	as in out or owl	oi = oi	as in oil
ay = a	as in day	ou = oo	as in wood
ee = e	as in eat	oo = oo	as in moon
eh = e	as in egg	uh = u	as in up
i = i	as in ill	zh = s	as in pleasure

Glossary

Aarad [Ahr'-ad]
son of Aeshone and Melne

Abaya [Ah-bae'-yah]
Draygon woman, wife of Kalleel

Abdoar [Ab'-dor]
fisherman on the Tok; captain of the Mer

Adal [Ah-dahl']
brother of Topek

Adayu [Ah-day'-oo]
Draygon warrior

adjnee [ahdj'-nee]
food - sweet, red, banana like fruit

Adjuwa [Ad'-joo-wah]
Draygon chief

Adujae [Ah-doo-jae]
river on which Adjuwa's village is located

Aeshone [Ae'-shon]
father of Aarad, husband of Melne

Aeto [Ae'-to]
Kroemaeon moon

aldayf [ahl-dayf']
food - a bitter tasting vegetable

Alleeya [Ahl-ee'-yah]
mother of Elluel

Allubet [Ahl'-loo-beht]
river south of Eltec

Almath [Ahl'-mahth]
wounded man found near the falls

Alna [Ahl'-nah]
village where Idar was born

Alnat [Ahl'-naht]
son of the cobbler

Altore [Ahl'-tor]
seaman on the Tel

andlen [ahnd'-lehn]
food - medicinal herb also used in cooking

Andore [Ahn'-dor]
Topan's vood

Annaya [Ahn-nae'-yah]
daughter of Boec and Mirranu

Anula [Ah-noo'-lah]
Draygon woman married to Ettak

Anyo [Ahn'-yo]
wife of Sethel, mother of Boec and Shend

Arganon [Ahr-gah-nôn']
city state three days north of Theo

Arman [Ahr'-mahn]
father of Shuman and king of Theo

artet [ahr'-teht]
food -a cereal grain

ashka [ash'-kuh]
wool bearing farm animal

Atoowa [Ah-too'-wah]
uncle of Elluel

Bak [Bahk]
fishing boat in the Alna fleet

Benfoar [Behn'-for]
carpenter on the *Tel*

Boaruf [Bor'-uhf]
seaman on the *Tel*

Boec [Bo'-ehk]
younger son of Sethel and Anyo

buk [book]
animal - mouse like creature

Burog [Boor'-ôg]
first mate on the *Tel*

cheshoh [cheh'-sho]
food - meat pastry

Crayoar [Kray'-or]
village three leagues east of Alna

Daeo [Dae'-o]
father of Tuac, Zhoh and Leyhah

Dennem [Dehn'-nehm]
father of Egome; Egome and Aarad's son

diu [dae'-oo]
smallest unit of Kallefandran coinage

Diud [Dae'-uhd]
seaman on the *Tel*

donect [do'-nehkt]
couger-like animal

Draygon [Dray'-gôn]
primitave tribe living near Mekul

Drevet [Dreh'-veht]
river along which Mekul is built

Dul [Dool]
fishing boat in the Alna fleet

edjah [eh'-jah]
uncle

edjeh [eh'-jeh]
aunt

Eduin [Eh'-doo-in]
river flowing into the Bay of the Pola

Egome [Eh'-go-may]
daughter of Dennam, wife of Aarad

Ehnek [Eh'-nehk]
Thean guard whos train Topan

Elem [Eh'-lehm]
grandfather of Idar

Elfad [Ehl'-fahd]
captain of the *Ket*

Elluel [Ehl'-loo-ehl]
Draygon interpreter on the Tellic

eln [ehln]
shrimp like sea creature

Eltec [Ehl'-tehk]
city twenty days south of Theo

Enon [Ee'-nôn]
Zet crewman who lives with the Draygon

Ensoar [Ehn'-sor]
went with Tennep to warn the farmers

Enuwa [Ehn'-oo-wah]
wife of Topan, daughter of Adayu

Ernoar [Ehr'-nor]
grandson of Marna, brother of Topan

Etoar [Eh'-tor]
villager who came to Alna with Morek

Ettak [Eht'-tahk]
fisherman on the *Mer*, husband of Anula

gamu [gah-moo']
an animal that gives milk

Glennoff Glehn'-nôf]
King of Arganon

gork [gork]
food - a poultry

Hallucantec [Hahl-loo-kahn'-tehk]
river on which Shentoar is located

Hannee [Hahn-nee']
wife of Morek and mother of Sepnoar

Hebdar [Hehb'-dahr]
captain of the *Von*

Hennek [Hehn'-nehk]
Boec's cousin, miller in Crayoar

Heshel [Heh'-shehl]
a plant having blue flowers

Hob [Hôb]
fishing boat in the Alna fleet

Huno [Hoo'-no]
Illiad's ashka

Idar [Ae'-dahr]
narrator of the story

Idool [Ae-dool']
son of Elluel and Setlat

Illiad [Il'-lee-ad]
wife of Idar, sister of Aarad

Jaygore [Jay'-gor]
wealthy merchant of Sefna

Jefta [Jehf'-tah]
soldier at Trenon, friend of Morek

kahl [kahl]
food - a hot cereal

kahlmek [kahl'-mehk]
alcoholic drink distilled from grain

kahtore [kah-tor']
Thean dice game

kalhu [kahl-hoo']
food - cereal grain like wheat

Kalleel [Kahl-leel']
Draygon worrior who was to marry Enuwa

Kallumtarra [Kahl'loom-tahr'-rah]
an inn in Shentoar

Kalnar [Kahl-nahr']
river and northern boundary of Arganon

karnel [Kahr-nehl']
food - traditional stew made in Terhal

Karnot [Kahr'-nôt]
Zet crewman living with the Draygon

kaylo [kay'-lo]
Thean game played with colored stones

Kebbit [Kehb'-bit]
cook on the *Tel*

keffan [kehf-fahn']
Kroemaeon profanity

Kellebet [Kel'-leh-beht]
cobbler at Mekul

kellec [kehl'ehk]
food - a fruit similar to an apple

Kellnor [Kehl-lnor]
farmer who sold his house to Aeshone

Kellon [Kehl'-lahn]
a crewman on the *Tel*

Kelna [Kehl'-nah]
Boec's cousin, daughter of Hennek

Keltoar [Kehl'-tor]
captain of the *Mek*

Kelyan [Kehl'-yahn]
seaman on the *Tel*

Kenneb [Kehn'-nehb]
seaman on the *Tel*

Kennec [Kehn'-nehk]
father of Idar, husband of Shahri

Keploh [Kehp'-lo]
the owner of the *Pola*

Keppoar [Kehp'-por]
captain of the *Son*

Kesset [Kehs'-seht]
island where Abdore's camp is located

Ket [Keht]
a Thean merchant ship

khansh [khahnsh]
food - an exotic fruit grown in Shentoar

killet [kil-leht']
a process akin to knitting or crocheting

kine [kaen]
food - cookie like pastry

klehden [kleh'-dehn]
a plant, something like cotton or flax

klenn [klehn']
a sea bird

Kohn [Kon]
Kroemaeon moon

kolat [ko'-taht']
folk dance done only by men and boys

Koron [Kor'-ôn]
medic on the expidition to Earth

Korpel [Kor-pehl]
grandfather of Boec and Shend

Kroemaeon [Kro-mae'-ôn]
Idar's language and culture

Kron [Krôn]
son of Zhen and Taya, brother of Narra

krumb [kruhmb]
food - a yellow leafy vegetable

Kuren [Koor'-ehn]
captain of the *Sep*

Kwel [Kwehl]
merchant ship on which Naemen sails

Kwellen [Kwehl'-lehn]
seaman on the *Tel*

kyte [Kaet]
leaping fish

Laron [Lah'-ron]
man in Idar's dream

laryat [lahr-yaht']
Kroemaeon betrothal ceremony

Lenyana [Lehn-yah'-nah]
friend of Egome, wife of Shend

Leyhah [Lay'-hah]
sister of Tuac, daughter of Daeo

Lot [Lôt]
fishing boat in the Alna fleet

mahlet [mah-leht']
lowest rank on ship, a cabin boy

maluk [mah-look']
strong meadlike drink from Eltec

Marna [Mahr'-hah]
grandmother of Topan, Ernoar and Setlat

mehalee [meh'-hah-lee]
a plant with orange flowers
Mek [Mehk]
Tenoar's ship before building the *Tel*
Mekul [Meh'-kool]
village built by the refugees from Theo
melmat [mehl'-maht]
a type of edible fish
Melne [Mehl'-nay]
mother of Aarad, wife of Aeshone
Menepe [Meh-neh-pay]
captain of the *Zet*
Menlo [Mehn'-lo]
wealthy farmer
Mer [Mehr]
Abdoar's fishing boat
Miku [Mi'-koo]
owner and captain of the *Tok*
Mirranu [Mir-rahn'-oo]
friend of Kelna, wife of Boec
Morek [Mor'-ehk]
brother of Aarad living in Teuwa
Naemen [Nae'-mehn]
runaway slave helped by the *Tel's* crew
Naleeya [Nah-lee'-yah]
daughter of Elluel and twin sister of Idool
Nar [Nahr]
Thean merchant ship lost at sea
narloo [nahr-loo']
food - cereal grain similar to rice
Narra [Nahr'-rah]
daughter of Zhen, sister of Kron
Narren [Nahr'-rehn]
grandfather of Tuac and Zhoh
nashcal [nahsh-kahl']
llama or alpaca like animal
Nef [Nehf]
Thean fishing ship

neffan [nehf'-fahn]
root vegetable

nodah [no'-dah]
dad, papa

nodeh [no-deh']
mom, mama

Nomlet [Nôm'-leht]
seaman on the *Tel*

nosha [no'-shah]
animal used like a horse

otlee [aht'-lee]
vegetable similar to onions or leaks

Otna [Ot'-nah]
a priest from Theo

pahdalla [pah-dal'-lah]
an evergreen tree

pallon [pahl-lon']
pastry - cake with fruit and nuts

pallunaroo [pal-loo-hahr'-oo]
Draygon blood feud

palne [pahl'-nay]
a plum like fruit

papool [pah-pool']
plant with orange flowers

Pellonek [Pehl'-lo-nehk]
second mate on the *Tel*

Penepe [Peh'-neh-pay]
tailor from Arganon born in Terhal

Pentra [Pehn'-trah]
trading colony of Arganon

pola [po-lah']
a mythical sea monster

Poran [Por'-ahn]
captain of the *Bak*

Porel [Por-ehl']
a farmer, father of Zherna

Prion [Pri'-ôn]
village four leagues north of Theo

Ruha [Roo'-hah]
river at the edge of Alna

Sefala [Seh-fah'-lah]
friend of Kelna and Mirranu

Sefna [Sehf'-nah]
pleasure port six leagues north of Alna

Selyupa [Sehl'-yoo-pah]
priest from Theo who does the Toharofa

Sennec [Sehn'-nehk]
captain of the *Lot*

Sennefen [Sehn'-eh-fehn]
seaman on the *Tel*

Senyal [Sehn'-yahl]
oldest son of Naemen

Sep [Sehp]
merchant ship in the Thean fleet

Sepnoar [Sehp'-nor]
son of Morec, nephew of Aarad

Seppan [Sehp'-pahn]
brother Aarad, also son of Aarad and Egome

Serret [Sehr'-reht]
one of the fishing islands

Sethel [Seh'-thehl]
inn keeper, father of Boec and Shend

Setlat [Seht'-laht]
granddaughter of Marna, sister of Topan

Shaffet [Shahf'-feht]
seaman on the *Tel*

Shahri [Shah'-ree]
mother of Idar, wife of Kennec

Shalmarra [Shahl-mahr'-rah]
country far to the south of Kallefandra

Sharn [Shahrn]
a fisherman, husband of Ulanna

Shellah [Shehl'-uh]
a Kroemaeon month

shen [shehn]
largest unit of Kallefandran coinage

Shend [Shehnd]
brother of Boec, husband of Lenyana

Shentoar [Shehn-tor']
city far south of Theo

Shoarnet [Shor'-neht]
Zet crewman who lives with the Draygon

Shufec [Shoo'-fehk]
captain of the *Hob*

Shuman [Shoo'-mahn]
last king of Theo

Son [Son]
fishing boat in the Alna fleet

tarrek [tahr'-rehk]
raft like boat

tarrope [tahr'-roh-peh]
drumlike musical instrument

tau [tau]
unit of Kallefandran coinage

Taya [Tah'-yah]
wife of Zhen, mother of Kron and Narra

tegga [tehg'-gah]
a bearlike animal that hibernates

Tel [Tehl]
Idar's ship

Telleg [Tehl'-lehg]
survivor found at Terhal

Tellon [Tehl'-lôn]
grandfather of Aarad, Seppan and Illiad

Tennep [Tehn'-nehp]
cousin of Mirranu

Tenoar [Tehn'-or]
owner and captain of the *Tel*

Tenwa [Tehn'-wah]
daughter of Aarad and Egome

Tenyah [Tehn'-yah]
primitive people living north of Arganon

Tenyata [Tehn-yah'-tah]
wife of Daeo, mother of Tuac

Terhal [Tehr-hahl']
village seven leagues north of Arganon

Teuwa [Tee'-oo-uh]
far western village in Theo

Theapan [Thay-ah'-puhn]
first king and founder of Theo

Theo [Thay'-o]
Idar's home city state

to'v [tov]
informal Kroemaeon greeting

Toarak [Tor'-ak]
nosha belonging to Aarad's family

Toarnon [Tor'-nahn]
captain of the *Yan*

toev [to'-ehv]
formal Thean greeting

toha [to'-hah]
Kroemaeon nature spirits, the gods

tohana [to-hah'-nah]
excamation calling upon the toha

Toharofa [To-hah'-ro-fah]
blessing of the fields

Tok [Tok]
Miku's ship

tolik [to-leek']
food - a vegetable similar to tomatoes

tolnah [tol'-hah]
grandfather, grandpa

tolneh [tol'-heh]
grandmother, grandma

Topa [To'-pah]
pole star

Topan [To'-pahn]
grandson of Marna, brother of Ernoar

Topek [To'-pehk]
Aeshone's hired hand

Topuwa [To'-poo-wah]
daughter of Topan and Enuwa

Torek [Tor'-ehk]
seaman on the *Tel*

Trenon [Treh'-nôn]
military outpost near Teuwa

Trohan [Tro'-hahn]
island where Miku's camp is located

Tuac [Too'-ak]
son of Daeo, brother of Zhoh

tuffel [tuhf'-fehl]
sea bird that hunts along the beach

Tullikan [Tool'-li-kahn]
friend of Idar in Shentoar

Ujedah [Oo-jeh'-dah]
healing woman of Alna

Ulanna [Oo-lahn'-nah]
wife of Sharn

Valnar [Val-nar']
warlike empire that conquers Theo

Von [Vôn]
fishing boat in the Alna fleet

vood [voud]
wolflike animal

Yan [Yahn]
fishing boat in the Alna fleet

zahrufa [zah'-roo-fah]
reed instrument similar to a recorder

Zayto [Zae'-to]
Kroemaeon moon

zehpat [zeh-paht']
Arganese pronunciation of zhehpat

Zet [Zeht]
fishing boat in the Alna fleet

Zhalleb [Zhahl'-lehb]
captain of the *Dul*

Zheh [Zheh]
bright star or planet

zhehpet [zheh'-peht]
a deerlike animal

Zhen [Zhehn]
farmer and close nieghbor to Aeshone

Zherna [Zhehr'-nah]
daughter of Porel, friend of Seppan

Zhoh [Zho]
son of Daeo, brother of Tuac

Zoar [Zor]
bright star or planet

zubah [zoo'-bah]
folk dance done in boy/girl partners

Printed in the United States
123935LV00003B/315/P